BREAKER OF FATE

R.M. Derrick

To anyone who grew up without seeing their fat body represented in books, especially in the fantasy genre. We deserve these stories too.

And to anyone struggling to make it through. You matter. Your story matters. Even if you aren't swinging swords at dragons. You're here, and I'm proud of you for that.

Author's Note

Breaker of Fate is an adult fantasy romance, and as such, deals with some heavy themes. In order to empower readers to make an informed choice, **please be aware you'll find the following content within this book:** explicit sex, profanity, violence, blood, death (battle and fight scenes), death of parent (off page, remembered), and suicidal ideation (point of view character - two instances with different characters).

Protect your mental health. Happy reading!

PRONUNCIATION GUIDE

Derica – Dare-ih-kuh

Reid – Reed

Pip – Pihp

Tedric – Teh-drik

Father Simond – Fah-thur Sih-muhnd

Balduin – Ball-dwihn

Justus Hadrian – Just-us Hay-dree-un

Nyle – Pronounced like the river Nile

Mazolan – Maz-oh-lahn

Callathe – Cal-lah-thay

Faelon – Fay-lohn

Sarenya – Sar-en-yha

BREAKER OF FATE

R.M. Derrick

CHAPTER ONE

Derica was one breath away from shattering.

Father Simond, a leader of the Disciples of the Loom, smiled, soft brown eyes sweeping over the gathered villagers. As in years past, he wore gray robes, his liberally silver hair catching the morning sunlight as he stood before the crowd. Derica noticed more lines weathering his pale skin this spring, surrounding his mouth and spreading from the corners of his kind eyes. She wondered if the past twelve months outwardly marked her as well and if he'd be able to see it. If he could spot the way her knuckles bleached or the way her eyes revealed a desire to flee.

Doubtful. Mrs. Hammond hadn't even noticed when Derica stopped in the bakery this morning. Unclenching her hands, Derica twined her fingers in the faded blue fabric of her skirt then fiddled with the belt around her waist.

Less than a hundred people—the town's entire population—milled about the square serving as Arlan's hub, assembled for the annual event. Derica's boots scuffed the pitted, crumbling cobblestone beneath her feet as she rose on tiptoe looking for Reid.

She knew he couldn't be in the bakery—Derica and Mrs. Hammond had locked up before wishing each other a happy Rite Day earlier this morning. A few people trickled from the inn to the square, but she didn't spy Reid's large frame and golden hair amongst them. The owner of the general store shooed stragglers out of the shop, her mouth twisted in aggravation, arms crossed menacingly. Derica's lips twitched as she swept the rest of the crowd with her gaze. A raven circled lazily overhead before alighting on the curled, wooden shingles of the inn's roof. From her vantage point to the west of the square near the well, sheltered from some of the crowd, she still didn't see him.

Her ankle rolled when she wobbled on a bit of loose stone, and she caught herself on the brick lip of the well. It was never more clear to Derica than on Rite Day how her small village was aging. Reid's family's farm stretched to the south, wide expanses of pasture that had existed for generations. To the east, the miller's wheat fields were beginning to sprout their yearly golden bounty. Squeezed between the forest to the west and the village to the north lay the old cattle farm.

The few businesses that called the tiny farming village home closed on this day every year. The event masquerading as a religious festival was really an excuse to cease work and bring everyone together. It was her mother's favorite day for that reason.

This would be the first Rite Day since Derica's mother passed.

Father Simond always officiated and had been for as long as she could remember. This year, it appeared he brought an acolyte along. A younger man in matching drab robes stood behind him and off to the side, lanky and dour. The acolyte's sallow skin tone suggested he saw little of the bright sunlight currently beaming down on the square, highlighting the only cheerful thing about him—his light blond hair. His eyebrows, darker than his hair by several shades, decorated his low forehead with severe slashes. His nose and chin formed surprisingly delicate points in an otherwise harsh visage. Eerily pale gray eyes bounced around the assembled population of Arlan while his thin mouth was pulled taut in distaste or impatience. When their gazes clashed,

Derica jerked her chin down and considered the scuffed leather of her half boots.

She didn't want anyone's scrutiny today. With every second, she felt more like an overstuffed cake pan in an oven. Any moment, she'd bubble over and spill out all the feelings rioting inside.

When someone moved beside her, Derica looked up. *Reid.* Derica mentally sighed with both relief and exasperation. She smiled in greeting but didn't meet his eyes. There was no one in all of Veridion she was closer to. If he saw the tension in her face and the poorly veiled grief in her gaze, he'd know. She stared at a spot above his left ear, watching a gentle breeze stir his golden hair. Two more people joined them before Derica could whisper a hello.

Pip, Reid's mother, touched her shoulder and squeezed her arm in greeting. Tedric, his father, stepped forward and gave her a quick hug, dropping a kiss on the crown of her head. Derica knew they meant to comfort, but it had the opposite effect—seeing them cracked something already brittle. Derica tilted her head down again and tried to gather herself, shoring up her armor, even as she realized she fought a losing battle. Reminders of her loss were everywhere—dark, oily fingers slipping through the crevices in her facade.

Derica looked to the center of the square. A group of three young adults stood in front of Father Simond. The father faced away from the crowd now, a gold sash draping over his shoulders—a proclamation of his rank within the Disciples. The sash's tails moved slowly on either side of his spine in the fingers of the wind. In his left arm, Derica spied the heavy tome he carried in the crook of his elbow.

"Welcome. I am delighted to see you all again this year," Father Simond began. "Surrounded by the rebirth and bounty of spring, we are here to witness and celebrate these young people as they acknowledge their place on the Loom, their duty to their fellows, as well as their loyalty to the Weaver and her Tapestry."

Reid leaned down beside Derica, breaking her concentration. "The father said to tell you hello," he muttered. "He's got some… interesting company this year."

"Oh?" she asked, eyes flicking to the acolyte.

Pip and Tedric moved away with murmured directions to find them after, leaving Reid and Derica by themselves.

"Apparently," he continued, "the Shredded are enough of a risk that Father Simond needed a group of mercenaries for protection on the road."

Arlan's miller turned with a thunderous frown and shushed them. Reid, although a head taller than the man, grimaced and ducked his head, mouthing an apology.

At the mention of the Shredded, Derica's shoulders tensed. She darted her eyes around the gathering in the square. The father calmly guided Mrs. Hammond's daughter, the miller's son, and Oliana's younger sister through the pledges of the Rite. Other than the dour blond acolyte, she didn't see anyone else unfamiliar.

She turned to Reid, pitching her voice barely above a whisper. "Mercenaries? Why not soldiers? Didn't the father come from Radley?"

Reid eyed the miller's back, wary of another reproach, as he shook his head. "Not soldiers. I overheard Neelson say they've all but locked down the castle town. All posted soldiers are to remain garrisoned there. The mercenaries must have been hired by the Disciples." Reid crossed his sun-weathered arms revealing dustings of gold hair as he pushed up the sleeves of his faded red tunic.

Neelson was the only tinker that ever stopped in Arlan. Yesterday morning, the dwarf made his customary visit to the bakery as soon as they opened. Over a pastry, he indulged in his favorite pastime—flirting shamelessly with the widowed Mrs. Hammond. Derica overheard the best gossip and news from Neelson while she kneaded dough at the counter, even if she almost strained her eyes from rolling them repeatedly at Neelson's wooing.

Mrs. Hammond had teased him about exaggerating his tales of the Shredded for drama's sake and then changed the subject, demanding to hear the latest court news from the capital instead. But the rumors of the Shredded scratched insistently in the back of Derica's mind—like shadows on the wall when you're small and freshly woken from a bad dream.

The Shredded were the stars of nightmarish tales the humans of Veridion told their children to scare them into good behavior. *"Don't wander off, or the Shredded will get you,"* and *"Naughty children are always found late at night by the Shredded"* were refrains from Derica's childhood. The stories terrified her then, and they did the same now at the age of twenty-four. In the last several years, the stories of the afflicted seemed to multiply. No one knew why.

Father Simond stepped behind the Rite participants, holding his hands over their heads in presentation. "May the benevolence and the wisdom of the Weaver hold and guide your thread on the Tapestry. May you enrich the lives of the threads you touch upon the Loom. From the Weaver's hand and back again, may you fulfill the destiny Woven for you."

Suddenly, Derica reached her limit. There was too much buzzing around in her mind, and the emotions she'd tried to keep contained all morning boiled over. She'd been foolish to think she possessed enough mental armor to take her through the day unscathed. She needed to be alone and safe, and she needed it right this second.

Derica didn't want to hear more about how the Weaver was so kind and good. Not when the god cruelly cut short the life of her mother.

"I forgot to do something at the bakery. I'll be right back." Not giving Reid the opportunity to respond, Derica wound through the crowd and away.

Reid's voice calling her name faded as she got farther away, the faces of the neighbors and friends she passed a blur. Once or twice, someone asked if she was all right. She tried to nod and smile, never halting to respond. Her breath came too fast as she squeezed through the crowd. Darkness encroached on the edges of her vision and her chest ached, the pressure almost suffocating.

Derica reached the front of the bakery and kept walking. Darting around and behind the building, she reached her haven.

The boards of the wooden porch were warped and rickety with age. Tedric built it for her mother, Eleanora, seventeen years ago. Eleanora had wanted a place to sit and watch over the garden that she and Derica planted when Derica was seven. On their hands and knees, fingers in the dirt, working on the garden together was Derica's favorite memory. Better than baking together. Better than reading together in front of their hearth in the winter.

Because it was a living remnant of her mother.

The small garden was a hodgepodge of flowers and vegetables. Tedric expressed complete bafflement to Derica once; it mystified him how Eleanora could keep track of which plant was which without markers of any kind. Honestly, Derica didn't know either.

She knew there was almost always something flowering or needing harvesting but claimed no organization or forethought went into the planting. Only love and enthusiasm.

Derica came here because she could still hear her mother's laughter in this garden. Derica felt her mother's fingers through her hair when the wind stirred it. It was easier to feel her presence here, instead of her absence. In this garden, the part of Derica that screamed at the unfairness of her loss went silent for a moment.

She sank to her knees in front of a spray of rioting daffodils. Bending down, she took the fragrance into her nose and closed her eyes.

And then she fell apart, tears dripping from her trembling chin, surrounded by the plants her mother had cared for.

CHAPTER TWO

D erica didn't know how much time passed, but it couldn't have been too long. Her tear-swollen eyes confirmed the sun still shone high in the sky.

She lay curled into a ball before the garden, cocooned in the scents of flowering plants and earth. If only she could weave them into a blanket and take them with her to her empty cottage, maybe it wouldn't feel so hollow and empty then.

A twig snapped behind her and Derica jerked up. Wiping still-damp cheeks, she looked behind her out of the corner of one eye, noticing a mountainous figure in dark clothing. Their arms crossed over their impressively wide chest, feet braced apart.

Then a voice like woodsmoke and twilight floated from the figure.

"I didn't think I'd find you here."

The words wrapped around her like a caress, stealing her wits. After an embarrassingly long silence, his words finally sank past the haze.

"Excuse me?" she asked.

"There's a man making a fuss about not being able to find a woman with red hair. Father Simond didn't want anyone searching by themselves, so he asked for help. Are you Derica?"

"Y-yes."

Derica stood and brushed dirt from her skirts. She turned to face the owner of that voice, noticing his barrel of a chest topped by even wider shoulders. Shorter than Reid by a few inches, he made up for what he lacked in height with width. She bet if she stood behind him, he might hide her oh-so-generous but petite frame entirely. The arms crossed over his pectorals were so muscled, she wondered how he pulled his black tunic over them. Fine, dark hair gilded by the midday sun covered his arms, becoming sparse on the back of broad, square hands.

Belts wrapped his slim hips and the hilts of weapons peeked up from holsters. Her eyes snagged on a glint of red near his right hip before he propped his hands on his waist. Coherent thoughts skittered from her mind.

Her vision ticked to the hollow of his throat. A thick, tanned column interrupted by a sharp Adam's apple led up to a pointed chin. Dark stubble matching the color of the hair on his arms shaded his square jaw. His bottom lip was fuller than the top, but not by much, and a hairline scar bisected the two in a silvery line from his left nostril down into the scruff to the right of his chin. The slight crookedness from an obvious past break improved a nose that was otherwise a little too hooked.

Derica breathed out faintly through her nose. The closer her gaze drifted to his eyes, the lighter her body felt. She realized she was slightly dizzy.

Finally, she lifted her eyes to his face and met a stare as dark as the images his smoky voice evoked. An electric pang shot through her chest when their gazes clashed, and her ears buzzed. Cocking his head, the man returned her inspection, something unidentifiable sparking in his eyes. His faintly amused gaze didn't dull its polished flint hardness, even as she resumed her mesmerized perusal.

Black eyebrows slashed above shining eyes. Thick, rich, dark brown hair scraped back from his forehead, secured in a low tail, exposing mismatched ears. The left was normally rounded, but the right was missing a notch of flesh at the peak.

The words tipped off her tongue without her volition. "Who *are* you?"

"No one. Come on." Abruptly, he turned and walked away.

She sputtered before blurting, "Wait!"

He froze, only turning his head back to look. "Why?"

She licked her lips and blinked gritty eyes. "I'm not ready," she croaked. Her ears went hot with the strength of her blush—the bane of every fair-skinned redhead's existence.

Silently, he walked back to her. She didn't meet his eyes, staring down at her boots instead.

He paused, a weight to his silence until he said, "Would you like to sit for a minute until you are?"

Derica's head jerked up in surprise.

He waved a hand to the patio ledge, and she jolted, moving to take a seat.

"One moment," he said, clasping her elbow before she bent to sit.

She waited while he frowned at the slanting, aged wooden structure.

"I don't think that's safe." He scrubbed his jaw with a broad palm and looked around. He wouldn't find anywhere else to sit.

"It holds my weight daily. I think it's plenty safe."

"But can it hold both of us?"

She folded her arms in front of her waist. "You don't have to stay." Derica didn't miss the dip his eyes made to the neckline of her tunic when the movement plumped her large breasts.

"Let me sit first, then. At least if I go tumbling to my a—the ground, I can charge the church extra." He sat gingerly, looking up at the awning above. "Or, I suppose, for a head injury."

"Oh, so you're—"

"The Disciples hired my companions and I to protect Father Simond on the road, in case he came across any Shredded." He pushed on the boards next to his hips. They creaked but didn't cave in—just like she told him they wouldn't. Nodding, he moved, allowing her to join him.

"And did you? Encounter any Shredded?" she asked, sitting.

The patio wasn't wide enough to allow them much distance. In fact, when Derica fully settled, the outside of her thigh brushed his. The warmth from the innocent touch was both comforting and oddly enervating. Derica stared ahead into the garden, focusing on anything else.

The mercenary shrugged his wide shoulders. "Only signs. Didn't see any, though."

"Have you before?"

He didn't answer, leveling a heavy look at her. "I don't think this line of conversation is going to help you feel any better."

She grimaced, face heating again. "You're right."

He leaned forward, resting his elbows on his knees. Her eyes traveled the wide expanse of his back and the way his shoulders flexed under the rough, dark fabric of his shirt. The sword strapped to his back would have been cause for unease normally, but she was oddly comfortable in this stranger's presence. Derica flushed and looked away, focusing instead on a single red tulip bouncing in a soft breeze.

Dark gaze on his hands, he asked, "Would you like to tell me why you were upset?" The question held no inflection or judgment.

Derica sighed. "I don't think we have the time for it all."

His eyebrows flew up as he turned to look at her. "There's that much to tell?"

This close, his voice had even more impact. It stroked down her spine and tingled her skin. Derica fought back a shiver.

"I have a feeling once I start, it'll all come tumbling out. How long do you think it'll be before someone else finds us?" she asked.

"It's likely we have a handful of minutes."

"I'd need two handfuls, at least," she sighed.

He chuckled, and Derica's heart stuttered. She didn't know if she'd ever heard a more pleasing sound.

"You're welcome to share—"

Pounding footsteps interrupted him. They hadn't even had a *thimbleful* of minutes.

Reid burst into the garden followed by Father Simond.

The mercenary stood, placing distance between himself and Derica. He pulled his back straight with his legs braced apart and hands clasped behind him. "Father, I found—"

Reid let out a grunt of surprise, and his blue eyes sharpened as they examined her puffy eyes. He looked her up and down, brows lowered in confusion and concern. "What happened?" He flicked his gaze between Derica and the mercenary.

The mercenary was completely unfazed by Reid's scrutiny. "I located your missing friend as Father Simond asked. She wanted to sit for a moment before rejoining the festival."

Reid's eyes narrowed, and he opened his mouth, but Father Simond cut him off. "Well, is she all right, Commander Hadrian?"

So, not just a mercenary. He was a *commander*.

"*She* can speak for herself, and yes, I am feeling better, thank you," Derica said. Truthfully, she wasn't but she would never say so out loud.

Father Simond walked toward Derica and stopped in front of her, his back to Hadrian.

"My child, I didn't mean to offend." He held a hand out and Derica stood. Grasping her elbows in the palms of his hands, he examined her.

Commander Hadrian shifted on his feet but remained at attention. If not for that shuffle, Derica would have thought him unconcerned. Meanwhile, Reid was watching the commander carefully.

For her ears only, Simond murmured, "Your first Rite without her. I'd tell you it gets easier, but the pain of loss can't be predicted or charted. I can say with certainty she wouldn't want you alone with your grief on today of all days, however."

Derica's lip wobbled and her vision went watery. Simond patted her shoulder and produced a cloth from his robe. He pressed it into her hand and stepped back, giving her a moment to collect herself.

Reid's expression said he desperately wanted to help but didn't know how. He rocked back and forth on his feet, clearly fighting the urge to offer comfort. She tried to convey her gratitude with a look of appreciation.

Witnessing a pain you were helpless to fight was hard. Derica knew this all too well after watching her mother slowly wither away from illness.

The longer everyone remained silent, the lower the commander's eyebrows sank over his dark eyes. His chest expanded on an inhale, his lips parting to say something, but Father Simond cleared his throat, drawing Derica's attention back to him.

"Well?" the mercenary murmured to the priest.

Father Simond turned to face Hadrian. "She appears physically fine, but maybe she would like to retire from the festivities with Re—"

The acolyte she'd seen beside Simond earlier rounded the corner of the bakery, joining them in the garden. His thin mouth compressed in impatience, he took in the scene quickly. His startlingly light gaze snagged on her puffy eyes, flicking down to the damp cloth in her hand. Immediately, he shot an accessing look at Hadrian, who bore the scrutiny with the same attention someone would pay a gnat.

"Father Simond, what goes on here?" asked the acolyte.

The older man sighed. "Derica, this is Balduin, my—"

"What did you do?" Balduin asked, staring hard at the commander.

If she hadn't been already watching him, Derica would have missed the way Hadrian's mouth twitched before he replied.

Voice as dry as sand, he said, "I located the woman Father Simond asked me to."

"And that's *all* you did?" Balduin made a show of looking Hadrian up and down.

"Now, what right do you have to think—" started Reid.

"Balduin!" Father Simond admonished.

The acolyte didn't care about being addressed like a naughty toddler. He was too busy exchanging thinly veiled sneers with the mercenary commander.

Derica ground her teeth and took a deep breath before responding. "If your worry is that this man harmed me, you could have asked *me*."

Father Simond had the decency to appear properly chagrined for his companion at least. Balduin wore the look men got when addressed by young women—a facade of politeness that communicated they would arrive at their own conclusions.

She continued. "To be clear, he did not."

Balduin deflated at that, murmuring an apology to Commander Hadrian. The mercenary said nothing, dipping his chin briefly. It was more a dismissal than an acceptance.

"I think," Derica said, looking at Reid, "I would like to retire for the rest of the day instead of returning to the square."

Reid nodded and stepped around Balduin to Derica's side, looping an arm around her back.

Looking at Commander Hadrian, she said, "Thank you."

His dark gaze softened slightly as he nodded in acknowledgment.

With a gentle touch to her spine, Reid led her away. When they were well past the square and halfway to Derica's home, she opened her mouth to unburden some of her sadness, but Pip called their names from behind.

"Reid Wariner, what is going on?" She waved her hand back toward the square with a jerk. "I heard you were looking for Derica. Derica, are you all right?"

When neither offered a response quickly enough to satisfy his mother, she focused on Derica. Peering at her eyes, Derica knew the minute Pip understood.

"Oh, darling," she clucked, pulling Derica into a hug.

A tear slipped from Derica's eye, rolling slowly down her cheek. Pip's motherly perfume of baked goods and sunshine enveloped Derica as the older woman's hand cupped her shoulder. Another tear came free, joining the first.

Derica opened blurry, watery eyes to find Pip examining her with concern. She then gently clasped Derica's hand. "Sweet girl, what's wrong?"

And, for the second time that day, Derica's composure dissolved.

Shaking and sobbing in the arms of the woman who had become her surrogate mother, Derica let it go. It all tumbled out. That she'd felt like fragile glass today. How Rite Day had been too much to handle. That she was irrationally terrified of the Shredded. And how she felt she had to pretend she didn't feel this way to keep from upsetting her friends.

Afterward, wrung out and hiccuping gulps of air, she felt lighter. Reid was holding one of her hands, slowly stroking his thumb back and forth over the back of her palm. Pip held the other, chafing it between hers.

Reid's mother reached up and dragged both her thumbs under Derica's eyes, brushing away the remaining salty tracks. Derica gently pulled away from Reid and clasped her hands in front of her navel. She looked down at her white knuckles, taking her first large breath.

"I'm sorry," she whispered.

"Why?" Reid sounded surprised.

Pip frowned at her but waited for an explanation.

"I'm sorry I can't seem to put myself back together. I'm sorry I fall apart like this." Her throat threatened to close, but she kept talking. "I'm sorry I'm such a burden."

Pip gasped. "Darling, you are *not* a burden. You're part of our family and that will never change, no matter what you do, where you go, or how old you get." She smiled wryly, flicking her eyes to Reid. "Just like this one." Reid started to protest and was hushed by his mother with a scowl. Pip ran a hand softly down the back of Derica's hair and pressed a kiss to her forehead.

Derica's vision went watery again, but she blinked it away. The sadness didn't suddenly vanish, but she was ready to put it away for now.

"I don't think I like the idea of you alone in your cottage tonight. Come to the house for dinner and then how 'bout you sleep the night in Algie's old room?" said Pip.

Derica nodded. Putting a comforting arm around her shoulder, Pip turned Derica toward the opposite side of Arlan and to the Wariners' farm. Reid grabbed her hand.

Buffered on either side by her friends—her family—Derica's steps felt lighter, as did the day's weight of grief. It may return tomorrow, but she didn't have to carry her burden alone.

By the time they reached the farmhouse, the sun had kissed the horizon, splashing hues of blush and gold across the darkening sky. Derica entered the Wariner family home after Pip, the clanking of pots and pans greeting them from the kitchen.

"Oh, no," Pip muttered, bustling away from the foyer.

Derica chuckled, looking back at Reid.

He rolled his eyes and grinned. "Pa must have left the Rite early, too."

Derica paused for a moment to soak in the comforting sights and sounds of Reid's family home. The midsize foyer, with its scuffed wood floors, transitioned into a hallway splitting the kitchen from the sitting room and its tiny hearth. Reid's older brother, Algernon's, vacant room was nestled across from the stairs to the second floor. It was a house full to the brim with familial memories and love.

As they entered the kitchen together, Pip chased Tedric away from the wood stove and the pile of pans he'd assembled on the scarred wooden counter. Tedric dashed behind Derica, bussing her cheek with a quick kiss. Derica laughed when his beard tickled, and her shoulders felt lighter again.

Tedric gripped Derica's upper arms, holding her before him like a shield between him and his wife. "Easy, woman!" he boomed over Derica's head. "I was just trying to help. I know I'm only fit for making slop. I wasn't trying to murder my family with my cooking."

Pip humphed, winking at Derica, before settling her hands on her broad hips. "And how would you know which pans I'll be needing for dinner tonight?"

"Don't they all just... work?"

Pip rolled her eyes and looked at her husband with warm exasperated love. "No, they don't, love. You've gathered me—" she looked to the counter "—three different pie tins and nothing to prepare a filling or dough in."

As his parents squabbled adorably, Reid shook his head and raised his eyebrows at Derica, pointing at the back door. She smiled, nodding.

When they returned from washing up at the basin on the back porch, Tedric was laying table settings, the worn plates and utensils mismatched, but lovingly so. Pip called Reid over to help prepare dinner but shooed Derica away when she offered to help.

Arguing with Pip would go nowhere, so Derica settled at the table next to Tedric. Like almost all the furniture in their home, Tedric had built it. The corner bore an indent from Reid's childhood—he and his brother had been chasing one another through the house when the elder slipped, assaulting the table with his forehead. Tedric had told the story for years after, saying his son was so hardheaded, he'd damaged the furniture instead of himself. The sturdy oak counter where Pip was currently preparing dinner had been an anniversary gift to his wife four years ago. Pip had cried when he'd presented it to her as she traced the tiny caricatures of their family enthusiastically, if not expertly, carved into the surface.

Reid was his father's exact copy, with the exception of the cleft in his chin—that came from Pip. Looking at Tedric, anyone could guess with fair accuracy how Reid would look in twenty years. Tedric was a study in living metallic hues—golden hair with silver streaks at the temples and straight, wide golden brows turned silver with time above intelligent blue eyes. Deep laugh lines spread at their corners, signaling a habit of smiling. A wide mouth above a square jaw led down to a suntanned neck and impressively still-wide shoulders. Reid was helping more than ever on the farm, but his father refused to work any less.

Tedric paused while laying place settings to catch Derica's eye and tilt his head in question. While Pip and Reid were more active and alert to changes in Derica's mood, Tedric wasn't any less invested in her wellbeing. He simply had different methods. When she gave a tiny smile as answer, he resumed his task.

Tedric was the best listener Derica knew. He never interrupted her talking to provide solutions or even ask questions. He let her spill every thought and secret while making her feel he was listening intently. And then he would give her the kind of hug that was so deeply shielding and comforting, her worries felt like they couldn't touch her.

They had a lot of those moments early after Eleanora's passing. Tedric sat and listened to all her anger, all her pain, and all her fear, leaving her feeling slightly more balanced, even if the heavy weight would return in a few hours or the next day. Derica didn't know what she'd done to earn such wonderful friends. Family, rather.

"You don't need to earn it."

Derica jerked her eyes up in surprise.

Tedric smiled, the lines beside his eyes deepening. "One of those thoughts that slips off the lips, was it?"

She nodded, swallowing a lump of emotion.

"You don't need to earn it," he repeated. "That's what genuine family is, blood or not. You have our love and support, regardless." And, because it was his way, Tedric reached forward, patted her hand, and then lapsed back into a comfortable silence.

When the meal was ready, he called for Pip and Reid to sit, then motioned for Derica to assist him in bringing the dishes to the table. As he passed his wife, he slung a still-brawny arm around Pip's waist and kissed her cheek softly. He brushed a sweat-dampened tendril of her brown hair behind her ear while Pip blushed like a maiden and swatted him away with a laugh.

Once Derica and Tedric finished laying the prepared dishes on the table and took their seats, Derica let the sights and sounds of family wash over her. Reid pointedly ignored his parents, who spoke to each other in low tones. Pip blushed again, and Tedric boomed a laugh. Reid rolled his eyes and stuffed a bite of bread in his mouth.

While filling her plate, Derica said to Reid, "Be thankful for every day you have with them, Reid. You're lucky."

Reid stilled, his head coming up to meet her eyes. He swallowed, gaze tight with contrition. "I am, and I do know that." He reached for her shoulder and gave it a firm squeeze. "They've always been your family, too, you know."

"She knows," said Tedric. "In fact, we'd trade you for Reid any day of the week."

Reid barked a wry laugh, another roll halfway to his mouth.

"It's true, darling," Pip said with a wink. "I honestly wish the two of you suited. I was so upset when nothing romantic ever developed between you." Her eyes switched between the pair.

Reid and Derica looked at each other. Derica's mouth twitched, then so did Reid's. He lost it first and threw his head back, laughing. His sides shook as he clutched his middle and continued to howl with mirth. Next to him, Derica dissolved into tittering giggles that became guffaws every time her eyes met Reid's. His parents waited calmly through the display.

Wiping his eyes, Reid gathered composure enough to speak. "Ma. Pa. I love Derica. We all do. But we're far better friends than we could ever be a couple. Other than that one summer when we were both thirteen, it's never something either of us entertained." He leaned over and placed a brotherly kiss against Derica's temple.

The summer he referred to, they both agreed to test if their friendship had a romantic aspect. After several exploratory kisses and some rather awkward experimenting, they determined they'd best forget thoughts of an amorous future and stick to their friendship.

"It'd still be nice to see more of Derica. Maybe get some little ones out of the deal," grumbled Pip.

Tedric patted her arm. "Pip, we see our darling girl plenty. She knows she's welcome here anytime." He pointedly looked at Derica until she nodded.

Reid echoed the movement. "Besides, after Algie visits with his four wee ones, you're both put out for an entire week. The family is fine, as big as it is now. Derica included."

"Just so. Now!" Tedric clapped his hands then rubbed them together. "Let's enjoy what my fine wife has made us tonight!"

In the lull of conversation later, thoughts of the Shredded invaded Derica's peace. Without her volition, the question was out of her mouth.

"Tedric," Derica said, "you've heard rumors about the Shredded around town, haven't you?"

Pip paused and looked at her husband, putting down her silverware. Reid continued to eat but gave his father all of his attention.

Tedric considered Derica with a frown before answering. "Why do you ask? Worried they've come around the farm?"

Silently, she nodded. "Have you ever *seen* one, though?"

Tedric laughed, the lines beside his eyes crinkling. "No." He shook his head, lips still curved. "No, I haven't. And I don't know that I ever will. Let me guess. Neelson was telling tales?"

Again, Derica nodded. Reid sighed.

"Derica," Tedric leaned forward over his plate, leveling his most serious look at her, "I don't think we'll ever see Shredded here. I know they're real. But I don't think they're quite the danger to anyone—or Arlan—that travelers make them out to be. Put the worry from your mind."

Afraid to ask if he was sure, Derica returned her attention to her dinner and let the conversation flow around her like water. Reid nudged her elbow and asked her to pass the platter of stewed vegetables.

Despite the readiness with which everyone else dismissed the matter, Derica had a hard time setting her fear aside. At least she wasn't alone in her cottage, without distraction or company. For that, she was thankful.

CHAPTER THREE

After dinner, they were all sitting on the back porch—Pip and Tedric holding hands on the wooden bench. Derica and Reid were leaning opposite shoulders against the same beam, feet dangling off the elevated platform—when Reid asked her to take a walk.

It wasn't an unusual request. They often walked together after dinners at the Wariner farmhouse, but the purpose was normally to get Derica to her cottage on the other side of Arlan.

Derica waited for Reid to grab a lantern from the hanger while she buttoned a cloak borrowed from Pip. The sun dropped below the horizon hours ago, and it was still chilly enough at night to need something warmer than her thin tunic and lightweight skirts.

It would have been oppressively dark outside if it weren't for the sliver of a moon casting metallic light onto the treetops lining the road. Reid crooked out his arm for her, lantern in the other hand.

She slipped her arm through his, and together they headed down the dirt road toward the village. Content to walk in the evening's silence, neither spoke for several minutes. Derica was warm from a good meal and several glasses of mead.

Distant lowing of cattle from the neighboring farm, the rustling of a gentle zephyr through the trees, and the occasional hoot or squeak from nocturnal animals filled the night air.

Reid's lantern lit the wood-post fence lining either side of the path before them. Beyond, it seemed to make the shadows outside the circle of light that much darker. She knew it was only farmland and pasture surrounding them, but her mind conjured formless nightmares nestled in the dark. Derica mentally chided herself, trying to banish her baseless apprehension.

A sudden cacophonous stirring of bushes came from the pair's left. Derica's head jerked towards the sound with a gasp, her arm slipping free of Reid. Rushing back to the forefront of her thoughts, her fears clamored. Derica's eyes darted, searching for the source of the commotion.

"Just a rabbit. Or a d-doe," she whispered. "Right, Reid?"

No response. She reached back for him. A chill skittered down her spine when she found empty air.

Derica's mead-fogged brain couldn't comprehend what she saw when she turned around. She blinked several times, hoping her senses were lying to her.

Reid's lantern sat, abandoned, in the middle of the road.

"R-Reid?" Derica called.

Warm breath tickled the skin of her neck.

"*Derica*," a voice wheezed into her ear.

Derica jumped and whipped around. She only saw the flash of his white teeth and tips of his golden hair, the rest of him cast in deeper shadow. It took her eyes a moment to adjust, but it quickly became evident his shoulders trembled the tiniest bit, and his teeth bit his twitching bottom lip. She darted her hand out and slapped his chest.

"You idiot! You almost scared me to death!" Derica cradled her stinging hand to her chest. Sometimes she forgot how much muscle Reid had from working on the farm.

"Ow!" he yelped. Reid rubbed the center of his chest, frowning. "It was a joke, Derica."

"Well, it wasn't funny." She snatched the lantern up and stomped away, not waiting for him to follow. Her heart was still beating like mad in her chest, despite the lungfuls of fresh air she steadily took, trying to calm herself.

"Derica. Derica! Wait, I'm sorry. I couldn't help myself."

The blond oaf plodded behind her until he drew even next to her, gently prying the lantern out of her hand. He looked over at her as they silently walked side by side again, but she refused to look back.

"I really am sorry," he muttered, waiting for her to return his gaze.

Giving in, Derica briefly turned her head, tilting her chin to meet his gaze, and nodded. She turned forward again but wound her arm through his. She'd die before admitting she did so to keep steady on her wobbly legs. He settled closer into her grip and blew out a long breath.

"At the bakery, I let Neelson's talk about Shredded get to me, it seems," she mumbled.

"The rumors can't be true. It has to be an exaggeration. Even then, it's probably thieves or highwaymen. True, I've heard more about them these last few months than ever before, but you know they're likely the product of imaginative, excitable gossipmongers? You heard about them from Neelson, after all." Reid bumped her hip with his and chuckled.

When she didn't respond, he gathered her close to his side and whispered, "I'm sorry."

The entire Wariner family went out of their way today to show Derica physical affection. She didn't know which of them figured it out first, but when she missed her mother badly, those embraces grounded her in a way nothing else did. Eleanora had always been demonstrative with her love, and it made Derica feel less alone to still have those moments.

Closing her eyes, she sank into Reid. She took a deep breath and squeezed him tight, then slipped out of his embrace. When she looked around, she realized they'd crossed the threshold of the town square. Relief swept over Derica seeing it abandoned now under the light of the moon. Both the general store and bakery were closed. The tavern was the only business to reopen so late to both travelers and town residents. Faint piano music floated through the open door.

Derica smiled. The melody meant Oliana, the owner's daughter, was minding the business, and it was empty tonight—she always came out from the bar to play when there were no customers.

Reid caught Derica's eyes and lifted his brows, silently asking her if they were going to keep up tradition. Reid had been walking Derica home from the farm since they were teenagers. Arlan was so quiet and so rarely had visitors, Oliana sat at the piano most nights. The tradition of dancing in the square began when Derica and Reid were adolescents with hopes of romance together. They continued it as a joke.

Reid set the lantern against the bricks of the well, wreathing the cobblestones beneath their feet in a bubble of light. He held a hand out and swept into a ridiculously exaggerated bow, golden hair aflame in the lantern light. Or, at least, his approximation of a bow. Nobles and the wealthy didn't frequent Arlan on their way to the castle town of Radley. At court, Reid's gallantry would likely be lacking.

He wiggled his fingers at her when she didn't immediately take his hand. Derica threw her head back and laughed, then placed her hand in his. He promptly stood and spun her into a twirl, swinging her skirts indecently high. His laugh joined hers, and he pulled her back into him, leading them into the silliest, most frantic jig. He kicked his knees up almost level with her ears, while she bounced around, chuckling and trying to avoid his legs. Oliana must have heard them, because she played a more raucous tune. Her tempo picked up, and the melody transformed into something fitting an evening whirlwind frolic.

After several bouts around the square, they were both drenched in sweat but grinning like imps. The door of the tavern opened, and Oliana smiled and waved from the doorway to the pair. Derica tried and failed to ignore the wistful expression in Oliana's eyes. Several years ago, Oliana would have joined them, snatching Derica's hand and stealing a sweet kiss in the middle of their jig.

A pang of guilt struck, lodging in her ribs. Derica should apologize for pushing Oliana away after Eleanora's passing, but with every day gone by, the conversation seemed harder and harder to start. Especially since Derica realized her feelings didn't run as deep as Oliana's to begin with. They waved back to Oliana. Reid bowed, making the woman's laugh trill into the square. When Derica smiled back, Oliana's eyes softened with sad acceptance.

Reid took Derica's arm, and with a shout goodnight, grabbed their lantern. They turned back to the farm, arm in arm.

Still a bit out of breath and giggling intermittently, Derica bumped her hip against Reid, bouncing him a few steps off the path. He was a giant—at least to her height of a little over five feet tall—standing a head and a half taller, but her waist was twice the size of his. She came from plump stock and had the breasts, belly, and hips to accompany her pedigree. Giggles turning into outright laughter, she reached out her hand to steady him back on the path. Up ahead, the torches marking the Wariner home came into view.

"Thank you, Reid. You always know how to make me feel better."

He smiled and dipped his head in a nod. "No thanks required."

When they were almost at the front door, Reid stopped her. "Derica, wait a moment. There's something I want to talk to you about."

She frowned but nodded, taking a seat with him on the raised platform of the porch. They both swung their feet, listening to the symphony of night surrounding them.

"I think it's time," he said.

Derica immediately knew what he meant. "You're leaving?" She searched his cornflower blue eyes, hoping she was wrong.

Since they were little, Reid had dreamt of going to Radley to apprentice to be a physician. When they grew up, life required they both set aside their adolescent desires. Derica took care of her mother from the time she was nineteen. About the time Eleanora fell ill, Reid's brother Algie eloped with a girl from the next village and left Tedric with all the work on the farm. Reid, who had been shadowing the only physician in Arlan to prepare for an apprenticeship in Radley, dropped everything to help his father instead. His relationship with Algie was tense now, and Derica didn't know how Reid stood to talk to him whenever his brother deigned to visit the Wariner farm.

"But what about m—the farm?" She breezed past the question she hadn't meant to ask. Derica refused to crack open the door to that particular emotion after the day she had. "Is Algie coming back?"

Reid's brows tugged down. "Actually, I think he is. He was whining in his last letter to Pa that they're too cramped in Idlewood with Seraphina's family." He linked his fingers together, leaning his elbows on his thighs as he stared into the night, gaze unfocused.

She swallowed down an appeal for Reid to stay. Her plea settled in the bottom of her stomach. Instead, she said, "Not a surprise with four children, all younger than three years old. Leaving the farm and your father like he did cost you. Because of him, you didn't get to become a physician."

Reid sighed, one thumb sweeping over the other. His shoulders were tight, the line of his neck straight as he stared down at his fingers. "No. Because of him, I chose to stay. I could have left. Ma and Pa would have happily seen me off, even if it meant the farm suffered. But now..." He shrugged, then looked at her, eyebrows raised. "You could come with me. We could go to Radley together."

"W-what?" Derica asked, nearly choking on her surprise. "You want us both to pack up and leave for the capital? What about the bakery and Mrs. Hammond?"

And leave the only place besides my home that holds memories of my mother? How can you ask me to give that up? And how can you leave me?

The unspoken questions remained tangled in her throat, and the tide of emotions threatened to drown her again. Derica couldn't weather another storm today.

She knew the second Reid saw it on her face. His lips pinched, and his blue eyes dimmed. "I'm sorry. That was selfish to bring up after the day you've had. It's not decided yet. I've just been thinking about it. We'll talk about it some more another time."

Her smile was brittle as she got up, bade him goodnight, and retired to the bedroom on the other side of the kitchen. Pip had already laid out a nightdress for her and lit the bedside lamp. Derica washed her face and hands mechanically in the basin, changed, then slipped between the sheets, hoping sleep would come swiftly.

Lips curling with distaste, the Savior reached into their pocket and pulled out the sachet the witch had given them. They didn't enjoy turning to the charlatans. But when their original methods hadn't yielded results, the Savior admitted to themselves that outside sources would have to be considered.

After all, when the credit was being given, the Savior would be appropriately recognized. As the party responsible for delivering Veridion from the enigmatic plague, they would receive their due. The Shredded were a problem they couldn't abide, and there was no one more determined to deliver a remedy to the humans of the world than them.

They pinched two fingers into the leather pouch and withdrew the rolled piece of vellum. Crouched before their lantern, they read the witch's instructions. Pulling another packet of supplies and implements from their other pocket, they diligently placed the runes, dried herbs, and talismans as prescribed. Then they stepped back.

The items lay in a neat circle, nothing out of place. To the north, a rune for protection; to the east, herbs for healing; to the south, a preserved butterfly wing for transformation; and to the west, dried snakeskin for renewal. Sat-isfied, the Savior knelt and prepared the small basin in the center. Tearing free the scrap of vellum with the words of intention—the witch's term for the spell—they memorized the words. They snatched a twig from the ground and opened the cage of the lantern, mouthing the words soundlessly as they brought the flame to the paper. Their whispered words fell over the prepara-tion, the last ingredient.

Doubt hovered in the back of the Savior's mind. The witch might have swindled them. With watchful eyes, they observed the fingers of smoke float-ing into the midnight air—the way they danced in the moonlight.

The Savior held their breath, waiting.

When the flame consumed the last of the vellum and all that remained was glowing ash, they wanted to hurl the stone vessel and grind the supplies into the ground. Nothing happened. The Savior should have known that an easy solution would be too good to be true.

Suddenly, a hush fell over the clearing. A ripple of air swept out from the center of the circle, moving the grass and pressing their clothing flat against the Savior's body as the current *wooshed* by.

The Savior froze. Their heart beat in their chest, a drum so loud they strug-gled to hear anything else. A minute passed. Then two. Nothing.

The blackened twig snapped in their hands. Not the witch's neck but it soothed the rage bubbling all the same. The Savior struggled to gather the supplies rather than fling them into the dark shadows cast by the surrounding trees.

On the edge of their vision, a shadow coalesced out of the darkness. The Savior stifled the nascent twitch of a smile and reached into their pocket for the last of the witch's items, determination renewed.

Their palm wrapped around a small, stoppered glass vial. Inside swirled a suspension of odd, orange, pearlescent liquid. When the Savior asked the witch what it was, the witch smiled and simply said, "Magic." The Savior had scoffed, but they took the vial anyway. Desperation was not a force many could overcome. Not even the Savior.

They turned and faced the shadow. It lurched into a beam of moonlight, and the Savior contained their shudder. Nasty things, Shredded. Tragic too, how a soul could become so diseased, they lost all sense of humanity and self.

It had white, milky eyes and skin leached of all color. The Savior had yet to learn if blood still flowed in the Shredded's veins. The few they'd captured hadn't yet been peeled open to examine. The Savior made a mental note to have the others determine the reason—a matter for when they returned to the capital, however.

Dirty and torn scraps of fabric hung from the monstrosity's skeletal frame, its pale skin visible in the night grotesquely stretched over sinew and bones. Patches of the dark hair on its head were missing, while blackened and wet wounds peppered its body.

The way the Shredded moved wasn't human—it navigated the ground between them like a mindless husk. The Savior wouldn't be fooled, though. The mindless appearance was a facade until it sensed prey. Then it skewed toward unprovoked and swift violence. While not much was known about the Shredded, the Savior's experiments provided *that* information, at least.

Careful to conceal the glint of the vial in the folds of their clothing, the Savior readied to lob it at the nightmare's feet. When the Shredded cocked its maimed head and tensed, the Savior pulled their arm back and let the vessel fly.

The sound of shattering glass was so loud in the quiet wrought by witchcraft, the Savior cringed.

At the creature's feet, the faintly orange pearlescent liquid transformed into smoke. The Shredded seemed unaffected, until the vapor traveled up its body in a way that was almost sentient.

The Shredded juddered and waved its arms about, like a child warding away insects. The smoke clung, snapping to its skin.

The Savior slowly stepped back, grasping their lantern and readying to retreat as they watched. When the smoke reached the Shredded's neck, it roared, the sound so entirely inhuman that the Savior couldn't even compare it to an animal. Unlike anything they'd ever heard before, the sound vibrated in the Savior's chest, kicking their heart into a gallop.

Snaking tendrils of vapor streamed into the Shredded's ears and nostrils. The Savior shuddered, tensing to flee but fighting the impulse. The experiment *must* be seen through to the end.

Like an insect in amber, the Shredded froze, halting its forward progress.

An ember of hope glowed in the Savior's chest, as one corner of their mouth curled up in delight. They had found it, a solution that could halt the plague sweeping Veridion.

The Savior stepped toward the humanoid monstrosity, smiling. They slowed when the thing's desiccated lips stretched into a grotesque oval, their blackened tongue wriggling like a worm on a hook. Just as suddenly as the Shredded had frozen in place, the spell broke.

The Savior started at the roar the Shredded loosed. Shaking its head like a mangy animal, the Shredded leapt. Hopes dashed, the Savior fled like a rabbit before a fox.

CHAPTER FOUR

L antern clasped in sweating hands, the Savior fled through the forest as fast as their legs could carry them. Phantom, foul breath tickled their nape as they pushed aside branches and tripped over exposed roots.

When the Savior stumbled from the clasp of the heavily wooded area, they hesitated, eyes flicking toward the buildings in the distance. Even if they could find safety there, they couldn't risk being seen.

The decision was plucked from their grasp when the Shredded burst from the trees at the Savior's back, giving chase. Galvanized, the Savior sprinted for the promise of security. As their feet ate up the ground separating them from the farming village, their eyes snagged on a humble cottage set on the outskirts of the village, but closest to the Savior. Changing course, they pumped their legs faster, lungs operating like a blacksmith's bellows at double speed as they sped for the cottage. Air stung their dry throat and their legs burned with the effort of exertion.

Something hooked the back of their clothing and the Savior pushed harder, ripping free. They reached the back of the cottage and dashed around, to the front door. The windows were dark, and it appeared empty. Their hand fumbled with the wrought iron door handle, jiggling it.

Locked.

Sweat dripped down their back, and they turned to look around. No sign of the Shredded, but nevertheless, chills skittered along their spine. The Savior wasn't naive enough to think they were safe. They were being *hunted*.

Setting their lantern at their feet, the Savior tugged and pushed on the door, to no avail. Finally, they turned their shoulder to the barrier, taking a step back. With a push powered by desperation and fear, they rammed into the thin wood. The lock creaked but didn't open.

Once more, the Savior threw themselves against the door barring them from safety, careful not to topple their lantern. This time, the door gave way as the lock broke, and they bounced into the small, one room building. Trembling hands snatched the lantern and immediately closed the door. The Savior fumbled with the bar, securing a reprieve.

The Savior leaned against the door, taking gasps of air deep into their lungs. Their knees knocked together, vision blurring slightly as the panic crashed down in waves, leaving them light-headed.

The witch would pay. The Savior should have known better than to turn to a harpy pretender.

Ragged nails scratched across the bubbled glass windowpane to their left, causing the Savior to jump, spinning in the sound's direction. Iron criss-crossed both panes, so the Savior dismissed the worry it would breach the borrowed haven. The door rattled in the frame and animalistic grunting floated through the wood.

The Savior edged to the right, cursing under their breath when they toed a fire iron laid against the wall. It didn't fall, but it danced back and forth briefly before stilling. Their fingers ached from their death grip on the lantern's handle as they swept a frantic gaze over the back wall. No windows. No doors.

No means of escape.

A kernel of an idea formed in the back of the Savior's mind. A combination of fear, anger, and frustration proffered the solution, but they snatched it with eager hands, regardless.

All they had to do was get free of the cottage and the Shredded outside, then return to their companions. The Savior repeated the gross oversimplification under their breath while they prepared their trap. With shaking hands, they set the lantern down in the middle of the dark cottage. Next, they returned to the entrance and slowly raised the bar keeping the nightmare at bay. The Savior grasped the door handle and opened it inward swiftly, staying hidden behind it, nestled in the L formed by the unbarred entrance.

Holding their breath, the Savior waited.

It wasn't long at all before a shadow swept into the cottage, an unnervingly *other* grace on display as it prowled inside. Lips fastened closed and lungs screaming for air, the Savior crouched, wrapping their hands around the fire iron. They edged to the end of the door.

With a snarl, the Shredded turned, readying to leap, gnarled hands poised to tear and rend. Moving faster than the Savior ever had before, they ducked through the door and slammed it shut from outside.

The Savior's hands fumbled, holding the door closed with one hand while they tried to steady the shaking of the other. A frustrated growl escaped them when they finally threaded the iron through the loop of the door handle, wedging it against the wooden house. The door rattled in their grasp as a roar from within threatened to collapse the roof of the little cottage.

Slowly backing away, the Savior took in great gulps of the night air as they allowed themselves to breathe for a heartbeat. They looked behind them, worried lights would stream from the front doors of the houses a good ways down the road.

When no splash of light beamed through the dark, the Savior allowed a sigh of relief past their lips. The fire iron rattled, and the door shook in the frame, but neither budged. Crashing and snarls filtered out from the inside of the building as the Savior retreated, edging back around the far end of the house, away from the village.

Glass shattered inside the cottage and the Savior grinned. Fire was a great cleanser of malady.

Pounding feet on the stairs outside the bedroom door woke Derica. The sun wasn't up yet, and it took a moment for the fog of sleep to clear—for her mind to register the tense conversation on the other side of the barrier.

"Tedric," Pip's voice was muffled through the door, "what do you think it is?"

"I don't know, but we haven't had anyone ring the village alarm bell in a good fifteen years. They wouldn't do it without reason."

The last time the town alarm was sounded, it had been for a fire in the miller's wheat field. Possible catastrophes rushed through Derica's mind, Shredded at the forefront.

Another set of footsteps boomed down the stairs.

"Ready, son?" Tedric asked.

"Yes," Reid answered.

Derica struggled out of bed and scraped her hair from her eyes, heart pounding. Now that she concentrated, she could faintly hear the clap of the large bell hanging in the town square. Scrambling for a dressing gown, she yanked open her door, threading her arms through the garment as she went.

Tedric was already through the front door, Reid's head visible over his shoulder dashing off the front porch steps as they rushed from the house.

Pip stood wringing her hands in the foyer and looked up when Derica's footsteps sounded on the wood floors. For a moment, they looked at each other, worry and alarm shared between them.

Pip stepped over, chafing her hands down Derica's upper arms. "It'll be all right." Derica knew Pip spoke more to herself, to ease her worry for her son and husband. "Come on, I'll loan you some fresh clothing. I imagine they'll need all the help they can get."

By the time they were both dressed and gathered the supplies Pip insisted on bringing—bandages, salve, and other medicinal sundries—fingers of dawn stretched golden rays above the horizon.

Neither spoke as they brought the Wariners' horses from the barn and hitched them to the wagon. Derica was less familiar with the process but took direction from Pip easily. Once they were both settled on the bench, Pip snapped the reins, and they were on their way.

The women maintained a tense but hopeful silence as they drew closer to the center of Arlan. Unfortunately, the glow of flames and rising black smoke became evident long before then. Derica's palms dampened, and she twisted her fingers in her lap. Pip's mouth tightened, and she flicked the reins, urging the horses faster. Other wagons and horses clogged the cobblestones paving the middle of Arlan, forcing them to halt and pull aside behind the bakery.

A fire line stretched from the well, villagers passing water-filled buckets down as a runner brought the empty vessels back, but Derica didn't see Tedric or Reid.

"Where are they?" muttered Pip, her eyes scanning the square. She clutched Derica's arm before she could join the fire line. "Come on."

The thinly veiled urgency in her command made Derica's heart stutter in her chest. It was almost enough to distract her from the odd looks her neighbors gave as they followed the queue.

Just as quickly as Pip had urged her forward, she suddenly stopped and planted herself in front of Derica with a gasp. Derica bumped into her with an *oof*. The older woman spun around and cupped her shoulders with shaking hands.

"What?" Derica asked, eyes wide in confusion and worry. "Pip, is it Ted—"

"Derica." Pip's face was white as a sheet. "Go back to the wagon and wait for me there."

"Wha—why? What is it?" She tried to peer around Pip's shoulders, but Pip moved with her, blocking Derica's vision beyond. Derica looked to the side, noting again the people in the fire line sneaking glances at her when they weren't passing a bucket. And then she realized exactly where the line led.

"*No!*" The yell vaulted from her lips as she dodged Pip and ran. Neighbors gawked as Derica sprinted down the path she took every evening home from the bakery. Smoke and ash hazed the air, smudging the dawn light. It suffocated both the nascent sunbeams and Derica's hope that she was overreacting. That the awful inkling propelling her forward was a figment of her imagination.

Derica skidded to a halt when someone stepped into her path. A growl of desperate aggravation rumbled in her chest. She batted away the hands reaching for her and attempted to flee from their grasp, but her struggles proved useless. Fingers like steel clamped her wrists and tugged her forward until a familiar hold cocooned her. It took a moment for his sunshine and grass scent—buried under the acrid smell of soot—to register.

Derica slumped into Reid's hold, her heart beating so hard she knew he had to feel it flutter against him.

"Derica," he croaked, "I'm so sorry."

Her breath hitched, and she pushed her cheek into his chest, fingers digging into the back of his tunic. "How bad is it?" Her whisper might not be strong enough for him to hear, but she couldn't bring herself to ask any louder.

His arms squeezed her harder, almost to the point of discomfort—like he feared she would break and the only thing keeping her together would be his hold. "We were too late." Reid swallowed audibly and his voice was a little stronger when he spoke next. "We tried to save it. Maybe if it hadn't gone up in the middle of the night... If we could have roused more of the town to the fire line sooner..." His shoulders slumped, curling in at Derica's temples as his chin settled on the top of her head.

There were times when emotions and events pushed her into reaction, like yesterday. There were others where the safest option was to close down, to withdraw.

Derica did the latter.

Sight and sound faded as she took small sips of soot-scented air against Reid's chest, allowing her breath to be her only focus. She recognized Tedric's smoke-roughened voice growing louder as he approached, felt his broad palm across her back, but his words were an unintelligible jumble to Derica.

Reid shifted and Derica turned her head to look, despite the nauseous fear curling low in her gut. Her home—the cottage her mother left her—was being consumed. The roof had partially collapsed, and flames danced along the blackened walls. The fire stopped just outside the cottage—the fire line was exerting their efforts to stop the spread—but it would have taken a population double Arlan's size to save her home in the middle of the night.

It was gone. Everything Derica owned lay in a blazing heap. The memories of her mother stored in the meager book collection in their bookshelf. The blanket she'd packed away because it retained a whiff of her mother's garden and flour scent. The perfume Derica scrimped and saved to gift Eleanora on her last birthday. Black smoke danced into the air above the misshapen remnants of her home. Derica didn't know what she expected to see, but the flaming, crumbling ruins of her cottage would be a sight that haunted her dreams for years to come. In the few seconds she glimpsed the wreckage, the image imprinted on the backs of her eyelids. Something to pull out and review when sleep eluded her—when every mistake and regret played across her closed eyes.

It was all gone.

Reid gently turned her away, mumbling to Tedric something like, *"She'll see it when she decides she's ready."*

Derica didn't think she ever would be. Every possession, every memory the little cottage held had been snatched from her limp fingers, stolen by flame in the middle of the night while she slept in her surrogate family home. A tiny voice, all the scarier for the softness with which it spoke, rang from the shadows of her soul.

I should have been inside.

Reid nudged her into a slow amble back to the wagon, Tedric on her other side. She couldn't bring herself to care enough to shrink from the pitying gazes of her neighbors and friends. Oliana called her name, and Derica didn't even acknowledge her with a look. Numb, she turned her chin to again glimpse what remained of her home out the corner of her eye.

Pulling Derica from her maudlin spiral, Tedric reached down, cupping his soot-stained palm beneath hers. With his other hand, he laid a small circlet of scuffed gold in her palm.

Her mother's wedding band.

She didn't recognize the sound that came out of her, couldn't tell which emotion, ripped free from the cage she'd locked them in, was responsible for the wordless cry. She only clasped the ring so hard, her knuckles bleached as she brought her clenched fist to her chest, over her heart.

Tedric spoke calmly and clearly into her ear. "Eleanora wasn't a collection of things or contained in those four walls. She's with you always." He fingered a skein of her red hair, holding it before her in pinched, blackened fingers. "She blessed you with pieces of her. In looks and in spirit. It's all right if that spirit dims once in a while. That's when you seek the shelter of others. In things that make your heart sing. If it takes time for those joys to light you up the way they once did, it's all right."

Derica tucked away his words for now. She was too numb to hear and absorb them. Dipping her chin, eyes vacant, she nodded and allowed herself to be guided away.

The fire line continued to pass water-filled buckets up the queue as they reached the wagon. Pip stood wringing her hands, brow pinched, beside it.

Tedric nodded, and they silently communicated as settled, married couples do. Tedric handed Derica up into the bench, Reid climbing up first to steady her.

Tedric patted her hand, looking up into her eyes earnestly. "I am so thankful you were safe with us."

CHAPTER FIVE

D erica twisted the scarred gold ring around her finger, the gleam of the metal stolen long ago by years of wear.

She had asked her mother once why she still wore the ring, after her father had abandoned them both.

Eleanora had replied, *"Because it's not a reminder of what's gone. It's a reminder of what was here."* A wistful, faraway look had crossed her face, like it often did in the twilight of her illness. *"The loss hurts. But don't let the pain steal the happy memories."*

Derica held onto those words with all her might, clinging to them as she knelt in the garden behind the bakery. She couldn't stand the pitying looks on everyone's faces, too much like the glances she received after burying her mother. So Derica hid in her private sanctuary, not even telling Reid or his parents where she fled hours after they returned to the farmhouse. As much as she loved them, and they her, the comfort they offered her was not what she wanted.

Not right now.

Something else Eleanora had said flitted through Derica's mind, remembering those last days together. *"Don't hide here, my love. Arlan is a lovely place with lovely people, but if you ever have the urge to go on an adventure—"*

Derica laughed, the sound more a choked rasp than anything. Her. *Adventure.* All Derica had ever desired in life was to read and bake. Or at least, that was her life before Eleanora passed.

"—but if you ever have the urge to go on an adventure after I'm gone, do it. Let nothing hold you back from living. Not grief. Not fear. Because as much as you will miss me when I'm gone, I can guarantee wherever I am that I will be missing you ten times more."

Derica spun her mother's ring faster. She had no tears left to cry. She was empty inside.

And homeless.

Of course, the Wariners had offered her a place, but Reid had already mentioned his brother's intentions to return to the farm with his family in tow. The farmhouse was about to be bursting at the seams.

"How can I leave this?" she whispered to herself, her gaze taking in the garden in the waning afternoon sun. "How can I leave *you?*"

The questions mirrored the ones she'd kept herself from asking Reid when he'd broached the prospect of leaving Arlan together. A breeze kicked up, ruffling her red hair and bringing the scents of flowers, greenery, and traces of smoke to her nostrils. A marriage of life and death.

Derica pushed the sleeves of Pip's borrowed tunic higher and reached down to pluck a weed. She let her thoughts scatter like dandelion fluff as she repeated the action, over and over, until a small pile of weeds occupied the ground next to her.

Dusting off her hands, she rose and curled up on the rear porch of the bakery. The building at her back was now all Derica still had of her mother's possessions. Derica had done her best to run it after Eleanora passed, but if Mrs. Hammond hadn't offered her assistance, she knew it wouldn't still be open today. It was both comforting and painful, continuing to operate their bakery without her mother.

"What if..." she whispered, "...what if I leave? What if I go explore somewhere I've never been?" Derica couldn't deny she'd hoped to somehow hear her mother's voice explicitly tell her to go. That leaving wasn't abandoning her mother's memory.

Then she remembered Tedric's words. Her mother's memory didn't reside in a place or an object. She carried it with her.

Derica looked across the back of the garden, to the east—to the road away from Arlan. "Let's go. Together."

By the time Derica returned to the farmhouse and burst through the door, she's made her decision.

Pip met her in the foyer looking harried, but her brow smoothed as she gathered Derica to her for a quick hug. "You worried us," she whispered before letting Derica go.

She swallowed, her nerves like a ball of honey stuck in her throat. "Where are Tedric and Reid?"

Pip pointed over her shoulder as footsteps sounded on the back porch.

"Is she back?" called Tedric, worry plain in his voice.

Derica grimaced and followed Pip into the kitchen. Reid pushed around his father and gathered her into an embrace. She remained stiff in his hold, afraid that if she relaxed, she wouldn't do what she intended next.

Reid held her away from him, studying her with a notch of confusion between his gold brows.

Derica didn't meet his eyes and gestured to the kitchen table. "Would it be all right if we all sat for a moment to talk?"

Reid, Pip, and Tedric passed around a puzzled glance, but they all sat.

"Derica," Pip said, frustration and concern threading through her tone as she reached across the table, patting Derica's hand, "you could have at least told us where you were going. We wouldn't have begrudged you some time alone to gr—"

"—to think," finished Reid, eyes darting to his mother.

Derica could tell by the tilt of his head he'd figured out something was brewing. But he waited patiently, giving her space to say the things she'd practiced the entire walk from the garden.

Taking a deep breath, Derica began her rehearsed speech. "I know this might sound rash and like I haven't thought this through." She licked her lips, continuing when all the Wariners sat expectantly, waiting for her. "And maybe I haven't. But I—the other night, Reid mentioned going to Radley together—"

Both Reid's parents' eyes snapped to him. He ducked sheepishly, then leaned forward. "I hadn't told them yet, Derica."

"Oh... well." She cleared her throat and spun her mother's ring around her finger. "Now might be the time to do that."

Reid watched her, looking for something in her eyes, as he rolled his lips between his teeth, stifling a smile. Whatever he saw erased some of the worry in his gaze. "Yes, I suppose you're right." With a shrug and a sigh, he said, "Ma. Pa. I know we've all talked about Algie returning." He waited for his parents to nod before continuing. "He's bringing Seraphina and the children. There's about to be very little breathing room to spare in this house."

Pip reached blindly to Tedric, and he grasped her hand. Still, they remained silent as their son slowly explained.

"I broached the topic to Derica the other day." He cringed, shooting her an apologetic look. "It probably wasn't the best time to bring it up, but," he shrugged, "you know how I get when I have a plan in my head."

Pip sighed and leaned into Tedric, nodding. Tedric stifled a laugh but couldn't disguise the sadness stealing into his eyes.

"I asked Derica to accompany me to Radley." Reid watched her now. "I guess she's decided that's something she wants to do?" At her faint nod, Reid raised a golden brow. "I need more than that, and you know it. Have you decided that's what you want? To come with me?"

Three pairs of eyes watched her, and Derica had never felt anything so heavy. Her swallow sounded like the impact of a boulder to her own ears. "Y-yes. I even arranged a few things before I came back here."

"You're sure?" he asked.

"I don't think," her eyes bounced around the faces of her surrogate family, "I have the luxury of *'sure'* right now. I'm not certain I ever will. Surety implies I know this is the right course of action. And..." she twisted her hands in her skirts to keep from fidgeting with her mother's wedding ring, "I don't know if that's true. But going to Radley is better than hiding here. If I'm honest, I've been hiding for a long time now. And I think this is the first step to remedying that."

Pip's eyes shimmered, and she reached across the table to take Derica's hands. "Wherever you go, you always have a place here. You know this." It wasn't a question, but an assertion.

"I do." Derica nodded.

Tedric looked at Reid while stroking the back of his wife's hand comfortingly. "And the same goes for you. Always has."

Reid dipped his chin. The love the three of them shared filled the room, and it tugged something raw in Derica's chest. He sniffled quietly and swiped suspiciously dewy eyes, then bestowed a smile like sun after a rainstorm on Derica. "This is going to be an adventure."

CHAPTER SIX

O nce the decision to leave had been made, Derica proposed they depart as soon as possible. All the Wariners looked at her askance, but she knew Reid understood the reason for her urgency. The softening of his eyes and his ready acceptance when she talked about leaving told her he grasped her reasons perfectly. Even a moment longer in Arlan with the knowledge of her loss was like holding scalding metal to bare skin.

She'd stopped on the way back to the farm and offered Mrs. Hammond the deed to the bakery. The older woman had balked, but after Derica let Mrs. Hammond know she desired a fresh start—something *new*—the excitement in the older woman's eye had warmed Derica.

Now there was so little holding her here and, with her mind made up, Derica couldn't focus on anything else. Her problems and her grief would likely follow her, but Derica chose to ignore that reality.

Readying for their journey would take very little time. She owned nothing but borrowed clothing and her mother's ring, after all. Pip and Tedric helped Reid and Derica pack and prepare, wearing poorly hidden sadness and shock. By midafternoon, they were loading their saddlebags and ready to depart.

She hadn't missed when Tedric slipped a half-bow and quiver into their packs, patting Reid on the back as he whispered, "Better to be prepared."

Now, Reid and Derica stood on the porch of the Wariner farmhouse, surrounded by his family. *Derica's* family.

Tedric and his son stood together, the older man smiling brightly, despite the shadow of melancholy in his eyes. He thumped Reid on the back and pulled him into a hug. Derica couldn't hear what they said into the other's shoulder, but Tedric's eyes shone with tears as he clutched his son to him.

Pip's gentle hands gripped Derica's shoulders. The woman, like a second mother to her, smiled softly, gaze flitting across her face.

"I expect letters when you two get settled. I want to hear about your adventures and all the new things you see and learn. I want reports about Reid and his apprenticeship. I made sure he's packed appropriately, and there's a meal prepared for you both when you stop for the night—"

As Pip talked about all she needed from them when Derica and Reid established themselves in Radley, Derica smiled broader with every word out of the older woman's mouth. She would miss Pip dearly. Derica could have never fathomed the circumstances that led to their departure. However, it would be a lie to say the tiniest kernel of excitement didn't blossom inside her at the thought of new experiences. Fear was there too—a thin coating. She kept repeating her mother's words, though.

Let nothing hold you back from living.

Pip's overly cheery and excessive instructions cut off when Reid and Tedric joined them. Reid wrapped his mother in his arms, and she buried her face in his chest. Pip's shoulders quivered, but when she pulled back from her son, her eyes were dry. She stroked her palm down her son's face, cupping his jaw. Reid stooped as Pip rose on her toes to place a kiss on his cheek before stepping back. Tedric gathered his wife against his side, rubbing his palm up and down her arm in comfort.

Reid bent and collected Derica's pack from the porch next to her, slinging it across his back beside his. His blue eyes searched Derica's carefully. "Ready to go?"

With a trembling smile at Tedric and Pip, she nodded.

Reid reached down and grabbed Derica's hand, and the pair moved off the porch, toward the horse Tedric saddled for them. Once Reid secured their packs on either side of the wide saddle, he swung himself up into it, then held his hand out to assist Derica up onto the horse, waiting.

Suddenly, her fear bubbled up, locking her legs and freezing her mid-step. She'd made a mistake. Everything was happening too fast.

Derica had been so proud of herself—so certain her mother would have been proud—when she told the Wariners about going to Radley. Now, her rising anxiety shook her certainty, threatening to crumble it into dust.

Sensing her hesitation, Reid leaned down over the pommel, pitching his voice low. "It's going to be all right."

"You don't know that. *I* don't know that."

"You're right. I don't. But you're not alone, Derica." He looked behind her at his parents, and the smile on his lips slid away. "I'm glad we're leaving together."

"Reid, I—is this the right thing to do?"

"For me, it is. I can't answer that question for you. Besides, aren't *sure* and *right* the same things?" He held his hand out to her again.

"Yes. I suppose they are." Her chest rose on a deep breath as she slipped her hand into his. Derica placed her foot in the stirrup as Reid helped her up into the saddle in front of him. His arms came around her waist to steady her as she settled into a comfortable position. Reid gave her a squeeze, then reached back to adjust the saddlebag on his left.

Her heart raced as she looked over her shoulder at Reid's parents, a riot of tangled emotion sweeping through her chest. They stood with their arms around each other, smiling at their son and the woman they'd all but adopted as a mist of tears wet their faces.

"Get moving so you reach the inn before the road is completely dark," Pip called with a wave.

"Ready?" Reid's voice rumbled against Derica's back as he waved back at his mother. She didn't know if she could throw a cheerful wave over her shoulder to Pip and Tedric. Part of Derica wanted to jump off the horse and run into their embrace. So, Derica simply nodded when they called their goodbye. She didn't look back.

Derica thumbed her mother's ring and settled back into the warmth of Reid's chest. With a comforting squeeze around her waist, he reminded her she wasn't alone. Before she had time to second-guess her decision, he flicked the reins, and with a last wave, they rode away from everything familiar and safe.

"They'll be all right. Algernon will be here tomorrow or the next day to help Pa, and Ma will be so busy with the kids, she'll hardly miss us." Reid's voice was cheerful, but she felt the hitch in his chest at the end of his statement. She reached over and laid her hand on Reid's forearm, entirely conscious of the fact he was leaving behind much more than Derica.

They both lapsed into silence, soaking in the cadence of the draft horse's hooves striking the packed earth. The rustle of the trees sang them a farewell as they rode out of Arlan and onto the road to the posting inn. Pastures and wheat fields gave way to dense forest that would thin out as they journeyed to Radley.

Ridiculously, she'd expected every step away from Arlan to give her a re-prieve—an emotional distance to match the physical, but that didn't happen. Thoughts and memories rampaged through her mind as the silence stretched. When she felt like the worries would smother her, Reid extended a lifeline.

"Did you tell Oliana you were leaving?"

Her mind stuttered onto a new track. "There wasn't time."

"Mmm." He waited for her to say more.

"I didn't want to hurt her again. She was so patient and kind af-ter—when—"

"I know."

"My feelings were never as big as hers," Derica sighed, guilt settling on her shoulders. "It was cowardly, but when we drifted apart—when I pushed her away—it was the easier thing to do. I thought I was being kind, but maybe it was cruel instead."

"Ma once told me grief is a solitary, winding path we often walk alone. For some, they're alone because they don't know how to reach out. For others, they turn from the hands they're offered. Neither is wrong. It's natural to seek solitude in pain. Animals do it. Humans are really no different. I think Oliana understands that."

Derica grimaced. "She does. If she didn't, she would have pressed for an explanation." With a deep exhale, Derica determined to fix her error. Oliana deserved more. "I'll write to her from Radley."

Given a fresh worry, Derica's thoughts pounced like a kitten on a ball of yarn. She thought out how to address her letter, what to say to confess her cowardice, and how to apologize while making it clear they didn't have a future together.

It took Derica most of a mile to realize Reid had worked his magic, giving her a safer, smaller problem to contemplate. The Weaver-damned, wonderful man.

When the posting inn came into view, Derica's ass was half asleep and her stomach was rumbling with every waft from the basket Pip packed them. Night was rapidly swallowing the last blush of sunset, and Derica shifted in the saddle, looking forward to a meal and some rest.

"Thank the Weaver," Reid sighed. She felt his stomach rumble against her back as well.

When they entered the courtyard of the inn, Reid hitched the bay, dismounting the animal first, then reached up for Derica. She slid down into his arms, thankful she wouldn't fall on her numb backside with Reid's help.

"Let's see if they have a room first, then come back for our bags." He nodded toward the large carriage alongside the inn and the rather impressive retinue of horses hitched to the posts beside their own. Derica's eyebrows climbed her forehead as she absorbed the surrounding scene.

She pursed her lips. "This could be a problem."

They'd left so late in the day and with the rumored threat of the Shredded, they hadn't planned on riding through the night to Radley.

Reid looked down at her, his brow gathered in grim contemplation. "Why don't you wait near the horse? I'll go see if there's any room. Maybe we can just occupy a table for the night if we have to. I can sleep sitting against the wall, I'm so tired." Reid's voice drifted off into a mutter, fading with him as he walked away and into the inn—but not before Derica glimpsed his under eyes, heavy and bruised with fatigue.

It'd been such a long day for them both, filled with stress, grief, and excitement. Derica felt a twinge of regret at her impulsiveness. She'd remember to thank Reid profusely when they were settled for the night.

Derica moved next to their horse, holding the reins and stroking the velvet soft nose of the massive beast. She looked around the courtyard, trying to puzzle out why there were so many here tonight. The carriage wasn't particularly fine. There was no insignia or coat of arms to signify traveling nobility. There were quite a few horses hitched in the yard, as well. Derica bit her lip, beginning to worry. She'd just assumed there wouldn't be any trouble finding a room available.

A breeze kicked up from the direction they'd come, sweeping down the road and into the courtyard. Derica stepped closer to their mount, shoulders tensing as she scrutinized the shadows crouched beyond the inn's torches. With determination, she mentally waved away lingering fears sparked by rumors of Shredded.

Derica cast a critical eye over the wooden two-story building. It hid its age well—until she spotted the cracked siding under a bright coat of paint and several shingles hanging from the roof, clinging by the power of prayer. Or possibly cobwebs.

The din from the dining room was so raucous it drifted through the bubbled glass of the windows. A gust of wind picked up and danced chilly fingers into the opening of her capelet. She tugged it closed and smoothed her hands down the breeches Pip hastily altered before their departure. Squinting in the dim light of the courtyard torches, she read the weathered wooden sign above the inn door as it swayed on its post.

The Dove & Dagger.

The horse huffed and pushed its nose into her hand. When no treats met the obvious ploy, the horse nudged her shoulder, sniffing down her arm. She laughed and yanked away from the animal. An almost dejected sigh blew her red hair back from her forehead.

"It's all right, I'll make sure you get a nice juicy apple when—"

The sudden swell of voices filtering through the open door of the inn caught Derica's attention, and out stepped Reid. Her heart sank at the look on his face.

Hands on his hips, he didn't look at her when he delivered the news. "No rooms. They don't have an open table in the dining room. There's not even an empty stool at the bar." He kicked a rock from under his feet and raked his hands through his golden hair. Derica stretched up to smooth it back into place, but he moved out from under her hands with a murmured epithet.

Reid paced up and back the length of the courtyard in front of the inn, alternatively pulling at his hair and swearing roundly. "No room at the inn. No room to sit inside. Don't want to risk the Shredded. Pa made sure I packed provisions for camping, so we do have a small tent. It could work. Shouldn't risk a fire, though. Right? Yes, a fire would be bad. It's not cold. We have food. A fire isn't needed, anyway. All right. We will be *all right*."

Derica just watched him pace and mutter. His hair became a truly impressive nest of snarls. By the time he worked out his frustration with long strides back and forth, he came to stand in front of Derica. His eyes looked a touch less wild, and his breath wasn't as quick.

"We're going to set up a camp just off the road. We have the food my mother packed for us and we won't need a fire. There should be enough moonlight tonight. I also don't want... unexpected visitors."

Derica frowned, unease sweeping back, climbing up her spine. "But the Shredded—"

"Won't be an issue if we don't have a fire signaling our camp position. Come on."

Reid nimbly leapt up into the saddle and threw a hand down for Derica.

When they were both mounted, Reid clicked his tongue and spurred their horse back onto the road. "We'll ride for a bit, away from the inn, and then see if we can't find a nice little spot for camp."

Sensing Reid needed to feel in complete control of the situation, Derica patted his arm reassuringly and let him lead. She turned her head to monitor his mood, and found his blue eyes glittering, scanning the wooded area on either side of the road. Aged trees towered on either side of the dirt road, so densely packed Derica squinted trying to pierce their shadows. A fair distance from the inn, where they could just spot the distant glow of the torches in the courtyard, Reid dismounted and carefully guided their steed through a break in the greenery.

The path opened up into a patch of verdant earth, wide enough to accommodate their small party and the horse. Reid hitched their animal to a tree and then reached up to help her dismount. She slid off the saddle to the ground. While Reid saw to the care of the horse, she gathered the basket containing their dinner and yanked free a blanket. Covering the ground with the heavy woolen quilt, she arranged their dinner.

They would set up their camp after they both ate something. Maybe it would improve Reid's mood. They ate in relative silence, comfortable with the lack of conversation. She noticed Reid's keen attention to their surroundings. His eyes flicked toward any sound, she assumed inspecting for danger. She agreed the absence of a fire would provide them relative safety from any late night visitors, but it was eerie in their little glade. The cool silver of the moonlight cast harsh shadows and made them seem deeper.

Finished eating, they quickly set up camp, although there was an almost constant stream of frustrated cursing from them both as they fumbled in the dark. They tried to set up the tent but were both too short-tempered and tired to work together properly. The night wasn't so cool to be uncomfortable in the open air, so they tossed it aside. They huddled side by side on their bedrolls and both succumbed to sleep quickly.

CHAPTER SEVEN

When Derica woke, the moon hung still visible in the sky. Reid's steady breaths puffed against the back of her head, the occasional small grunt or snore signaling he slept deeply. Their horse stood still and unbothered where they had tethered it. Everything seemed fine. Then it struck her.

The silence was what woke her.

No leaves rustled. No skitter of nocturnal animals accented the dark. Not even the hoot of an owl or the chirp of a cricket.

Derica slowly reached her hand back toward Reid. In sleep, they'd drifted closer together like two puppies seeking the warmth and comfort of another body. Patting until she found his arm behind her back, she gripped it in her hand, squeezing, then shaking him when he didn't immediately rouse. His snore cut off, and he shifted, mumbling blearily.

"Wake up," she whispered.

"What is it?" His voice was gruff with sleep in her ear.

"Do you hear that?"

"Hear what?"

"*Exactly.*"

Reid stiffened behind her.

"Do we have any weapons?" she asked.

"A half-bow, a dagger, and a knife. For hunting."

She hummed low, flicking her gaze around the shadows. "Are they still in the saddlebags, or did you unpack them?"

"*Weaver-dammit.* They're still tied to the saddle. We didn't need to hunt for dinner, so I didn't touch them. I should have laid them beside the bedrolls." The blanket rustled as he resettled. "It's probably nothing."

She took a large breath, tamping down her worry, then announced she needed to relieve herself.

"Take the dagger. Just in case." Reid sat up, rubbing sleep from his eyes. "I'll wait for you right here."

She crouched, slowly unfolding, holding her breath until she stood upright. Back rigid, she scanned around for any movement, sounds—anything to confirm the presence of danger.

"Derica, it's all right," Reid said, reaching up to touch her hand, offering her strength. "I'll whistle when I can't see you anymore, so you know when you have privacy. I'll be near, I promise."

She nodded and bent to ruffle through the saddlebags. It took less than a moment to locate the dagger and palm it. Her grip slicked it with sweat, but that couldn't be helped. Weapon in hand, she felt marginally better.

She moved away into the trees, frequently looking back toward the clearing where she'd left Reid. He whistled low once, as he said he would. Derica set the dagger within easy reach and, as fast as she could, she took care of her business.

As she straightened her clothing, movement on the edge of her vision snagged her attention. Fear dragged chilly fingers over her shoulders as she whipped her head around to look. A leaf falling from a tree branch. Heart still racing, she slipped the dagger into the belt at her waist and made herself take a deep breath. Next, she whistled to Reid, letting him know she was coming back.

Choosing her steps carefully, Derica watched the ground as she picked her way back to camp, stumbling over rocks and tree roots in the dark. Halfway back to their camp, a muffled yell broke the silence before cutting off abruptly. Jolting into motion, Derica stumbled back to where she'd left Reid in the clearing, finding it empty.

Her first impulse was to scream for him, and she barely kept her mouth shut, fearing any attention she'd bring with the call. Other than his rumpled blanket, there was no sign of Reid. Blood rushed loudly in her ears, and with every second that passed without Reid jumping out of the brush and revealing himself, her panic grew.

As smoothly as she was able, she walked to the bags and snatched the half-bow. Their horse shifted, tossing its head. She slipped the bow across her torso along with the quiver, leaving both hands empty. Then she pulled the dagger from her belt, wincing when the scrape of the metal against the buckle grated into the air. She froze and cast her eyes around the camp, hoping Reid was playing a prank again. There was no other acceptable reason for this. But if he was hiding, Derica detected nothing in the darkness.

The quiet of the woods was eerie and disconcerting. Reid normally wasn't such as ass though as to make her worry for his safety. Reid got his ridiculous satisfaction from tiny scares and hadn't ever escalated his pranks further.

This didn't feel the same. The niggling in the back of her mind wouldn't let her dismiss the thought he was in danger.

She stood near the horse, to one side of the clearing. The trees opposite her cast the deepest shadows in the moonlight. If Reid was hiding anywhere, it had to be there. She squinted into the darkness but didn't see a flash of blue eyes, no glint of his golden head.

Shaking herself into action, Derica moved toward the shadowy abyss, dagger in front of her. The closer she drew, the louder the voice in the back of her mind screamed. Adjusting her grip on the bone handle of the dagger, she stopped before the edge of the darkened copse. A bead of sweat dripped down her temple and dropped onto her collarbone. Steeling her courage, Derica licked her lips and stepped into the shadow's domain.

She blinked, trying to see anything in the pitch-black cast by the trees overhead, but it was all-encompassing. Derica stopped and stood for a moment inside the cocoon of darkness. She slowly turned her head to the left, then she looked to the right, swiveling her chin slowly. When her chin was almost perpendicular with the length of her shoulder, she saw them.

Two yellow, glowing eyes.

Shredded! her mind screamed.

Derica slapped her empty palm to her mouth to muffle her gasp. Her breath wanted to explode from her in fright, but she held it trapped in her lungs.

The yellow orbs might not be looking at her.

Yes. And the Weaver will bring your mother back to you if you believe that.

Derica's eyes slipped closed for a moment as she acknowledged her own hopeful stupidity. Derica popped them back open when a whisper of foliage announced the owner of those eyes moving. Coming closer.

The citrine-colored orbs drifted nearer in the shadows. One eye blinked. And then the other. Derica suppressed a shudder and a hysterical laugh, willing her body to remain still, hoping the creature wouldn't notice her. Reid would be the reason she died. Then morbid thoughts cascaded through the tumult of her fear—visions of Reid hurt. Or worse. Her hand spasmed around the dagger and she tightened her grip.

Still seeing nothing but the glowing eyes in front of her, Derica debated turning her back and sprinting to the horse. She could—she hoped—saddle it and mount quickly enough to ride away from danger. She could flee to the inn, bring back a party to search for Reid.

But she couldn't leave him. Not when she didn't know if he had been harmed by this creature, for those citrine eyes were not human. The gaze held an uncanny sharpness that enthralled as much as it sparked the desire to run.

The eyes grew larger. Frozen, she watched until it stood less than a foot away from her, its eyes a few scant inches above her own. She fought not to whimper and shrink, huddling down to the ground.

Realizing she still held the dagger, her arm thrust the blade forward on instinct. She slammed her eyes shut as she anticipated the impact of creature and metal.

Dizziness assailed her as something gripped her hand in a warm clasp and spun her body so she faced away from the golden-eyed source of terror. A thin arm reached around her, securing her waist, the other holding her wrist to control the dagger.

Damp breath brushed her ear as a silken voice stirred the hair at her temple. "Morsel, we need to teach you how to properly wield a blade. That was simply pathetic."

Derica gasped and shoved her hips back into her captor. She could tell whoever held her was slight, hardly taller than her, but they didn't budge. To her knowledge, Shredded didn't speak, but her panic refused to abate. The hands controlling her gripped like iron as she thrashed.

A disappointed cluck sounded in her ear. "I wouldn't try to get free. I don't want you harming yourself. Now, why don't you let go of the frightfully dull dagger and come with me? I believe we have your friend."

At the mention of Reid, Derica opened shaking hands and heard the weapon bounce on the blanket of leaves cushioning the forest floor.

"What a good girl. Follow me, and I'll take you to your giant."

The arms holding Derica slithered from around her. Free, she spun around to face her captor. Her hair fluttered around her head as the stranger in front of her plucked the half-bow and quiver from Derica's torso, leaving her defenseless.

"Well, I suppose if you're a decent shot, you could have done some damage with these," her captor said, voice dry as they blithely dismissed her weapons. "Safer too. For you, that is. If it had been anyone but me that caught you. Oh, and you've no reason to fear. I mean you no harm." They chuckled. "Badly done, to approach and not declare my intentions, but I was told to keep things quiet and I was afraid you'd run. A chase through the woods can make an awful racket."

Derica sputtered, shock choking her questions in her throat. *Who* was this person? Where was Reid? What in the *fuck* was going on?

Before Derica could ask, slim fingers grasped her forearm and tugged her farther away from her camp and deeper into the darkness. "Come along, morsel. I'm sure your man is tired of waiting for you by now."

Towed by her captor, Derica stumbled in the dark. Farther from the camp. Farther from where she'd last seen Reid. She almost dug her heels into the loamy earth beneath her feet, but the grip on her arm was far too firm and insistent to allow Derica to tug them to a halt. Or run away.

"I demand—!"

"Shh. You're safe and all your questions will be answered shortly. I'm taking you to your friend."

"But—"

"Great Spirits, have some patience."

Derica swallowed her protests and allowed herself to be led. No matter how hard she peered into the depths of the shadows, she could see nothing. She hesitated to trust this stranger, but there was little alternative. Even if she could escape, she couldn't navigate her way back to camp if her life depended on it. Her captor whistled softly in the dark. The tune held no malice, but it raised the hair on Derica's arms, and the skin on her arms pebbled into gooseflesh as they moved swiftly through the dark.

When she thought the whistling and oppressive shadows had stolen her wits, she perceived a glow. It grew larger and closer until Derica heard the pop and crack of a fire. Even with more light, she couldn't discern anything about her captor other than their height—the same, or slightly taller than Derica herself.

She followed them into a clearing, larger than the one she and Reid chose for their camp, and sucked in a relieved breath. Vision-hazing wrath crashed down over her as her gaze swept the clearing and its occupants.

Her cheery giant of a best friend sat, back propped up against a pile of saddlebags in front of the fire, holding a mug—presumably full of ale, given his smile and vaguely dazed eyes.

Elbowing her captor out of the way, Derica stomped over to Reid. The fire bathed her back in comforting waves of heat as she bent down, snatched the mug from Reid, and dumped it all over his traitorous blond head.

Blue eyes blinked up at her in shock as he swiped the foamy remains of the drink from his cheeks and jaw. "Weaver's tits! What was that for?!"

"I thought you were dead, or captured, or—or—you—" Derica's chest heaved, she was so mad. Her vision became watery as the well of her wrath was tempered by the fear her closest friend had been in mortal danger. Which made her rage stoke hotter.

Biting her lip to keep from sobbing and throwing herself into his ale-soaked lap, she chucked the empty mug at his chest and turned away. Derica tilted her head up to the night sky, breathing slow and deep as she blinked the banked tears away.

"Derica, I got up to check the other side of the camp and was startled by one of these fine people." He gestured over Derica's shoulder. "Thankfully, they didn't do any lasting harm." Reid circled his left wrist with the opposite hand, the nascent bloom of bruising evident. "By the time they towed me here, we'd already sorted ourselves out—all a misunderstanding. I was all turned around. They sent someone to bring you here to the safety of their fire."

The heat of her anger cooled and died. A drop of ale fell from Reid's chin, trailing onto his wet tunic. Derica's ears heated with embarrassment.

His eyes swept her up and down, a concerned frown crinkling his brow. "They didn't scare you, did they? You're all right?"

Derica stiffened, reminded of their audience. Other than the general height of her *guide* into this other camp, she hadn't focused on anyone other than Reid since entering the clearing.

As she swung her gaze around, she was startled to find Father Simond looking at her from across the blaze, his dour blond companion next to him. This meant...

"Welcome," a voice said from the left of Father Simond, the speaker hidden in shadows. "Take a seat next to your friend and enjoy some ale. You're lucky we have more after the bath you gave him."

Smoke. Twilight. A voice so distinct, she didn't think she'd ever forget it, no matter how briefly she'd heard it before.

She barely kept her head from jerking to search for the man the voice came from. As it was, she couldn't halt the nervous clasping and wringing of her hands in front of her.

Putting off acknowledging him—if she faced him, she might lose her capacity for intelligent thought—she quickly absorbed the rest of her surroundings. Old trees cast the clearing in shadow so dense, not a single beam of moonlight could have penetrated the bower made by their branches. A small cart, large enough for two riders and a small amount of cargo, stood by a group of five horses.

A man of average height—but intimidating bulk—brushed one of their mounts. Everything about him was golden brown: his short, curly hair, his eyes, his skin—except the flesh covered in deep blue tattoos. The ink swirled down his forearms onto his fingers and climbed the column of his neck above the collar of his tunic. He met her gaze, flashed a saucy smile and a wink before going back to grooming his mount.

That left...

Derica slowly skated her eyes back to the one who guided her here.

In the firelight, their heavily lashed citrine gaze sparkled with the depth of a tiger's eye gem. Their face was unlined, but their hair—both on their head and their brows—was so white, it glowed in the ruby hue of the flame. Plaited into a thick, silvery rope, their hair hung down to the small of their back. A slim blade of a nose highlighted high, full cheekbones and lips that were lush and shockingly red against the pale hue of their skin, its undertone faintly cool and blue.

Like sun-bleached lapis lazuli.

They wore simple, dark clothing that seemed entirely inconspicuous—until she noticed the knives glinting on their belt, a script she'd never seen before tooled into the leather. A necklace, the pendant a collection of small, tawny striped feathers, hung around their neck.

As she'd sensed before, their build was rangy and tensile. The grip she'd been towed by further informed Derica's visual inspection; their slimness hid massive strength. Strength banked for her benefit, it seemed. They could have hauled her bodily to this camp without undue exertion.

Those wide lips pulled into a genuine grin of mirth, and Derica stifled a gasp. Small *fangs* glinted from the edges of their smile. Two sets, one point shining in each quadrant of their sinful smile.

One yellow eye blinked. Then the other. In the full impact of the firelight, it was eerie and shot the impulse to flee skittering down her spine once more.

She squinted, and her captor suddenly stood right in front of her, their voice like silk and sin wrapping around Derica as their gaze swept her up and down.

"Hmm. Not quite what I pictured, but then again..." They trailed off, muttering. Their yellow stare pinned hers and up close, those eyes framed by thick white lashes mesmerized. Derica couldn't—didn't—want to move.

"Mazolan. Knock it off."

"It's all right, Commander, I only wanted to see something."

Derica frowned but continued to hold their gaze. Looking elsewhere proved impossible.

"You're frightening her." When they—Mazolan—didn't release her from their scrutiny, that smoky voice spoke again. "Maz. I said—" a hand grasped Derica and yanked her away, the spell broken, "—*knock it off.*"

She was turned, and then quickly released. Hadrian stood two paces away from her, a thunderous frown darkening his brow. Derica's arm tingled from that brief contact alone and she reached up to rub the sensation away. It was hard to believe the man who guarded her peace in the garden on Rite Day and the one who stood before her now were one and the same.

Turning to her, his obsidian gaze flicked to Derica's hand on her arm and his mouth flattened. "All right there?" His voice snapped, terse as his eyes flicked back up to hers. A bolt of awareness and something else shot down her spine, then wrapping around her chest. Derica's response stuck in her throat while she stared. This is why she'd avoided looking at him. This *pull.*

Derica searched her memory for something to compare this feeling—this fascination—to and came up empty. Warmth swept up her chest, rising to sting her cheeks, and still, she couldn't look away. It was a comfort to note Hadrian seemed to feel something as well, if the light in his eyes was any indication.

Reid got up from in front of the fire, tossing down the rag he'd found to dry himself. He stepped behind Derica and drew her into his chest. Even in his embrace, her muscles refused to loosen. She stood, wooden, in the shelter of his body.

As Hadrian glanced at Reid's hands on her hips and then back to her eyes, some of the heat in his eyes dissipated. Almost concealed in its dark scruff, a muscle ticked in his jaw. Derica blinked, breaking the spell, when Reid pressed a kiss to the top of her head, and she relaxed against him. Mazolan's gaze bounced back and forth between Derica and Hadrian, a keen light kindling in the depths of their eyes. Derica leaned into Reid, taking comfort in his nearness.

"Thank you for collecting my friend, Mazolan," Reid murmured.

Mazolan bowed with a flourish, a mocking tilt to their head, white braid swinging with the motion.

Hadrian drew himself into a military posture, chest out, hands clasped behind his back. "I was patrolling the perimeter of our camp when I discovered your friend thrashing around the woods. I mistook him for a threat and brought him back here. He couldn't direct me to your camp, so I sent our best tracker to collect you. Reid didn't want you left alone. I hope Mazolan didn't scare you." He frowned over at his companion. Mazolan smirked back, throwing themselves indolently on a spread bedroll.

"Where's the horse and their supplies?" Hadrian asked.

"Commander, there was no mention of collecting the woman *and* that monster of a mount and their detritus." Mazolan lay flat, one hand bent behind their head, one knee up, the foot of the opposite leg bouncing in the air.

Hadrian's posture, already rigid, became practically stone.

She eyed Mazolan uncertainly. Citrine eyes caught hers and twinkled impishly, a silken chuckle floating to her. She shook her head hard, unwilling to be caught in such a trap again.

The commander's rumbled growl turned into low muttering. She picked up only a few words.

"*Demon... Weaver-damned... of course... horse too.*"

"I can return for the horse," Reid said.

Hadrian shook his head abruptly and uncoiled from his stance. "No, Mazolan can direct me. *I'll* finish the job." He shot the last at his companion like a venom-coated arrow.

Mazolan flicked up one white brow and nodded at the commander. "Such chivalry!"

Hadrian walked to his subordinate and kicked the foot they bounced in the air. Mazolan frowned up at him, then nodded wordlessly in the direction they entered the camp.

The commander stalked into the shadows, quickly swallowed by the inky fingers of night. Derica watched him go, her gaze magnetized to his movements.

Father Simond, who had been observing the surrounding events with a placid smile, patted the blanket beside him. "Come, sit. Why don't the two of you rest together? I'm sure you've had an eventful night."

Balduin, the father's acolyte, frowned and his lip hiked up into the ghost of a sneer as he eyed Reid's damp tunic.

Derica and Reid looked at each other, silently conversing, before concluding it would be stupid to leave the safety of a larger group. At least, that's what Derica imagined they had agreed upon.

They would stay. For the night.

Together, they joined the father and his acolyte, Reid sitting between Derica and the others.

She looked over to where Mazolan lay, but the bedroll was now empty.

Before she had time to find her captor, their white head poked over her right shoulder. Derica squeaked as fangs gleamed far too close to her person for comfort. Reid's arm came around her and she pressed into his side.

"I look forward to getting to know you, morsel. Before the commander comes back to chastise me, I wanted to apologize." Their fangs gleamed as they smiled impishly before the expression melted away. "I'm sorry." Face stony and serious, they watched her, waiting. When she simply nodded, not knowing what to say, the twinkle popped back into their eyes.

Mazolan's braid slithered over their shoulder and swung down over Derica's, almost trailing into her lap. They drew closer and Derica leaned forward, her curiosity to know what they would say next overshadowing her trepidation.

"Your man has been so lonely without you. But not even he knows what you are." Mazolan's eyes became slits of piercing gold as they beamed into hers. Their voice dropped lower, becoming a whisper only she could hear. "You have forgotten. You have been lost for so long. Many times upon the Loom. Never together. Never connected at the heart like you once were. And you don't even know to miss it." They cocked their head, braid swinging like a metronome. A thread of melancholy underscored their last statement, knotting Derica's brows in bewilderment.

Mazolan's words didn't scare her—they weren't delivered with malice. It was the intensity that alarmed and confused her.

She had no idea what they were talking about.

"*Ahem.*" Father Simond cleared his throat, reaching over Reid to pat Derica's shoulder. "Mazolan, I think we should leave the dear child alone. Weaver knows she's probably had a fright, what with being separated from her friend. Clearly she was worried for his safety." He turned, addressing Reid next. "I believe I have a clean habit in my pack if you don't have a change of clothes with you, son. You probably don't want to sleep in those." He pointed to the ale stains still drying on Reid's tunic.

Reid politely declined, saying he'd have his clothing when the commander returned.

Mazolan, having been dismissed by Father Simond, slunk to the opposite side of the campfire, but even with the distance, she felt the intensity of their gaze on her skin like the rasp of uncomfortable wool. Derica refused to meet their gaze once more.

Reid wasn't her man, and he'd never been without Derica, not since they met as children. They'd been practically inseparable since they were five years old. She hadn't smelled ale on Mazolan's breath, but they had to be daft or drunk if they thought they knew anything about her life.

What they'd said about the Loom, though. That rang in her ears, echoing in her skull. And she didn't know why.

Commander Hadrian emerged from the dark, leading their horse, with a pack slung over each shoulder. Unerringly, Derica's eyes trailed him, but he didn't look at her as he hitched their horse with the others, then set the bags down behind her and Reid.

His onyx gaze flicked to the arm Reid still had around Derica before he stalked over to Mazolan and sat beside his comrade. The two whispered to each other, Mazolan gesticulating wildly while the commander seemed to be holding his temper in check. Derica strained to hear but didn't catch a word the two mercenaries exchanged. Hadrian turned away from Mazolan and settled his gaze on her and Reid. Realizing they'd been dismissed, Mazolan also studied the couple.

"So. What brings the two of you away from Arlan?" Hadrian's voice was flat, almost accusatory.

Reid patted Derica's shoulder and answered. "Traveling to the capital."

The commander swept his gaze up and down Derica, searching. He never met her eyes. "Unusual to camp on the road with such a small party."

"Unusual? I think the word is *stupid*," Balduin said, frowning at Derica and Reid like they were mangy, flea-ridden cats.

She picked at a loose thread on her breeches, returning his rude scrutiny across the fire.

"What would you have done? Turned around? The sun was already setting. I don't fancy travel on dark roads." Reid answered.

Balduin leaned back, crossing his arms. "Better that than be caught helpless by Shr—"

Father Simond cleared his throat and shook his head at the younger man.

"Lucky then, to have crossed paths," Reid said, nodding to Hadrian.

"You're sure you're all right? I gather you were quite worried," Hadrian asked. He indicated Derica with a tilt of his chin, still not making eye contact, instead looking somewhere to the right of her head.

She felt both apprehensive and compelled around him, and she didn't know why. She suspected he was bottled lightning and if the cork came free, she'd be struck. A sibilant voice in the back of her mind enticed her to confirm her suspicions.

"I'm unharmed, and so is Reid. That's all that matters."

"Good." The commander nodded and his shoulders lost some of their rigidity.

"How far are we from Radley?" asked Reid.

"About a full day's ride," answered Hadrian.

Reid stroked his chin, muttering under his breath to himself.

"My child," said Father Simond, "I don't think you should leave the safety of our group." He flicked a hand at the three mercenaries. "I don't know if the news has made it to Arlan, but there have been Shredded encounters near here. I don't mean to alarm you, but there's no better company to be in should danger appear."

"But you're paying for their protection, yes?" Reid asked.

Hadrian nodded. "The job was to escort Father Simond to Arlan and back to Radley."

"We couldn't possibly infringe on a service you're paying these people for." Reid grimaced and Derica knew he was thinking of their relatively meager funds.

"Well," said Simond, "you can't be planning to leave before the sun is up. Why not sleep on the matter and decide tomorrow?"

Reid considered a moment, then nodded. "That sounds fine." He looked at Derica to make sure he had her agreement as well. She dipped her chin, eyes feeling heavy with the weight of the last half-hour.

Father Simond lifted one gray brow and addressed Hadrian. "I don't know if two additional bodies to shepherd to Radley would increase the rates already agreed upon with the guild."

Hadrian shrugged. "Depends if there's trouble."

Father Simond waved a dismissive hand. "I'm sure I can get the church to agree to the additional expense."

The matter settled—at least to Derica's satisfaction for the night—she let her eyelids sink down into fatigued slits and leaned into Reid's side. He reached down and patted the side of her hip, curling his arm low across her back.

Hadrian's eyes were obsidian chips, glittering in the light of the flame as he stared at Reid's hand like it was the target at the end of an archery range. With focus and the smallest twinkle of violent intent.

Reid pulled his hand higher, resting it on the abundant curve of her waist, and Derica noticed the slight shift was enough for Hadrian's gaze to cool, the tension around his mouth smoothing a fraction.

Across the fire, he leaned his elbows against his knees, hands clasped beneath his stubbled chin. A few strands of dark hair had come loose from the leather thong securing it into a tail. Wisps curled against his temple, then shifted into his eyes with a cool night breeze.

Hadrian reached up, smoothing blunt fingers back over his crown to resettle the wayward strands. The flickering firelight lovingly limned his impressive biceps, the shadows casting their size into even greater prominence.

A curl of heat unfurled low in Derica's belly.

"May the Weaver see to our safety and comfort through the night," said Father Simond. He clapped his hands and walked to his bedroll. Balduin copied the action and followed without a word.

"Don't know the Weaver cares all that much about protecting us while we dream," muttered Reid. "Would be nice, though." He nodded to Simond in thanks.

"Are you cold, Derica? Here." Reid grabbed a blanket from their bags behind him and wrapped it around her. He pressed his mouth to Derica's ear and whispered, "*Weaver's tits, could this night get any worse? Are you comfortable staying here?*"

She nodded with a shrug. Leaving a larger group seemed like stupidity, given the events of the last few hours.

Hadrian twirled a stick between his fingers, watching as he wove it over and under each digit. "It's not safe to travel the roads at night without protection, and I very much doubt your hunting dagger and half-bow would be much protection during an encounter. In case you were considering doing something ill-advised."

With each smoke and twilight-laden word, Derica's stomach twisted, the flash of heat from a mere moment ago snuffed.

Hadrian smiled placidly at her from across the fire as he finally met her gaze. He slowly winked before crossing his arms behind his head and leaning back into the coiled bedroll behind him. The commander crossed his muscled legs at the ankles and closed his eyes.

"Nyle, you have the first watch," he said.

The silent tattooed one by the horses nodded and picked up a sword belt. Buckling it to his waist, he drifted from the clearing like smoke.

"The two of you can lay out your bedrolls in the back of the wagon," Hadrian said. "It should be large enough for your giant friend. It's the only privacy we can offer." Eyes still closed, he flicked a finger at the wagon beside the horses. It wasn't a particularly cold night, but the wagon would keep her off the ground.

Reid stood and held a hand down for her. They grabbed their supplies and prepared the bed of the wagon. The entire time, she felt a heat against her back, but she was too far from the fire. Before she finally settled into her bedroll, she realized it was the heat of two dark, mysterious eyes.

CHAPTER EIGHT

Derica woke for the second time that night. The smell of rain permeated the air, and a faint rumble of thunder rolled in the distance.

Next to her in the wagon, Reid snored softly on his back. One arm lay behind his head and the other was wedged between them, pinned against her side. So, it hadn't been Reid that woke her up. She tilted her chin down to look out the open back of the wagon. For a moment, she only saw the glow of the dying campfire. Blinking the sleep from her eyes, she concentrated past the thin trails of smoke rising from the smoldering embers.

Father Simond lay in his bedroll next to the remnants of the fire, asleep. Balduin's bright hair peeked out from under a small mountain of blankets beside the father. Ten paces away from the holy men, the mercenaries stood in a tight circle on the other side of camp. Their voices were so low, if she hadn't seen their lips moving, she wouldn't have known they were conversing at all. Each of the three stood in the same stance, feet braced apart, and arms crossed over their chests, alert, with weapons strapped to various parts of their person.

She struggled briefly, trying to decide whether to reveal she was awake and ask what was going on, or to wake Reid. When a distant howl joined the thunder, the commander raised a hand to his companions, and each turned to study the surrounding woods. Mazolan palmed their sword hilt and Nyle fingered the longbow perched on his shoulder. Hadrian reached behind his head, not pulling his sword free of the scabbard, but ready. The question, though, was ready for *what*?

The only way to get an answer was to ask.

Gently bumping Reid's arm, she sat up in the wagon, clutching the blanket to her. She was fully dressed, but the night turned cold with the storm rolling in. Moisture hung in the air, the perfume of impending rain tickling her nostrils.

Hadrian's obsidian gaze unerringly swung to her when she sat up, eyebrows slamming down over his black gaze as he let go of the hilt of his sword, arms falling to his sides.

Reid moved against her side, and then he sat up as well, rubbing his eyes and almost braining Derica with his elbow. She swatted his arm down.

"Ow!" he whined, cupping the bend of his arm in his other hand. "What's going on?" he asked, eyeing the mercenaries.

Making eye contact with the commander, Reid swung his arm around Derica's shoulders.

"He's quite easy to rile, isn't he?" Reid breathed into her ear. To Hadrian, it probably looked like an intimate hello after waking, and Derica fought not to shrug him off.

"Why would he care?" She was careful not to move her lips any more than she had to. Reid gathered her closer and spoke into her ear, exasperation dripping from every word.

"Woman, sometimes you really are blind. Do you remember the spring you finally realized Oliana felt *romantically inclined* toward you? I think she was days away from asking me what was wrong with you. She flirted with you at the tavern every single night. No one else. Only you. For two years."

"You were just jealous."

Reid nipped the top of her ear playfully, and Derica jerked. She almost shoved Reid away, but she couldn't help but notice how the commander went rigid across the camp. Even avoiding his eyes, she felt his stare like the blistering summer sun. Nyle snapped his fingers in front of Hadrian's face after he failed to respond to something Mazolan said, and the look the commander leveled on the tattooed mercenary could have frozen flame.

Reid chuckled into her ear. "Of course I was jealous. The only two women my age in the village were *you* and Oliana. And Oliana wouldn't even look at me."

"I know for a fact the blacksmith's daughter from Idlewood soothed your poor, bruised ego."

"Yes. Only after you finally came to your senses about Oliana, though. Don't think I don't know about the incident in the barn loft."

Derica's lips curled into a smirk. "Why, whatever do you mean?"

"You know exactly what I mean. As first encounters go, the loft was a choice. I returned your torn shift to you a week later, after I found it in there. I hope you enjoyed crushing my boyhood dreams. I was in love with Oliana, and you broke my heart."

Derica couldn't help it any longer. She let out a giggle, then so did Reid. It was so good to laugh. All three mercenaries turned to face them, brows not unlike the thunder in the distance—heavy and oppressive. They both shushed each other, grimacing at the attention they garnered, and sobered instantly.

Hadrian approached the wagon while Nyle and Mazolan went back to visually sweeping the forest at the edges of the camp. As he stepped around Father Simond, the holy man stirred and blinked awake. Upon realizing everyone else was alert, and the slight tension in the air, Simond sat up as well, shaking Balduin's shoulder. The blond man swatted his hand away with a growl and settled deeper into his blankets. Simond shrugged and said something to the other mercenaries, their conversation too low for Derica's ears.

"What's going on?" Reid asked Hadrian as he reached the end of the wagon.

Hadrian flicked him a look but settled his gaze on Derica. "What woke you?"

"I-I don't know." A distant clap of thunder, more a vibration in the ground than a sound in the air, rumbled in the clearing. "Maybe the thunder?"

The mercenary cocked his head, eyes narrowed. Studying her. So, she studied back.

She couldn't tell if he'd slept at all. His eyes were as alert as ever and his clothes were no more rumpled than when she'd drifted off. His hair was still severely scraped back into a tail, not one hair floating free around his jaw or temples, and she couldn't help but wonder if it would curl when loose.

"Were you patrolling this whole time?" The question was out before she knew she'd opened her mouth.

He nodded once with a shallow dip of his chin. "After Nyle's shift."

Derica almost asked if he'd slept at all to appease her curiosity, but she clamped her lips shut. She didn't need to engage with the man any further. Something told her she needed to be cautious and wary of him.

Reid leaned into her side as Hadrian's gaze shifted, and the absence of the commander's focus nearly made her lightheaded. She stiffened her spine to keep from slumping forward in relief.

"What's going on?" Reid asked again.

"I thought I spotted Shredded during my watch," Hadrian answered this time. "I wasn't able to confirm, but it's probably best if we break camp before dawn and travel earlier than planned to Radley."

Reid frowned, then looked at Derica, silently asking her opinion.

She sighed. "If there's danger near, the safest place is probably with a band of mercenaries and Disciples of the Loom, right?"

"Smart. Very smart." The commander's smoke and twilight voice was so dry, it nearly sapped the moisture from the suffocatingly humid air.

Reid scooted toward the back of the wagon, and Hadrian moved back to give him space. Reid's feet dropped to the ground before he turned to face her, shoulder to shoulder with the commander as they both held their hands out to assist her.

Derica hesitated, eyes jumping between the men briefly before she placed her hand in Reid's. The commander's offered palm rolled into a fist and sank to his side, muscles jumping in his jaw as he stepped back to allow Derica to step down.

Reid smoothed her sleep-mussed hair and then addressed the mercenary. "I'll help break down the camp."

Hadrian nodded, his expression flat.

"Come sit with me, child." Father Simond called, patting the ground next to him. Last night's campfire was a glowing heap of ashes now. "I'll only get in the way, and you got hardly any rest. Keep this old man company."

Balduin rose to his feet, moving to stand with Mazolan and Nyle.

Derica raised one eyebrow at Father Simond, then walked over with a smile. "You're hardly an old man, Father. Why, you can't be older than Reid's father, and he's still running around his farm like he's twenty years younger."

Simond's gray eyes twinkled at her, and he winked. She would have missed it, he was so quick. He leaned nearer, whispering. "Don't tell the strapping men, or they'll put me to work. Have mercy on this poor servant of the Weaver."

A laugh trilled from her, and Hadrian stopped packing saddlebags to frown at her. "Are you trying to call the Shredded down on us? Some quiet would go a long way to seeing us safely packed and headed to the capital." He didn't wait for an answer or acknowledgment, simply returned to his task.

She huffed, barely checking the urge to gesture rudely at his back. The only thing stopping her was Simond watching her.

Derica and the father passed the time with idle talk. Mostly, he questioned her about the state of Arlan through the previous year, careful to avoid the painful subject of her mother. When she asked about life in the capital, he answered fully and kindly, painting a picture of a vast town bustling with activity—a far cry from her own home.

During the half-hour it took the mercenaries and men to pack their camp, the wind kicked up, thrashing the branches above their heads and tearing at their clothes. The sky, at first steadily lightening with the impending rise of the sun, had darkened into stark black, clouds looming above heavy with rain. Flashes of lightning and ever louder thunder warned them to pick up their pace.

The mercenaries' movements became sharper and more intense as they tossed items into the wagon and prepared the horses.

With the cart loaded and hitched to two of the horses, Derica and Father Simond climbed into the wagon, she on the bench, and the father settled against a pile of bedrolls in the back. Reid saddled and mounted his horse, riding behind the cart, with Nyle and Mazolan on either side of the wagon. Balduin was trying to calm his agitated horse, but his vitriolic epithets and the way he jerked the reins were having the opposite effect.

Derica's thoughts scattered when Hadrian climbed up next to her and gathered the reins in his square hands. She hid her surprise at the commander deigning to drive the wagon. She'd assumed he'd ride—possibly patrol the road ahead. Driving the wagon didn't seem like a very *Mercenary Commander* act, but she bit her tongue and pinched her fingers together in her lap. She would not ask. She would *not*.

"Why drive the wagon, Commander?"

The moment the words left her mouth, she wanted to close her eyes and slide off the seat onto the ground and be trampled by the horses. The silence stretched, making her ears burn with embarrassment. Since she was small, Derica had felt compelled to fill silence. Most of the time, idle chatter and questions flew from her lips unbidden.

"Nyle, why does the commander drive the wagon?" asked Mazolan, smiling sharply, a flash of white in the surrounding darkness.

"The commander drives the wagon because he's the best horseman in this little crew. Those two—" Nyle pointed to the matched horses pulling the cart "—are the best pair we've ever had to pull our supplies. They're also the highest strung we've ever had. They calm for the commander when they won't for us."

She'd not heard him speak since she'd joined Reid in their camp. If Hadrian's voice was night and smoke, then Nyle's was a sensuous wind in meadow flowers and warm silk sheets. Her mouth hung slightly ajar. She couldn't help it.

Nyle, of course, noted her reaction and winked with a small smile.

Next to her, Hadrian threw a frown at his subordinate and snapped the reins. As the wagon pulled forward, she slapped her hands to the seat to stop from tumbling back into the wagon and onto Father Simond.

The wind whipped her red hair into her face as they moved, and she scraped it back behind her neck, holding it with one hand. Derica looked up at the ominously dark sky as they moved their caravan onto the road. The clouds above them were holding their rain, but for how much longer?

CHAPTER NINE

The howling wind calmed into a damp breeze after an hour on the road, and not one raindrop fell from the ominous clouds above them. The mercenaries and Reid were quiet, and the unnerving silence drove Derica mad. Simond and Balduin were the only ones to talk, even if their remarks were sparse and hushed.

She picked at a loose thread on her tunic. Derica knew if she started rambling to fill the foreboding stillness, there was no telling if she'd stop. Her shoulders tensed with every bump of the wagon in the pregnant silence, fraying her nerves with each passing mile. She'd expected the trees to thin, but they still lined the road densely, and combined with the clouds overhead, the environment pressed in around her.

When a warm hand rested lightly on her back, she almost jumped off the bench, pressing a palm to her thumping chest. She turned to see the kind smile of Father Simond.

"You seem a bit on edge, child. How about a story to pass the time?"

She nodded, a sigh of relief escaping her. Anything to lighten this Weaver-damned tension and feeling of impending doom.

She turned on the bench so her back was to Hadrian, her legs straddling the wagon seat. Father Simond took a deep breath and began weaving his tale in a calm, sonorous voice.

The Book of Fate tells us, since the beginning of time, the Weaver sat before the Loom and wove the threads of souls into the divine Tapestry. After millennia of repairing damaged threads, cleansing and renewing souls, determining patterns on the Tapestry, and tending the lives of the world, the Weaver yearned for earthly experiences of their own. This presented a problem, however. Without the Weaver's dedication, the reincarnation of soulthreads would halt. Each human thread—each soul that they held in their hands—was special and precious, full of such promise for the Tapestry. But the Weaver could not move about the world themselves. If they did not tend to the Loom, who would?

Time passed, and an idea struck the Weaver. What if they used the Loom to weave a piece of themselves into the Tapestry? This essence could sample all the wonders of life, and when it was time to return to the Loom upon their death, the Weaver would absorb every memory and experience from that essence. But when and how would they accomplish this? The Weaver would have to ponder this dilemma. Perhaps that pattern in the Tapestry had yet to reveal itself.

One day, while sorting and weaving, the Weaver discovered the soulthread of a mighty warrior, a thread with intense vibrancy, shine, and courage. The Weaver yearned to know him. There was a mystery to this Warrior that called to them enticingly. This was a life that needed to be experienced, not merely watched from the Loom. Determined, the Weaver reached into their hair of silver starlight and wove a piece of themselves into the Tapestry, forming a new soulthread with their essence.

The Weaver entwined the Warrior's soulthread with the one they had created.

When the Warrior was reborn, the Weaver sitting at the Loom saw he lived a courageous and heroic life. As the Weaver planned, the Warrior met the blessed soul created from the essence of the god. The Warrior was equally as spellbound by her as the Weaver had been holding the Warrior's soulthread at the Loom. Their enthrallment was mutual. The Warrior and the Weaver-blessed fell in love, as it was believed the Weaver intended. All said they loved so well and so hard, they must have shared a heartthread bond.

A bond so deep and true, they must be two halves of the same soulthread.

After the pair lived a long and love-filled life together, the one blessed by the Weaver's starlit hair lay on her deathbed, holding the hand of their Warrior. She looked into his eyes and thanked him for the love they shared, knowing she had to return to the Weaver and bring all of their experiences to the god who created her. They would not meet upon the Tapestry again, for hers was not a thread meant to see the Loom again.

The Warrior raised the hand of his fading beloved to his cheek and cried with rage. He did not want to go to his next life knowing the soul sharing his heartthread would be missing from the Tapestry, never to encounter them again. Once the Weaver reclaimed the Weaver-blessed's soulthread, they could never again walk Veridion together. Seething anger took hold, and the Warrior decided he would subvert the Weaver's will.

Leaving the bedside of his beloved, the Warrior desperately searched for a solution to tie their soulthreads so tightly, one could never be separated from the other—not even by a god. He had heard whispers of the time before the Weaver created the Tapestry of Fate, when many creatures roamed the earth: demons, faeries, dwarfs, griffins, mermaids, and all other manner of magical beings. Surely one of these magical beings held the answer the Warrior sought. The birth of humans in Veridion had forced these other beings into the shadows, where they were safe from the violence and persecution of the insidiously bountiful race.

Finally, after searching leads and inspecting rumors while racing against the clock, he found a demon. The Warrior begged the demon to manipulate Fate and trespass into the Weaver's domain. They agreed, not out of kindness, but because the Warrior consented to pay any price in his desperation—the price to be named after the Warrior's agreement. Once the deal had been struck, the demon smiled, and the Warrior listened with horror as the demon explained the terrible cost the lovers would pay.

To guarantee the binding of the their souls, the Weaver-blessed's thread could not rejoin the Weaver in their realm. The pair would always share their reincarnated lifetimes, and the catalyst would be death. Not just any death—death at the hand of the Warrior. The demon enchanted the Warrior's most prized dagger, the blade glowing with magic as they instructed the Warrior to take the life of their beloved with the weapon. The dagger, wielded by the Warrior with love in their heart, would sever the Weaver-blessed's chain to the god.

The demon's final enchantment ensured the dagger would always find the hand of the Warrior in each lifetime, never to be lost. Devastated by the price they would pay but determined to see his love in the next life, the Warrior thanked the demon and prepared to rush back to the Weaver-blessed's bedside.

Before he could depart, the demon issued one last important warning: should the Weaver-blessed's death be caused by something other than the dagger, the lovers' threads would not be reincarnated together upon the Loom. Natural death, an accident, war, famine, or any other earthly danger capable of ending a human life would circumvent what the magic was meant to do. The Warrior and his love would be doomed to live apart until they shared the Tapestry again.

Despite this warning, the Warrior was desperate to bind his beloved to him in all lifetimes. He would end the Weaver-blessed's suffering and join them on the Loom in the next. How did the end matter when they could live happily together in every life?

The Warrior hastened back to the deathbed of his lover, frantic to reach her before the last breath rattled from her chest. When he found her still clinging to life, he was intensely relieved. Seeing her face once more however, the Warrior made the decision not to tell his beloved of the demon's deal. Deep in the back of his mind, *he doubted the Weaver-blessed wanted to be bound to him forever, especially if she knew the cost.*

The Weaver-blessed held out her arms one last time as she felt the end of her thread upon her, and the Warrior fell into her embrace. He framed the cherished face of his beloved and brought her to him for a final kiss. As their lips touched, the Warrior gripped the hilt of the bespelled dagger and, with tears rolling down his cheeks, inhaled the Weaver-blessed's agonized gasp as the weapon slid home. With wet eyes, the Warrior looked into his beloved's and promised they would find each other in the next life, no matter what.

The Weaver's essence residing in the blessed one reacted to the terrible pain and betrayal. In those last breaths, a second spell—or rather, a curse—was layered over what the demon had created.

The Warrior had attempted to do what only the Weaver was allowed: to direct the Fate of another. Divine punishment crashed down over the Warrior, ensuring he—unlike every soul rewoven into the Tapestry of Fate—would remember not only each lifetime but every gruesome death of his beloved by his hand. For his audacity, he would be cursed with an immortal memory, ceaselessly haunted by his past lifetimes while searching desperately for his beloved. The demon's spell guaranteed the two would find each other, if only for the Warrior to end the Weaver-blessed's life. Forever chained by links of love and betrayal.

CHAPTER TEN

But for the clop of the horses' hooves and the dull roar of the wind, quiet pressed in on Derica after Father Simond finished his tale. She licked her lips and tasted salt. Derica reached a finger up to her cheek and realized with embarrassment she'd been silently weeping. She knuckled the evidence away before the commander or the father could see.

"What an incredible tragedy," she said. The wind tore the words from her lips as soon as they were spoken. Not fast enough to evade the mercenary at her side's hearing, it would seem, though.

"A tragedy," Hadrian murmured. His low voice cut through the bluster of the weather, wrapping her in visions of night dark eyes and throaty whispers. The fine hairs on her arm rose, and she suppressed a shiver despite the heat of his body mere inches from hers.

Turning back to sit facing forward once more, Derica cut her eyes over to him. His posture was somehow rigid and loose at the same time while he moved with the roll and jostle of the wagon, but his knuckles were white where they wrapped around the reins. His mouth set into a thin line, the muscles in his jaw ticking out a pulsing rhythm. The sharp, flinty look was absent from his eyes as they scanned the road ahead. Hadrian was far away, in contemplation of what, she wasn't sure.

Balduin's blond hair caught her attention, the acolyte riding closer, listening intently. "The Disciples tell this tale to illustrate the hubris of man and the foolish wish of the Weaver to know what it is to live in this mortal realm." Balduin's voice rang with conviction and piety. "The divine and human domains are not meant to intersect."

"Fools." Hadrian's voice whipped out, his knuckles clenched further around the reins. The horses weaved briefly, swaying Derica on her perch. Hadrian cursed under his breath and efficiently settled them back into a calm, unified trot.

"Commander Hadrian, do you have thoughts on my parable?" Father Simond's question was cool, reminding Derica of the quiet intelligence of a spider plucking the strand of their web to entice a fly.

Hadrian tilted his head one way, then the other, stretching his muscles. "The Warrior damned them both to an eternity of torment. For what? Love?" He sneered the last, his eyes coming alive with the predator sharp awareness they had been lacking.

Mazolan pulled their mount up next to the wagon, considering each occupant before winking at Derica, and then addressed the commander.

"You humans and your soft hearts. It's almost enough to put a demon off their dinner." They lifted a hardtack biscuit to their mouth and bit. Red lips pulled into a grimace and they leaned over their horse, preparing to eject the offending mouthful.

"Don't." Hadrian's voice was low, but firm. "Don't waste the supplies."

Mazolan straightened in the saddle and chewed with a look of dejected reluctance, as their previous statement finally penetrated Derica's thoughts.

"D-demon?" Her hands clenched on the seat of the bench.

"Finally! An answer to your burning question, eh, morsel?" Maz's smile was a fierce glint of teeth in what little light there was, glee twinkling in their yellow stare.

Balduin sniffed from the back of the wagon. "Commander, must that thing be so *smug*?"

Hadrian's spine snapped straight, and he slowly turned his head to pierce the acolyte with a steely, obsidian look. When Balduin dropped his eyes, cowed, Hadrian turned to Simond. "The church hired the best crew, Father. That includes my comrade, who happens to be the best tracker in the land. And a demon." One dark brow lifted, pausing for a moment to allow his words to suffuse the air. "If you'd like, we can settle our account and part ways here." He pulled back on the reins, slowing the horses.

Father Simond paled to a shade of gray, nearly the same color as his robe. Balduin jerked his head up, sputtering.

Father Simond collected himself quickly. "No, Commander Hadrian. I'd like to make it to the capital, please."

Hadrian flicked the reins, and the horses resumed their previous pace. "As you direct. Please, no more slander about my crew. I selected them myself and am quite proud of their achievements. I value their employ."

Derica gaped at him, and Mazolan let out a delighted titter. Hadrian dressed down a Disciple of the Loom—a father no less—as if there were a naughty child.

"My thanks, Commander." Mazolan executed a shallow bow from atop their steed. "One could say you're quite Warrior-like yourself, the way you protect our little crew."

Hadrian rolled his eyes and sighed. "Did you have something to report, Maz?"

"No. I heard the dear father telling one of my favorite tales and had to listen. You see, I've heard the story many times and each time every holy father tells it a little differently." Their mouth hitched in a one-sided smirk. "It's funny how humans hold on to stories and how they change over time."

Father Simond flushed. "I can assure you, this account has been faithfully retold exactly as it's written in the Weaver's doctrine."

One white brow rose and the look Mazolan leveled on the father was so frosty, Derica shivered where she sat. "Is that so?" When the father didn't respond, Mazolan dismissed him, focusing their attention back to Hadrian.

"You don't think the story has changed over the years, Commander?"

The tail of Hadrian's hair danced in the fierce wind of the storm, dark strands brushing against the nape of his neck as he clenched his jaw. The dark clouds above them still refused to unleash a single drop of water, but the temperature was dropping steadily, the air charged. On either side of the road, the foliage whipped in great undulations with each lash of the wind. The slap of leaves and branches was a staccato cacophony counterpoint to the bass of thunder overhead. The only answer he offered his comrade was a low grunt. Derica frowned at the mercenary beside her. She couldn't pinpoint what caused his tension, and the mystery dug sharp talons into her brain, demanding she find the answer.

Mazolan drifted closer on their mount, drawing even with the commander. "Commander, I seem to remember a slightly different tale being told when I was a wee demonling." The expression they wore brought to mind a mischievous, frantic wolf cub, snipping and snarling at the alpha, and Derica couldn't help but eye Hadrian, wondering if the alpha ever snapped back, but Hadrian's stoic visage told her she wouldn't see that happen now.

She jolted at the thought. If she had her way, she wouldn't *ever* see it. She shouldn't want to see this band of mercenaries again after they reached their destination.

Mazolan's glee ratcheted higher with every moment of silence from Hadrian, and her eyes darted back and forth between the two. "I'm sure the tale has differed over the years. It's inevitable with oral stories," she said, hoping to stymie the rising tension.

Mazolan's attention snapped to her, and they snared her in their citrine stare again.

"But this one is quite, quite interesting in its *modifications*." With every word, their gaze bored into hers. "I would dearly love to be there when you learn how drastically. Your reaction should be nothing short of delicious."

"What does that mean?" Derica asked, not breaking Mazolan's stare as her frustration bubbled over. "You've been watching me like the star circus act since you terrified me upon meeting. I would dearly love for you to cease."

Mazolan barked out a delighted laugh and Hadrian's deep chuckle reverberated through her chest. The strand tethering her eyes to Mazolan snapped, and she shifted her gaze to the dark-haired mercenary. A ghost of a smile tilted his lips while fine crinkles on either side of his night dark eyes appeared.

"Someone else who can only stand so much cryptic drivel from Mazolan. How interesting." His woodsmoke voice curled around her and she mentally waved it away, straightening her shoulders and sitting taller on the wagon bench.

"*Most* interesting." Mazolan appraised her, and she bristled. "You know, Commander, I think this one has promise." They saw her reaction and clucked their tongue, leaning towards her with a grin baring their fangs. "That was a compliment, morsel." Not waiting for her to respond, they kicked their horse into a faster canter and abandoned the wagon to patrol the road ahead.

Derica sputtered at the brief dismissal. "Are you sure you're proud to have Mazolan in your company? They seem a bit... irrepressible," she said.

Hadrian's lips twitched briefly before he gave way to laughter. The sound erupted from him in great gales, one arm wrapped around his belly. If his chuckle teased her desire, his outright laugh laid a wood pyre in front of it. One spark and it would consume her in an inferno.

His mirth tugged up the corners of her own mouth, and she couldn't help but share in his amusement. When he quieted, he wiped moisture from his eyes and grinned at Derica. She sucked in a breath, heart stuttering.

He was devastating when he smiled like that.

She looked away, suddenly needing to check in on Reid.

"Irrepressible is a bit polite," Hadrian said, and Derica didn't dare turn back to look at him again, willing her heart to settle. "I've never met a demon who could respect authority. Anarchy is hereditary to the race, I believe."

She hummed noncommittally, turning to the back of the wagon. With a deep breath, Hadrian returned his attention to the reins and the road ahead. Peering over the back of the father's head, she skipped over Balduin's eerily pale stare, spotting Reid riding next to Nyle. The two appeared friendly, chatting as Nyle's eyes scanned the trees and bushes alongside the road.

Reid saw her looking and waved with a sunny grin, his white smile a beacon in the dark cast by the rain clouds overhead.

Despite the fact that the storm held, Derica couldn't dismiss the pervasive, uneasy feeling that clung to her, and couldn't pinpoint its cause. Yes, she was distressed by her visceral reaction and inconvenient curiosity about the mercenary next to her, but this felt like more. Her eyes darted to the dark forest all around them, searching for *something* to attribute her disquiet to. A stray red hair floated on the wind, tickling her nose, and she reached up, smoothing it behind her ear.

She sat facing backwards, staring out over the scenery as she watched the clouds roll in the distance while the wagon bumped along the road, the air growing heavier with each passing moment. Hadrian whistled piercingly between his teeth in two shrill bursts several minutes later, and Nyle kicked his horse, quickly approaching the carriage. Derica shifted to see the commander and Nyle exchanging looks, and then Hadrian indicated her with a tilt of his chin. Nyle's mouth pulled into a thin line at whatever he saw.

"What?" she asked, righting herself on the bench.

"Derica, I need you to jump on the back of Nyle's horse quickly and ride with him for a moment." His words were soft but clear, like one might address a spooked animal. She frowned, eyes scanning their surroundings as she puzzled over what was going on.

Another hair tickled her nose, and she brushed it away. Her fingers tangled in more hair as she attempted to clear the strands from her view. Then she realized what the mercenaries were reacting to.

Her hair stood up in a red halo around her head.

Her eyes darted to the sky, remembering the words Tedric had pounded into their brains so many times as children. Lightning was about to strike. Her hands trembled as she lowered them to her lap and nodded with a jerk.

Nyle rode around the wagon next to her and held out a hand. His curls swirled wildly around his head, and the image would have been funny if she wasn't terrified.

Without wasting a moment, she placed her hand in his and allowed him to help her into the saddle before him. When she was seated, his arms banded around her as his breath stirred the hair at the crown of her head. She smoothed her hair down for him, holding it flat to her nape, to keep from obscuring his vision.

"Go," Hadrian commanded.

Nyle kicked his horse into a fierce trot. Even as distance grew quickly between their horse and the rest of the party, she heard the commander respond to Reid's shouted question, assuring him she was going to be all right. Derica glanced over her shoulder, watching as Reid moved to follow her until Hadrian ordered him to stay back, then yelled for Mazolan.

Mere seconds later, Mazolan passed Nyle and Derica, riding back to the wagon as they talked to themselves. "Why the fuck do *I* have to get the priest? Who decided the demon needed to help the *holy men*? Sick joke..." The wind snatched their voice as they rode farther away.

Reid appeared next to them, pushing the larger horse to keep up with Nyle's sleek mount.

"Are you all right?" Reid had to yell to be heard over the cacophony of the storm now, wind rattling the trees around them and the clatter of hooves on the dirt road.

She nodded jerkily at him.

Her cheek stung as an icy droplet struck her skin. Another pelted the top of her head. Then the sky let loose.

Derica's hair was drenched and plastered to her head in seconds, the storm stalking them for miles finally pouncing with a vengeance. The loudest rumble of thunder they'd heard yet rolled above them, slowly gathering until it was deafening.

Hadrian.

She clutched Nyle's arm and tried to twist to see over his shoulder, but rain was already clouding her vision. Hadrian was a darker speck in the already oppressive black of the storm-fraught landscape. His silhouette popped into and out of her view with the cadence of the horse's trot, waves of stinging rain moving with the wind like surf near a coast.

A flash of blinding light burst from the sky with a boom. The horses screamed, and the *creeeeak* and *whump* of a falling tree echoed up and down the road. The horse beneath Nyle and Derica reared. Nyle calmly and firmly pulled on the reins to control the animal, all the while maintaining a secure grip on her waist, so she didn't slide sideways out of the saddle.

Reid wasn't fairing as well. He frantically tried to soothe his mount, but she was rearing repeatedly, rolling her eyes and stamping her hooves in fright. The horse kicked the air with their forelegs a final time, then shot into the woods to the right of the path.

"Maz!" Nyle yelled as a dark streak flew toward them and stopped at their side. Father Simond clutched Mazolan's waist from behind, face stoic but pale. Balduin rode behind the pair, already sallow complexion practically ghostly now.

Mazolan pointed a long, manicured finger at Nyle. "No! The priests are enough. Now the *pig farmer*? It's too much!"

Nyle remained silent.

Mazolan dropped their accusatory finger and looked up into the sky. The torrent of rain slicked their white braid back, the ends streaming thick trails of water onto the saddle, and, consequently, Father Simond. "Argh! Why? *Why* do I let the commander talk me into this shite?!" Mazolan raged. When they tipped their head back down, they flicked a look promising vengeance to Nyle and kicked their horse into a gallop, heading toward where Reid disappeared into the foliage.

Derica gripped Nyle's forearm and squeezed. He bent his head down to her. "Yes?" he said.

She turned her mouth and spoke into his ear, hoping he could hear her above the sound of the torrential rain. "What about Hadrian?"

He stiffened behind her, and they both turned to look back toward where they last saw the commander and the wagon. Derica squinted into the black, blinking like mad to keep the rivulets of rainwater from running into her eyes. Nyle spotted him first.

"Shit!" he barked. His hands gripped the reins and swung their mount around. Nyle kicked the beast into a gallop. Derica squeezed her eyes shut, gripping the pommel before her like her life depended on it. In fact, it very well may. She cobbled together silent prayers to the Weaver, anything to help their mount keep its footing in the mud. She felt no shame for her sudden piety. Fear and worry blotted out everything else at this moment. With each great stride of their mount's hooves, the tableau in the distance became clearer to Derica, making her stomach clench and her heart flutter in her chest like a frantic bird in a cage.

One of the two horses hitched to the wagon lay on its side while the other remained upright, pulling at its harness in terror. The commander stood in between both, trying to calm one while accessing the condition of the other. Nyle pulled up several paces from the scene under a tree and handed her the reins before sliding off the saddle. Her hands clenched the leather in spasms, shaking. Her fingertips tingled, not from the cold, but from her body's response to so much stimuli and fear.

Part of her felt like it floated outside of her body, watching this all unfold.

Nyle bent and retrieved a dagger from his boot and sawed at the wet leather of the harness tethering the animal that stood upright. With his comrade handling one horse, Hadrian crouched in the mud next to the downed horse who breathed heavily, breath fogging the air as its eyes rolled in its head. Hadrian ran his fingers down its head, neck, and then withers, checking for injuries before laying a hand over its nose, worry and affection plain in the care he showed the animal. He reached for his dagger next, and she couldn't watch. Derica slammed her eyelids closed, whipping her head to the side as she prayed the animal's end came swiftly, hoping the storm would muffle the sounds of its scream.

When she heard nothing but the symphony of the storm, she cautiously opened one eye, and then the other. The animal stood, and it appeared healthy, if a bit dazed. Hadrian sawed at its harness, water dripping down his face and teeth clenched.

Nyle was holding the reins of the horse he'd successfully cut free when eerie howls rent the air. "Fuck," he snarled. "Commander! We have company. Shredded."

Hadrian didn't look up, a grimace of fierce determination twisting his mouth. The howls rang through the air again. Derica turned her head toward the sound, helpless to stop herself, as her blood froze. Derica thought nothing could terrify her further than this storm, but what she saw coming toward them on the road almost stopped her heart.

A pack of Shredded—*five* in number—barreled toward them.

CHAPTER ELEVEN

N yle vaulted onto the back of the nearest cart horse. Hadrian tossed him the tethers for the recovered horse, then zipped to where Derica sat astride Nyle's mount. The commander reached for her, and dazedly, she slid into his hold while panic rioted through her mind, paralyzing her limbs. Hadrian secured the other horses' reins to Nyle's cart horse as well, and the commander gave a sharp jerk of his chin.

Nyle's answering smile was a vicious flash of white teeth in the darkness. "Like the Wardgard job, then?"

"But with one added distraction. Go," the commander ordered.

Nyle's amber eyes flashed with determination as he nodded to Hadrian. He snapped his reins, bellowing, and all three horses rode off *towards* the Shredded.

Confusion lanced through her alarm, eyes scanning from where Nyle and the horses were to Hadrian at her side. Was Nyle the distraction, or was she?

But words were lost to Derica as her heartbeat raced wildly, threatening to bruise her ribs. What combat training did she have? *None.* She could beat a ball of dough into submission with a rolling pin, but that was it.

Firm hands circled her wrist and pulled her into the thick bushes and low tree branches before she could voice her *many* worries. Glancing back, she saw two of the Shredded peel off and follow Nyle, but three continued forward after Derica and the commander.

"Well, fuck," he grunted, emerging through the brush. The branches and snarled hands of the bushes pulled at Derica's clothing, snatching and snagging her tunic and breeches.

She hissed at the sting of a particularly thorny branch slash fire across one shin. With every plodding step into the darkened foliage, Hadrian urged her faster until they sprinted headlong, feet slipping in the mud. Between the storm and the dense forest, Derica could barely see her hand in front of her face, but Hadrian pulled at her wrist, and she had no choice but to trust him. His grip disappeared, and a panicked cry rose in her throat, cut off when wide palms framed her waist and hoisted her over something unseen. Buried beneath her terror, Derica marveled at how easily he maneuvered her—she was not waif-like in the slightest.

"Come on, it's a little farther." Hadrian's woodsmoke voice tickled the shell of her ear. His grip returned to her wrist, and they were sprinting forward again. Feet pounded as they burst into a clearing barely more illuminated than the absolute pitch black of the trees they'd come from.

Hadrian towed her in front of him and pushed her forward. "Go! There's a cottage up ahead in that direction." He pointed in front of her face so she could see. "When you reach it, bolt the door and don't move until I come for you."

She saw the flash of metal as he drew the dagger at his hip, then the sword from his back. He turned to face the direction they came from, feet planted, deadly blades poised. Waiting. Hadrian met her eyes and the fury there would have been terrifying if she didn't know he directed it at the terror rushing toward them.

"I said *go!*"

Derica's heart kicked in her chest. She reached out to pat his shoulder, in comfort, gratitude, or encouragement, she didn't know. He was a *mercenary*. He didn't require any of the three from her. She snatched her hand back and turned around, dashing in the direction Hadrian had pointed.

Raindrops pelted her in cold, stinging strikes, soaking her hair as it flopped into her eyes, and she tossed her head to clear her vision. Rocks and other forest debris almost tripped her several times, but Derica stayed upright, thank the Weaver.

Guttural snarls echoed from behind her, made all the more terrifying when wrapped in the chaos of the storm. She tamped down the urge to look back and pumped her legs harder. A ragged moan of relief escaped her lips as a rustic cottage came into view, the wood siding dark with rainwater and the windows lightless. The little flame of hope in her chest flickered out. She had wanted to find and bring back help for Hadrian, but this cottage was empty. Hadrian appeared to be a competent mercenary, but, even still, three Shredded were too much to handle alone. A frustrated cry, a mixture of fear and impotent anger, spilled out of her, but she didn't slow her run as she approached the building.

Derica threw her body into the door of the cottage, half expecting to rebound off and into the mud beneath her feet, but the wood gave way beneath her shoulder and she almost fell onto her ass, anyway. Breath sawed in and out of her lungs as she reached behind her to hold the door open, looking for Hadrian.

A flash of steel in the dark thirty paces from the cottage signaled the commander's position. Despite the pounding of rain on the roof, she could still hear snarls and grunts from the attacking Shredded.

"BAR THE DOOR!" Hadrian bellowed, loud enough to be heard over the deluge.

Derica stepped back, door thudding closed, and pulled the heavy beam down into its brackets, then halted as she turned in a circle. There were no other entrances. Hadrian didn't intend to join her in the shelter.

The ass shouldn't be left to die because he was a prideful idiot.

Muttering at her own stupidity, she looked around for any weapon she could use. Small bed, ramshackle wood table, tiny hearth. Her eyes snagged on the fireplace, noticing the coal shovel and fire iron propped against the brick lip. Wet breeches pulling at her thighs, her half-boots squelching, she hopped over and wrapped a hand around the fire iron. She tested the weight and nodded, satisfied this would work.

At least if she was indulging in idiocy, she'd be armed, dammit.

With a deep breath, she unbarred the door and ran back outside. The rain-drops struck in icy, piercing pellets against her back and on the top of her head as she let the sounds of fighting draw her to Hadrian. Her hands trembled as she drew closer to the sounds, cursing her stupidity, but unwilling to remain alone in the cottage, imaging his gruesome, needless death. When she neared enough to see Hadrian through the curtain of pounding rain, she stopped and drew the fire iron into both hands, holding it out straight in front of her chest.

Hadrian slashed a dagger with one hand to hold off the two Shredded circling him to his left. The most aggressive of the trio attacked relentlessly from his right, barely held off by the sword Hadrian wielded in the other hand. She could see dark liquid—blood—streaming from a gash where his neck met his shoulder. Despite the injury, he lunged and parried, keeping the Shredded from making ground against him.

She crept closer, hoping the dark and the pounding rain would give her the element of surprise. Derica hesitated, considering whether to engage the duo on the left or the aggressor on the right. Better to distract the most dangerous element, she thought. She veered to circle around behind the lone Shredded, her heart lodged in her throat.

Hadrian grunted in pain as one of the two on the left darted in when he was distracted, scratching a shallow furrow along his spine. She moved faster, feeling an urgency to have this done. Derica was cold, wet, and scared. She threw stealth away with a flash of anger and ran toward the back of the most aggressive Shredded. Drawing the fire iron back next to her side, she rushed forward, aiming between its shoulder blades.

She yelled, hoping to disorient, as she thrust the cold iron into the back of the Shredded. The resistance was jarring, as was the sound of flesh giving way to metal. The Shredded howled into the air and stiffened. Over its shoulder, she made eye contact with Hadrian. His eyes widened, and his mouth firmed into a fierce grimace. He turned back and slashed out with both weapons at the two on the other side. With a spray of dark blood, they both fell, too distracted by the yell of the third to halt the attack.

The length of the fire iron was the only thing keeping the enraged Shredded from Derica. It pulled forward, trying to dislodge the metal from its back, but she held tight, grunting and gritting her teeth. The commander finally faced the last remaining Shredded, and each step toward Derica and the creature made the Shredded thrash all the harder. Hadrian's wrath pulsed in the night, undiluted by rain. Dark hair streaming down his head and neck, plastered flat against his skull by the sleet. He bared his white teeth in a snarl. With a flick of the wrist, he twirled the dagger in his hand, fist cocking back, the point of the blade toward the Shredded, sword gripped tightly in his right. With three steps, he stood in front of the enemy, both hands in motion. He thrust the sword into its chest with the ease of practice and training.

Derica felt the impact, shoulders jerking as the Shredded was forced back on the fire iron, but she miraculously kept her feet planted in the mud.

The Shredded howled, the sound morphing into a wail of pain as Hadrian's pressure on the blade increased. The wailing ceased. He stepped back, pulling his sword free, and the Shredded pitched forward, taking Derica's weapon out of her hands. With a wet squelch, it fell face-first into the soaked ground, unmoving.

Hadrian crouched next to the prone form and lifted his dagger to the base of its skull. Derica looked away, knowing he meant to ensure the creature didn't get back up. Waiting a moment, she turned her head back to the commander, who now crouched between the other pair, completing his task. Then, he stood and held his dagger blade into the rain to be cleaned, followed by the sword. When the water dripping from them was clear, he shoved them both into their scabbards—the dagger at his hip, the sword behind his back.

His slate black eyes glittered with remnants of battle rage as he stepped toward her, but he was gentle as he took her hand, and nodded to the cottage. They hurried to the building, Derica's body sluggish between the numbing cold and ebb of adrenaline.

Hadrian opened the door and ushered her through first, before shutting and barring the entrance. The clink of metal and the snap of leather, followed by a thump next to the door, disturbed the eerie silence of the cottage, his sword in its scabbard propped next to the door frame. Derica stood in the center of the one-room home, only flashes of lightning streaming through the single window to light the dark space. Footsteps sounded, then the slap of wet hands on wood as Hadrian rifled through the home. Next came the squeak of old wooden drawers and the rattle of their contents. A thump against the table, and then the strike of a flint.

The commander walked past her to the hearth, his stark face illuminated as he shuffled logs into the fireplace. A moment later, the flame caught, and the increasing blaze revealed the cottage.

CHAPTER TWELVE

D erica's teeth chattered, the clicking mingling with the crackle of the fire and the thunder outside the small cottage. Hadrian rose from his crouch in front of the flames, and strode to face her. Derica had become even more numb. She stared without seeing at the center of his chest and wrapped her arms around her waist, desperate for some warmth as she shivered, her wet clothing rapidly cooling in the dry shelter of the cabin.

A flash of red streaked into her vision, jarring her enough to make her blink and focus. A bead of blood ran from Hadrian's wound in the crook of his shoulder and neck, disappearing into his soaked, dark tunic.

Her brown gaze met his. "You're bleeding."

"Nice of you to notice." He flicked his fingers at the bloody slash. "This is what happens when stupid women don't listen when I order them to run. And this?" His thumb hiked over his shoulder, to the slash he took along his spine. "This is what happens when the same stupid woman rushes in to aid a man trained in combat," he snarled in her face, their noses almost touching.

A drop of rainwater ran from his hair onto the slope of her breast. The cold didn't register against her numb skin, but his statement stirred feeling of another kind, anger rising in her chest.

"What kind of idiot *man* thinks he can hold off three crazed Shredded by himself?" The words whipped out between her numb lips without thought. "I wasn't going to leave you to die!"

Blood roared in her ears, drowning out all other sound in the room.

A flush of temper traveled up the commander's throat, red flagging the tops of his cheekbones as he leaned in. They were sharing breaths now, they stood so close. Derica's heart pounded a wild rhythm as she refused to step back.

"Take those wet clothes off, *now*," he breathed, reaching down to grasp her hands.

"I will *not*!" Derica stepped away from his hold, anger turning to outrage.

"I didn't mean—" he growled in frustration and scraped wet hair off his forehead. He stared at the ceiling and took a deep breath, held it for a moment, then gustily blew it out. Hadrian reached for her hand again and held it up in front of her face. She could see the contact but didn't feel his fingers on hers. "You have to get warm. You're hardly shivering now. We *have* to get you warm." His voice was gentler, but just as brittle, and Derica got the sense he struggled to keep from baring his teeth at her as she slipped unfeeling fingers free of his hold. Hadrian moved closer, agitated and muttering, blotting out the light from the fire.

Voice wooden, she nodded at his wounds. "You're the one bleeding."

He scoffed. "And I've bled before from wounds during a fight. Nothing to warrant concern. It's amazing you have such fire when you're so cold." Hadrian came even closer, and the damp fabric of his tunic rustled. "You can't even feel me holding your arms."

With a gasp, her chin tipped down to look. As he said, he cupped her elbows in his grasp, and the realization was enough to shatter the anger coursing through her. When she looked back up, his eyes were tight, his expression serious.

"If you don't take those wet clothes off, there will be consequences. If your concern is for your modesty, I understand, but your health should come before propriety. You have nothing a man my age hasn't seen countless times before."

Derica resisted the urge to snarl about braggarts and the notches on their bedposts, but stopped herself, letting the words sink in. Really listened to what he said. Her shoulders sagged on a sigh. He was right. She licked her numb lips and nodded.

"I'll—" She cleared her throat and tried again. "I'll need your help."

Surprised black eyes twinkled at her in the fire-lit cottage. By degrees, the surprise warmed into something else, and his heavy gaze shot a frisson of excitement and a little fear down her spine. The fear... was not of him—that had evaporated after the fight outside—but what *she* might do or say next.

"Is that so?" Hadrian's voice was a quiet rasp. His lips slowly pulled up into a shadow of a lopsided smile, and Derica was sure if she could feel her knees, they would have gone weak at the sight. "Go stand in front of the fire." Hadrian nodded to the hearth, and she moved stiffly to stand before it.

Hadrian's footsteps echoed in the quiet as he stepped behind her. She felt pressure more than sensation as he held her steady. He hooked a finger through the wrists of her tunic. "Raise your arms," he instructed.

Derica did, and he worked the soaked fabric up and off until he set her tunic away, leaving her in her under-tunic, stays, and breeches.

He unpicked the laces at her back. The fabric gaped around her shoulders but clung like a second skin to her damp bust.

"Done," he said, hot breath feathering over her nape.

She turned her head over her shoulder. "Turn around."

His feet shuffled as he turned his back, moving away from her.

The tips of her fingers and her toes stung as she stood near the warmth of the fire, shivering. If she didn't want his help to get completely undressed, she had to see this done now. Struggling with the wet fabric, trying not to scream in frustration, she finally wrestled free from her stays.

She almost toppled into the fire trying to kick out of her breeches. Afterward, her under-tunic was easy to fling away, the slap of soaked fabric on the wood floor announcing her victory. Wood scraped across the floor, and she jumped as the commander issued his next order.

"Get in the bed. Wring out your hair first as best you can. I didn't find any extra linens. We don't want the bed any more wet than we'll make it."

Nude, she walked toward where he'd dragged the bed closer to the fire, shaking harder. Then what he'd said finally penetrated her thoughts.

"We. What do you mean 'we'?"

"You expect me to sleep on the floor? In my wet clothes? What was the point of saving me if I die in this cottage of exposure?"

Her lips pursed. They were in an untenable situation, and they'd have to manage, so she hummed a non-committal ascent and continued to the bed. As she examined the sheets for signs of vermin or other unwanted inhabitants, she heard another slap of soggy fabric.

Hurriedly deciding it was safe enough, she pulled the sheets up and tucked herself beneath them, teeth clacking together. The sound of bare feet on wood preceded the gust of cold hitting her bare side as the blanket lifted. She huddled farther to the side of the straw mattress and slammed her eyelids shut.

She stiffened her body to keep from rolling into the dip as he slid under the blanket with her. Derica's face heated as she tried to keep her quickening breaths from filling the interior of the cottage.

Icy skin brushed her arm, and she gasped.

"Sorry," Hadrian murmured, his voice trembling the slightest bit and Derica frowned, feeling the way he shivered. He was shaking almost harder than she was.

"If the point is sharing body heat, that would require touching." As soon as the last word was out of her mouth, a grunted chuckle answered her.

"Are you comfortable with that?" he asked.

"Yes."

She gasped when the mercenary's bulky arm turned her to her side, facing away from him. Cold, damp skin plastered against her back. His thick thighs curved under hers, but he politely kept some space between their hips. His arm slid under her side and settled tight around her waist, careful not to touch her breasts. They both trembled from the cold, but her sense of feeling was returning with each passing minute. The skin of her back burned with more than the tingle of blood returning to the area.

"How's this? All right?..." His low voice wrapped around her, goosebumps raising the hair on her arms. Not from the cold. Not from the cold at all.

"Y-yes." Derica meant for her answer to come out nonchalant, but it was a throaty murmur instead. The tips of her ears grew hot with embarrassment.

"Good," he grunted. "May I?" He held a hand up several inches away from her upper arm. When she nodded faintly in response, he laid his palm against her arm and chafed quickly. Warmth built, tingling between his hand and her skin.

Derica twitched when the fingers below her breasts stroked her skin in slow, soft circles. She stiffened, and the stroking halted until she leaned her back more firmly into his chest. The blanket whispered over their skin as Hadrian shifted behind her.

"Wha—" She coughed, banishing the husk from her voice. "What's your first name?"

"Justus."

Casting about for anything to focus on other than his heat at her back, she asked the question bouncing around her mind, attempting to stymie the riot of sensations he was waking. "What happened on the Wardgard job?"

Justus laughed and his hot breath slipped through her damp hair, stroking her nape. She couldn't have suppressed her answering shiver if her life depended on it. His arms tightened around her. Derica slammed her eyes shut and swallowed an inappropriate and unwelcome purr of satisfaction.

"In Wardgard, we were contracted to locate, subdue, and then deliver a local criminal. What the contract *didn't* state was that this criminal had assembled their own small army. When we found our bounty, we were—as you'd imagine—unprepared to fight a score of semi-competent thugs and bandits. So, we decided to distract and separate."

"And?"

Justus's smile was plain in his voice. "We completed the contract and charged the client three times their offered sum for the trouble. Restrained and bleeding—minimally—we brought the mark and their accomplices in. The client squabbled, accusing us of extortion. Nyle threatened to release our captives instead." He shrugged, shifting the mattress momentarily. "He has a gift with words—sparse but effective. The purses we brought back to the guild were fat. Mazolan upset Alondra, the head of our guild in Radley, when they 'borrowed' some funds from the treasury to purchase a celebratory wagon of ale." His smoky chuckle blanketed her, calling an answering laugh from her.

Despite the cold, and the panic she'd experienced the last day, Derica couldn't deny that there was something alluring about this man. She fidgeted with the simple gold ring she wore. After her mother's passing, her grief had frozen her in amber, and now fine cracks were spider-webbing across it. Derica knew she could repair them if she wished, but...

She wanted to feel something other than heartbroken.

She wanted to glut herself on something pleasurable, decadent, and indulgent. She'd never desired anything more after the last several days of sorrow and today's terror.

Maybe Derica would regret her decision later, but she couldn't seem to stop herself from moving against his heat at her back.

Her breath stuttered as his fingers at her waist started tracing larger circles. She strangled the moan threatening to drift from her lips. Feeling had finally come back to her limbs, and her shaking was now barely a shiver. Justus's chest radiated heat down her spine, and the steady beat of his heart thumped against her skin. Heat coiled low in her belly and her cheeks stung as blood rushed into her face—it was a wonder her face didn't glow red in the dim firelight of the cottage. She made every effort to get her breathing under control, but her concentration frayed with each heated puff of breath on the back of her neck.

He stopped rubbing warmth into her arms and brought up one large, square hand to brush her red hair out of the way. His touch was surprisingly gentle, his fingers the slightest bit cooler than her skin. He settled his arm back around her waist and she couldn't have halted the movement of her hips back into the cradle of his body if she'd wanted to. The small movement pushed her flush against the hot, rigid length of him.

Justus's nose buried in the bend of her shoulder, and his groan reverberated around them.

"Derica, it's nothing personal," he whispered. She trembled in his embrace, thighs rubbing together. "You're an attractive young woman. You're naked. I'm naked. There are no *expectations* that anything should result from this situation." He paused, and his hands loosened their hold on her waist. "In fact, I think we're both warm enough now. I can turn over and we can forget about this. Our clothes will be dry in—"

The rustle of the woolen blanket and the shifting of her body on the mattress cut him off as Derica turned to face him. She left a small sliver of air between their bodies, but the tiniest movement forward by either party would result in her breasts mashed into the sparse hair coating his muscular chest.

The flicker from the fireplace cast Justus's face in harsh shadows. This close, she could see the fine ring of gold circling his irises, the contrast to his midnight eyes highlighting the metallic oddity—the glinting molten intensity.

In less than three days, she'd lost her home to fire, abandoned the place she grew up, and thought she'd lost Reid. She desperately wanted to succumb to this man's visceral lure—to be pulled out of her mind and away from her emotions by something purely physical. Throwing off the shackle of her caution, Derica let the thoughts she'd been caging find their way free.

"Commander, we're *both* adults. I think we understand the situation." She felt more than heard the groan he strangled in his throat.

She reached her hand toward his shoulder, the blanket slithering down her arm until the tops of her shoulders and breasts were exposed to the air. His eyes flicked down, back up, and then quickly down again as his gaze sharpened with hunger. His tongue darted out and licked his full bottom lip, the sheen flickering with the pops of the fire behind them. When the tips of her outstretched fingers grasped the top of Justus's bulky shoulder, his whole body shuddered, and she realized how rigidly he'd been holding himself away from her.

Her gasp and his groan wrapped around each other in the space between them when his hands shot to her wrists and yanked her into his front. Her ample softness cradled all his hard edges. His burning length almost seared her skin.

At a snail's pace, he tilted his head to hers, watching. He wouldn't find any hesitation or rejection. Justus moved into her, trailing his hand down to Derica's knee. He hooked the bend of her leg and guided it up onto his hip. At the same time, he drew the tip of his nose down alongside hers, breaths mingling in a heady cloud of desire before his lips pressed a soft kiss to the corner of her mouth.

With the meeting of their lips, all thought of slow left Derica's mind with the force of a blazing inferno. Her core was molten as she circled her hips into the cradle of his.

"*Derica*," he groaned out, before sinking into the kiss—all teeth, tongue, and velvet wet heat.

Before her last coherent thought left her, she asked, "Contraceptive potion?"

"I've had mine this month." He looked her in the eye, making sure his answer was heard and satisfactory. At the wicked slant of her smile, his eyes heated.

Derica clutched both his shoulders, not knowing if she wanted to pull him on top of her or push him down and slide herself above him. Her indecision mattered little the next moment when his hips nudged hers flat against the mattress. She lifted her legs so her soft thighs grasped his hips, her ankles crossed above his ass. On either side of her head, his biceps bracketed her face. Wisps of his dark brown hair, black in the low light of the fire, hung into his dark eyes, their molten core shining into hers.

It *did* curl when it was loose.

One of his arms left her vision as it grasped the soft skin at the side of her stomach, callused fingers leaving a trail of sparks and heat until he was cupping one breast.

"A treasure," he murmured before bending his head over the plumped offering. The scrape of his stubble made her clench her eyes shut, the sensation making sparks blink against the back of her eyelids. Firm, wet heat tugged her nipple into his mouth and she arched into him with a moan. Every lave of his tongue and tug of suction on her taut peak increased the melting fire at her core.

Derica's moan turned desperate as she sought the pressure of his thigh, anything, against her. She untangled her legs behind him, trying to gain leverage to bring him into better alignment with her.

Cold air shocked the tip of her wet breast as his lips came free with a pop.

His hands pushed her hips flat into the mattress, stilling her frantic movement. He leaned over her and nipped the shell of her ear.

"Slow down. We have all night." His twilight and woodsmoke voice had her clenching and whimpering, squeezing him between her thighs. He'd yet to bring the heat of his rigid cock into contact with her, and she ached for it, but he had her pinned so effectively, Derica couldn't make him move.

"One of us would like to come soon," she panted. She'd hoped for a throaty purr to spur him into action, but it came out more achingly needy than anything.

A dark chuckle echoed in the shadows. Justus dragged the flat of his tongue from the bend of her shoulder up the side of her neck. Her hips tried to twitch up, but she was still firmly under his control.

"And one of us shall," he rasped into her ear. "Soon. But first, I want my other treasure."

His head trailed down in front of the breast that had escaped his attentions so far. Derica tried to arch harder, to place her flesh in his path sooner.

"Ah-ah," he crooned, shaking his head and trailing the ends of wavy, dark brown hair over her skin. "I said *soon*."

His head shifted over to the center of her chest. The hand holding her hip flicked to her center, then lightly grazed a path of fire up to her sternum, trailing her wetness up onto her soft abdomen. Her legs trembled on either side of his hips, breath sawing in and out of her lungs harder.

His fingers splayed, thumb touching one breast, his pinky the other as his palm pressed flat against her sternum, firmly pushing until her back lay completely flush with the mattress. She was too focused on her emptiness to protest. She ached for him.

Justus joined their mouths in another tangle of tongues, and the hand not on her chest cupped her ass. His teeth lightly scraped her bottom lip as he squeezed the flesh overflowing his palm.

She couldn't take it anymore and raked her nails up his sides, growling her frustration into his mouth.

His hips slammed into hers and she finally had the heat she wanted, his cock pressing against her. Derica was so wet, she could already slide him up and down against her clit with the tilt of her hips.

"*Fuck,*" Justus grunted.

His palm wrapped around her nape, over her birthmark. A hot sting started to build under his hand, but her heart beat with such frenzied rhythm, it muddied the pain. Her hips moved faster, mindlessly chasing the completion she sought as she ground against him.

Derica felt the damp of Justus's forehead against the curve of her neck, then the firm clamp of his teeth. His tongue laved the sting away before he pressed an open-mouthed kiss to the column of her throat. His hips jumped against her at the hoarse cry she couldn't contain. Justus's hand clenched in an almost bruising grip on her ass. He let go after one more almost punishing squeeze and pinched her clit lightly before strumming it with a broad thumb. Simultaneously, he curled a finger inside her, pressing on just the right spot. The mix of sensation tipped her over the edge.

She moaned her ecstasy, and he swallowed every sound.

As the waves of pleasure broke softly around her, the pain centered on her nape came into sharper relief until she gasped and pushed free of Justus. She sat up, hand flying to her neck, feeling for injury.

"Are you all right? Did I hurt you?" He brushed his hands up and down her back and limbs, searching.

She gulped air and rubbed the mark on the back of her neck. Her mother had described the birthmark to her, and she imagined it looked the same now as it did then. They hadn't owned a mirror, let alone two, so she'd never seen it herself, but it was a two-inch, slightly raised horizontal slice of strawberry-colored skin in the very center of the back of her neck. When she brought her hand forward, there was no blood on her palm.

Justus got off the bed and crouched in front of her, a hand bracing each shoulder. His eyes flickered over her hand.

"What happened?" he asked, gaze sliding back to her neck. He brushed aside her hair lightly, turning her head and looked. "I don't see—"

Justus's words suddenly cut off, and his whole body jerked. He pulled away, hand dropping as his mouth flattened into a firm line and his face cleared of all expression. Derica lifted her hand to her neck, interrupting his focused gaze.

"Just a birthmark," she shrugged, searching his face, but his dark lashes fluttered down, shuttering his gaze. The heat and passion suffusing the cottage a moment ago was gone. With a deep breath, he opened his eyes, now chips of black ice as he reached an arm behind her hip and pulled the woolen blanket over her, covering her from shoulder to knee.

"I need to patrol. I didn't make sure there weren't any other Shredded who followed us and not the other group." His voice was flat and entirely devoid of feeling, Derica could barely convince herself this was the same man who'd had his hands all over her body moments before.

She flicked her eyes down to his erection, still rigid, and confusion frothed her thoughts.

Following the direction of her gaze, he cocked his mouth into a semblance of a smirk, but his eyes were still black, empty pits.

"Don't worry about me."

Turning his back to her, he walked over to the clothes he'd draped next to the fire, and Derica couldn't help but watch the muscles flex and pull in his broad back as he got dressed. The shallow slash down his spine was a thin, red ribbon, bookended by light pink marks from her nails. Clothing donned, he moved to the door and belted on his sword. He paused before picking up his dagger, clenching his fists open and shut, and Derica's brow furrowed. His nostrils flared as he grunted out a breath, then swiped the weapon and belted it to his hip like the metal burned his hands.

Staring at the door, his back to her, his shoulders rose, head high as he said, "I'll be back. Bar the door."

A gust of frosty air was her only companion a moment later. Derica woodenly got up and barred the door as Justus bid, blankets wrapped around her naked form. Her emotions churned as she walked to the window a few feet from the door and looked out.

The rain hadn't completely stopped, but now fell in a light mist. Long enough out there, and the commander would come back soaked, just as before.

A movement at the tree line drew her gaze, a dark figure looming, but one she recognized immediately. Justus braced both hands on the wide trunk of a tree at eye level, his forehead pushed into the bark. His shoulders slumped, and he appeared to be breathing like he'd sprinted a mile, shoulders heaving. Then he stilled, lifted his eyes to the sky, and roared. Birds flew into the air and streaked away like feathered shooting stars.

Derica jerked and ran back to the bed. Panting, she settled so her whole body, head too, was under the scratchy, warm fabric. She slammed her eyes shut, telling herself the tears dripping down her temples into her hair were from the stress of the attack. They surely weren't because the mercenary with the midnight eyes had rejected her.

CHAPTER THIRTEEN

J ustus never thought he'd be so blessed, or so cursed, to find his other half
during this lifetime.

He walked mechanically into the dark trees surrounding the cottage, not
seeing anything in front of him. All of his energy went toward containing the
shock, horror, fear, and hope coursing through his body at the discovery he'd
made.

Derica was the other half of his heartthread, the one he'd been searching
for.

This explained why he'd been unable to shake thoughts of her since walking into that garden. It explained the bolt of unexplainable joy and terror that
struck him as soon as he looked into her doe-brown eyes.

It had been five long, lonely lifetimes since he'd last seen, touched, held, or
loved the being he treasured most in existence.

His heart beat like a drum in his chest and a gray haze invaded the edges of
his vision as the mist soaked into his clothes. His feet tripped over something
in his path, and he reached out blindly to halt his fall, palms striking damp
bark. The scrape barely registered. He leaned into the trunk of the tree, bringing up the other palm, and rested his forehead against the bark.

Against the still, safe harbor of the pine, Justus realized he was shaking. He groaned raggedly into the night and closed his eyes. Never could he have imagined *this* was how the job the Disciples of the Loom hired him for would have turned out. Meeting *her*.

Five remembered lifetimes of despair, loneliness, rage, and helplessness crashed into him in waves. He shuddered under the onslaught, a roar swelling in his chest before escaping from his mouth. Lightheaded, breathing heavily, he turned his back to the tree. Bark stung, scraping exposed skin as his tunic rode up. The scabbard on his back screeched in time with his descent to the wet forest floor. He sat propped against the trunk, the rain-soaked ground wetting the stiff fabric of his mostly dry breeches.

Justus tipped his head back and stared into the cloudy, dark maelstrom of the sky. The heavy rain clouds had loosed their deluge and were now impotent puffs of remembered wrath. The midafternoon sun hid but tinged the sky the faintest hue of gold. Birds and forest-dwelling animals rustled and croaked melodiously, as if the world cared not about a discovery so momentous. It shifted *everything* for him.

The Warrior and Weaver-blessed were once again together.

He scrubbed the heel of his rough palms over his closed eyes. Her taste was still in his mouth, her scent still in his nose. He was drunk off it. Giddy. And, at the same time, petrified.

Justus reached down to his hip and unsheathed the dagger—the cursed thing he could never escape. Even without the Weaver-blessed, the dagger always found him in every lifetime, a reminder of every sin committed against his love, every flash of betrayal as the light left their eyes—destined to meet again in the next life. Until the Warrior had failed to meet the terms of the magic.

Until they were too late.

Some people dismissed the Disciples doctrine as just that—doctrine. Justus knew better. The Warrior knew they had been touched by the Weaver's hands before being Woven into the Tapestry. He remembered his past lives, unlike the other human souls of Veridion. Sometimes, his head was so full of other lifetimes and memories, he struggled to hold onto Justus.

He flipped the blade in his hand, pushing the pad of his thumb along the hilt, feeling the grooves of the tiny script carved there. Justus raised the blade before his eyes, staring hard at the reminder he couldn't escape. The dagger was made of dark metal, a shade darker than pewter. He still, to this day, didn't know what it had been forged with or by whom. As many times as he'd been Woven among the threads of the Loom, and as many times as he may yet be Woven, Justus didn't hold out hope he would find the answer to the riddle. The Weaver-blessed had once told him the weapon was a beautiful lie—it was damnation masquerading as salvation. If he was honest, every lifetime of separation from the Weaver-blessed was almost a reprieve—he couldn't face the decision to end his lover's life if they never met.

Yes, he was lonely. Yes, his heart ached with every beat for its other half. Five lifetimes was such a long time to wait to be together again.

Every time he wielded the dagger, ending the Weaver-blessed's life to keep them together, it inevitably blackened a part of his soul. He couldn't bring himself to think exactly how much time passed since he'd first damned them to this forsaken cycle of love and betrayal, and not once did he even have to sharpen it. He rubbed a calloused thumb against the edge of the blade, dispassionately watching a bead of crimson well.

His self-hatred whispered that the bones of his love honed its edge—prepared it for his next betrayal.

Numb, he sat until the sun finally peeked through the fading storm clouds.

Justus trailed his fingers back to the hilt and gripped it, knuckles flashing white in the growing light. The guard was simple—sturdy, but not ornate. Dark metal, the same as the blade, stretched neatly and purposefully on either side. Sufficient protection from an opponent's counter-strikes. The darkest ruby he'd ever seen—in any lifetime—capped the pommel and tiny demonish script wrapped the hilt.

No demon he'd ever encountered would decipher the script for him, out-right refusing his requests. Justus didn't know if the words held the spell binding him to his love, or a way to cut the tie entwining them, and he'd likely never know. Mazolan wouldn't even tell him.

Everything changed after he failed to uphold his duty to the magic. As the demon told the Warrior, if they failed to end the Weaver-blessed's life with the dagger, they would not be tied to the same reincarnation cycle upon the Loom. The Warrior had grown lax, certain they would be able to protect their lover from any threat. Five lifetimes ago, the Warrior watched, helpless, as the Weaver-blessed's life was extinguished. The Warrior held onto their hope, certain the cyclical way the Weaver operated the Loom would deliver them back to the Weaver-blessed. After three journeys among the Tapestry, the Warrior's faith abandoned them.

Justus knew what it was to experience perfect love. And he knew what it was to watch that love wither and die in his beloved's eyes as blood coated his hands—as the heart of the Weaver-blessed beat for the last time. That final look of shock and betrayal, in all its forms and figures, was a cascade of memory that threatened to drive him mad with shame and grief.

Early on, Justus had wondered if he deserved to be whole. He'd slept with any willing woman, drowned himself in every liquor, jumped into every fight or battle with the niggling hope he wouldn't see the following dawn. Nothing cured the ache in his soul or filled the black abyss in his heart. None of it mattered. Nothing changed.

Eyes fixed on the blade that tormented him so, he slowly brought the tip of the blade toward his heart.

Justus's awareness seemed to float outside his body. He saw the glint of the blade in the cloud-filtered sunlight. He saw the white knuckles, *his* knuckles, gripping the hilt. And he saw the slight tremble of those fingers, the blade bouncing beams of light with every waver. In all his many lifetimes, he'd never tried this approach.

What if he quenched the blade in the blood of the Warrior?

What then?

Awareness still outside of himself, he saw his chest hitch and his muscles tremble with wrath, fear, or relief—he didn't know. They all swirled around him. The overarching feeling of self-loathing cocooned them all in sticky, sickly threads.

He didn't want to repeat the cycle. He didn't want to love her.

Derica.

He should set them both free. A just man, a *good* man, a *worthy* man would do it.

But he was none of those things.

Flipping the blade into his fingers, he drew his arm back fast as the lightning that had nearly struck him and let the weapon fly. He didn't look to see if it hit its target, but he heard the thud of blade and wood, and the singing metallic vibration as the hilt quivered.

He roared again into the sky, this time holding back none of the pain, none of the loathing deep in his heart. It scalded his throat, stung his vocal cords, as it rang from deep inside. If there was anything deeper or more intrinsic than a soulthread, that's where his pain lived. No matter how long he yelled or how loud, it never left him.

The echo of his agony rang in the air. Chest heaving, breath puffing in visible clouds, Justus hunched back into the tree trunk, soaked breeches clinging to the backs of his legs. Eyes slipping closed, Justus made a concerted effort to keep from crumbling under the weight of the clamoring emotions swirling within. He'd survived lifetimes with this pain and suffering, this loneliness. He could—he *would*—continue to live with it.

For Justus Hadrian vowed he would not dance this dance again. He *refused.*

In fact, he'd lived until now—rather, the moment in the cottage—entirely accepting he would never find his Weaver-blessed lover in this life. He'd let go of the hope they lived in the next town, or their eyes would meet in the next crowded tavern. Letting go of hope had been like shrugging off an immense yoke.

Justus had stepped out of the shadow of hope, and into the light of living fully this lifetime. Previously, he'd isolated himself. He'd not allowed anyone close because he only wanted his Weaver-blessed love.

When he let go of his suffocating expectation, he had found friendship and surcease from the loneliness with first Mazolan, then Nyle, and Alondra. Never before had he allowed himself companionship, and, now, it felt as if reality descended with crushing, violent intent.

The scrape of leaves and forest debris centered Justus. He dragged his heels back and pushed his forehead into his upraised knees. He propped his chin on his knees, opening his eyes to view a forest gilded by the sun.

Little by little, Justus allowed the scents, sounds, and sights around him to push down his internal turmoil. He focused on the cold, wet fabric wrapping his legs, the scrape of bark, and the dance of new sunlight on the surrounding trees. Justus breathed in the scent of rain-damp linen, muddy earth, and leaf-strewn forest floor. Birds chirped and sang, their song shrill and cheerful.

The entire time, he laid mental bricks around the yawning chasm of longing and despair at the center of his being. *I will not pursue her. She will never learn who we are to each other. I will let her go.*

With every brick, his breathing came easier. With the last?

He felt nothing.

Not happy, not sad, not lonely.

Nothing.

The truest test of his internal armor would be the sight of her.

With deliberate movement, Justus unfolded from his seat against the tree trunk, brushing off the leaves clinging to his clothing. He fingered the empty scabbard at his hip knowing the damned enchanted blade would find its way back to him. It always did.

Rage and pain beat at the brick walls, but he ignored them.

Starting back to the cottage, Justus hoped the brick walls he erected would suffocate his love, his pain, his anger.

Because he would not do it. He would not love and then end Derica.

Even if his soul cried out for hers as it withered away to nothing.

Justus was a coward.

He'd reached the cottage and called through the door to Derica, saying they would remain here through the night. Or rather, *she* would. Justus would patrol.

His uneventful, soggy evening served to provide the distance he required to reach an equilibrium again. But now, with his fingers grasping the cottage's iron latch, Justus's mental fortifications seemed insufficient.

As quietly as possible, he opened and closed the door of the cottage. He winced when the hinges whined, the high-pitched squeal jarring in the quiet. The hinges were still damp from the rain.

Palms on the closed door, he stared at the dark wood and black nails. The ultimate test of the walls he'd erected inside himself lay behind him on the bed in front of the dying fire. Justus would admit only to himself how much he feared that test. But from the clawing grasp of fear sprang bravery. At least, that's what he would tell any green mercenary.

The truth was much less poetic.

Fear was a naked woman under a wool blanket. It was the smell of her skin and the feel of her hands on his back. The taste of her lips on his. That fear would draw him in and bind him to her. It would mark the beginning of their long journey to untold suffering.

Fear was the unstoppable force of Fate.

He quieted the voice screaming to sink back into her embrace, to take the happiness he'd so long been without. Justus slowly turned on his heel and faced the interior of the cottage, his heart stuttering, hands curled at the sight that greeted him.

Derica lay on her stomach in the middle of the bed. Fiery red hair spread over the single pillow, the strands blazing in the light streaming in from the window. The wool blanket gathered at the small of her back, hiding the wide hips and ass he'd feverishly clutched earlier

His nails pricked his palms as the phantom memory of sensation tingled the flat of his hands.

Her pale skin lacked the bloom of rose he'd barely been able to discern in the firelight before, but the brightening sunlight highlighted freckles spattered across her back, a mole in the center of her spine. His mouth watered as Justus imagined kissing and nipping his way up her lush body to that mole.

He swallowed a groan as he adjusted himself in his breeches and quickly scanned the rest of her. Derica, with the side of her face plumped beneath her by the pillow, facing the door. Severe, straight eyebrows several shades darker than the shoulder-length wealth of flame haloing her head. Spiked eyelashes the same color as the slash of her eyebrows kissed her plump cheeks. Her rosebud mouth was slightly open, a tempting shade of summer-ripe peach.

Justus nearly jumped when Derica suddenly brought up one arm and tucked it under the pillow. What it revealed...

He surely had to be drooling now. The sides of her bountiful breasts plumped against the tick mattress, spilling away from her torso. The remembered sensation of petal soft skin stroked his lips. Justus scrubbed his mouth with his palm, banishing it.

"Justus?"

His eyes snapped to her face. Doe brown eyes stared at him hazily. Derica scrunched up her button nose and slipped her hand out from under the pillow to stifle a yawn.

With each blink, those eyes became more aware, and he braced himself for what would come. Justus expected a barrage of questions.

Instead, he got *frostbite*.

The sleepy warmth lighting her soft brown eyes dimmed and chilled. Derica pulled the blanket up her back, hiding her luscious body. Her lashes swept down, shuttering her gaze. She sat up, careful to keep the parts of her he was most eager to see in the daylight securely hidden beneath the thick blanket.

"I was half worried you'd abandoned me here alone last night." All the soft rasp of sleep was gone from her voice. Part of him cheered while the walled-off part of him roared in frustration. It would be so much easier to maintain his resolve not to pursue her if she spurned him.

"I wasn't far." His voice was hoarse, his throat still raw from loosing his pain and frustration.

Derica flicked a questioning gaze at him and Justus carefully kept his features blank, devoid of his inner turmoil.

"Near enough to be close should there be danger. Far enough away... to be far." He sounded like an ass. He couldn't have said far enough to avoid his outbursts disturbing her.

Far enough to make it difficult to come crawling back to you. Not far enough to banish the compulsion to return to you.

He'd spent most of the night torturing himself with memories of her deaths in their shared lives. Recalling the light leaving the Weaver-blessed's eyes more than cooled his ardor—it had shriveled his heart.

"You could've left me a weapon. I could've taken care of myself. If you hadn't returned, I'd planned on finding Reid on my own." She paused, her eyes sweeping over him, and he fought the impulse to go to her, to sweep her into his embrace and let her heart beat against him like a healing balm.

Her brown eyes snagged at his hip.

"I couldn't have handled the sword, but your dagger—" she flicked a finger at his belted scabbard "—could have protected me just fine. It's a beautiful blade."

Justus brought his hand to the scabbard on his belt, knowing what he would find. When his hand made contact with the steel hilt, he couldn't stop his eyes from slipping closed or the grinding of his teeth. Inside his mental brick walls, he screamed in rage.

A rustle of fabric on the bed made him snap his eyes back open. When he focused, Derica stood in front of him, only an arm's length away wrapped in the woolen blanket, her shoulders and arms free above it.

She stared at the jeweled hilt, an enigmatic expression on her face. The longer he watched her, the hollower her stare became. Her hand slowly lifted towards the sheathed weapon. The instrument of their anguish.

Heart kicking like a bucking stallion, he jerked back out of her reach.

The Weaver-blessed sometimes remembered their shared history on their own. Other times, they remembered through contact with the Warrior, or more rarely, the dagger. In one lifetime, the Weaver-blessed had even been the one who delivered the cursed blade to the Warrior. How cruel a curse to deliver themselves and the weapon meant to end their life to the hand that would bring the killing blow.

While Justus and the Warrior were one and the same, he had also learned to separate himself from his past lives. It was a game he played with himself.

When the loneliness became unbearable, he would sit on quiet nights and stare up into the sky, wondering what it would be like to simply be the mercenary, Justus Hadrian, not the Warrior, damned and blessed.

His hand clenched around the cold, dark steel of the dagger. The ridges of demonish scrollwork pressed into his palm, a familiar bite.

Justus focused back on Derica, his heart beating against his ribs, as if eager to be held in the palm of this woman. She'd held his heart in every life they'd been together.

But not this time.

She stared at him with wide, confused eyes. Hurt flashed across Derica's face, before her gaze shuttered and she stepped back. It took every ounce of will he possessed not to step forward, kneel before her, and offer apologies while begging for the opportunity to court her. Justus locked his knees and thinned his lips. His hands shook, and he fisted them together behind his back, assuming a military stance.

"Your clothes should be dry by now. I'll stand outside while you get dressed and then I can track the others. Hopefully, the rain wasn't hard enough to wash away tracks in the trees. If so, I should at least be able to get us back to the road." His voice was leaden as he turned on his heel, not waiting for a response, and then walked out of the cottage. He stood with his back rigid against the side of the door frame and dropped his head back to lie against the sun-warmed wood of the structure.

Justus would damn himself to eternal reincarnations of pain and loneliness rather than be his love's end one more time.

CHAPTER FOURTEEN

Derica jerked her arms into her tunic, struggling with the fabric, stiff with dried rainwater as it was.

That man.

He had some *nerve*.

To have experienced such intense pleasure in the arms of an enigmatic stranger, much less a dangerous mercenary, and then to have that mercenary storm off into the misting dark, cockstand straining the front of his hastily donned breeches... She didn't understand it.

Hadrian—for she wouldn't think of him as *Justus* any longer—was dumber than Reid's brother, Algie, if he had expected a warm welcome when he came back to the cottage. Adrenaline combined with this strange pull she felt to Hadrian might have influenced her actions, but Derica would not castigate herself for taking her pleasure how and with whom she chose. Life was precious and fleeting. She refused to regret grabbing for experiences as they presented themselves. At least, that's the woman she endeavored to be after leaving Arlan.

She wouldn't choose to have an experience with him again, though.

They would find Reid and the rest of the traveling band, and then she would never see them or *him* again after they reached Radley.

With a sharp nod of her chin, she ran her hands down her thighs, smoothing the rumpled fabric of her breeches, grimacing when the wrinkles remained. Dressing completed, she strode towards the door with purpose. Derica flung it open and promptly had it shut in her face after a rather unsettling thud.

Masculine groaning came from the other side.

Served the ass right if he'd been peeking at her through the door.

Cautiously, she pressed the door open and stepped out into the bright morning light.

Jus—*Hadrian* stood with his head tilted back, hands covering his nose. He blinked up into the sky, the sheen from his watering eyes catching the light.

"Weaver-damnit, woman. I was coming to check if you needed help with your clothing."

Derica blinked. After his bizarre behavior yesterday, and then his stilted manner this morning, she hadn't expected polite courtesy from him. She refused to raise her estimation of him, however. The bare minimum would not impress her.

She stepped up to his big body and batted his hands away from his nose. Reaching up, she grasped him and tilted Hadrian's head so she could see the damage. "It's obvious you've broken it before. I don't know what you have to be worried about." She pressed gently on one side of his nose, then the other with her thumbs.

He didn't wince, but his eyes tightened in discomfort.

"One more break isn't the problem," he said. "It's the swelling. It makes it difficult to fight when your face is throbbing, and your vision is limited." Hadrian's voice was low, and the puff of his breath on her hands sent gooseflesh rippling up her arms.

Derica cleared her throat and swallowed a twinge of guilt. She would have a slight crisis of conscience if the oaf got himself killed because of the injury.

"I'm sorry. If you had knocked, you could have avoided this inconvenience."

His husky laugh stroked her forearms, and her core clenched. She hurriedly dropped her hands and backed away to a safe distance.

"Next time, I—" His lips pinched closed before finishing.

She cocked one eyebrow, studying his closed expression. Derica waited for a hint of the warmth and fire she'd experienced—for a softening or indication he felt the same persistent tug she did. When his countenance remained stony, she sighed. "There will not be a next time."

His eyes shuttered further. He nodded, gazing at the forest behind her. Derica searched his face, but for some reason, she didn't think the nod was in acknowledgment of her statement.

Hadrian pointed to her muddy, scuffed kid boots, changing the subject. "Will those hold up to some walking?"

"Is there an alternative?"

"I could carry you?" His midnight eyes flared with an ember of desire and then cooled so abruptly, Derica almost thought she imagined it.

"No. No. I shall be fine." She would die before she let this man carry her through the forest to Reid. Even if the image of her wrapped around his body, pressed to his broad back, tingled like a caress across her skin. Her body may crave his touch, but Hadrian's abrupt departure from the cottage the night before had confused her. In the light of day, he was a smoldering cinder to the bonfire of intensity she'd experienced in his arms.

The metallic clink and the rustle of leather accompanied Jus—*the commander*—adjusting the sword strapped to his back and patting the dagger belted to his waist. His lips twisted into a hateful sneer so briefly, when Derica blinked next, it was gone.

Turning away, she cast her gaze to their surroundings, finding nothing familiar. The trees dripped sparkling crystals of dew onto the still-muddy ground. "How will you find the others?"

"Well, as part of my many talents, I also happen to be a damn fine tracker. The only thing to make it a challenge will be yesterday's storm."

Retreating behind waspishness, Derica rolled her eyes. "Get to it, then." She gestured at the dense forest in front of the pair, jerking one auburn brow up. "Let's see this *prowess*."

Hadrian stalked forward, muttering, not even looking to see if she followed.

Trotting to keep up, barely letting more than a few feet separate them for fear of losing her way, she watched as Justus transformed into the hardened warrior she'd witnessed before. His obsidian gaze sharpened, his body moved with silent but intimidating grace. This man was a weapon, but forged of what, she wondered? Every pause to examine the bark of a tree, every time he knelt to examine the ground before them, Derica watched. It was impossible not to. Again, she felt that draw to him. With enormous effort, she pulled her avid gaze away and looked around. Nothing about the densely forested scenery was familiar, and she had no clue what direction they were moving relative to the road or the cottage and its shelter.

You found more than shelter there.

A hard shake of her head banished the thought. Derica didn't want to remember.

Her eyes flicked back to him without her conscious direction, and she found him still, kneeling. As if sensing her eyes on him, he looked up, expression filled with such hunger, but his midnight eyes also reflected an intense pain.

Then she blinked, and it was gone. Hadrian's face was a stone mask, hard and sharp like flint. Was this the face he wore into battle? Because, if so, his enemies must regularly piss themselves in fear. It made her knees tremble, while also sending a thrill of liquid heat to her core.

But Derica would not examine her reaction too closely, refusing to acknowledge this draw to someone she barely knew. She might pull it out and review it at a later date, but not now. Not so soon after being carelessly abandoned last night.

"It shouldn't be too far now. I think we're close," he said. Hadrian rose from his crouch and walked deeper into a copse of trees, heavy with gnarled branches, the wood still wet from the storm.

A figure shot out of the foliage and launched directly at the mercenary. Derica's scream lodged in her throat as she startled and tripped, falling onto her ass. It took her brain precious seconds to catch up with the scene her eyes witnessed.

The attacker headed straight for Hadrian, hands tipped with sharp, glinting black claws. Hadrian moved smoothly and sinuously out of the way, throwing a hand out to snatch the back of his attacker's tunic, and indolently tossed them onto their back in front of him. The attacker's chest hitched as they struggled to pull in air, their claw-tipped hands folded onto their chest. A flash of fangs and wry yellow eyes glinted in the sun peeking through the trees.

"Good morning, Commander." Mazolan's voice came out choked. "Just—ahem—trying to keep you on your toes. I'd hate to see you become rusty. Glad to see you survived those Shredded, by the by. Oh, and look, if it isn't the lovely Derica. Hello, morsel. You look a bit *different* this morning. A glow, I'd say you have. Yes, a nice—"

"Mazolan, get the fuck up and stop blathering." Hadrian hiked up a disdainful eyebrow and stepped near the prone demon to offer his hand, impatiently waiting to haul his mischievous subordinate up.

Trying not to groan at the sting of her scuffed palms, Derica stood and brushed off what she could of the damp ground she'd landed in, hoping there wasn't a muddy ass print on the back of her breeches. She didn't want to meet the rest of their company looking a mess, even if it matched the tangle of emotions she was after the cottage.

Hadrian and Mazolan stood close together, the demon giving a report on the events after they were separated. Maz saw her watching, and, with a nod, pointed back into the dense copse behind them without stopping their report.

Derica didn't have to be told twice. She desperately needed to see Reid was whole, and then she wanted some space from Hadrian. Hopeful for the first, and aware of the current impossibility of the second, she turned on her heel, swatting branches and leaves away from her face. After trudging through the muddy brush, she entered a small clearing, similar to the one the mercenaries had camped in before.

With a cry and a teary wobble of her chin, she spotted Reid immediately and rushed over for a hug. Reid grinned, gathering her to his wide chest. A closer inspection revealed he was all right. If their grips were too tight, or a trembling was discernible, neither acknowledged it. Derica closed her eyes and breathed slowly, listening to Reid's steady heartbeat. It was the most comforting sound in the world right now.

Reid smoothed the hair at the back of her head in slow strokes. "You're all right?" he murmured into her fiery hair.

She nodded, unable to speak past the lump in her throat. Her relief at finding Reid alive and unharmed competed with the comfort she felt after the tumultuous time she had with Hadrian. Derica knew she was safe with Reid. Always.

She squeezed his waist tighter and burrowed her face into his chest.

"Are you sure?" Reid gently held her away by the shoulders, scanning her with his cornflower-blue eyes. No matter how intensely he scrutinized her, he wouldn't find any injuries. All the same, his blond brows bunched further into a knot the longer he stared at her face. She didn't know what he saw, but Reid knew her better than any soul in the world. There was very little she had ever successfully hidden from him.

"What happened?" Reid's voice was flat and hard.

"Nothing." Her voice didn't warble, but her eyes misted at his concern. Reid's gaze sharpened, and then his brow set into a darker scowl. He pulled her into his chest again as he looked to the entrance of the clearing where Hadrian entered with Mazolan.

Hadrian's gaze immediately found her in the circle of Reid's arms and the expression that flitted across his features was dark possession distilled. Her heart galloped in her chest and continued to run riot even after the mercenary smoothed his expression to placid passivity.

Reid stiffened around her, and his hands locked behind her waist.

"What did that ass do? He may be a mercenary, but I'm bigger than he is. That counts for something." Reid spoke low enough no one else could hear, but Mazolan's sharp smirk hinted they caught the exchange. They looked between Derica and Reid, to the commander, and back again, the twinkle of mischief in their yellow eyes edging toward gleeful. It sent a frisson of wariness down her spine.

"You're well, Reid?" Hadrian said. His eyes were dull, and the question held no inflection.

Reid nodded, radiating protective aggression. Hadrian moved his hands to his hips, one curled around the dagger she'd never seen him without. The ruby at the pommel glinted in the sun, and Derica's gaze snagged and held on the blood-red jewel. She couldn't seem to look at anything else.

Until Mazolan strolled up to her and stared with undisguised interest, the way one might observe a bug in a meadow on a lazy sunny day. With singular, rapt focus.

"All right there, morsel?" They flicked a no-longer-clawed finger at the commander. "What were you looking at before, hmm? The commander's dagger, wasn't it? Beautiful weapon. Demon made, in fact. If you've never seen demon script before, I'd be happy to show off my people's craftsmanship. Can't read it for you, though. Quite old. Not even I, with my overwhelming intellect, am able to decipher it. You may find it *familiar*, though. Morsel, why don't you—"

"Mazolan, stop talking and help Nyle ready the horses." Hadrian's command served all the purpose of a cracked whip. The demon immediately shut their mouth, and with a mocking bow to Derica, moved off to assist in preparation for getting back on the road.

Father Simond and Balduin, who had been standing with Nyle over near the horses, walked over to them. The older man frowned in concern at Derica.

"I'm so glad you're unharmed, my child. How did you fare the last day?"

"Fine, Father," she said. She avoided mentioning anything more about how she passed her time with the commander.

Balduin, with his regular sourness, merely swept her up and down with an intense look before dismissing any further interest.

"Have you eaten?" asked Father Simond. "I believe the two of you didn't have the benefit of supplies to break your fast this morning." He showed her over to a small area they had prepared to take meals. He sat her down on a folded blanket and started digging in the bags. "It's not much, just some hardtack biscuits. But we have cold, fresh water from a nearby stream and plenty of it. Nyle tells me we aren't far from the castle town and then this shall be behind us all."

Nodding, Derica accepted the water skin Father Simond offered her with one hand and the biscuit with the other. The chilled water was sweet on her tongue and she spent a good while relishing the kindness of Father Simond and the brief chance to simply rest.

Until she looked over at Reid and the mercenary commander.

The two still stood exactly where they were before the father led Derica away, staring daggers at each other, jaw muscles ticking, bodies rigid with contained challenge. Reid's protective streak at times frustrated her. At others, it warmed her heart. This time, it was a mix of both. She was a grown woman. Reid had clearly picked up that something had happened between them. Derica was still bruised enough emotionally from the last few days to allow him puffing up like an enraged peacock. If the added benefit was a shift in the commander's attention from her to Reid, who was she to direct it back?

He clearly didn't want her, anyway.

For whatever reason.

She shook the gloomy thought away and crammed a stale biscuit into her mouth. The loud crunch might drown out her ridiculous self-pity.

"How did the two of you pass the night?" Father Simond asked kindly.

Derica choked on the biscuit.

Simond moved around her and firmly thumped her back. "I'm so sorry. I should have waited until you were done with your meal."

Derica coughed and then took a swig from the waterskin. Wiping her mouth with the back of her hand, she replied, "No, it wasn't your fault, Father. The commander dispatched the Shredded with a little assistance from me, and then we were fortunate enough to have found an empty cottage to shelter us through the night."

The priest frowned, his mouth dropping open in shock. "You assisted, my child?"

Balduin, having drifted nearer, put down the pack he held and gaped at Derica. "What business did you have jumping in to assist a trained fighter?"

Derica straightened her shoulders. "It was the commander against three rabid assailants. So, I decided to help. We're both alive and well." She stared directly at the acolyte, daring him to censure her for helping protect her own life or the life of another. After a tense moment of silence, the man dipped his chin in a shallow nod and cleared his throat.

Father Simond frowned at the younger man. "I'm sorry you had to do that, Derica. You were very brave."

He meant well, she was sure, but her temper flared, regardless. She didn't need a pat on the head from a Disciple of the Loom. She had little patience for a man's judgment, even less when it was wrapped up in holy vestments.

"I may have lived all my life in Arlan, and I may not be worldly or have the benefit of mercenary training, but defending myself wasn't bravery. I simply did what I needed to stay alive. If the commander got injured or killed, my chances of surviving the night would have diminished."

A gurgling cough behind her made Derica turn her head toward the sound. Reid and the commander stood behind her, but it was Reid's pale face that announced he had been the origin of the cough. He came forward and knelt in front of her, searching her eyes again as he gently clasped the hand still holding half a biscuit, appearing to need the contact.

"I am so incredibly glad you're all right. Were either of you—"

"I'm fine, Reid. Whole and unharmed." She clamped her lips shut before she thanked Hadrian out of polite habit. He deserved thanks, but she couldn't bring herself to voice it right now.

"She saved my life."

Derica would have dropped her food if Reid hadn't been clasping her hand. She stared up into midnight eyes watching her with intense focus. Realizing her mouth hung open, she snapped it shut, but couldn't force her eyes away from Hadrian's earnest gaze. Surely, she'd imagined being praised by the mercenary who played her body with masterful hands and then abandoned her for some unknown reason.

CHAPTER FIFTEEN

J ustus stared down at the woman who had saved his life. In the light of his discovery of who Derica really was to him, he'd almost forgotten that. Pride for her swept through his chest. She didn't have any training, and yet, this courageous woman had stepped in to even the odds of his fight against the Shredded.

The shock on her face when he acknowledged her was almost insulting—he could give credit and thanks when it was due. But this incarnation of the Warrior and the Weaver-blessed had a lot to relearn about each other, he supposed.

No.

You will not *relearn her.*

You will stay *away.*

Derica doesn't deserve the end you'd force on her. The years of happiness you might share aren't worth the eternal torment of bearing the weight of betrayal and hurt one more time in the eyes of the Weaver-blessed.

Shoving the yearning ache down into the depths of his cold, lonely heart, Justus cleared his throat and inclined his head to Derica, making sure his countenance was passive.

"Thank you," he said. "I know I chastised you for interfering, but without your help—I can acknowledge I would have come out of the fight with more than a few bothersome scratches."

Derica blinked wide, doe brown eyes, the flutter of her auburn lashes glinting like heated gold in the sun. Reid nudged her hand. Justus wasn't sure if Reid wanted to prompt a response to his thanks, but the blond certainly seemed attuned to Derica, and his attitude toward Justus had shifted dramatically.

It was no matter. Justus had no intention of pursuing anything with her. If his soul silently screamed at the absence of its other half, it wasn't anything he hadn't already borne for five lifetimes. If the Weaver sat above, orchestrating all of this on the Loom, maybe she wanted to see his suffering peak this span upon Veridion. Maybe she *wanted* him broken.

He had already learned the goddess wasn't all-powerful. A demon's spell had circumvented her will before. Justus was confident in his ability to do so again.

"Derica?" Reid prompted.

Her friend's nudge snapped her out of her surprised stupor. A frown gathered her straight brows and Justus stifled a grin. A delightfully contrary creature was the other half of his heartthread, and he couldn't help but look forward to whatever she would respond with.

Her face smoothed, and she murmured, "You're welcome."

Now *his* brow pinched. *You're welcome?* He'd heard the set down she'd delivered moments before. He expected... more. But then, he didn't deserve more, did he?

He nodded to Derica, then the priest, and finally Reid. The last watched him with a satisfied gleam, like he knew Justus hadn't gotten the back and forth he desired from Derica.

Pushing the whole encounter to the back of his mind, Justus joined Mazolan and Nyle near the horses. If his back was slightly too straight and brow still pinched with frustration, so be it. Justus would see them all to Radley and then he would not seek her out. He would accept the next paying mission, no matter what it was or how dangerous. He *had* to keep his distance.

Nyle and Mazolan had already saddled the horses and packed. Inspecting the animals for injuries, Justus was satisfied to see they all appeared well and calm. Even Reid's draft horse, who wouldn't have been used to the noise or terror of battle, seemed fine.

"Maz, where'd you pack the salve?" Justus asked.

"Commander, did one of those nasty Shredded get you?"

"Just throw me the damn salve, demon."

Mazolan clucked their tongue and reached into a bag. They tossed the metal tin at Justus, and he snatched it out of the air.

"You two must have had a night. You're usually only this snippy after a night of excess at the tavern. As I know there was no swilling at a tavern last night, it must be something *else* that's got the dear commander in a kerfuffle—"

Nyle didn't look up as he adjusted a bag on his horse's saddle. "Maz, for the love of the First, shut your gob before the commander runs you through."

Mazolan humphed imperiously and fiddled with the bags on their own horse.

Justus unbelted the sword strapped to his back and reached behind his neck, yanking the back of his tunic up to his shoulders, the cool morning air pleasant on his bare skin. The scratch he'd sustained along his spine wasn't bleeding as far as he could tell, but it pulled a bit with movement, likely having scabbed over. The slash at the bend of his shoulder caused a bit more pain, but also wasn't bleeding.

With a scowl, he realized he needed to scrub out the wounds. It wouldn't be a novel experience for him, only one he couldn't do alone—and it would sting.

Nyle flicked him a look, then raised his brows questioningly.

For all that Mazolan filled every silence with endless prattling, Nyle was the quiet, steady one of their crew. He was slow to anger and quick to offer help.

Justus's two comrades struck a harmonious balance together, where alone they would drive some mad. Despite their differences, they cared for each other and him like family. Justus had been lucky in that, at least. Someone you could trust at your back was hard to come by. Multiple someones was indeed a blessing.

Justus bent down to snatch a full waterskin from the pile of supplies and nodded to Nyle. Nyle pointed to a large rock and Justus walked over to sit, making sure his tunic remained up and out of the way.

"It'll sting, same as always," Nyle said. Justus heard the rustle of cloth and handed back the water skin. The splash and fall of water followed. "It'll be cold, too."

Justus grunted his acceptance. The warnings weren't necessary, but he didn't fault the tattooed mercenary for his kindness.

The damp cloth was a shock of cold at the center of his back, but he held still. The sting would come. Ah, yes, there it was. Nyle pushed firmly in rough, scrubbing strokes. Justus grit his teeth and let himself wander away from the sensations.

A flash of flame-red hair across a pillow, throaty moans, and the soft cushion of her skin rose to his mind, and Justus lacked the willpower to shove them away.

Red glinted at the corner of his vision, and then he stared into those doe eyes. He blinked, realizing she stood in front of him, not a phantom lover conjured to lure and besiege his control. Derica looked between him and Nyle. Concern flitted across her features and then she left, returning with her blond giant in tow.

Lovely.

"Why didn't you mention your injuries needed tending?" she asked.

Justus sighed. "It's nothing a thorough cleaning and some salve won't handle. Don't concern yourself on my account."

"We're quite used to handling scrapes and injuries on the road. Nothing we haven't done a hundred times before," echoed Nyle.

Derica turned to Reid. "Will you examine it?"

Reid searched her eyes and then nodded.

Great. This would be even *more* painful now.

Nyle stopped his ministrations and stepped back, handing Reid the damp cloth. With a clap on Justus's shoulder, his comrade returned to Mazolan. Derica remained in front of Justus, eyes flicking back to her friend every few seconds.

"Well?" Justus shot over his shoulder.

"Derica, can you gather my kit from our bags please?" Reid said.

She nodded and hurried off to fetch the requested supplies.

The rustle of Reid's clothing sounded in Justus's ears. Then came the warning he'd been expecting since walking into the clearing with Derica.

"If you've hurt her in any way, visible or unseen, I will end you," said Reid, voice low and full of gravel.

Justus's lips twitched, surprised by the gentle giant's hidden depths. His respect for Reid rose, although they weren't any closer to forming a close and abiding friendship, however. No. Absolutely not.

Justus turned his head and let all the frustration show on his face. "Try," he growled, "and you will force me to deprive her of what appears to be a dear friend."

"If I get one good blow in, it'll be satisfying enough for me," Reid answered.

A surprised bark of laughter escaped Justus. "You don't appear to be an expert at unarmed combat. Are you sure you could manage one blow?"

"For her, I could manage anything," Reid said.

Reid's statement wiped all mirth from Justus's expression, echoing the mercenary's own feelings.

For her, anything. Even forsaking her so she could live free of this curse.

Grudgingly, Justus's respect for the man inched higher. Weaver-dammit. He didn't want to like this man. Reid had had Derica's smiles, her touch, her warmth for years. He had everything Justus coveted but would not allow himself.

Reid must have seen some of the torment in Justus's eyes because he carefully searched Justus's face. For what, he wasn't sure. His intent not to harm Derica? The possibility of violence?

Derica returned, eyes dancing between the two men. She handed Reid a small leather pouch, and he took it without breaking the thread connecting their gaze.

"Everything all right?" Derica asked tentatively.

"Just asking the commander how he came by the injury," Reid said.

"Shredded," he grunted.

Reid nodded and then dug into the bag, pulling out strips of linen bandages, a small jar of... was that honey? And a tin of what was likely a liniment or unguent. The powerful aroma of the item wafted to Justus even with the lid closed.

"Don't worry, Reid is the best physician's assistant Arlan ever saw," Derica said.

Justus's attention snapped to her. Was she trying to comfort him? His traitorous heart warmed in his chest, but he quelled it with the ice of his determination never to see her eyes burn with betrayal before dulling into lifelessness. He would not be her end.

Justus grunted and faced forward. "Well, physician's assistant, proceed. We need to get on the road."

He shouldn't have done it. The man treating his wound made sure Justus wouldn't forget his warning anytime soon. The unguent slathered on the slash down his spine stung for hours. And it smelled like cat piss.

CHAPTER SIXTEEN

D erica sat in front of Reid on their horse, riding beside the mercenaries and their wagon. The sun warmed her crown, and the steady sway of the horse pulled heavily at her eyelids, tempting her to drop her head back onto Reid's shoulder and sleep.

"You can, you know. Sleep that is."

She started, jerking against Reid. His soft laugh rumbled against her back as he reached forward to settle her again. "I don't know what happened last night, but you can tell me now, or sleep and tell me when we get to the city," he continued.

She gritted her teeth and sealed her lips so the sigh building wouldn't escape. Derica could tell Reid about the Shredded and leave out the events at the cottage. Desperately, she wanted to tell him. There wasn't anything her closest friend couldn't soothe with a talk. Even if the problem couldn't be solved with talking, Reid took such care listening, his patience and concern were always a balm to Derica. *Always.*

"I'll tell you now," she said in a low voice.

They were far enough away from the wagon, and Hadrian was out of earshot. She briefly searched for Nyle and Mazolan, finding them on opposite sides of the cart, quiet but alert to their surroundings. Mazolan rode closest. Briefly, they caught her eye and winked a golden orb at her. She frowned, and the demon flashed a fanged smile.

"Wretch," she mumbled.

If demons possessed better hearing than humans, she didn't know, but Derica wanted to get the story over with. So, she quietly launched into the tale of the previous night's events.

"And when you found the cottage?" Reid prompted after she relayed the details of the fight. He didn't bluster or chide her for jumping into the fray. He knew better.

"The commander lit a fire, and we slept."

"Derica." It was a reprimand.

She remained silent, trying not to stiffen in the saddle before Reid, but he knew her too well. Even as she thought she succeeded in throwing him off the scent he flicked to the top of her right ear. Derica squeaked and turned back to glare.

Reid cocked a golden brow, his steady gaze not reproachful, but waiting. Rubbing at her tingling ear, she knew why he'd done it. Her ears blushed before the rest of her face. Anyone who knew Derica knew to watch her ears.

"We don't lie to each other. Do we?" A hint of hurt tinged Reid's question.

"No," she said on a sigh and began—in such a hushed voice, Reid had to bend over her—the remaining tale of the cottage.

When she finished, her ears were practically aflame along with the rest of her face. Warmth even crept up from her chest to her neck. Placing a hand over her warm skin, Derica thought she must look like a tomato from the tip of her head to the top of her decolletage. Reid's silence didn't help. As her truest friend, she didn't really believe he'd shame her for her behavior, but she needed him to say something.

"There's something wrong if the man stopped so abruptly," he said, voice dryer than a desert at noon.

She let out a shocked snort of laughter, one she hurriedly stifled when Mazolan looked over at them. They raked gold eyes over them both, noticed nothing amiss, and turned back to chatting with Nyle over the back of the cart.

"I do hate to be crude, Derica—"

"Since when?" she mumbled.

Reid continued as if she hadn't interrupted, "—but someone doesn't just stop in the middle of the act and leave without significant reason. It's not *human*. You are sure he is? Human?"

They both faced forward and watched the commander's dark head where he sat, driving the mercenaries' cart.

"He looks human to me," she said.

"Felt like it, too?"

She tossed an elbow back into Reid's hard stomach, his answering grunt puffed onto the back of her head.

He patted her thigh. "Jesting, of course."

Derica heard the smile in his voice. All the tension, all the fear of his judgment, leaked out of her, and she felt both calmed and deflated. Her tension was the only thing keeping her upright, she realized. Confusion, anger, and tiredness rose to the surface, ready to overwhelm her. Since the moment she met the mercenary, Derica had felt unmoored. It was as if he shook the foundation of her life and she was in freefall, with no idea where or how she would land. It was exhausting.

She slumped back into Reid and let her head fall to his shoulder. If she tilted slightly, the top of his head blocked the glare of the sun. Allowing her eyes to slip closed, she breathed deep.

Reid adjusted his grip on the reins and his arms around her. He pressed his lips to the top of her head. "Sleep. I'll keep you safe."

"I know, Reid. I know."

Derica woke with a jolt to the clatter of wooden cart wheels, the indecipher-able chatter of a crowd, and the squawk of chickens. Blearily, she rubbed the sleep from her eyes and looked around. The sun sat half below the horizon, a deep, golden disk gilding their surroundings.

How long had Reid let her sleep?

She opened her mouth to ask, but he slipped off the horse behind her.

"Good. You're awake. Stay with the horse and Father Simond. I'm going with the commander and Balduin to secure our clearance into the city." Reid didn't wait for her response, but followed Hadrian's dark silhouette to the side of a heavily guarded bridge. Balduin trailed them, curling his lip as they passed wagons full of squalling livestock and playing children.

A small caravan of covered wagons sat ahead of them on the road, also waiting for permission to enter Radley.

Derica's eyes traveled the length of the line awaiting entry, and she blinked in surprise at the wealth of guards patrolling the outer walls. Was this all because of the Shredded?

"It wasn't this bad when we left, morsel."

Derica jumped and almost slid off the horse. Her heart beat at her ribs like a manic bird, and it took several gulps of air to calm herself enough to reply.

"Oh?" It wasn't the witty reply she hoped for. It was, however, the best her brain supplied to her lips at the moment.

Mazolan chuckled, their yellow eyes shining with mirth. "Yes. When we left Radley two months ago to accompany the holy men on their journey, the city was not even half as well-guarded."

Derica wasn't certain, but the demon's tone seemed mildly concerned by this change, even if it didn't show on their face. "It seems the Shredded we encountered were not a singular incident. Where do the fool humans think they come from, morsel?"

She opened her mouth to answer, but Mazolan kept talking.

"Rhetorical question, of course. You don't know." Their eyes trained on Derica, and she was at once terrified and fascinated by their singular attention. Several times, the demon had held her gaze, and each time she felt as if she was being tested or examined. Her very soul felt stretched out for them to examine, and Derica couldn't help but wonder what Mazolan saw when they looked at her.

"But I think you will soon, morsel. Very soon." Mazolan looked over to where the commander and Reid stood, and her relief at the absence of their regard was a heady thing. With a whoosh, she exhaled, realizing she hadn't taken a full breath the entire time Mazolan had appraised her. It soured something in her stomach to recognize the fear in her reactions to the demon. They weren't human, but Mazolan had done nothing to hurt her. So where was this apprehension coming from?

"Morsel, demons naturally unsettle humans. Don't be ashamed. You're simply human." With a fanged smirk, they turned back to Derica. Their eyes scanned her from head to toe. "Aren't you?"

Derica jerked, the second time she'd felt as if Mazolan had read her mind, and unsettled enough to mumble a, "Y-yes!"

Mazolan hummed. "We shall see. I think you are quite *unique*, morsel. For now... yes, 'unique' fits. We shall see what that uniqueness really is. I do believe our dear commander already knows. I'll be sure to be on hand when you reveal your secrets."

"*What* secrets?" With every word out of the demon's mouth, Derica's confusion deepened. Her brows clashed practically halfway down her nose.

"The best kind. The world-changing kind." With a wink, the demon walked away, leaving Derica with her jaw practically on the ground, completely and utterly bewildered by their conversation.

A shadow melted out of the darkness to Derica's right, and she again yelped, clutching the pommel to steady herself.

"Easy! Easy." Nyle grabbed the reins of her horse and held one arm out, ready to catch her should she topple from her perch. "I didn't mean to startle you. I forget what Mazolan can do to someone's nerves if they're not acclimated," he ruefully chuckled.

She cleared her throat and nodded, trying to compose herself. Nyle seemed the calmest of the mercenary group. He was like a human nerve tonic. Where Justus was watchful and always poised to take action, Nyle was a slower hand—no less capable—but less quick to action and violence. The night of the attack, he'd been a steadying presence. A thank-you danced on the tip of her tongue, but then he spoke.

"What did Mazolan say to unnerve you so?" The blue tattoos on the backs of his hands winked in the shadows as the sun dipped below the horizon. His amber gaze unnerved her as he waited for her answer.

"Some nonsense about how I'm unique and they want to be around to find out exactly how."

Nyle released her from the vice of his gaze, instead watching his palm stroke the draft horse's mane in slow, rhythmic movements. "Hmm. That's quite interesting, even for Mazolan. They normally can't be bothered with humans they don't know."

Derica chuckled awkwardly, not sure how she was supposed to respond.

Nyle changed the subject, putting her off-center further. "You wouldn't know this, because you haven't been around the commander long, but he's different since we left Arlan. He's faced foes much more dangerous than those Shredded we encountered and come out of battles with more serious injuries than a few scratches. It wasn't the battle that caused this shift." Nyle focused on her again, and she fought not to hold her breath, freezing like prey sighted by a predator. "I think... it's you. When I met him, the commander was a flame seeking a powder keg. Over time that frantic energy calmed, and he grew to be who he is today. A strong man who values his comrades and their friendship.

But, even then, he held a part of himself away—there was a distance in his eyes. When he looks at you..." He sighed, lapsing into silence while raking his hand through his curls.

"What?" she asked, brows rising as she fought to breathe in and out normally. "What could I have possibly done to affect your commander so strongly?"

"I don't know. But that distance disappears when he looks at you. There's something else there too, though. And Hadrian," he nodded to where Mazolan, Reid, and the commander all stood near their cart conversing, "is like a brother to me. I don't think there's a person in Veridion I share as much history with. And when I say he's different around you—after meeting you—you can believe me." He stepped back from her and inclined his head in a polite nod before leaving her alone with a maelstrom of thoughts.

Derica needed away from this. From Hadrian, his cryptic demon, and his devoted "brother". A scream of frustration threatened to escape. Her hands shook and her heart pounded. Her temper caught fire.

That man.

Justus had the gall to play her body masterfully, wring pleasure from her, and then subject her to interrogation and confusing discourse with his comrades?

After he'd left her naked and aching for him for no discernible reason?

No.

She wouldn't have any more of this. She and Reid would ride across that bridge and lose themselves in Radley. Unlike Arlan, the capital was enormous. Surely the mercenaries would go back to their guild, or on another job, and there would be no danger of crossing paths.

Derica needed this confusion and theater to end. Enough was enough, and she'd reached her limit. She wanted the comfort of a soft bed, a hot meal, and the peace Hadrian's absence would bring her.

"Reid!" she called.

He turned to her, frowning. Hadrian turned as well, scanning the surrounding area for threats, she supposed. She barely quelled the desire to roll her eyes. No one would have the audacity to attack the gates. The *heavily guarded* gates.

She motioned Reid over, and the commander followed.

Her frustration pulsed beneath her skin, clamoring for release. Her ears must be beet-red.

Reid passed his eyes over her and immediately noticed something off. He hurried to her side, taking her hand. "What's wrong?" he asked, searching her eyes.

"I can't—I'm overtired. Are we taken care of? Can we enter Radley and find a place to rest, Reid?"

Hadrian stopped behind Reid, peering over his shoulder at Derica astride their horse. "What's wrong?" he asked.

Derica gritted her teeth so hard, it surprised her they didn't squeal or grind to dust in her mouth. Thankfully, Reid answered for her.

"Nothing," he said, not looking away from her. "We've got everything we need to enter the city. We'll bid you farewell here. Thank you for helping us reach Radley." Reid's eyes flicked down, noticing the way her tense posture loosened and the sigh of relief she couldn't contain. He didn't wait for a response from Hadrian, but walked back to the cart, picked up the one bag that wasn't already on their horse, and returned. He tied the pack to the saddle and swung up behind Derica, gathering her to his front and reaching around her for the reins. In his embrace, Derica felt her anger drain, replaced with bone-deep weariness.

Justus stepped closer, almost brushing the fabric of her breeches.

"Farewell, Derica." Smoke and twilight wrapped around her, trying to steal into her soul. To do what, she didn't know, but she shrugged it off and inclined her head to him in a shallow nod. Refusing to meet his gaze, Derica stared ahead as Reid guided their mount over the bridge and into Radley.

If she felt a sting in the vicinity of her heart, she ruthlessly ignored it.

CHAPTER SEVENTEEN

Six Months Later - Radley

Light streamed through the stained-glass windows above her as Derica sat next to a cot, sponging a refugee boy's forehead. The child had been mute since he arrived with a small group of elders and other children, his silence swallowed by the bustle and hum of the church around them.

A passing acolyte deposited a fresh basin of water and a stack of clean cloths near her before bustling away to bring supplies to the others.

The threat of the Shredded had grown since Derica and Reid left Arlan, and Radley, with its walls and highly defensible location, took in more refugees every day.

When Reid and Derica rode into the city six months ago, the physicians' guild had instantly accepted him into their ranks, desperate for more people to treat the sick and injured as they entered Radley. He was given lodgings and work immediately.

Derica, on the other hand, was adrift. She hadn't been prepared to walk into a city swollen with sanctuary seekers. Available permanent lodgings were scarce, and, unlike Reid, she didn't have a useful skill during a crisis such as this. After seeking out three bakeries for work, Derica had discovered vendors of the city were subject to rations—as were the citizens. Bakers didn't have the ingredients to make—much less peddle their wares—to people who hadn't a spare gold piece.

Luckily, Balduin had given Reid directions to the church before they'd parted ways, and they hadn't questioned the oddly social behavior from the dour man, thankful for the assistance in a strange city. She and Reid had found the church after many wrong turns—despite Balduin's information—and Father Simond had given her work in the Disciples of the Loom's infirmary. Unfortunately, or fortunately in this case, Derica knew how to dress a wound and maintain a clean sickbed from her time taking care of her mother. She was shocked to see the church overwhelmed with refugees, all needing assistance, and Father Simond was grateful for her assistance. He even offered her a place to stay before Derica could ask.

For six months, Derica's days had been filled with taking care of the sick and injured in small ways, watching as the church received overwhelming numbers of refugees—most without means or relatives to seek shelter from within the city.

Derica rarely saw Reid until the end of the day when she'd make her way to the physician's guild, where the more critically ill in the city were sent. Exhausted, they would catch up while sharing an almost luxurious dinner provided by the guild's cooks. Reid would share letters and news from home, while Derica provided a sympathetic ear to complain to about improvised field medicine.

As always, Reid could read Derica so well, understanding when her duties reminded her too much of caring for her mother. Each time, he offered her a distraction—a book, a walk around the city, and even showing her an overgrown herb garden the guild cultivated medicinal plants in. The first time he showed it to her, she burst into tears, the emotion and stress she'd attempted to shut away spilling out. Apologizing profusely, Reid mopped at her face with a clean edge of his tunic, but Derica had waved him away with a watery laugh, thankful beyond words for a piece of home.

As she sat beside the small boy, her mind drifted to the garden, smelling the sweet aroma of lavender as she felt the dirt beneath her fingers, lulling her into a sense of calm even amidst the chaos of the improvised infirmary.

"Miss?"

Derica jumped in her seat and turned. An older woman stood behind Derica, sharp elbows and thin arms jutting from her worn clothing as she wrung her hands, biting her lip. Her eyes bounced back and forth between Derica and the boy.

"Yes? Can I help you?" asked Derica.

"Elyhan, how is he?" The woman brushed back a hank of her gray-streaked hair from her dark, sunken eyes.

"Were you part of the same group entering Radley?" Derica pointed to the opposite side of the cot and an empty chair. "He's been silent since I've been caring for him. A familiar face might help him find his voice."

The woman hobbled to the other side of the bed, limping on one leg. She sank onto the offered seat with a weary sigh, gaze locked on to the boy—Elyhan—the entire time. "Yes. We came from a small hamlet near Ittiron."

Derica bent down for a fresh cloth, dipping it into the clean water the acolyte deposited. She wrung it out, then returned to bathing Elyhan's forehead. He stared, unblinking, at the vaulted stone ceiling of the church. Derica had assumed his care when she overheard a priest telling an acolyte that they couldn't determine what ailment he suffered from. She knew then his affliction wasn't physical, but emotional. The boy looked young—six or seven—but was so thin he might have been older. His dark hair fell past his shoulders in matted clumps, green eyes dull and listless. After removing the dirt from his face, Derica had uncovered what she suspected was youthful suntanned skin when not jaundiced by traumatic events.

"Elyhan?" the woman called softly, taking his hand in hers.

He blinked, but didn't turn his head or respond.

"It's your Ama." She blinked, tears sheening the woman's eyes. "Ama is here. You're not alone."

Derica continued to stroke Elyhan's forehead soothingly. "You're his grandmother?" Derica asked in a whisper, afraid to spook either Ama or Elyhan.

"No." Ama swallowed, biting her bottom lip until it bleached white. "She didn't make it. We didn't believe the rumors when we first heard them, thinking they were exaggerated children's tales." She huffed a bitter laugh, her dark eyes hardening. "My husband insisted they were real—that he heard stories about them driving our sheep back from pasture from other farmers. I thought he had enjoyed a pint too many and then repeated drunken blather." She knuckled away a tear. "He was the first to go missing. After three days, when we'd already searched the hamlet and surrounding area, he returned. But he was... wrong." Ama dissolved into silent sobs, shoulders jerking as she grieved.

"Ama..." croaked a little voice.

The older woman gasped and leaned over Elyhan. "Yes. Yes, Elyhan. I'm here."

Elyhan stared at her with dry eyes, but his small hand gripped Ama's, knuckles blanching with the strength of his grasp. "Don't be sad. There's too much sad right now."

Ama choked on a sob while Derica's eyes misted. She kept silent as she set down the damp rag. "I'll give you both some time together," she murmured, before standing and moving away.

Derica's back ached, and her shoulders were tight—the physical manifestation of the toll of the months caring for patients like Elyhan. Rolling them, she retreated down the hall toward the room they stored the aid supplies in. Her movements pulled the chest of her tunic taut against her bust right as her nape itched, warning her a familiar gaze was on her. Derica immediately dropped her shoulders, hunching them inward as she walked faster, and cursed under her breath when she heard her name.

"Derica!" Balduin huffed, running to reach her.

She turned, blanking her face. "Yes?"

"It's almost time for the dinner bell. Did you pick up the supplies from the market today?" His pale eyes stayed on hers, but she knew it was his gaze she'd felt sweeping her body. Derica had often found him watching her in odd, unsettling moments during her months in Radley.

She ground her teeth for a moment before answering. "No," Derica bit out, struggling to keep her tone neutral. "It's not my day to make the market run."

"But I told Tarin to ask you to deliver them today."

"Why?" She couldn't keep herself from snapping. "No one bothered to let me know." She crossed her arms under her breasts unconsciously in her anger. When his eyes flicked down, up, then back down, lingering, she strangled her growl of frustration and lowered her arms.

Footsteps rang down the hall and Derica stepped to the side to allow others to pass. Balduin followed. Her jaw ached from holding back her anger, but Derica was glad to see it was Father Simond approaching, saving her from Balduin's unwanted attention.

"Derica," he greeted. "Balduin." He looked between her and the acolyte, eying Derica's tense shoulders and Balduin's thinner than normal mouth. "Is everything all right?"

When Derica opened her mouth to answer, Balduin cut her off.

"Father, Tarin was supposed to send Derica for the supplies today. She didn't retrieve them."

Her head threatened to explode at the hubris of pious men, but Father Simond proved he had Weaver-given sense. "You said nothing about anyone letting her know that was her duty. And why was the schedule change made? I didn't order it."

Balduin coughed, eyes darting around. Before he could answer, someone else called her name.

"Derica!"

Her head whipped towards the door of the church, the father and the annoying acolyte forgotten as a huge smile split her face at the sound of Reid's voice. This was earlier in the day than he usually came to see her.

"Go," Father Simond said with an indulgent smile "Thank you for your work, child. Balduin and I will sort out the supply miscommunication. Your help has been invaluable to the Disciples of the Loom, but please take advantage of your free time. The city is quite full with current events being what they are, but there is still much here to see and do. Go experience the finer things Radley can offer, both you and Reid."

Balduin squawked the beginning of an objection but Father Simond quelled him with a look.

"Thank you, Father," she nodded, brushing her hands down her gray skirts, pleasantly surprised and a little touched to have her efforts recognized and rewarded. But the father was right; she rarely took time away from her duties at the church. Spinning on her heel, she walked away without acknowledging Balduin, feeling his eyes burning a hole between her shoulder blades.

As Reid walked to meet her, his flaxen hair was a bright mess on the top of his tall form, and the dark, bruised signs of fatigue under his eyes hurt Derica to look upon. But his cornflower blue eyes twinkled with such happiness and friendship her worry about him shuffled to the back of her mind.

Derica could always read Reid's moods, and he was clearly excited about something this evening. Her dearest friend gathered her in a quick hug that smelled like medicinal liniment and sunshine, then held her away from him.

With a grin, Reid said, "Come with me. I have a surprise for you."

Seizing her hand, he led her out of the church before she could question him about his mysterious surprise. She laughed, all the tension leaving her as they walked down the church's steps and out on the street.

"Where are we going? You have to tell me."

"That would ruin the fun. But have you heard about the Winter Fête?"

Derica cocked her head. "No. It sounds like something for nobility, anyway."

"No, it's for all the people of Radley," Reid said, flashing her a smile as he tugged her through the foot traffic of the cobblestone streets. "Musicians, traders, and performers come from all over Veridion each year."

"How are performers going to make it here when the Shredded are attacking in packs?"

"I heard from the captain of the city guard that they are sending out patrols to make sure any travelers for the fête make it into the city safely."

Derica frowned and muttered, "Spending that manpower on patrols for a fête instead of protecting incoming refugees is certainly a choice." She tugged on her hand, making Reid slow. "That's not where we're going. Right?"

"No," he chuckled. "It's not for at least a fortnight, I think." His white teeth flashed in the lengthening shadows. "This will be *much* more fun."

CHAPTER EIGHTEEN

Derica followed Reid closely as he wound a zigzagging path through the alleys of Radley. As they walked, the alleys squeezed tighter and the sturdy brick buildings she was used to seeing vanished, replaced by crumbling, tilting stone structures. After the eighth turn, Derica glanced over her shoulder, worried she wouldn't be able to find her way back to the church. They'd turned off the main road through Radley to avoid carriages and wagons, opting for alleys meant solely for foot traffic. Shops and residences blurred as they passed, squat stone buildings varying in color and decoration. The structures stretched next to each other, becoming taller and narrower the further they walked. Despite being in the city for the last six months, she only knew the immediate area near the church and the market. Each day was a stark reminder of how little she'd seen in her life, never having been to a city or village much bigger than Arlan.

The sinking sun brought with it chilled tendrils of air that slipped through Derica's threadbare cloak. Underneath, the simple top and skirts she wore were new purchases with her stipend from the church, but they provided meager warmth as the days grew colder. She made a mental note to slip off to the clothing stalls at the market and find something better suited for winter.

"Where are we going?" she asked for the second time.

Reid laughed lightly and shook his head. "You'll see."

As the shadows grew longer, casting the corners and nooks of the back streets in darkness, Derica grasped the back of Reid's shirt, fearful of getting lost. Navigation and directions were not her forte.

Immediately, the thought brought Hadrian to mind, remembering how he'd tracked their traveling party six months ago. The night at the abandoned cottage and the sight of his chiseled body in the firelight flashed before her eyes. His husky voice full and deep in her ears as he told her about Wardgard that day in Arlan as she stood in her small botanical sanctuary, a rock to shelter herself from Rite Day. Derica forced a harsh breath through her lips and banished the images and confusing feelings, refusing to let herself focus on the insufferable commander. There was little point—she'd likely never see him again.

Derica suddenly smacked into Reid's back with an *oof,* not noticing he'd halted.

"All right there?" he asked with a quirked brow, reaching back to steady her. With Reid's help, Derica stayed on her feet, avoiding ricocheting onto the ground.

"Fine." She combed her red hair back from her face and moved beside Reid, following his gaze. The wonder before her hitched her mouth into a blooming, giddy smile, banishing any lingering thoughts of Hadrian. Reid mirrored her joy, a satisfied grin and his white teeth glowing in the increasing blanket of night.

She blinked, wondering if the mirage would dissipate. "How did you discover this?" she breathed, awed.

Reid towed her out of the narrow alley and into the wider street before them.

"I heard some of the younger apprentices whispering about the Winter Fête and plotting to sneak out. I listened until I figured out where the traveling

performers and merchants camped within the city, then came to collect you."
He gestured before them, and Derica soaked it in.

Brightly colored banners above matching tents and gaudy covered wagons
lined both sides of the avenue. A wooden platform stood at the far end of the
street, a performer on stage, entertaining a small crowd gathered in front of
the platform.

Derica's eyes roved the area, searching for anything familiar to give her an
idea of where they were in the city. Wherever they were had to be in an older
part of the city, farther from the castle. This area didn't have any of the ornate
oil lamps along the streets that surrounded the castle. Here, there were only
torches and lanterns hanging from poles beside tents and wagons.

The dancing waves of firelight made everything seem vibrant and mysterious at dusk. Tides of shadow swept in, alternatively hiding and revealing stunning flashes of brilliantly dyed fabric banners. The smell of grilling
meat wafted to them on a gust of chilled winter wind and Derica's stomach
growled.

Reid frowned down at her. "You haven't eaten dinner?"

She blushed, smiling with chagrin. "No. I was too busy at the church. There
was another influx of refugees this morning. I hadn't had a chance to eat
anything since breaking my fast this morning."

"Well, let's fix that then, shall we?" Reid waved a hand forward for Derica
to proceed him down the street.

Slapping a hand over her still grumbling stomach, she moaned in gratitude
and strode into the dizzying wonder of sights and smells.

Roughly half an hour later, Derica and Reid ambled side by side, taking
bites of the palm-sized meat pies they held wrapped in paper. Derica wanted
to look everywhere at once. Smell all the delicious food, touch all the sump-
tuous fabrics, see all the performances. She felt, at once, overwhelmed and
enervated with excitement. Her cheeks ached from smiling so much. If Reid
didn't have the same ridiculous grin stretching his lips, it might embarrass

Derica to display such joy over a simple gathering of performers and merchants.

Arlan was too small a village to draw traveling caravans. They were lucky to see a tinker visit with their eclectic amalgamation of "rare and unique" wares. Pip used to humph and remark that their *exotic* inventory likely came from two villages over. Didn't stop her from coming back from the tinker's cart with Reid in tow, his arms weighed down with the gifts and trinkets his mother had purchased.

The smile slid from her face at the thought of Pip, and her heart ached. Weeks had passed since their last letter to Reid, and Derica was beginning to worry about their safety in Arlan. The dark circles under Reid's eyes weren't from his apprentice work alone. His unspoken worry for his parents ate at him, as much as he tried to bury it in his work and caring for others. Derica felt much the same.

A bump to her shoulder from Reid almost saw the last bite of her meat pie fall to the ground. Derica squawked and clutched it in both hands. The flaky crust with its savory filling, while doing shamefully little to alleviate the creeping chill of the night, was far too delicious to drop.

She looked at Reid while popping the last bite into her mouth, raising her brows in question at his steady gaze.

Reid laughed and pointed to the tent in front of them. "What do you think? Should we have our fortunes told?"

A simple wooden sign hung from the top of the tent. "Fortunes," it said, burned into the plank in plain lettering. Scarlet silks draped the tent, made all the more vivid by the lanterns as large as Derica's torso—quite a feat given the breadth of her bust—hanging from twisting, wrought iron posts on either side of the tooled leather flap serving as a door. Squinting at the leather, she noticed scenes in gold thread stitched upon it. The Loom, and the Weaver behind it. A silhouette of entwined lovers, wrapped in a swirl of golden thread, a thinner line connecting the chest of each person—a heartthread pairing, she supposed. Other, smaller designs were whorls of stars and runes she didn't recognize.

Derica looked at Reid, watching him inspect the tent as well, noting the way he seemed to have relaxed tonight. This evening was a distraction. A way to pull both their minds out of the mire of worry they'd been living in for months. Even if Derica was hesitant, she knew Reid needed this night.

With the smack of leather on silk, a young woman burst out of the fortune teller's tent. Derica and Reid jumped to opposite sides of the entry to avoid being bowled over by the slight, but agitated woman. She stormed between Derica and Reid without looking at them, muttering heatedly beneath her breath. *"Charlatan fey,"* Derica thought she said.

Reid and Derica looked at each other, wordlessly communicating as they so often did. She raised her eyebrows, silently asking if he still wanted this little adventure. He considered for a moment and then nodded, shrugging.

The leather tent flap danced in the young woman's wake. Derica reached out a hand to sweep it aside when a cloaked figure pulled the partition back.

They were of middling height—taller than Derica but shorter than Reid—and the light of the lanterns didn't penetrate the shadows of their hood. The hand holding back the leather flap was small-boned, with thin fingers. Silently, the cloaked figure stepped back and glided the opposite arm out, bidding them enter.

Reid took a deep breath and entered first, keeping an eye on Derica and the person holding the tent open to them. Derica followed warily.

The smell of pungent herbs permeated the space. A small replica of the lanterns outside the tent hung from the center of the ceiling above a circular table laden with bundles of dried herbs, a stone bowl, and neatly laid stones with the same runes tooled on the tent's leather flap.

"Please, sit," the cloaked figure said, a voice like soft wind drifting through a meadow. As Derica and Reid sat, the fortune teller—for that's surely who they were, no one else occupied the tent—rounded the table and sat before them.

Movement so smooth it was hypnotic, the fortune teller reached up and lowered their hood. Derica couldn't have gasped with surprise if she'd wanted to, her breath stalled in her lungs as her brain tried to decipher what her eyes beheld.

Most noticeable, and a sure reason Derica's heart was galloping in her chest, were the pointed ears peeking through hair as dark as ink.

Fey.

Derica blinked, shock making her thoughts sluggish.

Every story Derica had ever heard of the race said fey didn't come into human towns and villages. As a rule, they hated all the other races of Veridion and sequestered themselves on their island—away from the other beings they deemed beneath them. The fey famously believed humans bred like rabbits and died as easily. An infestation of vermin, they called them.

If the stories were true, the only thing keeping the long-lived fey from waging war against humans was the sheer difference in population. Despite being long-lived—or maybe because of it—fey reproduced at a glacial pace when compared to humans. They didn't deem the risk of conflict worth the possible cost to their numbers. But every human knew, one day, that concern may not be enough to keep them safe from the threat of war with the ancient, shape-shifting race.

The enmity between humans and fey had reached such a crescendo, conflict sparked anytime fey and human mixed, so both races had learned to keep to themselves. A single fey in a human city took their safety into their own hands. Should the Radley guard learn of their presence, the fey would face imprisonment or worse. When her shock ebbed and allowed her to move on, she took in the rest of the fortune teller's delicate features. Dark skin like umber reflected the glow of the lantern. A feline face with a small nose and wide, full lips. Brown eyes—more amber—almost seemed to reflect the firelight like a cat's. A delicate, pointed chin. Her lips pulled into a calm smile, dimples appearing in both cheeks.

Derica's mind and heart calmed infinitesimally. Surely, no evil could be wrought by such a graceful being with gorgeous dimples. With a start, Derica realized the fey fortune teller was beautiful. Derica hadn't noticed anyone in such a way since *him*.

"My name is Sarenya." Watching her speak was almost as entrancing as listening to her. Her voice was soft, like the satin draping her tent, and had the same grace and elegance with which she moved. "I do not claim to change fate as woven on the Loom. I simply read the pattern the Weaver has made for you. Ten gold pieces and you will know what your immediate future has in store." Sarenya settled her slim hands on the table and waited for either to agree or leave.

Reid, just as taken as Derica, it seemed, spoke first. "But the fey don't worship the Weaver."

Derica jerked in her seat and swiveled her head to look at the dolt. The fortune teller wasn't hiding the fact that she was fey, but for Reid to acknowledge it so cavalierly was another thing entirely. He knew what he'd blurted could put them in danger. *Would* put them in danger.

His throat bobbed as he swallowed nervously, too frozen to try to smooth over his blunder.

Derica's heart raced in her chest as she swung to the fey, thinking of how she could backtrack through Reid's words. But she blinked in surprise when she found Sarenya smiling softly, dimples shadowed in the flickering lantern light, seemingly unbothered by Reid's words. Before Derica could launch into a speech to try to rectify Reid's gaffe, Sarenya laughed throatily. "You're correct. We do not. *But* humans do. And if you are learned enough in magics, a human's fate—as woven by your god—can be read."

Reid frowned. "But the fey don't—"

Derica slapped her palm over Reid's mouth. "Thank you for the explanation," she said to Sarenya, praying Reid wouldn't open his mouth and insert his foot again. "We would like to have our fortunes read. Is it ten gold pieces each, or for the two of us together?" Derica asked, acting as if Reid hadn't almost tried to tell a fey what they did and did not do.

Sarenya didn't need to be told what a fey did. She *was* one. And for whatever reason, this fey was telling fortunes in a large human city. If Derica and Reid didn't upset her, they could have their fortunes told and leave, forgetting they'd ever seen the lone fey. This was the safest plan. If they left now, Sarenya might think they planned to turn her in, when that was the furthest thing from Derica's mind. Derica held Sarenya's smiling gaze and tried not to fidget. She lowered her hand, Reid opened his mouth, and Derica pinched his side, hard. He muffled a yelp, glaring at her, but thankfully, closed his mouth once more.

The fortune teller bounced her gaze briefly to Reid and came back to Derica, considering. "I'm feeling generous this evening. My last reading was *lucrative,* but combative. I can read your fate as many times as you would like, but the fate I see never changes. I am a fortune teller, not the Weaver." With a feline smile, she added, "Who am I to turn away gold when repeatedly pushed across my table? Ten pieces to read both your fortunes. A discount, courtesy of my last customer."

Reid reached into the pouch tied to his belt and laid ten gold pieces on the table in front of them. Sarenya scooped them up the moment they hit the table, tucking them away inside her cloak. When Sarenya lifted the fabric, a brightly colored tunic of deep blue satin flashed, in contrast to the red satin walls of the tent. Her chest was modest but daringly displayed by the low neckline of the garment, the skin on view smooth and luminous in the lantern light. Reid shifted in his chair, and Derica hardly kept from rolling her eyes.

Flash tits—or the suggestion of them—and men turned to idiots quicker than Neelson spread gossip back home.

When Sarenya settled her cloak back, her wink said Reid's attention did not go unnoticed. Derica pinched his side again under the table, hoping he understood her silent order to behave.

"You, golden one, you shall be first," Sarenya pronounced, staring into Reid's eyes.

CHAPTER NINETEEN

G ranted the fortune teller's sole focus, Reid blushed, nodding with a gulp. "Wha—" his voice cracked, and he cleared it, starting again in a deeper voice. "What do I do?"

Sarenya slid a dark, smooth stone bowl toward Reid. "Cup your hands around this bowl. What I do will heat the stone, but it will not burn you. Do not release it until I am done."

Reid nodded and cupped his large hands around the bowl. Sarenya studied his grip, then moved the bundle of pungent herbs into the well of the vessel. She struck a flint and lit the bowl's contents. Small, delicate wisps of fragrant smoke rose into the air between Reid and the fortune teller. Next, she picked up the pile of pebbles marked with runes. As she moved them into the center of the table, Derica noticed they were a pale, yellowed white. Staring at them harder—

Derica's blood drained from her face.

Those weren't stones or pebbles. They were bones—human knucklebones, she guessed. The flattest side of each piece had runes carved into it.

"Fear not, no one was harmed in the making of my scrying runes," Sarenya assured, voice calm, and Derica shifted in her seat. The fortune teller's attention remained solely on Reid and the implements before her. Derica didn't know if Sarenya reacted to her apprehension or if she gave such a speech during each reading.

"Close your eyes, golden one," said Sarenya.

"Reid," he corrected.

"I know who you are," she said, but her voice had changed, now sonorous and deeper than it had been previously. Almost sensual. *Foreboding.*

A shiver skittered down Derica's spine, raising gooseflesh along her arms and prickling her scalp.

Sarenya focused her attention on the trails of smoke rising from the bowl's well. Reid squirmed next to Derica, his fingers drumming nervously against the stone bowl as he clasped the vessel. Derica quietly scooted her chair closer to his. Their arms brushed, and Reid settled, some of the tension in his shoulders dissipating.

Minutes ticked by, Derica's unease blossoming with each passing second as Sarenya's eyes watched the dancing tendrils of fragrant smoke before the fortune teller finally spoke. "You are a piece on the board, golden one. You stand tall and proud behind... someone of incredible power. I see nothing but fiery light and power when I look at them. I see you, bathed in the glow—limned in gold." Sarenya's lids fluttered closed, and her brow pinched. "Friend, adviser, and protector, all at once, to this person. I am sorry, for I see the path ahead is not smooth or safe."

The fortune teller gasped, and Derica reached for Reid's wrist, squeezing.

Sarenya's eyes flitted behind her eyelids. "Golden light extinguished, faded like a flame snuffed."

Trepidation tickled the back of Derica's neck. The air felt heavy with something powerful, coating the tent interior, stealing into her lungs with every breath. Part of Derica wanted to jump up and exit with all haste. But the spectacle and power before her was mesmerizing, calling to something deep inside her—some separate, ancient part.

Derica twisted her hands in her lap as they waited several minutes, the silence in the tent eerie and oppressive. Sarenya spoke no more, her eyes still shut.

Reid swallowed audibly. "Is that all?"

Tension melting off of her like water off a bird's wings, Sarenya opened amber eyes. "What else do you wish to know, golden one?" she replied.

"Well... whose light di—extinguishes?" He paled. "Mine?" Reid croaked. "And any details you can give about *who* snuffs that light would be helpful. It would be nice to know who to avoid if I cross their path." Reid chuckled weakly,

"They..." Sarenya trailed off into silence, expression growing faraway.

Derica looked at Reid, and he met her questioning glance by straightening in his seat, giving her a firm nod. It seemed they were both committed to sticking this out. It wouldn't do to prod the fey. They didn't have anywhere else to be, so patience would be the best course of action.

"...They mean you harm. They seek the one you protect. They will use trickery, violence, or charm to get what they want." Sarenya's voice was layered now. Another, like her own but deeper, wreathed her words. Again, a tingle skittered down Derica's spine, but her curiosity was stronger than her disquiet.

"And what do they want?" asked Reid.

Derica turned back to him. If she couldn't clearly see the pallid complexion of his face, she would think him unconcerned with the events of their reading. Pride thrummed in her chest witnessing Reid's bravery. Even if Sarenya was putting them on, hearing portents of death would unnerve anyone, but Reid still sat with his back straight, shoulders back.

Sarenya's hand came up suddenly and Derica caught herself before she flinched back into her seat. Graceful fingers stirred the wisps of smoke in the firelight, and for a moment, Derica thought she saw the outline of a man in the patterns formed.

In her mind's eye, she saw the silhouette of Commander Hadrian on the night of the storm and the Shredded attack, dagger and sword in hand. Derica shook her head and blinked. The pattern in the smoke was gone.

Reid leaned forward and repeated with a measured tone, "What do they want?"

Sarenya reached down to the knucklebones on the table, scooped them into her palm, and rolled them across the table before her, all without looking. When the last piece settled flat, she tipped her head down to read them.

Derica flicked her eyes down and almost let a gasp slip past her lips. While she couldn't read the runes, the way they lay in a perfect circle before Sarenya, alternating runes facing up and down, was startling.

"They want what all evil beings want. Power." Sarenya's layered voice stated the fact as if Reid should have known.

Reid shifted in his seat. "Can you be more speci—"

Derica cut him off with a poke to the ribs. Three questions of the fey fortune teller were probably three too many.

"More specific?" Sarenya asked, voice returned to normal. Her eyes were clear and focused on Reid across the table again. "No, golden one, I cannot. I see only what the magic shows me of your pattern on the Loom. The meaning is yours to find." She looked down at Reid's hands still clasped around the vessel. "You may release the bowl. Please exit the tent and wash in the trough around back. The energy from the reading is not something you want to carry with you, trust me."

"Will you be all right?" Reid asked Derica in a whisper.

"Fine," she answered with a smile.

Reid's brow furrowed, but he set the bowl down and exited the tent with one final worried look back at Derica.

"I don't think there's a call to wait for your companion. Let us start your reading," Sarenya announced, clearing the table of the runes and setting the bowl with its smoldering herbs aside. She reached to her other side for a pitcher and drizzled a small amount of water into the vessel, putting a halt to the smoke. Sarenya straightened back up with another bowl in her hands, identical to the first, and placed it on the table before Derica.

"As the golden one did, so shall you," Sarenya directed. She rearranged the scrying runes before her and picked up another bundle of herbs. Derica placed her sweaty palms on the smooth, cool—for the moment—stone vessel.

As before, Sarenya placed the herb bundle in the well and lit it. The herbs slowly took the flame, the dried leaves and flowers curling into perfumed ash.

Sarenya's chest expanded on a large inhale and her shoulders shimmied, shaking off the previous reading. Her exhale sent the nascent smoke wisps into a wave, sweeping towards Derica. She flinched, blinking her eyes shut, but opened them again immediately. The smoke was not irritating and—she sniffed—not the same blend the fey woman had used for Reid.

This smoke was sweeter, with the tiniest sting of mint in her nostrils.

When Derica focused on Sarenya, the fortune teller again sank into the same almost trance-like stare as before. Derica's palms slicked the sides of the bowl as nerves tensed her neck and shoulders. As Sarenya had warned Reid, the bowl slowly warmed in her palms, but it wasn't anything more than the heat of laying in full sunshine on a summer day.

"You are—" Sarenya paused, tugging Derica's attention away from the bowl and back to the fey. "You are not what you appear, are you?" Sarenya asked with a tilt of her head.

Derica frowned and opened her mouth to ask what that could possibly mean, but the fortune teller continued without waiting for a response.

"You have lost a piece of yourself. Or rather, you *are* the lost piece. You have so much inside you. So much hides in your dark corners—in the shadows of your memories. And in those shadows..." Sarenya's voice dipped into silence.

Derica's heart kicked as she leaned forward, not wanting to miss a single detail. Not one part of her fortune so far had made a damn bit of sense to her. She couldn't help but think this might have been a waste of ten gold pieces, but then Sarenya scooped up the runes in her palm.

"In those shadows—" She tossed the scrying bones onto the table in front of her.

Derica inhaled deeply, bracing for the words to come.

But she never heard the rest of Sarenya's words. The herbs she drew into her lungs chased the world around her away. The woman before her, the bowl in her hands, the chair beneath her—it all became ephemeral. Derica's vision tunneled and the tips of her fingers tingled.

And then Derica was somewhere else.

Some*one* else.

CHAPTER TWENTY

*C*allathe fought, back to her lover, weapons arcing through the air trailing crimson ribbons of gore.

The dark metal of her opponent's helm seemed to absorb the harsh midday sun of the battlefield rather than reflect it. The clang of metal and the tang of blood permeated the loamy marsh.

Sweat slicked her blond hair to her head, her biceps burning with every swing of her sword and parry of her shield. Her braid danced with her movements as pants and grunts escaped her clenched teeth.

Nothing and no one would get through her to attack her lover—not while she still drew breath.

This may be a war for the city of Asterfeld, but she fought this war for him. *Only she could guarantee Faelon would return alive and whole. The earth could swallow Asterfeld, and Callathe wouldn't shed a tear, as long as Faelon was spared. His subordinates laughed, calling her the Warrior's bodyguard, but she saw the hungry way they watched her in the mead hall after a battle, as well as the begrudging awe when they witnessed the fury of her blade in battle.*

Faelon grunted, the sound echoing in his brushed bronze helmet over her shoulder. His back pushed into hers, and she snapped up her shield to avoid a slash to her midsection.

"Faelon!" she shouted over her shoulder. "A dead man can't win a war. Neither can he experience the pleasure of my bed this evening."

Through the slit in their helmet, Callathe saw her opponent's eyes widen at her lusty rebuke. Their surprise was just the opening she needed, not wasting a second as she slashed her blade down and swiped at their vulnerable inner thigh. The fighter yelled, stumbling forward, but before they could fall, her blade, crimson with the lifeblood of the bodies laying scattered around them, gracefully slit their throat.

The death of another christened her blade.

"Callathe, you can't keep using innuendo as a battle tactic," Faelon grunted in between the clash of steel at her back.

"Why the fuck not? It works." Her lips pulled into a feral grin, and she motioned for the next opponent to step forward, the sigil on their helmet indicating they were a lieutenant in Hederon's army. Their eyes bounced around as she settled into a ready stance. The officers were always her favorite—unlike the other fighters, Callathe chose not to wear a helmet into battle, wanting her opponents to know exactly who they fought. Her reputation preceded her onto the battlefield and her identity was another weapon in her arsenal.

Those who approached her in combat were stepping into the den of a lion. They would either prove their prowess or succumb to her claws. Callathe had yet to fight an opponent she couldn't best.

She bared her teeth at the lieutenant, hoping to goad them further with the sight of her figurative fangs. Others' underestimation was her favorite weapon before a battle. During? It was anything she could lay her hands on. Innuendo. Hubris. Incompetence.

Faelon liked to tell her he fell in love with her across a battlefield. He always said she drew his eye with her fighting prowess, but it was her mind and the way she played with her opponents—ferreting out their respective weaknesses—that pushed him off the cliff into an all-consuming passion for her.

Every fight was different. Why should Callathe approach each with the same tactics? That was just asking for death.

And if there was anything she yearned for, it was life. And the man behind her.

The lieutenant hesitated, and no one else stepped up to challenge her. She was only guarding Faelon's back at the moment. That wouldn't do.

She tossed down her shield and reached back to Faelon's hip with her left hand, her fingers wrapping around the hilt of his dagger. It sang on its way out of the scabbard. Callathe brandished it before her, satisfied when the dark ruby in the pommel complemented the blood adorning her steel sword. Both weapons raised before her, she took a step away from Faelon, towards the lieutenant.

With a mocking smile, she deliberately reached out one booted foot and drew a line in the soft ground. She stepped over the line and again motioned for the soldier.

You will not cross.

"Callathe," *Faelon snapped,* "We don't have time for games."

"I always *have time for games, Warrior. If you would hurry up and end this battle, I wouldn't have to keep myself entertained.*" *Callathe flourished her sword and wagged Faelon's dagger at the lieutenant. They snapped with a cry of rage and rushed her.*

Poor, dead idiot, *she thought.* What was Hederdon using as a training regimen for these officers?

A gleeful laugh erupted from her, ringing over the marsh, turning heads and stilling blades as she moved. Callathe saw the ripple spread out around her and laughed harder.

She may mete death on the battlefield, but no one could say she was not fully, incandescently alive.

The lieutenant, on the other hand, was entirely blinded by rage. Really, Hederdon was a mess. When the battle ended, she reminded herself to tell Faelon to exile the surrendering soldiers. They would only embarrass his army.

Slinking under the lieutenant's guard in a move so naturally fluid, she stepped into and past their guard in a second. Her sword reached around and down to sever the tendon at the back of their ankle. The officer fell forward with a roar of pain, fingers almost touching the line drawn in the dirt. Callathe silenced them with a quick thrust of the dagger between the bones at the back of their neck.

Breathing no harder, Callathe wiped the blade on the lieutenant's leathers, then turned to study Faelon. Finding only minor flesh wounds—scratches, he would say later when they were bathing—but nothing to cause alarm, she returned to his side.

Faelon engaged not one, but two opponents. She'd hear about this later as well. He would call it telling, *but the puffing of his muscled chest would reveal it for what it was.*

Bragging.

Callathe would properly praise him and his prowess—after they fell on each other to slake the lust the heat of battle never failed to stir up.

She eyed the ring of bodies and the buffer of space around them, noticing it had grown. The tide of battle was beginning to turn. Asterfeld would see the back of Hederdon's army as they fled in defeat within hours, she predicted.

Swords clashed, drawing her attention back, and Callathe couldn't help but admire Faelon's prowess. His dark skin was slick with sweat and the grime of battle where it peeked through the bronze armor protecting his chest and wide shoulders. A man so large shouldn't move with the grace he did. As she spun to appraise the fight, he snapped up a booted foot and kicked one of his assailants to their back. Without letting his other opponent land a hit, Faelon reached to the small of his back and plucked a sleek throwing blade. With only a second to eye the shot, he let it fly. The prone soldier gurgled a spray of crimson as the throwing knife sank like warm metal through butter into the soft underside of their jaw.

Callathe whistled low, eyebrows hitching up. He had *been paying attention when she was teaching him how to throw. A delightful surprise.*

Faelon must have sensed her gaze on him. He unerringly turned his head, meeting her eyes and flashing a quick smirk, before he turned and was again her fierce Warrior. *Callathe smiled and stepped over a slain Hederdonian soldier that had fallen into her path.*

When her trailing foot lifted over the body, a slick hand snatched her ankle. She couldn't have stifled her squawk of surprise if she wanted to as she fell onto her stomach, fingers clenching hard around her weapons. A fighter without her weapons on the battlefield was a walking corpse. Faintly, she heard Faelon call her name, but she didn't have the luxury of reassuring him at the moment.

She kicked back hard and pushed her shoulders up from the ground. Fire raked her back, low and towards her right hip. Callathe hissed through her teeth and forced herself to keep moving. Breath coming in pants and back burning, she turned. The soldier she thought a corpse—the amount of blood slicking their armor certainly supported that perception—levered themselves up, as well.

Either way, they would be a corpse in a few brief moments.

Callathe steadied her grip on her weapons and sunk into the quiet place in her mind she only found during battle. The agony in her back faded; screams, the metallic symphony of war, and all extraneous distractions shuttered from her focus.

"You've made a mistake," she whispered.

"No. I will end the Warrior's Witch. I will be a hero to my countrymen." Under all the grime, the soldier was male and quite young. He held a discarded sword of Asterfeld make. Their blades curved slightly, a contrast to the thinner, pin-straight blades the Hederdon army used.

"Is that what they call me? I'm sorry to disappoint, but I'm merely a woman with intellect." She stepped closer and added, as if in confidence, "Between us, I've never understood why the witches are so hated. They keep to themselves." Callathe flicked a pointed look at his groin. "I also know that without them, human men would have nowhere to turn to cure ailments of flaccidity."

The young soldier's jaw dropped, and his face colored crimson with fury. "Die, witch!" He launched himself at her.

Callathe let all the humor fall from her face and became Death. True Death. Not the fading of a life to return to the Weaver, lovingly woven back into the Tapestry, ready for their next reincarnation. Death was the ultimate end. A concept humans rejected.

Not Callathe.

Her eyes tracked every movement the young soldier made, met his blade with one of hers every time. Despite her slip into battle meditation, the burning from whatever wound he'd inflicted to start the encounter slipped through. She could feel the warm trailing fingers of blood down her flank until the back of her right leg was slick with moisture.

Callathe was about to strike the killing blow—distracting with her sword, while positioning the dagger to sever his jugular—when she slipped. Her right heel skidded out from under her, and her eyes flew wide as she fell. The flash of satisfaction in the soldier's eyes was the last straw. On her way down, she tossed away her sword and yanked the collar of his armor. As they fell together, she arced the dagger down the side of his neck, flaying open his artery. Hot blood splashed her face and chest as her back hit the ground of the marsh.

His weight on top of her pushed every bit of breath from her lungs. She twisted out from under his body, yelling through her clenched teeth when the ground scraped her back. Black dots swam in her vision and she sipped air. Her lungs wouldn't fill like normal.

"Callathe!" Faelon dropped next to her. "Where?" He patted her neck and chest, finding no injury.

"Not... mine," she managed between shallow inhales.

"Weaver-dammit, Wildcat. Do you know you almost killed me when I saw you go down—the first time? I couldn't get free to you. When you fell the second time—" The panic in Faelon's voice made her ache. Usually, it was her fussing after him. He was the one she worried about and needed to protect.

"Only a flesh wound on my back, Warrior. I slipped in my own blood. What a pathetic way to go down."

Faelon placed one broad palm high against her back and carefully levered her into the crook of his arm.

"Let me see," he said, gently tilting her farther over her hips. The tail of her blond braid, tinted pink and brownish-red with blood, swung free over her shoulder. She watched it swing back and forth, the motion oddly slow. Callathe felt more than heard the shouted exclamation from her lover when he saw her back. His hands shook—or was that her?

Everything spun, and she blinked hard, trying to right the world.

The clank of metal seemed far off and Callathe watched as Faelon's helmet bounced across the ground.

Vertigo smacked her between the eyes when Faelon lowered her flat, supporting her head in his hand. His face—his gorgeous face—swam, and she closed her lids hard to clear her vision. She needed a clear picture of him.

Her mouth was dry. Swiping a tongue out to wet her lips, she turned her head and spat as she tasted the copper of the soldier's blood.

Faelon's hand spasmed cradling her skull, "No, no, this isn't how it's supposed to end. This isn't how it should end at all. We're supposed to be old and gray when I'm faced with this decision. We're supposed—supposed to have children. And grandchildren. I wanted to see—" Faelon's gruff speech stalled in his throat.

She looked into his dark eyes, seeing the thin gold band circling his pupils that was only ever visible when she was this close. Callathe loved that about him. It was a feature of his that was just for her—a secret. Black lashes that would be the envy of any beauty framed those dear eyes. They were wet.

Callathe lifted a hand to his cheek, stroking her thumb across his broad cheekbone. She couldn't feel his skin. Not the texture, not the warmth. Faelon reached up and held her hand to his cheek with one of his, then turned his head and pressed a kiss into her palm with his wide mouth. She couldn't even feel the brush of the beard he'd grown on the long war campaign.

Callathe complained to him endlessly about the burn of it against her skin. He said the marks told anyone with eyes she was his. She'd scoffed but smiled when he strutted around the camp, petting the marks on her skin in passing or looking at them with hungry remembrance.

What she wouldn't give to feel them on her skin one last time.

"My Warrior. I love you. Think what we would have missed if I hadn't stopped myself from killing you in battle when we met. You were too impressive to kill. Then I discovered your incredible kindness—" She coughed, and Faelon's wide brows slammed down. A tear dripped down his cheek into his beard, sinking claws of regret into her heart.

"I knew then," Callathe whispered. "That I had found my heartthread, and I was whole again." If he hadn't been holding her hand to his face, it would have slipped away. All her strength deserted her. Faelon never would, though.

She hoped he found joy again after she was gone. Callathe wanted to think he would smile again. Without her.

Callathe tried to move her thumb and stroke his lips. She watched as not even a twitch moved the appendage. Her vision clouded and Faelon brought their foreheads together. His breath hitched. Their tears mingled on her face.

Faelon pressed the tenderest kiss to her lips. When she would have deepened it, happy to give him her last breath, he gently laid her flat and leaned over her, reaching toward something off to her left.

That wasn't important right now. She needed her last sight to be him.

Faelon bent over her, his head hanging down into the crook of her neck, his knees on either side of her hips—holding himself up to avoid limiting her breaths. If she could have moved, she would have tugged him fully against her. Callathe wanted to feel his heat, savor his life as hers deserted her.

"Forgive me, Callathe. Forgive me."

"For what?" It came out a whisper.

"I can't do this without you. Every time, I try. I try to let you go. And I can't. When I think of never knowing you—whoever you will be next—it's unbearable."

If she could, Callathe would frown. "What—"

"All I ask is that you forgive me." Faelon placed a rough kiss to her forehead, cradling the back of her head with one hand. Dark red glinted in the other.

She opened her mouth to answer: anything, but he shocked her into silence with the expression of utter despair on his wet face.

"Please, Callathe, when you find me, forgive me."

A sudden impact to the back of her neck was all she felt, and then Callathe drifted away.

"—is the end of everything as you know it at the hands of one you love," finished Sarenya.

Derica felt unmoored. It took moments before she understood what Sarenya said. Moments where scenes of battles and strangers clung, refusing to be shaken loose. The air inside the tent was laden with tension. She stared at Sarenya, too afraid to tell her what Derica had seen, or ask what it meant.

Sarenya watched Derica, gaze sharpening progressively with every second of silence.

"Is there nothing more? Anything about..." Derica's voice was hoarse. She licked her lips, swallowed, and tried again. She was proud of the fact her voice did not waver, but it wasn't particularly strong, either.

Taking a deep breath, she closed her eyes.

A flash of deep red flitted through her mind, and they popped back open.

That dagger... it couldn't be.

"Anything about a battle?" she croaked.

"As I said before the reading, I can only see what the Weaver has created for you on the Loom. I cannot change or alter your fate. That is all my magic will show me of the future in store. But..." The fortune teller cocked her head, considering Derica.

Derica leaned farther over the table. "And there was nothing of the," she swallowed, hesitating to voice her question, "the past?"

Sarenya shook her head. "I did see something I don't know how to make sense of. It means nothing to me, but perhaps it will mean something to you. If not now, possibly when this fate comes to pass. I saw your hands holding a frayed thread. In the next moment, the thread was made new, like it had never been damaged."

Derica frowned down at her hands, having forgotten she held the stone vessel. The warmth from it soothed, even as she struggled to make sense of what she had seen.

A frayed thread? That meant nothing to her, either. But a thread didn't sound particularly dangerous or frightening.

Derica supposed she should be thankful for a fortune that wasn't entirely ominous, but she was left with more questions than answers. She wanted to ask about the battle. She wanted to know who Callathe and Faelon were, and why she saw them. The words stuck in her throat, unable to move past a block made of reticence. Reticence to reveal what she'd seen. A small voice in the back of her mind urged her to be careful with the memory and whom she shared it with.

Sarenya gently pried the vessel from Derica's grasp and smiled softly at her. When she spoke, her voice was low and sweet. The same tone and cadence one used to speak to a skittish animal. "This is all I can see for you. I'm surprised your friend isn't back yet."

As the fortune teller finished, Reid parted the flaps of the tent and peeked inside. He blinked a few times, adjusting to the dim lighting of the tent.

"You didn't wait for me, did you?" he asked with a grimace.

Sarenya cleared her throat before Derica could answer. "I hope the two of you had a lovely lark. Now I must tidy my tent for the night," Sarenya said, pouring water over the smoking herbs as she'd done before. She rose from the table and stood inside the tent across from Reid, holding open the other side of the door flap.

As dismissals went, Derica supposed it wasn't the *most* rude she ever witnessed. She stood up and smoothed her skirts down her hips, not looking forward to the cold walk back to the church. Stepping through the opening, Derica looked over her shoulder, her gaze snagging on the runes still laying on the table.

They were arranged in a vertical line, with an upside-down V-shape near the bottom. Derica halted in her tracks, dread thrumming through her veins.

She'd been so focused on the vision or dream, she had forgotten Sarenya cast the runes.

Faintly, she heard herself ask, "What does that symbol mean?"

Sarenya looked to the runes, then back to Derica, a flash of fear sparking in her eyes.

"What does it *mean*?" Derica repeated, nausea roiling through her belly.

"Death," Sarenya said, her voice tremulous and somber. "It means death."

CHAPTER TWENTY-ONE

T he moon rose high above the buildings as Derica and Reid walked silently together through the back alleys of Radley. Derica felt changed after seeing the fortune teller—like she was too much for her skin to hold. Maybe Reid felt similarly altered.

She flicked a look next to her, noting his puckered brow and mouth tight with tension. Their evening of fun transformed, tainted with ominous foreboding.

Chest tight, Derica didn't yet want to speak about her reading, and Reid didn't push her for the information. Though each stewed in their own oppressive speculation, the comfort of Reid's presence soothed like a balm, as always.

She slipped her hand into the crook of Reid's elbow, seeking some warmth in the chill of night. He looked down, blinking, and placed his palm over the back of her hand. Reid brusquely swept a thumb over her knuckles and it both grounded and comforted Derica. For the first time since stepping out of Sarenya's silken tent, she took a full, deep breath.

"The next time you promise to take me somewhere fun, I don't know if I'll be able to believe you," she muttered.

Reid huffed a wry laugh. "I'm not capable of fortune-telling myself. If I could have anticipated how our little jaunt would have gone, I might have taken you to the little bookstore I found close to the physicians' lodgings instead."

"Why wasn't that the first choice?" gasped Derica.

"Because I wanted something a bit more stimulating than a quiet bookstore."

"Nothing is ever more stimulating than a good book."

Reid looked at her askance, eyebrows raised.

"Fine," she waved him off with an eyeroll. "Some things can be. But rarely do I ever feel more engaged in a task than I do when I'm reading."

"I remember when Ma gave you your first book," Reid said with a smile as he walked confidently navigated the alleys, steering them in a direction Derica hoped was towards the church. "By the end of our tenth winter, you'd read that book cover to cover nearly a dozen times. If books could talk, that one would have surely begged for a reprieve. It was positively unrecognizable after you finally finished with it."

"First of all, if books could talk, I'd never want to speak to another person. Second, books are meant to be read and enjoyed. Where else can you escape inside a haven of words and stories so fantastically exciting your troubles melt away?" She could use a book right this second, in fact.

Reid's blue eyes flickered with something like confusion. "What do you mean?"

"You've never read a book with such vivid words, the world in the text formed inside your mind? Never been so deeply affected by an author's prose, your breath stalled in your chest and your heart soared or broke because of words on a page?"

Reid considered, biting his lip. "I got hold of a medical text once. That's about the most fascinating reading I've ever experienced. You mean to say you *see* what they write in books?"

"Doesn't everyone?"

"No. I'm quite certain they don't," Reid paused, thumb stroking her knuckles absently as they lapsed into a contemplative silence.

Yeowlllllll!

Derica and Reid both jumped as a screeching feline came from behind and tore past them into the alley. When the streak of dark fur vanished, Derica stood clutching her chest, heart pounding hard and fast against her palm. Reid appeared in the same condition.

"A fright after that reading is—" Reid cut off when an ominous shuffle and moan came from behind. He stiffened, and Derica's eyes grew wide. She both desperately wanted to turn her head to inspect the source of the sound and run back to the church as fast as possible.

Head turning without her conscious volition, Derica found herself inspecting the alley behind them.

The redbrick buildings on either side of them were pitted, their exact hue hidden by the gentle glow of the moonlight. The alley was surprisingly free of detritus or litter, unlike several others they'd already been through. A large wooden crate half as tall as Derica stood at the other end of the path, likely belonging to a business occupying one of the buildings. Flimsy wooden doors were sparse and scarred.

She wondered if anyone would hear, or care, if a murderous criminal attacked them.

Reid shuffled next to her. "It was probably the wind."

She turned to face her friend. "*What* wind, Reid?" Derica licked the tip of her finger and held it aloft before her. No wind; not a single pathetic gust.

Reid paled. "Weaver's tits, woman, let's get back to the church." He reached out to clasp her hand. Shadows wavered in her periphery, and Derica whipped her head around to the large humanoid figure shuffling out from behind the shipping crate at the other end of the alley.

The figure didn't speak, taking halting, juddering steps toward the pair. The moonlight struck the crown of their bent head, illuminating a snarled mess of medium-length light brown hair. Everything else about them was cast in deep shadow or obscured by baggy, torn dark clothing.

"He-hello?" called Reid.

The figure didn't halt their slow progress. No answer.

Reid stepped in front of Derica, and she grabbed his waist as she peeked around his back.

"Do you need assistance? Are you hurt?" he tried again.

"*Need...*" a rasp of a whisper floated to them. The voice was scratchy and gruff like the speaker had been without water for a cruel amount of time. Derica's heart twinged. Whoever this person was, they needed help.

She made to step around Reid and halted when he slashed down a brawny arm.

"No. Something isn't right," he muttered to her, not taking his eyes off the figure now roughly six feet away. Reid took a slow step back, pushing Derica with him.

They matched the pace of the figure before them, maintaining their distance of six feet. The figure did not slow down, speed up, or halt their movement.

"What do you need?" Derica called.

"Derica," Reid admonished.

"*... need... blessed... need... healing...*" the figure answered, head still bent—cloaked in shadow and diaphanous, dirty fabric.

Derica opened her mouth to offer to take them to the church when suddenly the figure lurched two great strides forward. Fast as lightning, they reached around Reid and snatched Derica's wrist in a grip unyielding as iron. She cried out and tried to flinch away, but they had her trapped like a rabbit in a snare.

Reid tried to push the figure away, but only succeeded in yanking them all around and rattling Derica's brain.

"*Please... please... help,*" the voice rasped.

Derica stilled. The figure hadn't harmed her. They weren't harming Reid. She reasoned a cool head would get them out of whatever kind of mess or misunderstanding this was.

"Reid," she called, keeping her eyes on the pleading figure, "it's fine. I'm fine. I don't think they mean us harm. Do you?" she asked.

The figure tilted their head in a jerky denial.

"See? It's all right." Derica flicked a look to Reid, and he slowly nodded, scrutinizing the figure with a menacing squint that promised harm should they be lying.

Reid stepped back from the figure and wrapped one arm, deceptively gentle, around Derica's back. With his hand hidden behind her, Reid's fist clenched the rough spun cotton of her tunic. To yank her away and behind him should things devolve, she supposed.

Derica slowly reached out her other hand and gently pried the shackle of dirty, stick-thin fingers off her captive wrist. The figure let her, not moving, or protesting.

When they separated, Derica pulled her hands back and clasped them together in front of her. The figure's arm hung limp at their side, the explosive energy of their lunge for Derica a moment earlier so absent it might have been a figment of her imagination. There was an air of deep pain and dejection—of exhaustion—about them now. Their head was still bent, hiding their face and eyes from Derica.

She waited for them to look up—meet her eyes.

The silence grew heavier, the tension in the air a near palpable pressure against her skin. Reid fidgeted next to her, but moved not an inch away from Derica.

Slowly, *frustratingly* glacially, the figure raised their head. Derica barely contained her gasp and forced herself to remain still instead of turning and sprinting away in fear.

What looked back at her made her knees quake and her palms sweat. Her stomach roiled with sudden nausea and surely every drop of blood in her body shot straight to her toes. Briefly, black dots swam in her vision. When she blinked, Reid gathered her more firmly into his side, body as stiff as a board. He tensed to run or respond to the threat revealed in front of them.

One of the Shredded.

Derica squinted into the darkness. Or, she supposed, someone who appeared on the cusp of Shredding.

Now, Derica could admit to not paying attention the night Shredded attacked their party on the road to Radley. She had been preoccupied with staying alive and then making sure Hadrian had stayed alive, too. The way the Shredded looked was the last thing she'd been concerned about. But there appeared to be something *less* about this being—person? What did one call someone who was not *quite* Shredded?

Oh, her stomach was a grinding, clenching mess of fear regardless of their unfinished Shredded status. Derica took a steadying breath and shuffled her feet nervously. Reid squeezed her waist but remained silently vigil.

The figure had sallow, thin skin, and gruesome, bloody scratches—from what looked like claws—down their cheeks. The wounds trailed all the way down their face but stopped before the sparse, scruffy bush of a beard, the same shade as their light brown hair. Their slim, blade-like nose made the gauntness of their blood-streaked cheeks all the more emaciated-looking.

Milky eyes—their previous color indeterminate in the sparse moonlight filtering into the alley—stared in Derica's direction but couldn't seem to focus. They wet their dry, cracked lips with a filmy tongue, and Reid shuddered beside her.

"Please... help... you... can help," they rasped, barely louder than a whisper. Derica's throat ached at the sound of their voice. Speaking seemed painful for them.

"What is your name?" she asked, keeping her voice clear and as steady as she could. If her question warbled the slightest bit, she doubted anyone would blame her. Who could say they'd had a conversation with someone who appeared to be Shredded?

"*Name?... None... Only pain. Help.*" Their rasp deepened, growing slightly in volume. They reached one hand up and snagged the neck of the dirty, damaged tunic covering their torso. With three skeletal fingers, knuckles protruding under the skin grotesquely, they scratched down their chest, dragging the fabric with the movement.

Derica covered her mouth to silence her cry of alarm. Reid's hand spasmed on her hip, almost bruising.

Their chest was as sallow as the skin on their face—ribs, and sternum visibly outlined under skin so smeared in streaks of dark dirt and Weaver knew what else. Her eyes teared seeing the three bloody, possibly inch deep, slashes across their sternum, trailing diagonally from one side of their chest to the other.

It wept blackened blood. Their nails caught a small patch of light, blood of the same color caking the jagged ends. Derica halted herself from wiping the wrist they'd held in that hand against the fabric of her skirts.

"*Hurts... Wrong... Need fixed. You fix. Please...*" they said. It wasn't a question. As they stepped closer to Derica and Reid, a waft of sour sweat, the coppery tang of fresh blood, and the scent of the pounds of dirt on their person assailed her nostrils.

As much as Derica wanted to run, her feet stayed rooted in place, the need to do something for this person a clamoring, pressing urge. "We can help you get to the church. The Disciples might know what to do to help you—to heal you. I help tend the sick there. Maybe you've seen me there? I—" She paused, glancing at Reid. "We can guide you there. My friend is an apprentice physician. We can clean your wounds, get you some food, and hopefully make you better. Or we can help you back to Reid's guild."

Her inane prattling sounded like just that. She'd never heard of someone who became Shredded being healed. The person before her didn't have the mindless, violent bent of the afflicted. But she hoped there was a chance—however small—they could be made whole again.

"Derica," Reid muttered, "I don't know if the father would like it very much if we showed up at the church with *them* in tow."

"Are you turning your back on someone who needs healing, Reid Wariner? Is that not in violation of the Physicians Code? 'To help the wounded, heal the sick' etcetera, etcetera?"

Reid sighed. "If anyone could heal them, I think I'd have heard of it. I don't want to see their descent into the affliction prolonged."

"No... no Disciples... no phys-physicians." The figure lifted one bloody, gnarled finger and pointed at Derica. "You."

"I—I can't help better than Reid." She shook her head, huddling into her friend's side.

"Help!" they rasped, voice tearing from their throat, before flinging themselves at Derica once again.

Reid gripped the fabric at the small of Derica's back and tried to yank her behind him, but her assailant already latched both hands around her forearms as she'd raised them to shield herself. With a yelp, she stepped back, pulling away so hard she twisted her ankle. Derica lost her balance, falling to the ground with her attacker on top of her. Reid's broad hands whipped out in the corner of her vision, whether trying to catch her or tear away her assailant she didn't know.

Either way, they slipped to the ground with a shock of expelled breath and the sound of bone hitting cobblestones. Derica couldn't breathe, dazed, while spots danced behind her tightly closed eyes. She tried to raise her arms to protect her face, her heart, her throat, but her attacker was on top of her, pinning her down. Her skull throbbed where it struck the cobblestones, ears ringing with a high-pitched whine.

She tried to blink away the black spots in her vision. The ringing in her ears grew louder, coming in and out, interspersed by thumps.

Thumps?

She'd let her mind wander and paid for it. Derica cried out when nails raked the side of her neck. The sting cleared her vision, but did nothing for the ringing. But why the thumping?

Opening her mouth to shout for Reid, she struggled against her attacker, blinking in shock as the high-pitched whine transformed into the song of metal leaving its sheath. She blinked again and the gleam of a wicked blade of dark metal was separating Derica from her assailant, held at their throat.

A voice like woodsmoke and twilight growled, "Release her. *Now.*"

The crazed ghoul on top of her didn't even flinch when the blade nicked their throat. Viscous, dark blood spattered Derica's chest, and she fought not to gag.

The rustle of weapons and clothing preceded the weight of her attacker disappearing. When Derica planted her hands on the ground and slowly levered herself to sitting, she was sure she was hallucinating.

Justus Hadrian held her attacker pinned by the throat against one of the brick buildings lining the alley. Mazolan smirked next to Reid, who wore the most thunderous scowl she'd ever seen grace his face. Nyle stood on the other side of Reid, at attention, hand on the weapon at his hip while he watched the commander and his prey.

For that's what it was. The monster of a moment ago was now not the most frightening thing occupying the alley. Commander Hadrian was.

Aggression practically rolled off of him. His shoulders raised and fell rapidly, his profile limned in silver light as his nostrils flared and his obsidian gaze burned with wrath.

"*No-no-no-no-no-no-no-no,*" the figure pinned like a moth to the brick repeated over and over, distress and frustration ringing in every rasped syllable.

Hadrian flexed his broad hand around their throat, black blood shining as it oozed through his fingers. "Quiet," he hissed.

Derica shuddered on the cobblestones. She pulled up a knee, preparing to stand when fingers gripped her elbow.

"Hello, morsel. I've missed you." The flash of Mazolan's fangs twinkled in the moonlight as they helped Derica up, gently steadying her. Citrine eyes swept her up and down, an uncommon gleam of concern flickering in their depths before they allowed her to stand unassisted. Still, they held slim-fingered hands out ready to catch her, Mazolan's unique, pale blue skin a beacon in the moonlight. She looked down to wipe her dirty hands on her skirts, and when she looked back up, the world spun. Mazolan gathered her closer, supporting her while Derica waited for the dizzy spell to pass.

She tried to step towards Hadrian, but Mazolan's grip transformed into a steely shackle.

"Ah-ah. Let the commander have a minute. He needs it," Mazolan said.

"Wha—No! They need help, not whatever *that* is," Derica insisted.

"The commander won't kill them, no matter how much he may wish he could," Mazolan said, before calling out, "Right, Commander?"

Hadrian growled and menaced all the more aggressively.

Derica tugged harder, forcing Mazolan to either let her go or restrain her. Fortunately, they chose to let her go.

"Fine. This should be entertaining, at the very least," Maz muttered, hands raised in defeat, white brows lifted high

Mazolan followed Derica closely, hands ready to catch her should she falter. Reid and Nyle stood on the other side of the commander, speaking in quick, low back and forths, every other turn gesturing at Hadrian and then Derica. Nyle gripped both of Reid's shoulders and talked until Reid calmed. Well, deflated was a more apt description.

When Derica halted at Hadrian's shoulder, Mazolan was two steps behind. Her hand shook as she gently laid her fingers on the commander's arm.

He growled at first contact, but she kept her hand still, even as his bicep bunched and jumped with the effort to hold her attacker aloft. By now, they were limp against the wall, still muttering "*No*," repeatedly, but all the fight seemed to have leaked out of them.

Derica was about to open her mouth to tell Hadrian she was unharmed when a warm trickle of blood from the scratch on her neck rolled past her clavicle. With her free hand, she tentatively poked at the weeping scratches, determining they were fairly shallow. Dropping her hand back to her side, she turned so, should the commander face Derica, he wouldn't see her injury. The deflated assailant shifted milky eyes to her, eerily focused and intent on her, to the exclusion of the very great danger Hadrian presented.

"Thank you for your intervention, Commander, but I think you can let them go. They don't appear to be a threat now," she said, speaking calmly and slowly, even though her heart beat a rapid tattoo against her ribs.

Without turning his head, Hadrian responded, "I'd say that attitude is what caused the little scene we came upon. I think I'd prefer to leave them where I have them now."

"*Please*," the pinned attacker rasped, holding out a skeletal, gnarled hand to Derica, palm up.

Derica couldn't say what made her place her hand in theirs—whether it was some buried instinct or the adrenaline from moments ago—but she reached out.

"No!" Hadrian spat, unable to release his prey and risk her further injury.

Behind Derica, there was a distinct lack of sound or reaction from Mazolan, even as Nyle cautioned Reid to stay back.

As soon as her fingertips made contact with the sallow, bony hand, the world around Derica vanished.

The only thing in front of her, all she could see, was a glittering, golden thread floating in the air. It was as long as she was tall. At the top of the glowing filament, the golden color faded to a sickly yellow, where it sprayed in ragged tatters.

She could see and perceive what was before her, but couldn't control her limbs. Instinct puppeted her hands while Derica simply watched. The compulsion pressed, blotting out her will and taking control. She extended a hand, drawn to the damage, compelled to smooth it—helpless to do otherwise.

Her hand remained steady and sure as it reached for the damaged part of the thread. When she closed her fingers around the filament, it writhed and pulsed and stung, how she imagined holding lightning would feel. Despite the shock, her body didn't react, like a wall separated her mind from her body.

Placing her other hand farther down the thread, she prepared for... something. Meanwhile, Derica's senses ratcheted higher with the increased crackle and snap of the thread's lightning. She didn't know how her hands held steady with such overwhelming, searing pain crawling across her nerve endings, but her body didn't react to it.

Fighting to stay focused, she watched as her hands moved without conscious thought, slowly smoothing the frayed edges of the thread. As her grip passed up the filament, its sickly yellow pallor transformed into a gold as brilliant and vibrant as the bottom length.

Reaching the end, Derica watched in shocked awe as the thread transformed and repaired.

A soulthread healed, came a whispered voice, very like her own.

She didn't have time to marvel at what happened. In between one second and the next, Derica was back, standing near Justus and her attacker.

Her knees buckled, but she didn't fall, someone supporting her from behind.

"That was *quite* something, morsel. Absolutely fascinating. We need to have a little chat soon," Mazolan purred in her ear.

Derica's hand was still extended, wrapped gently by a gnarled, steady grip. She held her breath and looked up, searching for their eyes.

A gasp of surprise hitched from her throat as eyes of warm brown met hers, no longer milky. Gone was the sallow tint to their skin, too. Caked in dirt and blood—malnourished, certainly—but they were no longer on the cusp of Shredding.

"Thank you. *Thank you*, my lady." Their voice was still a rasp, but there wasn't pain in it now.

Hadrian looked at her, his expression a shifting kaleidoscope of incredulity, wariness, and awe. At the end of the roiling emotions, Derica might have even seen a flash of longing. For her?

Heavy footsteps moving closer had the commander tensing and Derica jerking back, pulling her hand free.

"No! I won't stand back one second longer." Reid stomped to Derica's side, nudging Mazolan out of the way. Nyle followed calmly, unbothered by having his charge slip his tether.

Reid gently clasped Derica's shoulders and turned her to face him. He carefully lifted a knuckle under her chin, tilting her head up and to the side to inspect her wound. Reid hissed angrily and glared at Mazolan, then Nyle. "Why wouldn't you let me near her? She needs this wound seen to immediately. We—*I* need to get her back to the guild so I can clean and bandage her wound." His hand holding her shoulder trembled slightly, his grip spasming, like he wanted to pick her up and dash for the guild.

Nyle answered, voice level and soothing, "Reid, we've seen a lot of wounds in fights and battles. The bleeding isn't excessive. Derica is in no danger of expiring from those scratches. You know this."

Derica blinked, pleasantly surprised to feel Reid's trembling hand steady and his shoulders drop into a more relaxed posture.

Reid nodded. "I still would like to get her cleaned and bandaged as soon as possible."

"We will clear up whatever *happened* here and then the two of you can be off."

"The commander may have something to say about that actually, Nyle," Mazolan said breezily. Nyle frowned over at them and Maz rushed to clarify. "Oh, not the seeing to morsel's wounds, of course, but the two of them leaving unescorted. Say, Commander, why don't you let the poor fellow down?

They don't appear to be a danger anymore. Funny how that happened. Quite curious, in fact—"

"Mazolan," sighed Nyle.

Maz shrugged their shoulders, mouth ticked up in a little smirk as their white braid blew in the slight breeze.

Derica turned her head to watch Hadrian slowly release her assailant. He didn't step back, nor did his posture relax.

Hadrian was the same, and yet different, from the last time Derica saw him. There were dark hollows under his cheeks and eyes. The facial hair she was used to seeing him with had been allowed to grow into a short beard instead of a shadow of one.

"Who are you? Why did you attack the woman, and what happened to you?" Hadrian fired the string of questions with rapid precision and his tone warned the answers he received should be satisfactory. *Or else.*

"My name is Braiden," he said, slowly wringing his bony hands together. "I... I don't know what happened to me, nor why I attacked the lady. All I know is I was sick. I saw her pass by, and it was as if the Weaver guided her into my path." Braiden sank down onto his knees, and Hadrian clenched his dagger tighter, shifting closer to Derica.

Reid scowled, tucking Derica into his side. She allowed herself to lean into his warmth, finally feeling some of the strength return to her limbs. Unfortunately, the wound at her neck chose that moment to sting with the heat of a blacksmith's forge. She flinched.

"Are you all right?" Reid asked, alarmed.

Four other pairs of eyes focused on Derica, waiting for her answer.

"Ye—" she paused and winced at the pain of the skin of her throat moving with speech, "—I am fine. Or I will be soon. Commander, can we please hurry and get back to the church? Surely, the guild isn't necessary for so tiny a scratch, Reid. I would dearly love the comfort of my bed."

Hadrian turned at her question. His eyes searched the wound at her neck as the skin near his temples tightened, mouth hardening into a tight line. When his gaze met hers, it was like glittering black ice.

The commander gave a clipped nod, sheathed his dagger, and bent to haul Braiden to his feet. Hadrian jerked his chin at Mazolan and shoved the dirty man at the demon.

"You see to him. I'm sure you're dying of curiosity to find out more about Braiden and what happened to him. You have the time it takes to walk to the church to find out everything." With that, Hadrian stalked off. Derica blinked in surprise, shocked at his brusque dismissal. She didn't know what she'd expected to happen if they crossed paths again, and more than once—if she was honest—there'd been daydreams of softening eyes and profuse apologies for his cold behavior at the cottage. Derica shook the embarrassing thoughts away and leaned more firmly into Reid.

A wry smile on his face, tattoos looking like whorls of shadow on his bronze skin, Nyle waved out a hand to Derica and Reid, indicating they were to follow the commander.

Reid humphed, but gently led Derica forward. With a deep breath, she rested her head on his shoulder and let him guide her toward a bath and her bed.

CHAPTER TWENTY-TWO

THREE MONTHS PREVIOUS

The world spun, and the light narrowed to a claustrophobic tunnel around him. Justus shook his head, trying to clear his vision. The movement didn't right the world. If anything, it brought about some nausea.

A hearty slap on his back nearly sent him somersaulting to the sticky plank floor of the tavern.

What was its name? The Salty Fish? The Slapping Tentacle? Something nautical and idiotic...

"Oh, Commander," Mazolan said, sliding into the seat at the bar next to Justus. "Drowning our sorrows again, are we?"

"We're not on a job, last I checked," he answered, leaning over his mug. *The Slippery Pearl? No. Not that either.* "My free time is mine. If I want to spend it at the bottom of a bottle?" Justus shrugged. "It's nothing you and Nyle haven't done on occasion."

"*On occasion.* You've been doing your best to pickle your internal organs for three months. Normally, your vices are a bit more... varied. When was the last time you buried yourself between two gorgeous thighs?" Mazolan said. They nodded toward Nyle, seated at the end of a bench in the corner of the establishment, the tattooed mercenary holding a woman on each thigh. His head nestled in the crook of one's neck while a hand palmed the other's breast. Both women were flushed with pleasure and very much enjoying their night, it seemed.

Fiery hair and soft, plush thighs flashed through the whorl of Justus's mind, but he didn't attempt to shake the thought free—he had learned his lesson a moment ago. That would only set everything spinning again.

Instead, he grabbed the tankard in front of him and poured the dregs down his throat.

Mazolan's sigh coincided with the thump of the empty vessel on the scarred wooden counter. "Sometimes I wonder why I bother with you. Most of the time, you're good for entertainment; an excellent commander, fighter, and comrade. It's been a good long while since you've shoved your own head so far up your arse you've forgotten what you're about."

"Maz," Justus guffawed, "we both know why you 'bother' with me, and it's not for any of those reasons." Justus looked around the raucous dining room, finally spotting a serving maid as he waved his tankard in the air and smiled. "It's because the demons won't have you." He leaned in, lowering his voice. "You found the only human willing to employ you, and you've been clinging like a fucking barnacle every day since."

Mazolan went still as death on their barstool.

Well, fuck.

Eyes like chips of golden ice threatened to freeze Justus where he sat, which would be quite impressive given the glow of warmth the ale gave him. If anyone could freeze a human solid with contempt, though, it would be Mazolan.

"An animal in pain is the most dangerous beast of them all. Be careful you don't maim everyone who cares about you," Mazolan said before they got up and glided through the crush of boisterous patrons, halting at Nyle's side. Maz dipped their head, saying something in Nyle's ear that made him frown.

With an absentminded flick of his wrist, the two occupants of his lap got up and sought other enjoyments for the evening. Mazolan sat down opposite Nyle and the two bent into a conversation that appeared quite serious.

"Another ale, mister?"

"Huh?" Justus jerked his head to the barkeep on the other side of the counter, then slammed his eyes shut when the world tilted and whorled.

The Spinning Squid. That *was the tavern's name.*

"I said, another ale?" the barkeep asked, his emphasis spraying spittle onto the scarred wooden bar. He grabbed a dirty rag and buffed it away, or maybe into the wood.

"Yes." Justus slapped two silver pieces down on the counter.

The nipple Justus rolled his tongue over was the wrong shade of berry. His lips were numb, and he didn't know what the owner of the nipple's name was, but he knew it was the wrong color.

In fact, everything about her was wrong. Her hands too bony, even as they gripped the back of his head. Her waist too small, pinned between him and the wall. Her thighs too thin as they wrapped around his waist.

Worst of all, her soul wasn't the other half of his. Even here, Justus couldn't seem to escape *her.*

"Derica."

"*What?*" the nipple's owner asked.

And her voice was *much* too shrill.

"My mama didn't teach me much, but she taught me you never let a man dip his wick if he calls you by the wrong name." She pushed his shoulders back, tugging up her bodice and sliding her legs from around Justus's waist.

Perfectly serviceable nipples, actually. He was sure she had two too many though.

"Ironic," Justus slurred. "I don't think you asked *my* name before you were mewling your pleasure against that wall."

A flash of enraged blue eyes was all that preceded the ringing slap to his cheek. In his daze, he entirely missed the knee that slammed into his balls.

"Fuck!" He cupped himself and curled around the pain, teetering.

"Pig!" She spat on the ground in front of him. As the swish of skirts and the stomping of small feet faded, Justus let himself collapse onto the ground, turning to prop his back against the wall. Gingerly, he drew his knees up and propped his elbows on them. He lowered his aching head into the cradle of his palms, closed his eyes, and breathed through the lingering pain.

The slow thump of boots several minutes later announced a visitor. With his luck, it would be a friend of the nameless woman come to teach him a lesson. Justus readied to lose himself in a bout of fists striking flesh, then sighed. Even with his eyes closed, Justus knew this man's approach anywhere.

"Weaver's tits, Nyle. I've already had it from Mazolan. I don't need it from you, too."

"Doesn't seem that way. I'm pretty sure those weren't the Weaver's tits you were sucking a moment ago. From what I heard, you didn't know who they belonged to."

The most galling thing was, there was not one ounce of censure in Nyle's voice. He spoke pure fact. Nyle never used emotion to convey how wrong you were, but simply spoke with pure, damning truth and let you boil in your own guilt and shame.

It was a good thing Justus was so anesthetized against that right now. Eight tankards of ale could do that.

Was it eight? Could've been nine. Ten even. Lost count after five, really.

"I didn't say anything sooner because you needed some time. We've been pushing hard since the Shredded became such a problem, especially after escorting Father Simond back to Radley. You, even more so than us. This behavior couldn't possibly have anything to do with a lovely redhead, could it?" Nyle asked. Justus didn't bother opening his eyes, but the rustle of cotton and the muffled thump of another back against the wooden wall announced his comrade joining him on the floor.

"What does it matter? You and Mazolan have never cared whom I fuck, how often, or when. In fact, that little shit asked me when the last time I—" Justus dropped his hands and squinted through the haze of alcohol, "—I'd buried myself 'between two gorgeous thighs.' I'm trying to follow their advice. If Mazolan thinks a quick roll in the sheets will cure my mood, who am I to nay-say them?"

"I think Maz was trying to get you to confront the *real* problem. Which might be closer to who you were *last* with, instead of when, hmm?"

"She's not a fucking problem," Justus snarled, turning his head to glare at Nyle.

Nyle waved his hand in front of his face and blinked. "Benign First, you're ripe. The morning you'll have will not be fun."

"And tonight was?" Justus laughed.

"It could have been. If you weren't a complete ass."

"Better than a half-ass," he snickered.

Nyle slapped the back of Justus's head, and his ears rang. "The question you need to ask yourself, Commander, is: if she isn't the problem, then what is she?"

Even drunk as he was, the answer presented itself immediately and demanded to be voiced.

"The solution," Justus sighed. "She's the solution. She always is."

Nyle's head tilted in curiosity at the word "always," then he shrugged and said, "Well, there you go." Pushing to his feet, Nyle reached a hand down to help Justus stand.

Justus stood. Locked his knees. And swayed into Nyle.

He had the forethought to say, "Nyle, if you ever tell Maz about this, I will skin you alive," before he passed out, falling into the other man's arms.

CHAPTER
TWENTY-THREE

J ustus felt Derica's eyes on him as he strode down the alleyways of Radley toward the church. Her gaze burned.

Deliciously.

Angrily, he shook thoughts of her from his head. There could be nothing for them. Justus may have let Mazolan and Nyle talk him into returning to Radley, but knowing he was in the same city of his heartthread had chafed. Mazolan, if asked, would insist that chafing was excitement.

But the demon couldn't have been more wrong. At all.

If that bricked-off part of his heart screamed in want at the very back of his mind, it wasn't loud enough to keep Justus from blocking it out. He thought about the blood of his beloved coating his hands, the elixir of their life seeping away—because of him.

Throughout their shared lifetimes, he'd justified his actions with any logic. It was a mercy; they had lived their lives, and his betrayal was an insurance they would see each other again. If his soul blackened a little each time—if he saw the bloodstains on his hands even when they were clean...

All the more reason to let his beloved go.

Nyle glided up next to him, matching his pace as he navigated the dark alleys.

"You don't have any questions about what happened? How a Shredded could be healed miraculously?" Nyle asked quietly.

"Nearly. Not Shredded, but nearly."

"Even more curious then, wouldn't you think?"

Oh, Justus had a theory, but not one he would share, so he grunted non-committally instead.

Justus's hand had felt the change travel through Braiden's body as he held him pinned to the wall, the nearly-Shredded's flesh starting at barely warmer than a corpse, waxy, and half-dead. Then Derica had touched Braiden's hand. A moment passed, and he held a slightly dirty, malnourished man against the brick wall where the nearly-Shredded had been. Justus had felt the thrum of his rapid pulse. Braiden's skin had warmed rapidly to a normal temperature, and previously milky eyes cleared like clouds melting on a hot day, leaving nothing but endless sky.

If Justus hadn't known who Derica was, he would have been hard-pressed not to call it a miracle.

But Justus and the Weaver weren't on the best of terms. He maintained she threw every obstacle in his path to punish him for keeping the Blessed-one from her. These obstacles were what made him such a fine Warrior. Over the years, he'd learned to calculate for every hitch—every point of suspected weakness. Then again, maybe the Weaver knew and was satisfied with his torment. Like a superstitious sailor, maybe his belief was a kind of self-ful-filling prophecy.

"Mazolan will find out what happened. You know they will. A dog with a bone is not as tenacious as they are," Nyle said.

"They can certainly try. I don't know that Braiden will be able to tell us what happened," Justus murmured.

Nyle hummed, the sound lyrical in the dark of the night. "What would Derica have to say, I wonder?"

Justus would like to say that he was always levelheaded. And normally, he was. But finding Derica, his heartthread, had woken up parts of him that had slept for far too long. Parts howling with anger, parts raging with the pain of a heart missing its other half.

In between one step and the next, he shoved Nyle against the wall, forearm braced against the mercenary's neck. Nyle didn't struggle and, other than the faint look of shock in his eyes, nothing indicated he hadn't predicted this reaction, much to Justus's annoyance.

"Whoa! Is that really necessary?" shouted Reid from behind them.

Justus turned and leveled a stare at the golden farm boy, prepared to tell him to shove his concern up his ass. But the words stuck like glue on his tongue after he caught a glimpse of red hair gilded in a shaft of moonlight.

Derica's eyes were closed, her head resting against Reid's shoulder. Justus's muscles bunched, locking to keep him in place. He desperately battled the desire to gather her against his chest and carry her to the rest she'd pleaded for. A cough escaped Nyle, and Justus moved, dropping his arm.

Nyle stood before him, righting his shirt, no censure in his stare—no anger.

It was fucking annoying.

More than ever, Justus wanted the earth to open up and swallow him whole. He wanted to seek one of those physicians they only talked about in hushed voices—the kinds that performed life-threatening surgery and removed maladies of the mind by boring holes into people's skulls.

He wanted to rip his beating heart out of his chest and lay it at Derica's feet, beg her to take the ache away.

"Everything all right now, gentlemen?" Reid asked in a hushed tone.

"Fine," answered Nyle, not looking away from Justus.

Everything *was* fine, because Nyle saw through Justus, saw the tension riding the commander so hard he could barely focus. And forgave him.

Again, it was fucking annoying.

It also warmed him. Not that Justus would ever admit it.

Justus held out his hand, and Nyle clasped it, a silent apology offered and accepted in the span of a moment, before they resumed their path toward the church.

"Commander, I had better not be missing anything interesting!" Mazolan yelled up from the back of their party where they walked with Braiden.

"Nothing, Maz. You missed nothing," Nyle tossed over his shoulder as he clapped Justus on the back.

The scuff of boots and a hearty *oomph* made both men turn around, hands on their weapons.

"I wasn't even done with my questions yet!" whined Maz. "Humans are really the most inane creatures. You'd never catch a demon fainting," they grumbled. Braiden had, indeed, passed out and Mazolan must have been feeling kind because they caught him against their chest. "Healer boy, come take a look at this one," they called, "I want it known that I didn't harm a hair on his filthy human head."

"But—" Reid started, eyes darting down to where Derica leaned heavily into his side.

"Give the morsel to the commander. The smelly one needs your attention more," Mazolan pronounced.

Justus barely heard the chuckle Nyle couldn't stifle beside him.

Reid's gaze narrowed, and the look he leveled at the commander... If looks could kill, Justus would be dead on the cobblestones. It's a good thing those wrathful blue eyes didn't have any genuine power.

Justus moved forward to take Derica into his arms, his heart racing, his palms itching for the softness of her skin. His lungs filled, anticipating the perfume of her hair.

"She's half asleep," Reid said, gently slipping his hold free and waiting for Justus to replace him at Derica's side. "Just guide her while she rests her eyes. Get her to her bed at the church, then I'll come clean her wounds, and be there to comfort her in the morning." As much as Reid's closeness with Derica filled him with envy, Justus begrudgingly admitted to himself the man would make a fine physician.

Derica murmured sleepily, and Justus slowed, careful not to jostle her as he wrapped a hand around her waist, bringing her cheek to lie in the crook of his shoulder.

With one last stare promising swift retribution should anything else happen to Derica tonight, Reid walked over to Mazolan, struggling to prop up a limp Braiden.

Justus's heart kicked when Derica burrowed closer into his hold, clumsily reaching one grasping hand around his back and tangling her fingers around his belt.

A brick in his wall crumbled at the touch.

Reverently tilting his head down until the hair at her crown tickled the tip of his nose, he promised himself one lungful. One deep breath to take her scent into his body. Tomorrow, he would continue to operate as he had been, putting distance between them once more. Radley was a large city. Justus would not seek her out. He would not follow her on her errands for the church. He would *not* watch for her safe return to the church after an outing with Reid.

"When was the last time Mazolan let someone lose consciousness during an interrogation?" Nyle asked.

Justus jerked his head up and blinked at his comrade, an odd, unfamiliar warmth climbing up his cheekbones. "What?"

Nyle smiled knowingly, then nodded to where Maz and Reid held Braiden between them, his arms draped over their shoulders.

"I asked you when the last time was that Maz let someone pass out during questioning? I don't think that's ever happened. Can you recall a similar situation?"

"No," Justus answered, "I can't."

"Mmm, that's what I thought. Maz does know that handy little trick for cutting off blood to the brain, though. Long enough to knock someone unconscious." Nyle turned and walked off, whistling a bawdy sea shanty.

Justus snapped his head over to Maz, careful not to jostle the woman in his hold.

With a flash of fangs in the moonlight, Mazolan smirked.

CHAPTER
TWENTY-FOUR

N yle ran up the steps of the church and pushed the heavy door open.

Justus stopped at the foot of the stairs and smoothly swung Derica up into his arms, cradling her to his chest. She murmured, sinking into his embrace as her hands circled his neck.

His fingers clenched as he fought to breathe evenly. This bone-deep rightness was the feeling he'd mistakenly sought in all the wrong places three months ago. He'd been trying to supplant the angry, wretched wound in his soul with meaningless physical pleasure and drink. These were the sleep-soft curves he'd wanted in that tavern. A deliciously heady weight that caused claws of need to scratch insistently. Enough bounty to overflow his hands.

More than that, this was the heartbeat he wanted to hold against his chest, each thump knocking down the walls he'd built, determined to ease the torment he so ruthlessly hid. As much as he knew he didn't deserve the peace she brought him, Justus also recognized the futility of the battle he fought. It was impossible to let go of his other half once he'd found them.

Looking down, Justus allowed himself a moment to trace her features with his eyes. Any sane person would balk when confronted with the intensity of his feelings. It had been so long since he'd navigated carefully wooing the Weaver-blessed, learning the new landscape of their being while knowing their soul almost better than the Warrior's.

Justus knew it was useless to attempt to let Derica go.

But he had to.

"Are you just going to stand there?" Maz quipped from behind, snapping Justus out of his reverie. "Some of us—*me*—have to deal with a slightly less perfumed dead weight."

Justus lifted one foot, moving up the stairs with care so he didn't jolt Derica awake.

"I can take—" started Reid.

"Quiet, healer. You should be used to the stench. Or become used to it. Stinky calling, medicine. All those liquids and squishy bits," said Mazolan. Justus practically heard the demon's full-body shudder.

Reid huffed a weary sigh, his sole response.

Justus stepped over the threshold of the church and moved aside to let Maz and Reid in with their charge. "Where?" he asked Reid.

"Over there." Reid pointed with his chin towards a small alcove. "Her cot is the one in the corner. I'll wake one of the Disciples and have Braiden attended, and then I'll come see to Derica. Get her comfortable."

Maz's face screwed up into an expression of distaste at the mention of the Disciples, then cleared into a look of sinister glee. "Do you think they've ever had a demon here before? Doubtful, as demons don't worship your silly Weaver. Would they consider my presence blasphemous? Delicious..." Maz's chatter trailed off as they accompanied Reid to deposit their charge.

"I'll wait here then," said Nyle, sitting down with a tired groan in one of the few long wooden pews. He crossed one leg over the other and flung his arms across the back of his perch, softly whistling another nautical tune.

Justus gently hoisted Derica higher in his arms and she grumbled adorably. He steered them toward the alcove Reid directed him toward, careful to keep silent.

A door preceding the alcove opened slowly and out stepped Father Simond.

The father stopped when he noticed Derica in Justus's arms and then rushed over.

"Oh my, what happened? Is she all right? What are you doing here, Commander?" Simond fired rapid, concerned questions.

The way Derica lay turned into his chest, her injuries were hidden from the holy man.

"Derica and Reid ran into some trouble in an alley. Fortunately, my comrades and I came upon them at the right time. She'll be fine after Reid bandages her wounds, with some rest," Justus said.

The father wrung his age-wrinkled hands together. "Thank the Weaver you were there to intervene. Her wisdom and mercy are great to have Woven such a rescue."

Justus bit his tongue to avoid disparaging the holy man's deity. Why such an attack would be fated in the first place didn't reveal the Weaver to be a wise and merciful god to his mind.

"Her cot is this way?" Justus asked, hoping to stop the old man's worrying.

"Oh! Oh, yes. Bring the poor girl here," Father Simond said, bustling off.

Simond led Justus through the doorway Reid had pointed to and then wound through an orderly arrangement of cots full of sleeping refugees.

"I knew the city was full and getting more so every day, but I didn't know there were this many seeking safety," Justus murmured. Shame burned the back of his neck as he realized how his pathetic, inebriated escape into the bottom of a tankard had blinded him to what was going on.

"We will soon run out of room to take them in," said Simond, voice ringing with pity and sadness. "We do all we can to keep them fed and warm—give them a place to rest their weary bodies and hearts. The Weaver leads them to us, and we bring them her comfort."

"Mm-hmm." Justus dipped his chin in a skeptical nod. It wasn't the Weaver bringing these people to Radley in droves. It was the growing threat of the Shredded.

No one knew what caused the soul sickness, transforming neighbors into nightmares. Until tonight, Justus hadn't ever seen one of the afflicted who wasn't a walking frenzy of violence and anger. The fanciful whispered they were undead, enchanted by the malevolent fey to take back the lands the humans had stolen from them.

Justus wasn't a healer or physician, but he had fought Shredded close enough to know they were men and women—living, breathing people.

Or, at least they had been, once.

And tonight, he'd seen one healed.

Father Simond stopped at the last cot, nestled in the corner. Justus thought of his room at the mercenary guild—the privacy he enjoyed and was thankful for. Derica had been living here without that luxury for the last six months. Three of those months, he'd been in the same city and unable—unwilling—to seek her out, even though his soul urged him to do exactly that every day.

It was more an ache than an urge, really. Holding Derica in his arms gave his soul the peace it craved. If Justus laid her down a bit too quickly, if his hands shook, he told himself it was the excitement of an unexpected Shredded encounter and the subsequent miraculous healing he'd witnessed.

He extended one trembling finger, moving a strand of her red hair from her forehead. Tucking it reverently behind her ear, he let himself imagine that she was his, and he was hers once again. The ache in his chest became a crushing weight of guilt as he imagined all the blood—*her* blood—that had coated his hands over the lifetimes.

Justus wasn't worthy to occupy the same room, much less touch her.

His foolish heart had forgotten the consequences of his love and his own weakness. With a deep breath, he solidified the brick wall—already cracked and crumbling around his yearning. Fuck, why wasn't doing the right and just thing easy?

"Commander?"

Justus blinked and jerked his hands away from Derica. He took two large steps back from her cot, almost tripping onto the sleeping form in the neighboring bed. As he righted himself, he automatically settled into a ready stance—hands clasped behind his back and legs braced—and smoothed all covetous and self-pitying thoughts from his face. "Yes, Father?"

"I asked what happened in that alley?" The holy man frowned in concern at Derica's form.

Her chest moved up and down at regular intervals, but her brows twitched above her closed eyes here and there with... distress? Justus hoped not.

"We came upon her," he nodded to Derica, "and her companion, being attacked by an individual who appeared, at first glance, to be Shredded."

Would it cause a panic to tell the father about Braiden's seeming return to normal? Would it endanger Derica to tell Simond? The Disciples of the Loom were notoriously twitchy about magic. They distrusted anything they could not credit to the Weaver and her benevolence. Even worse, what if they decided Derica was some vessel sent by their god? That was entirely too close to the truth to be comfortable. No, better to frame it in a way that assured the father no one really understood what happened and leave it at that. Justus would stay here until Reid came to treat Derica's wounds and they would... form an understanding about what happened tonight. For the benefit of all involved.

"*Appeared* to be?" asked Simond, a frown further wrinkling his aged brow.

"Yes, but it was clear after I restrained the attacker he was nothing more than a confused, injured man. Maybe he thought he was in danger, or maybe he thought he could gain something from attacking Derica and Reid. Mazolan interrogated him on the way to the church."

Upon mentioning Maz, the father's lips pinched slightly.

"We wouldn't have brought him here if we thought he was dangerous. I think the man was simply sick and disoriented. When he—Braiden—realized what he had done and whom he harmed, he was contrite," Justus said. At one point, he was sure his tongue kept moving, even though his brain wasn't quite sure what the plan was. That often happened with his muscles during a fight, but never his words.

Justus flicked a look at Derica. At least she wasn't awake to witness his babbling. A mercenary commander should never babble. He left that to Mazolan.

Reid entered the alcove, carrying a pail of clear water, a clean linen cloth, and a small pile of fresh bandages. Both Justus and Simond watched him pick his way through the cots and sleeping refugees. Reid didn't halt until he'd walked by the pair and knelt at Derica's bedside, pulling free Justus's favorite little tin of liniment. He had the stench of it carved into his nostrils, even all these months later.

"Reid, the commander told me what happened. You're unharmed?" asked Father Simond.

Justus couldn't see Reid's face, but the other man's shoulders tightened, and his back tensed. With shame? Or anger? A tiny little voice, sounding suspiciously like Mazolan, whispered maybe the two had become romantically entangled in the six months since he'd last seen them. As soon as the thought came, he mentally waved it away. It was no business of his.

"No. The attacker went for Derica, and I couldn't get to her in time." Reid's voice was tight with emotion, but his hands were gentle as he turned Derica partially onto her stomach, exposing the side of her damaged throat. Reid's fingers brushed her hair back and away from her nape. His familiar air lit a coal of jealousy in Justus's stomach. His hands itched to haul the man back.

"Father, will you please hold a candle behind my shoulder? I need more light here," said Reid.

"Oh, of course, my child." Simond carefully grabbed a lit taper and maneuvered around Justus until he stood behind Reid's shoulder. "How is that?"

"Much better. Thank you."

In the flickering candlelight, it first appeared like a reflection from Derica's fiery hair. But after several blinks, the mark remained, and it wasn't a trick of the light. A line of crimson-colored skin about the length of Justus's forefinger slashed horizontally across the back of Derica's neck. Behind the mark—almost like a faded port-wine stain—was the shape of a starburst.

Father Simond's eyes weren't so old that he didn't notice. The holy man gasped, and the candle shook in his grip. "Is that—what is that?"

"She was born with it, Father. A birthmark, nothing more," answered Reid. Nothing in Reid's manner or voice announced he believed otherwise.

But Justus knew.

It was the mark of the Weaver-blessed, and they carried it in every lifetime. He'd seen it at the cottage, of course, but it was as jarring to see now as it was then. Locking down every muscle in his body and keeping his face blank, Justus watched Simond.

"That doesn't look like any birthmark I've ever seen," said the father.

"I assure you, it's not from a wound. Derica's always had it. I'd be sad to learn the church holds onto archaic ideas about curses and marks of evil." Reid turned slightly from Derica. He leveled a blue-eyed stare at Simond, strongly encouraging a denial of such outmoded thinking.

It stung to see the protection that had been Justus's honor to perform in all other lifetimes upheld by Reid.

"Of course not, my child. None of the Disciples would judge another because of their appearance."

"As long as they're human." Justus couldn't call the flat words back. He'd blame the lack of forethought before speech on Mazolan's influence, but the attitude of the church had long been an injustice to his thinking. Veridion's other races worshiped a wide and varied pantheon: the fey had their Primordial Stag, the dwarves their Mother Mountain, the witches their blasphemous Benign First, and the demons had a confusing host of spirits for every day of the week, season, and purpose under the sun. The Disciples condemned them all as heretical and an affront to the Weaver. This stance was another point in the enmity between humans and the magical races.

Father Simond frowned, a flicker of something in his eyes there for the span of a blink and then gone. "The Disciples welcome all to the teachings of the Weaver. However they may come."

Justus couldn't tell if the father spouted sentiments by rote or if it was something he personally believed. He'd seen the way Balduin curled his lip up at Mazolan when he believed no one was paying attention while they'd been on the road together. It stank of prejudice then and didn't engender faith in Simond's doctrine of acceptance. On the road, the father piped up, redressing the younger man for his attitude, but Justus remained reluctant to put stock in Simond's acceptance.

Reid and Justus shared a look, revealing they were both skeptical, but the blond silently shrugged and went back to tending Derica's wound. Justus watched Reid work, glancing at the father every so often. Simond appeared entranced, focused on Derica's mark with an enigmatic intensity that was hard to decipher.

As Reid twisted the lid on his salve, Justus held his breath preemptively. When the father didn't flinch or wrinkle his nose after Reid opened the jar, Justus ventured a sniff.

The bastard.

The faint smell of rosewater and honey pleasantly overlaid a generic medicinal aroma. Justus had been stuck smelling like cat piss for days on end after Reid tended his back months ago. The stench seemed to meld to his skin and clung in his nostrils for nigh on a week. Mazolan and Nyle had complained endlessly, refusing to ride downwind until it faded with repeated and frequent bathing.

"...you can't go this way," a harried voice insisted.

Justus looked over his shoulder to see Balduin walking backward in front of Mazolan, arms spread as he tried to herd the demon away. Justus sighed, scrubbing his jaw with a palm.

"It appears my feet are carrying me in this direction. So I would say I *can* go this way. I believe the phrase you want is: you aren't *wanted* this way. And I am well aware of that," Mazolan drawled, continuing to move forward.

Balduin blustered, his sallow complexion making the ruddy flush of anger on his cheeks all the more vivid. "You can't—I—It's forbidden—"

Mazolan leaned toward the acolyte, teeth gleaming. "By whom? The Weaver? I rather doubt there's an edict recorded somewhere disallowing demonly beings from entry to the church. Do toddle along and find it for me, however, if it does exist. Having you buzz around like an annoying horsefly is tiresome."

Nyle walked behind the pair, tattooed hands in his pockets, a faint amused twinkle evident in his tawny eyes. Justus caught his gaze and jerked his chin at the acolyte. Nyle nodded. He smoothly stepped around Maz, laid an arm around Balduin's shoulders, and turned on the charm that was his hidden weapon.

Mazolan's fangs flashed in a smug grin, sauntering around Nyle and the acolyte until the demon stood at Justus's side.

"Commander," Maz nodded, surveying Reid tending to Derica and Father Simond's watchful gaze.

"What did you find out?" Justus asked.

"Oh, very little compared to what I suspect you know."

"Mazolan," he sighed, "I—"

"I know, I know. How could you know anything? You didn't do anything to Braiden. Other than hoist him up against a brick wall by the throat. He's fine, by the way. Not even a bruise. Quite interesting that, wouldn't you say? Miracles upon miracles for the boy..." Maz droned on.

Justus ground his teeth and breathed through his nose, letting Mazolan's words float around him. An ache settled in his temples, and he stifled a third sigh in as many minutes.

The absence of Maz's chattering focused his attention.

The demon's citrine gaze was trained on Derica, their body predator still. Maz's eyes slid to Justus's, and a smirk hitched one side of their mouth.

"An interesting mark. Was she born with it, Reid?" Maz asked, not looking away from the commander.

"Yes," Reid replied absently, adjusting the bandages against the side of Derica's neck.

"Mmm," hummed Maz, one pale eyebrow winging up. The look told Justus he was in for a harrowing inquisition to shame the questioning Braiden had faced.

Nyle stepped behind his comrades, the acolyte nowhere to be seen. "How is she?" he asked quietly.

"She would be better if we let her get some rest," announced Father Simond, waving his hands to usher them away from her bed. "Reid, have you finished? You need the rest too, my boy."

Simond helped Reid gather his supplies, but Justus didn't move with the others. Someone should be here if Derica woke.

"I can see you're set on playing guard, Commander," said Simond.

"Yes," he nodded.

The father's lips pinched, and he wrinkled his nose at Justus's tunic. "I don't know that Derica would find your watch soothing. You could stand a wash and some rest yourself. I assure you, she is safe here."

Justus opened his mouth to argue, but the father raised his hand, cutting him off.

"I can look after her while she rests. My evening has been much more relaxing than the one you lot appear to have had. I will be near should she need anything."

With a grunt and a last look at Derica, Justus forced his legs to carry him away.

CHAPTER TWENTY-FIVE

The Savior strolled down a dimly lit stone hallway. They halted in front of a heavy oak door decorated with antiquated, heavy locks. From the depths of their hooded robe, the Savior pulled a key ring of matching wrought iron. Dull clangs bounced in a discordant echo down the long hallway.

Finally, the oak door swung open, revealing a weathered stone staircase descending into a yawning maw of shadows. They grabbed a small torch lighting the very top of the stairs and moved into the stairwell, the heavy door closing behind them with a thud. Nothing but the bob of the firelight and the sound of their footsteps joined them in the long descent.

The hitch of their shoulders indicated their breaths were coming quicker, but their pace remained steady as they reached the bottom landing and moved under an arch, finally entering a large room lined with bookshelves. The smell of vellum and damp permeated the space.

The Savior knew the tomes were safe in this vault. They had lived here longer than the Savior had been alive. Hundreds, maybe even thousands of years.

As they moved farther into the chamber, more bookshelves lined the walkway and the walls of the vault. They were careful to keep the torch high and away from the ancient wood and the precious, leather-bound books. Gilded spines winked in the firelight here and there, flashing like dancing fireflies in the dark.

So many books, so many words. But they sought the one at the very end of the chamber.

A sigh of pleasure escaped them when the corrugated marble pedestal melted from the darkness into the torchlight. The slim, leather-bound volume atop the podium seemed entirely unremarkable.

The light bounced, making monsters in the shadows, as the Savior reached over the pedestal and rested the torch in a nearby sconce.

Fingers betraying their nerves with the slightest tremors, the Savior reached out and gently stroked the aged hide of the cover. No gilding, no tooling, no markings of any kind announced what was inside.

Reverently, they lifted the cover and began to read—to search.

As long as this vault had been here, so had this volume. In fact, there were rumors this was the sole reason their compatriots built the chamber. To house and protect its precious, sacred knowledge.

They looked for something quite specific this time. The Savior forced themselves to turn the pages carefully, lest they tear or bend the paper. Hand-drawn illustrations and looping script passed by. Smudges of dirt, ink, and unsavory stains spoke for the long life of the volume before coming to reside here.

There.

Carefully smoothing the pages flat, the Savior inspected what they found. What they had come to confirm.

On the left side of the page, the journal's owner had drawn a mark in exquisite detail. A starburst and its overlaying horizontal slash. On the right was a slanted and halting text entry. The hand that had penned the scrawl must have been overwrought, but the artist's rendering opposite had the clean lines and dedicated shading of a cool head.

They always wondered what the artist and writer had felt when creating this entry. How much time passed between the drawing and the written entry? Why is it that not a single page in the volume bore a date? Did the writer ever intend this book for the eyes of others?

Bending their hooded head closer to the page, the Savior squinted at the handwritten note.

"I have doomed us. I saw love transform to hate, and it shattered something in me. In the next lifetime, I will earn forgiveness. And then I will watch the transformation again when it is time to take up the blade."

Humans were not meant to manipulate what fell into the Weaver's purview. The Savior believed themself tasked with setting the balance right.

For only then would Veridion be healed.

Derica woke because of a dull burn and an aching stiffness in her neck when she tried to turn over. She blinked into the dimly lit alcove for a moment before the reason for the pain came back to her. With a sigh, she lifted a hand and gingerly poked at the bandages on her neck, wincing when the movement caused a zing of sharp pain.

Someone cleared their throat on the other side of her cot. "My child, I'm glad to see you're not so much the worse for wear," said Father Simond, his voice quiet and soothing to Derica's ears.

She lay on her side, her back to Simond. Tentatively bracing one hand against the thin mattress of the cot, she intended to shift and face him.

The squeal of wood on the stone floor preceded the father's gentle grip on her arm. "No, there's no need to make yourself uncomfortable on my account.

Please, remain still. Reid was falling asleep on his feet. I sent him off to seek his own rest with the promise that I would see to your comfort. Young men need their sleep."

Derica's lips twitched at the image of Father Simond sending a droopy-eyed Reid off to bed like a toddler.

"As for the others," the father continued, "they are likely comparing notes after speaking with that poor boy—Braiden, I think his name was?" He patted her arm carefully and with another wince-inducing squeal of wood on stone, settled back into his chair.

Her eyelids fluttered shut at the mention of Braiden, the tableau of her hand in his grip and the... soulthread she'd somehow touched. Possibly even healed.

Against the back of her closed eyes, her mind was a jumble of questions. Underneath it all was a simple, sterling satisfaction. It settled comfortably and contentedly in the hurricane's eye of her thoughts. The dichotomy induced a pounding in her temples.

Derica must have made a noise. Simond leaned over her and shifted her hair away from her forehead before laying a cool, damp cloth above her brow. "Reid said you might be uncomfortable despite his treatment. I find with the sick and searching, talking helps keep their mind away from their troubles, whether they're physical or spiritual. Would you like to talk, Derica?" She couldn't see the father's face, but she imagined the holy man had a gentle smile deepening the lines around his eyes and mouth.

"I-I don't even know where to start. This evening has been..." she paused, pressing the cool cloth to her forehead to quiet her racing thoughts. "It has been something else, that is certain." A tiny voice in the back of her mind cautioned her against speaking about the events in the alley. Especially to a Disciple of the Loom. Father Simond had provided Derica with a haven in the chaos that had been her life since fleeing Arlan with Reid. Still, the words to explain the night she'd had were a tangled snarl in her throat, unwilling to flow from her lips.

"Quite all right, my child. In times like this, the Weaver gives sage advice. Begin with one thread. Don't approach the problem of the whole Tapestry. Start with one small thread," he said.

A hysterical laugh echoed in the jumble of her mind. One small thread had been the start of all of this. And Derica couldn't discern if what happened was reality or some hallucination in a dark alley, the product of fear and lingering anxiety from the fortune teller's reading.

Her eyes snapped open, and a jolt ran through her body.

I saw your hands holding a frayed thread. In the next moment, the thread was made new, like it had never been damaged.

Gooseflesh raised on her arms, and her scalp prickled. Sarenya had spoken true. That, or she'd known exactly what Derica would hallucinate.

"Derica?" Father Simond's question seemed to come from far away. "My child?" At the touch of his fingers on her shoulder, his voice became clear, and her breaths came easier.

"I'm sorry, Father. Woolgathering."

"Only to be expected after the experience you had. You seem to be doing very well, considering."

"Considering?" Derica frowned, and a lance of pain struck between her eyes. Forcibly, she cleared the expression from her face. She didn't dare turn to face the holy man and search his face for his meaning.

"I mean only that you've had more excitement since leaving Arlan, hmm? The Shredded and a new city have forced quite a few unfamiliar and frightening experiences into your life, I suspect. You're not alone in that. I've noticed the refugees here find comfort talking about their homes." The shifting of robes signaled the father was settling in for a lengthy chat. "Why don't you tell me about Arlan? My annual trips to your lovely village can't tell me everything about the town. I get to see so little on Rite Day myself. I'd love to hear more about the place."

"There's not much to tell. You saw the entire village. Either on the way in or the way out." Derica mentally slammed a door on thoughts of Arlan. She still battled swells of mourning for her home and the memories she'd left there.

"No, no, my child. That way lies only dark thoughts. We're trying to coax them out from the shadows and into the light. Tell me..." he hummed in consideration, "tell me what your childhood was like. You've known Reid since you were children, yes? What was the lad like as a boy? Did the two of you get into mischief at every turn?"

An image formed over the chaos of her mind, and Derica almost sighed in relief. Maybe the father was right. Maybe some mindless reminiscing was all she needed to calm the maelstrom. The words weren't a tangle or a snarl, but flowed like fresh, clear water from a well pump.

"Reid and I were not the little terrors of Arlan. That job belonged to his older brother, Algernon." Her nose wrinkled of its own accord at his name. "Algie was never a bully to his brother or the other children of Arlan, myself included, but he was always—" She wondered how to say it without sounding like a bully herself, "—Algernon was always weighing everything and everyone. And he always found them wanting. Arlan was too provincial. His family was too happy with their lot in life. Algernon was that way as far back as I can remember. Everything could have been bigger, better, and more efficient if Algie was in charge. Reid and I left him alone. He didn't want to play games with us. He wanted to scold his brother about what he needed to do to grow up to be important." She chuckled, looking back. For all Algie's dissatisfaction, as an adult, he'd moved one village away and produced some children. Seemed rather normal and ordinary to her.

"And while Reid's older brother was terrorizing Arlan with his expectations?"

"We were content. I helped my mother in the bakery during the day, and Reid helped his parents around the farm. In the afternoons, we would play with the other children."

"Sounds charming indeed. What about your father?"

Derica shrugged. "He left when I was a baby. I don't remember him. My mother was all I had. Other than Reid and his family." Her heart twinged at the mention of her mother, and she battled back the melancholy that swept over her.

"A man that leaves his family is not one to find favor with the Weaver."

"From the little my mother said of him, he wouldn't have cared for her favor. He left us for another family."

"The Weaver—"

"Thank you, Father, but I long ago stopped worrying about him. I was a lucky girl to be raised by a woman like my mother. Her hugs smelled like sweet pastries, and I never went to bed without the knowledge that I was her world." The last word choked from her tight throat, her eyes misty with tears of remembrance.

She missed her mother. Every day. It was an ache that she suspected would never leave her heart. A piece of it always missing. Derica worried her thumb over her mother's ring, the warm metal soothing.

"She has returned to the Weaver's hand for her next turn on the Great Tapestry of Fate. The Weaver is lucky to have your mother at her side," Father Simond said.

A pang struck her chest, and for a moment, Derica couldn't breathe. Then the comforting fire of fury swept through her chest.

The Weaver didn't deserve her mother. The Weaver had seen fit to take her mother from her too soon, had allowed a wasting disease that slowly and cruelly sapped the life and vitality of the most vibrant woman Derica had ever known. If the stories of the Weaver were to be believed, then this had always been her mother's fate, and it filled her with helpless rage. Before Derica could sink into the molten pool of acerbic anger, Father Simond bent over her to change the cloth at her brow.

"My child, I know and recognize well the pain of one angry at the Weaver for what she 'took' from them. Again, that way lies only more pain. Remember, we were trying to banish the shadows with light and sunshine."

Derica tried to nod. Maybe her chin dipped the slightest in assent, or maybe it wobbled with emotion. She wouldn't examine it too closely. There lay more shadows and anger.

"I bet your Eleanora came up with the most charming story to explain your birthmark. Am I right?" She could hear the smile in Simond's voice, and unbidden, an answering one came to her lips.

"She did." Derica's bandages pulled and stung as she reached up unconsciously to stroke the mark. "I wonder if she knew she was sick from the time I was little. My mother told me we'd met before on the Loom, and my birthmark was the kiss she'd placed on me the very first time we were mother and child. It was there so she could find me again." A tear rolled from the corner of her eye and into the pillow beneath her cheek. "I hope it's true. I hope I see her again."

Derica almost jumped when the father touched the hair at her nape, brushing it over her shoulder. Cool air touched the mark she knew was there. Despite his habitual kindness, she held her breath. Her mother had warned her to be wary of religious men because they often saw evil in anything that was not their idea of perfection.

A finger lightly tapped the skin at the back of her neck. "All these years, and I never knew. A mother's love is a beautiful thing. You carry a reminder of her always then, don't you?"

"I do. If she hadn't warned me against displaying my mark, I would wear it openly and proudly through life. She cautioned that some might call it a witch mark, or an ill omen from the fey, dwarves, or demons. Humans may not have magic—forgive me for saying so, Father—but they do have religious fervor."

Derica's eyebrows rose into her hairline when Simond chuckled softly, and said, "That we do. That we do. Do you feel like you can—"

The approach of footsteps interrupted him. "Father Simond, I fetched—"

"Not now, Balduin. Derica needs her rest."

"But—"

"You can wait for me in my office." Father Simond was normally so calm and level-headed; it was shocking to hear him snap at the younger man.

Derica could swear she felt Balduin's beady eyes on her back. She fought the urge to shudder and huddle into her blankets. Reaching her hand up, she moved her hair to cover the mark. She heard Balduin retreat, and the absence of his regard was visceral.

"I'm sorry about Balduin," Father Simond sighed. "He's so eager to learn and rise within the ranks of the church, I think he forgets common decencies. It's unbecoming at times. I'm working on it with him. Now, are you comfortable? Do you feel like you can rest again?"

"I do, Father. Thank you." As his footsteps on the stone floor faded away, Derica drifted into sleep, the smell of sweet pastries tickling her nose a second before dreams blanketed her.

CHAPTER TWENTY-SIX

J ustus stood propped against the outside of the church. He'd sent Maz and Nyle back to the guild. They'd both given him knowing looks, then strolled off, heads bent together—probably speculating like old maids.

The sun felt like a warm blanket on his shoulders and the crown of his head. When it disappeared beneath the horizon at dusk, it would take all its warmth with it.

Justus hated winters in the city. He much preferred the crisp, clean air of the wilderness, where the hush of falling snow or the whisper of the wind could lull him to sleep beside a campfire. The quiet was the best of all.

Radley made his ears ring. There were too many bodies—too many voices—crammed into the vast castle town. Even now in the early morning hours, the city was alive. The city's main thoroughfare ran parallel to the church, and the clatter of cart wheels and horseshoes on cobblestone battered his ears. This is why he preferred the guild's tunnels for navigating the city. He'd never seen Radley this full.

The Shredded were a threat that needed to be dealt with, and soon.

The conversation Justus, Nyle, and Maz had last night after leaving Derica's bedside nagged like an insistent fishwife. Mazolan had pried for details while

Justus had prevaricated. Nyle had observed it all with keen eyes—less vocal, but always discerning. In the end, Justus escaped their questions and theories without spewing his secrets and his guilt. Thoughts and worries still plagued him all night long. When his eyes were open, Justus's mind conjured Braiden's transformation and all its implications. When they were closed, he saw Derica and what they'd done in the cottage those many months ago. He could still taste her—smell her. The hunger prickled underneath his skin, a draw that wouldn't abate. Awake, it filled him with worry. Asleep, it tormented him with an unslakable thirst.

Breathing out harshly through his nose, Justus shook his head hard before letting his skull fall to the warm brick behind him. The rap was grounding, but it still couldn't banish his worries. It might help if he went inside the church and verified that Derica appeared healthy and on the mend. Justus could practically hear Maz in his ear, telling him to succumb to his asinine human feelings.

He pushed off the wall when he spotted Reid running toward the church. Justus's heart lurched and began a gallop. Images of a bloody, feverish Derica flitted across his mind. Before he could demand answers, Reid started speaking rapidly.

"A large party was attacked west of Idernockt. Refugees are hurt, and we're already spread thin caring for the sick and injured in the city. Will you tell Derica where I am and why I can't be with her today? Also, let her know I left fresh bandages and salve with Father Simond last night, just in case." Reid huffed, hands on his knees as he spat out the words.

Justus's teeth clicked shut, and he simply nodded.

Warning bells rang in his head as he accepted Reid's tired thanks and watched him trot back toward the physician's guild. It was like Justus hovered outside his body, watching himself casually and calmly stepping through the massive doors of the holy building. He bargained with himself as he walked down the center aisle between the cramped pews. If he found Father Simond, he would deliver the information to him; he wouldn't have to set eyes on Derica.

But it was fiery hair Justus scanned the church for.

Clusters of refugees, priests, and acolytes dotted the interior of the hallowed building. It was certainly calmer and quieter here, but a melancholy air of sadness tinged what was an otherwise peaceful atmosphere.

Justus resolved to talk to Alondra when he got back to the guild—find out what the status of the city really was and where the Shredded threat stood currently. People from surrounding areas were arriving daily in caravans seeking refuge. There had to be a solution that would combat the threat directly instead of treating the symptoms.

And Justus would keep Derica far, far away from it.

He'd walked the entire hall and hadn't spotted her. Maybe she was still lying in bed—resting, hopefully. The commander retraced his steps to the alcove the father directed him to last night and finally saw her.

Derica was dressed and sitting on the side of her cot, staring through one of the wide, high windows lining the north wall of the building. She watched a large raven hopping along the sill, black feathers shining dark blue in the bright sunlight. Justus turned his eyes back to Derica. Her stillness unnerved him. She wasn't ever frantic or brimming with energy, but all the times he'd been near her, she could never keep still—or quiet.

It stoked a rage in some corner of his mind. He wanted to find the source of her melancholy and rip it to shreds. Shoving the primitive impulse aside, Justus drifted nearer, then stopped. Clasping his hands behind his back, he cleared his throat, preparing to deliver Reid's message. Before he could announce his presence, Derica started talking.

"Reid, I'm scared." The words were soft, and her voice trembled as she continued. "I don't know what happened last night. I don't know what I did—if I *did* anything. I saw..." her voice trailed off.

The polite thing to do would be to correct her about who stood behind her. But a voice suspiciously like Mazolan's crooned, *let her talk.*

So, he hummed an affirmative, hoping she would continue.

"What I saw... What I think I did... It's not possible. It can't be possible." Derica's voice faltered, and Justus locked his knees to keep from going to her and offering whatever comfort she would accept.

He was determined to keep his distance. There would be no relationship here.

Comforting her was not his privilege.

But burning coals of agony lined the bottom of his stomach as he forced himself to stand and witness her pain and confusion.

"Reid, what do I do?" she whispered. "What can I do? What if Braiden was a fluke? He wasn't quite Shredded, but clearly on the cusp of becoming one... Neelson—" She cut herself off, and, this time, he couldn't stop himself from moving closer. He didn't halt until his shins bumped the other side of her cot. He watched her back tremble with stoppered emotion. Justus reached out a hand, but curled his fingers into a fist before touching her shoulder. It wasn't his comfort she sought, but Reid's. Justus's presence was merely an intrusion on her grief.

Despite his remembrance of their past lives, he couldn't recall the Weaver-blessed ever exhibiting power. But in their shared lifetimes, the Shredded had never existed before. The creatures were a new shadow over Veridion and, while he could kill them, that didn't seem to staunch their increasing numbers.

Derica gulped, taking a deep breath, and her voice was much steadier when she continued. "Neelson heard rumors the fey did this—that they're behind the Shredded. I can't see how that can be true. No one knows what causes the affliction, and the fey have kept to their Isle for hundreds of years. I've heard rumors they're building an army to take back the mainland, but surely, they would come with a navy and infantry. Subterfuge seems too delicate for them." She huffed a laugh. "Granted, those stories also came from Neelson when he was drunk in the tavern."

Justus chuffed low, hoping to prod her into happier memories.

"Pip used to give him the dirtiest looks when he would drink one pint too many and start his tales. Do you remember?"

Justus grunted. His mouth tugged up at one end.

Derica's laugh was watery but light and free. It eased something in Justus's chest.

She continued, "What about the time she chased him around the dining hall with a wooden spoon when she found him telling us the tale of how he bedded a dwarven shield maiden? We were, what? Seven, I think. Oh, she was so mad." This Neelson liked tall tales. Dwarven shield maidens were celibate.

"I miss Pip. I miss Tedric. I hope your parents are all right, Reid. I don't know what I would have done after my mother died if it hadn't been for you and your family. They *have to* be well. We can't be without them, too."

He clamped his mouth shut to halt the questions that threatened to pour forth. She was alone? What about her father? What had her mother been like?

In every lifetime they were together, getting to learn the Weaver-blessed all over again was a privilege. Things were new and different every time they met. But the love that grew between them was always a tie as strong as diamonds were hard. It varied in facets and cut, but it was always the shining highlight of his existence.

Until his greed got the better of him and he succumbed to his selfish need to keep the Weaver-blessed with him in the next life. Justus may meticulously clean his demon-made dagger, but he would never see it as anything other than drenched in his love's lifeblood.

Derica's sweet voice penetrated his self-loathing, and he pushed away the suffocating regret.

"—I don't want to imagine what would have happened in that alley if Jus—the commander and his people hadn't shown up."

A thrill coursed down his spine at her almost-use of his name.

Derica's eyes returned to the raven. "Have you seen them? I hope they haven't done anything to poor Braiden," she continued.

Poor Braiden? Justus thought, his head rearing back in surprise. Braiden was currently fine and, other than being painfully malnourished, he showed no ill effects from his affliction. Derica, on the other hand, had a neck that was half-covered in snowy bandages blotched with dried blood. Justus couldn't have halted the irate grumble that came from his chest if he wanted to.

Derica's head turned slightly, and Justus froze. He wanted to hear more, wanted to know everything about her, and he knew the second she saw him, this little subterfuge would halt any genuine conversation they could have. He'd backed himself into a corner by not announcing his identity, and his only hope was to listen to what he could, then slink off and deliver Reid's message to Father Simond, leaving Derica none the wiser. His lack of guilt over this intrusion should have made him feel lower than a slug, but the drive to be near Derica overrode much.

Derica laughed. "Oh, stop. Braiden hurt me, but I don't think he was in control of his actions. I'm sore and stiff, but the salve you left is helping. Father Simond helped me change my bandage this morning."

Justus frowned. The blood on her bandages could only be a few hours old, if that, and shouldn't have needed changing yet. He'd make sure Reid was the next person to change her dressing. The Father may not have attended it correctly. That voice—Mazolan's Weaver-damned voice—whispered, *it wouldn't be unusual for a less than day-old wound to bleed onto a fresh bandage.* He breathed slowly in through his mouth and out through his nose, trying to release the disproportionate reaction to her injury.

Glancing at the windows above, Justus watched as the raven took flight, leaving its perch, and Justus wished he could do the same. He didn't know how to extricate himself from this one-sided conversation. Justus was sure Reid wouldn't disappear in the middle of a conversation with a wounded, emotional Derica. He didn't have to know the man well to guess that.

Justus could sit down and see what happened. Maybe she'd be irate. Maybe she'd yell and tell him to leave. Or maybe... maybe she wouldn't. Having a conversation wasn't an invitation for friendship or a relationship. He could walk right back out of this church after he relayed Reid's message.

Sighing, he turned and sat on the other side of her cot. His weight tipped her backward enough for their arms to brush. Justus burned at the contact, instantly remembering carrying her in his arms last night. The alien urge to thank Mazolan for their ridiculous interference struck and was then forgotten when Derica turned her head.

She blinked at him, face gone slack with surprise. "You're not Reid."

"No," he said, searching her eyes for something. Happiness? Curiosity? He only knew this was the first time they'd really spoken since parting ways six months ago.

He wanted to ask about last night.

He wanted to ask about her mother and her life in Arlan.

He wanted to know every little detail about her, but the questions burned, stuck in his throat.

"I should have noticed I wasn't talking to him. You were far too quiet to be Reid. Why did you let me...?" She swallowed the rest of her question, pink blossoming on her cheeks.

With a sigh, Justus shrugged. He didn't have a reason he would willingly voice. His cheeks felt warm, but he blamed the heat of the sun streaming through the windows.

"Maybe I'm still rattled from last night." Derica shook her head with a self-deprecating laugh.

"That wouldn't be wrong or weak. Last night was," he searched for the right word, "shocking, I'm sure."

"Where's Reid?" she asked.

"He found me outside the church and asked me to tell you he's needed at the physician's guild—a large party of injured refugees arrived today."

"Oh." She looked down and twisted her hands. "I hope they all end up all right. I have faith in Reid."

He hated this. Hated the pull he felt toward her. Hated that he couldn't let himself succumb to that pull. He knew the other half of his heartthread sat next to him, and it was elating and soul-crushing at the same time. Justus was determined to alter the end they always met. If he didn't let himself love her, if she didn't love him, maybe they could escape their fate.

You dumb human, Mazolan's voice rang in the back of his mind.

Better dumb than a murderer, motivated by selfish greed. Justus believed the only reason he hadn't recognized Derica that day in Arlan was because of how long they'd been separated from each other.

That was a lie.

He had felt something when he found Derica in the garden.

Justus had closed himself off to the possibility of finding the Weaver-blessed because he'd lived five lifetimes without them. Every pass on the Loom without meeting his heartthread made his hope dim and his guilt intensify.

He cleared his throat. "I'm sorry—for intruding. It wasn't my intention to hear words that weren't meant for me." Another lie, he thought to himself.

Justus turned his head a fraction, peering at Derica out of the corner of his eye. She continued staring down at her hands, watching as her fingers plucked a loose thread on her skirt.

When she lifted her face, the confusion and barely concealed fear in her eyes twisted his heart. The words that came out of his mouth next originated somewhere in that vicinity, because they surely weren't planned.

"I think you need to get out of here." Justus flicked a hand at the austere stone walls of the church alcove. "I think you need a distraction. I need to pick up an order for the guild in the market and then deliver it. Would you like to accompany me?"

I approve, idiot, sang Mazolan's voice.

And that's how Justus knew it was a terrible idea. But he couldn't call back the words. He couldn't pluck them out of the air and stuff them back into the walls around his heart.

The look of wary happiness that flitted across Derica's face made him feel like a fucking bastard. He could spend the afternoon with her, serving as a stand-in for the comfort of the preoccupied Reid, and survive. The trick was not to say or do anything to reveal how very much Justus wanted to be more than that to Derica.

He rose from the cot, walked around to stand in front of her, and extended a hand. "Shall we?"

He held his breath, determined not to flinch or twitch a muscle if she rejected him. It would be the more sensible course of action for her.

Justus's hope may have dimmed, but it was still there—a faintly glowing ember. That glow flickered brighter when she placed her hand in his.

Mazolan's elated laugh echoed from the back of his mind.

CHAPTER
TWENTY-SEVEN

As they made their way to the market, Justus was careful to maintain a buffer of space between them. Getting too close to her fried his senses and dulled his wits. Yet that was entirely the reason he'd invited her to accompany him. The casual but maddening brush of her arm against him on the cot earlier had eroded his will.

If Justus looked into the shadowed alleyways surrounding their path, he was almost afraid he'd find a grinning Mazolan.

Justus didn't allow himself to search. That Weaver-damned demon wasn't his concern at the moment.

She was.

Derica maintained pace with him easily. The thick fabric of her skirt and the heavy hooded cape she wore to hide her bandages draped over her curves. The hem of the cape ended below the substantial swell of her breasts and the bounce of the material was distracting in a way that threatened to cause an embarrassing reaction.

Justus concentrated on walking and breathing. Thinking was out of the question at the moment. He completely abandoned conversation because he couldn't think of anything to say that wouldn't stoke the fire of his obsession. Instead, he focused on the strike of his boots on the bricks. Justus led them into a circuitous path through back alleys to avoid the crush of people and traffic. The back of narrow homes formed the walls of the alley. In a few turns, they'd cross into the shopping district.

Now, he regretted his choice. They'd passed only a handful of other people in the few minutes they'd been walking, and Justus didn't know how to alleviate the weighted silence hanging between them.

"Commander?" Derica asked from his side.

He turned his head, but his tongue refused to operate properly, so Justus resorted to what Nyle called his favorite form of communication: grunting.

"I'm curious," Derica ventured hesitantly, capturing a stray red hair from her face and tucking it behind her ear, "I've been by your guild, and I never see anyone come in or out. It's rather odd."

His heart stuttered in his chest. She'd looked for him, even after how he'd treated her at the cottage? Nothing else she could have admitted would have shocked him quite like this veiled confession.

Derica felt the draw, too—or that's what his heart screamed, beating against the brick wall he'd hidden it behind.

His mouth quirked into a semblance of a smile. It was foreign and out of place when talking to anyone other than his comrades. "We have other ways of getting in and out of the guild." Justus would have told her about the tunnels and the hub that the mercenaries had created beneath the city, but he thought better of it. He had every confidence the underground tunnels couldn't easily be discovered or breached, but they remained that way because no guild member spoke of them.

"Oh. That explains that, then." She nodded, and they lapsed back into silence as they passed a huddle of bedraggled children.

"Things can't continue this way," Derica murmured, brown eyes tightening at the corners.

"No, they can't," he agreed. Justus continued to lead them forward, but he turned a second later, walking backward and whistled to the tallest child. When their head jerked up, he flipped them a few gold coins. "They'll find room for you at the Tawny Owl, two blocks north. Tell the proprietress that Hadrian sent you."

The child nodded, a smile brightening their face. The others crowded near, hands reaching to hold the coins.

Facing forward again, Justus caught Derica blinking at him. "What?" he asked. Again, an unfamiliar heat climbed up his cheeks.

"That was kind."

"No, it was too little. It'll keep them warm and fed for a while, though." He shrugged, nervously putting his hands on his belt. When the dagger hilt bumped his wrist, the smile tugging at his lips melted. Silence descended again, the quiet weighted. They turned again, shops starting to intersperse the homes as the shopping district neared.

"Anyway, that doesn't seem like a good business practice for the guild. An entrance no one uses? Comes off a bit... mysterious and foreboding, doesn't it?" she mumbled.

That surprised a laugh out of him. "Ah, but that's what people want from a mercenary guild."

Derica's chin jerked up, and she stared at Justus. The tops of her cheeks colored, her enticing mouth hanging slightly open.

Gazes locked, they drifted to a standstill. Justus reached out his hand and crooked a knuckle under Derica's chin. She clicked her mouth shut at the touch, eyes sweeping down with a hitch of breath. His traitorous thumb swiped across the curve of her lower lip. The petal soft skin entranced his vision, seeing the way the peach-tinted flesh yielded. He didn't feel in control of his hands. Or his words.

Soft and low, he said, "That's what's expected of us. The complexity is the draw for our wealthy clients. It's a bit like wanting most the things you are denied."

He hadn't meant to say that. Those words implied something else. But now they lay between them, both a lure and a dare. To whom, he wasn't sure.

Derica's pupils expanded, and she swayed toward him. He snatched his hand away when he felt himself begin to lean down, aching to sip from her lips.

She was fucking intoxicating. This is how things spiraled out of control in the cottage.

He scrubbed a hand across his face. The rough scratch of Justus's stubble served to ground him enough to wake himself up.

"Yes, I can see how the curiosity and mystery is compelling," Derica breathed faintly.

Justus grunted and forced his feet to carry himself farther down the alley, renewing their trek to the market. He'd made sure to pick a route that wasn't well traveled.

Now, that seemed like folly.

Justus prided himself on his prowess in a fight, but around one woman, he was defenseless. He'd forgotten.

He'd allowed the passage of time without her to dull his memory. Justus remembered every lifetime, as he'd been cursed to. But the color of those memories had started to fade. He wondered how much of that was a conscious attempt to step away from the guilt and grief that followed him wherever he went.

"Ugh, wait! I'm coming," Derica called from behind.

Justus flinched, glad she couldn't see his face. Her words conjured her hoarse shout of pleasure as she came undone under him.

"Wait," she panted. The scuff of her shoes on the cobblestones announced she was right behind him. His tunic pulled from behind. His only warning was a rough *oof* before her body tumbled into his back.

Quickly, he braced his legs and kept them from crashing to the ground. For a moment.

Justus turned at the same time Derica pulled back, hand still twisted in his tunic. Her unexpected hold unbalanced him, his weight on the very edge of his heels, and they fell.

"Fuck," he grunted, clamping his arms around her sides and tugging her so he'd fall first. He managed to curl his head into the crook of her neck, and his shoulders took the brunt of their weight. Justus lost his breath. For a moment, he couldn't pull air back into his lungs.

"I'm so sorry! Oh, let me—" Derica cut off as she braced her hands on the ground next to his shoulders and attempted to push herself up and off of him.

Justus clutched greedy hands above her waist. Fuck breathing. He wanted this while he could have it. He would let her go in a moment.

"Don't," he managed, "move."

Derica peered down at him, her mouth pulled into a guilty grimace. Her hair floated along the sides of his face, tangling in his beard. Justus breathed in through his nose, filling his nostrils with the scent of lavender soap and soft woman.

"I'm so sorry." Her hands gently sifted through his tied-back hair, searching for injury from the crown of his head to the base of his neck. It sent licks of fire down his spine. If his shoulders weren't screaming in pain, he'd close his eyes and move her hands to something else that wanted stroking. "You're not bleeding. Can you move? Let me up. I can't be helping you breathe."

Later, he would blame her injury, or his, or the combination. But at this moment, all the reasons not to sink into her touch and savor the feel of her plush curves deserted him.

"I can breathe fine." Justus slowly skated one palm from high on her hip to the valley of her spine until he clasped the back of her neck, mindful of her bandage. Justus watched her eyes and listened for the tiniest hesitation or rejection.

If she accepted this, if Justus stopped trying to stifle this firestorm of desire, that's all it would be, he told himself. He had been empty and cold inside for so long. He would burn in the flames, and then watch her go. Justus wouldn't let the heat touch her.

If anyone was to be consumed, he was determined it would be him and him alone.

It was penance.

"Did the fall hurt your neck?" he asked. His thumb stroked her nape, wrapped in the silk of her flaming hair. Such gorgeous fire. Derica's head sunk closer, the curtain of her hair shutting out everything around them. All he could see and feel was her.

Something inside him unfurled and relaxed for the first time in lifetimes.

"N-no." Her breath hitched, and she swiped her tongue across her top lip. His eyes tracked the movement and lingered for a moment before coming back to meet hers.

They were sharing breaths, filling each other's lungs. Her pupils were blown, and Justus could feel her heart beating like a bird's wings against his ribs.

Justus moved his hand until his thumb grazed the edge of her mouth. "Are you sure?" His voice sounded rough. If he could manage a clear thought, he might have been embarrassed by exactly how rough.

Somehow this moment felt pulled out of time.

He wasn't a mercenary, determined to stay away from the woman he desperately wanted, and she wasn't the Weaver-blessed.

It was this thought that allowed him to grasp her chin and slowly, ever so slowly, guide her lips down to his.

The fervor at the cottage had been missing this lethargic indulgence. Derica's lips touched his tentatively. He was careful to let her control the pace and movement of the kiss, the pressure like the barest sweep of a rose petal across his lips.

His half-hard cock stirred, and he fought the urge to clamp her hips and grind into the soft, ample heat of her belly. Justus held himself still, the hand now on the back of her neck barely exerting any pressure. Its purpose was more to satisfy his thirst for the feel of her skin than to keep her from pulling away.

Justus realized he was being teased. The pressure of the kiss hadn't deepened. What was her game?

Derica pulled away, and he restrained himself from snatching her back and unleashing the inferno of his lust.

Her breath puffed onto his damp mouth. "Do you always seduce women on alley floors?" she asked, auburn brow quirked.

It felt like a challenge. So, he met it.

"I do not. I wouldn't call this a seduction. Would you like to see what that looks like?"

If she wasn't lying on top of him, he would have held his breath, waiting for her answer. Justus maintained a normal rhythm of air in and out of his lungs and kept his face blank. She could leave him here, and they would go to the market like nothing happened. Or he would escort her back to the church. Either way, if she stopped this, he would abide by her wishes.

But if she didn't...

The stroke of her hand against his cheekbone startled him. He'd been watching her doe-brown eyes for anger or distress.

Her thumb swiped an entrancing path. Justus's eyes fluttered, and he struggled to keep them open, lips pinched to stay the sigh of relief trapped in his chest.

"Yes, I think I would," Derica mused, tilting her head to the side. Watching.

His tongue wanted to spill forth honeyed words full of tender promises. It didn't matter that it would end with tragedy. It didn't matter that it would end with her blood once again staining his hands. His heart wanted to give her the words. The ones that would tie her to him, bind them in a way that ensured their painful ending.

If Derica felt the tension in his jaw or saw the desperation in his eyes, he hoped it seemed the interest of a man too long without a warm body in his bed.

Justus choked the words down, tucking them behind the brick wall, as well.

He would worship her body and pray at her altar. It would bring some surcease.

And that was all he would allow himself.

He gently clasped her hand and helped them sit up, then stand.

"Come with me," he said, reaching out his hand.

CHAPTER TWENTY-EIGHT

Derica thought this was madness, but the most delicious kind. She was a frenzy of need, and she needed to feel something—*anything*—to assuage the uncertainty she felt waking up this morning. Satisfying the hunger that had plagued her since that first taste of Justus in the cottage.

Justus's warm hand held Derica's in a steady grip as he led them through alleyways, away from the market. Her heart thudded in her chest, both from the adrenaline rush of healing someone on the cusp of Shredding last night, and at what she knew was coming next. Where he was taking her.

Memories of their last time flooded her as she followed him, the thrills that had skittered down her spine as his voice and hard body wrung such pleasure from hers. She knew he could make her feel alive—could make her body sing. Despite the bizarre reaction he'd had to their ill-advised—but explosive—coupling in the cottage, this felt different, and she was willing to succumb to his pull. The alleys grew narrower and narrower, turn after turn, and she wondered how his broad shoulders didn't get stuck. Justus navigated them with ease and familiarity. His steps never faltered as he pulled her along.

He looked back over his shoulder more than once, raking her body with hot, assessing looks. Firmly under his thrall, she was helpless to do anything but follow.

Her eyes dropped to their entwined hands. His fingers looked right, grasping hers. Like the contours of her fingers were made for the peaks of his. Like they were two halves of a whole. Her heart raced at that thought, but she knew better.

No matter the magnetic pull between herself and the mercenary, she understood there was no future for them.

No, this would be an itch scratched. A fire doused. A mercenary was not the home for her heart. And a homeless refugee who lived in a church was not the ideal partner for a mercenary.

There was no romance here—no soft words or warm feelings. None that were felt by them both. True, there was a draw, but she dismissed it as simple attraction. The only thing she would learn about the man in front of her was how much pleasure she could find in his arms. She held no claim to his history, nor his future.

She let her eyes rove over the width of his shoulders, down his broad back, to his slim waist. His belts and weapons made his size even more menacing. And yet, he was always incredibly careful and deliberate when he touched her.

"Where are we going?" she finally asked, still following him blindly.

He squeezed her hand. "A little farther," he murmured over his shoulder.

They rounded one last corner, and he stopped in front of a battered wooden door almost indistinguishable from the surrounding bricks. "We're here."

Derica raised her eyebrows skeptically, glancing around the alleyway and back at the door. She wasn't under the impression he was trying to woo her, but if this entrance led into some seedy, flea-ridden love den, he'd feel the sting of her palm before watching her walk away. She'd wander her way back to the church on her own if she had to.

With a quirk of a smile that had her clenching her thighs, Justus unlocked the door and pushed it open. He nodded for her to enter, and she hesitantly stepped over the threshold.

It was like being back in the cottage as he followed her into the dark building. She listened to clinks and rattles as he searched for a flint. The flare of the flame illuminated his midnight eyes and broad cheekbones as he lit a lantern, revealing the interior.

She blinked in surprise to find a neat but rather austere apartment. A large four-poster bed nestled in the far corner of the room, clearly spacious enough for the man next to her. And a partner. At the foot of the bed was a wide, wooden chest. Under her feet was the only item of noticeable luxury in the space—a plush, handwoven rug that whorled with intricate patterns and swirls of blues and grays. With its size and quality, Derica guessed it cost an alarming sum.

"Where are we?" she asked, still taking in the details. A basin and shaving implements sat on a rough wooden counter opposite the end of the bed, but the rest of the space was bare of clutter or keepsakes.

"The apartment I keep in the city," he answered from the doorway. Derica flicked her eyes toward him, spying him rubbing a hand over his jaw. "When I can't stomach the guild, I come here to get away. I don't see it as much as I would like."

Understanding sparked as she glanced around the sparsely decorated space once more. "A mercenary doesn't spend long in one place, do they?"

"No, we don't."

The rug muffled the sound of his steps. He clasped the tops of her shoulders, his chest brushing her back. An inch closer and his hips would cradle the top of her ass. She could feel the heat of his body as she turned her head and looked up to watch his face.

Justus's expression was solemn, but the fire of his lust shone in his obsidian eyes. It awakened an answering fire within her.

And she couldn't wait to burn.

His palms skated down the tops of her arms until he grasped both her hands in his. With a tug, he brought her back flush to his front. Justus's heat almost singed. She inhaled a gasp as his hard length burned like a brand through their clothing.

"This is where I come to be alone," he rumbled, a wry curve tugging his lips. The reverberation traveled through his chest, and she melted against him. He groaned, his hands slipping from hers and settling on her hips, walking them toward the bed.

At the side of the wide bed, Justus turned and guided her to sit. He stood between her legs, and her uptilted chin pointed at his chest. With a flick, he freed the button holding her cape closed and let it flutter to the ground.

Silent, Derica watched the way the lantern light moved across his broad hands. The play of his muscles under his forearms and hands as they undid the various buckles and sheaths securing his weapons to his body. The clang of metal and the brush of leather filled the space of the apartment. It was loud enough to hide how her breath came faster with each passing moment.

The wink of a red gem—the pommel of that strange dagger—briefly called to mind her vision, but it was forgotten in the next moment. Justus reached behind his neck and pulled his tunic off.

The expanse of scarred, lightly furred skin would have made anyone's mouth water. In the cottage, she hadn't seen much of him in the dark. At least, not like this. Witnessing his strength and beauty added to this encounter. It stoked the pyre of her need into an inferno.

He reached for the belt at his waist.

Derica put a hand out. "Let me?" she asked.

Eyes blazing fire, Justus nodded and dropped his hands. She loosened the belt's clasp with trembling fingers, guiding it through his pant loops, heat spreading through her body. He sucked in a breath when her fingers brushed his stomach. As she tugged the laces at the front, she sought his eyes for permission.

He dipped his chin. A muscle ticked at the side of his jaw, and his fisted knuckles whitened when she concentrated on untangling the threads. Derica's lips curved into a small smile at his obvious impatience.

It was a rush of power to have this strong man stand before her, holding himself still while she set the pace. She only hoped the power wouldn't become addicting.

When the placket fell open, Derica found herself grasping air as he stepped back. He toed off his boots and shucked his breeches like they were filled with burs.

She struggled not to laugh but choked on her amusement when he stood, shoulders back and spine straight—displaying his bare body for her perusal. Her eyes widened, taking in all of him. Derica's hands itched to trace the cuts of his muscles and the silvery scars that swiped here and there over his impressive form. Before she could do anything, Justus stepped forward, then knelt at her feet.

"Now, you," he said, gently grasping her foot and slipping it free of her boot. He repeated the action with the other.

Today she'd opted for stays paired with a loose, wide-necked tunic of soft blue tucked into her heavier, winter skirts. She reached behind her back for the clasp. The movement thrust her generous breasts forward, tugging the fabric taut.

Justus groaned, and watched hungrily, crouched in front of her.

"Too slow," he murmured, inching closer. "Much too slow."

Without waiting another moment, his hot mouth was on her breast, tonguing her nipple through the fabric. Dizzy with desire, her fingers fumbled on the clasp, but she managed to get it undone before moving her hands to the back of his head, urging him for more.

"Oh, there will be more," Justus said, lifting away briefly before moving to the other breast.

Derica realized she'd spoken the request aloud, but she couldn't be bothered to feel embarrassed. Her greedy fingers spread through his hair, pulling it free of its tail. Loose, it brushed the tops of his shoulders. The dark curtain reflected the lantern light, and seeing her fingers tangled in the deep brown strands incited something ferally possessive inside her.

Having this man who was always so contained naked and on his knees for her was an aphrodisiac of a whole new kind. She'd never felt so wanting and empty.

His hair slipped through her grasp as he stood and gathered her tunic.

"I want you bare," Justus growled, guiding the garment off and then whipping it away to flutter to the rug behind him. He deftly tugged her stays free, and they joined her tunic. The flat of his palm on her clavicle pressed her onto her back.

Her skin touched the bed beneath her, and Derica sucked in a breath. The sheets smelled like him. She watched as he tilted her hips up and drew her skirts down, leaving her only in her thin lawn pantalettes. Then, they too floated to the ground behind Justus as cool air kissed her pebbled nipples and revealed just how wet the insides of her thighs were.

"Much better," he said.

Reclining with her legs hanging off the bed, Derica watched as he stood in between her thighs. He kept far enough away, teasing the ache he stoked, but she still felt his heat.

Justus's hands circled Derica's ankles. Then he dragged his grip up her legs to her calves, cupping the backs of her knees. With every inch he moved his callused palms, he left a wake of tingling desire. Her core lay exposed and his eyes on her glistening pink skin were like a physical stroke.

Shifting his body in front of her, he settled his hips into the cradle of hers. His obsidian gaze glittered, the thin golden band circling his pupils twinkling in the dim light. The sight of it spurred the liquid heat in her veins faster. The ache in her core intensified, and she shifted her legs, trying to cross her ankles at his back.

Justus's hands gripped her hips, pressing her firmly but gently into the bed beneath her, halting her movement.

"No," he breathed, his eyes closing momentarily, jaw clenched. "Not yet."

Derica reached for his shoulders, desperate for the weight of his body on hers. For him. For this.

Again, he shook his head, keeping out of her range—this time with a wicked smirk on his full lips, his eyes black fire.

Using his weight, he kept her still and slid his hands down her legs, trailing his rough fingers reverently over every bump and hollow. His eyes followed the entire slow journey, wicked satisfaction evident in his dark gaze—watching her shiver under his hands. It made her burn hotter.

When he firmly clamped both ankles in the shackles of his grip, Justus flicked her a hungry, enigmatic look. The smirk playing at his lips beckoned her to taste, to bite, to consume. Holding her stare, he dipped down momentarily to watch her tongue swipe across her lips.

Derica saw the tick at the corner of his jaw. He was as wound up as she was, despite the control he projected. Her mouth slid into a smirk of her own. Justus's gaze sharpened on her face, eyes narrowing. The next moment, he hiked both her ankles onto the wide plane of his shoulders. Gooseflesh danced up her legs as he turned his head, his hot breath puffing against the inside of her ankle. Then warm lips, soft like sun-warmed silk, pressed to her skin. Her lungs hitched in her chest, and her core clenched.

He hummed against her, dragging his kiss down. The scrape of his dark stubble and the softness of his lips had her grinding her hips back into the mattress, seeking something—anything—to ease the ache Justus ratcheted higher.

Reaching the bend of her knee, he halted—only to turn to the other leg and replicate his journey from ankle to knee.

By the time Justus reached his destination, Derica's breaths came in short pants. She fought to keep from moaning her frustration.

Despite the desire pooling in her core, she refused to let her control shatter before his. Derica needed to see him undone. To make the perfectly controlled man who was a living weapon become nothing more than sensation and pleasure in her arms. She would not lose herself in this alone. They would both drown in this maelstrom of feeling. Derica would not allow him to hold himself back.

"I need—" she panted. "I need—"

"Yes? What is it you need?" Justus's tongue lapped at the dimple beside her knee. A stream of warm breath blew across the wetness and she arched up, desperate for the teasing to end.

Derica decided this was enough of his slow torture.

She surged up, fisted one hand loosely in the hair at his nape, and pulled him down on top of her. Justus puffed out a surprised chuckle, white teeth flashing. The curve on his lips and the crinkle at the corner of his eyes suggested he thought he was still in control.

With a hand still speared into his thick, dark hair, she guided his mouth to hers. As they exchanged breaths, teeth and tongues clashed. Derica smiled as she wound her calf around Justus's trunk of a leg. He groaned and ground into the apex of her thighs. She almost abandoned her plan when his hot length roughly caressed her bare clit.

His loss of control was too strong an enticement, though.

A quick shift of her hips and a shove to his broad shoulders, and Derica flipped their positions. Justus's delighted bark of laughter reverberated from his chest into her palms.

She sat astride him now. Looking through curtains of her red hair and down into heavy-lidded midnight eyes, Derica took a moment to assess the mercenary.

A ruddy flush colored the tops of his cheekbones and his wet lips shone in the glow from the lantern. His hair was a wild tumble, loose from its usual severe tail, and the strands tangled in his darker stubble. He looked wanton, but his eyes were still too clear. Too sharp. She wanted to see them hazed with pleasure—lost to sensation.

The thrill of having this powerful man at her mercy had her practically dripping in anticipation.

Derica traced the silvered scar slashing from beside his nostril to his full, lush lips with her forefinger. She cupped her hand beneath his chin and guided his jaw up. She stared into his onyx eyes as she bared the long, tanned column of his throat. He tensed, his hands rising to her hips. Broad, callused palms tightened on her bare skin, grip firm enough to warn her Justus didn't appreciate this loss of control.

"What—"

"Shhh," she cut him off. Derica bit her lip to restrain her feral grin.

She leaned down into his chest, her breasts pillowed against the deliciously hard plane, and ground her clit against his rigid erection. She kissed the hollow at the base of his throat and flicked her tongue out to taste.

Justus's palms spasmed on her hips and then moved to cup her ass, guiding her into a rougher grind.

She trailed her lips to the side, sweeping a path of damp caresses until she closed her teeth over the sensitive lobe of his ear. Derica bit down slowly and firmly while dragging her tongue over the heated flesh.

His chest expanded on a gasp and Derica exhaled sharply when he jerked his hips up into her. Derica was still—barely—in enough control herself to draw back and assess him.

Justus's breath sawed from between his clenched teeth, brackets of strain framing his delicious mouth. His hips restless and rocking beneath her, his gaze slightly unfocused as it trained on her lips. Lips that felt swollen and buzzed with the scrape of his stubble. Swiping her tongue leisurely across them, she watched him fray further. It prompted a thrill of dark satisfaction—almost enough to launch her into her first orgasm. She was determined there would be many.

Leaning back so she could trail a lazy hand down his hitching chest, she traced a path to her prize—slowly—through the furrow bisecting his stomach created by the ropes of carved muscles.

With a wicked grin, she realized she held mastery over his body. And the feeling was decadent.

At the flash of her smile in the dimly lit room, the steady rock of his hips lost its rhythm. It edged over into desperate—this side of frantic.

Finally.

Derica flattened her palm an inch below his navel, entirely neglecting the impressive erection standing proudly beneath. She stilled his movement long enough to show him her whims were law at this moment.

His desire was incandescent behind his midnight stare. It stole her breath, threatening to banish the control she was barely clinging to. Derica wanted—*needed*—a few minutes more of this power.

She trailed a finger down, slowly, while watching his control disintegrate under her touch. Derica gloved his cock in her hand. Staring down into his enraptured gaze, she firmly dragged her grip up before twisting her wrist when she met the head. His full-body shudder of pleasure accompanied a hoarse, ragged groan of surrender.

Shifting her hips higher, Derica gave him the reins. "Now," she breathed.

Hot, hard palms clamped her ass and pulled her roughly down onto his length. She tossed her head back and followed his guiding grasp until he was seated fully inside her.

Then the world spun when Justus rolled Derica under him. The scrape of stubble at her throat and the damp lips dragging at the skin beneath her ear had her desperately clenching her core around him.

"Did you have fun? Do you think your teasing deserves a reward?" His woodsmoke voice curled around her, a sibilant hiss. It both promised and threatened retribution. She felt the impending tremor of her orgasm and jerked her hips, chasing the sensation.

Justus held her pinned against the pallet. She raked her nails up the jerking muscles of his broad back and clamped her teeth on the top of his shoulder. With a muffled curse, he pulled away and slammed into her. He slipped his thumb down, strumming her clit.

That's all it took. Her vision narrowed, and she keened when she catapulted into crashing waves of pleasure. Justus stayed unmoving, propped above her and fully seated inside her, watching the tremors subside.

When Derica inhaled a deep breath and met his eyes, what she saw awed her. Midnight eyes lacked his previous fervor. Instead, he looked at her with wonder and affection. It was like he battled this softness and finally surrendered. The mood shifted with that one caress. His lips brushed her ear as he bent down over her.

"I was a fool," he rumbled. "There's no fighting this."

Derica frowned at his words, but then the tip of Justus's nose stroked down the side of her throat and he began to move again, slower—with reverence. His lips sipped at the shallow dip in the middle of her collarbones and she forgot her confusion. He placed the softest kiss there. Derica's vision misted with unexpected tears.

"There's a pull—a tie to you I don't think I could ever ignore," he rumbled into her ear, breath labored. "Wanting to ignore it means nothing. Every fiber of my being wants to hold you, touch you, care for you. Until the universe is dust around us, that's all I could ever want." With every word, every thrust, he stoked the fever in her blood higher. His lips moved further, seeking her jutting nipple. Justus's hair trailed over her sensitized skin, leaving consuming fire in their wake. He continued, "From the day I set eyes on you in Arlan, my whole being wanted nothing but you. I fought it. Weaver knows I fought it. Endeavoring to stay away from you is like asking a starving man not to eat at a feast. Impossible. *Absurd.*"

Derica's eyelids drifted shut to the hypnotic cadence of Justus's voice. With his words, he banished the urgency she felt. She was no longer trying to glut herself as quickly as possible on the pleasure he offered.

Now, she was like the poppies that grew behind her cottage as a child, blooming fragrant and sweet under the heat of the summer sun. Her limbs were languid. The scrape of Justus's beard and the tug of his teeth at her breast was a bright counterpoint to the lethargy that stole over her. Raking her fingers up the broad plane of his back, she arched her plush curves into his hard chest, purring at the dichotomy of their bodies.

Without moving his mouth from her nipple, Justus growled against her skin and pulled almost completely from her body, then sharply plunged back in. Derica gasped in ecstasy, eyes slipping closed—feeling the beginnings of a second orgasm mount.

"You still with me? You looked a bit like a cat napping in the sun." His voice was full of wicked pleasure and decadent promise.

Derica opened her eyes and found his fever-bright gaze breaths from her own.

His soft words and gentle lips couldn't hide Justus's reaction to her. Sweat trickled down his temples and highlighted the delicious dip above his top lip. As she watched, a bead traveled the path of his scar. Grasping his nape, Derica flicked out her tongue, tracing the course of the salty drop. His moan reverberated against her mouth and then Justus was kissing her with such single-minded intent—like she was precious air and he was a man drowning. They began moving simultaneously, the rhythmic sound of passion-damp-ened skin a staccato beat that filled the small room.

Justus's hand threaded through Derica's flame-red hair, tenderly cradling the back of her head. It was a sharp contrast to the way they writhed together everywhere else their bodies met. He trailed blunt-tipped fingers down to the base of her neck and tilted her head up to meet his eyes.

Obsidian irises greeted her stare. Despite the intensity of his continued thrusts and her frenzied grind to take them, his voice was a calm, cool thrill up the center of her spine. "You are the sun to a man starved of warmth and light. You are *everything*, Derica."

For a second time, tears stung her eyes. A drop escaped and trailed down her cheek. He kissed it away and leaned back. A callused hand reached down to her clit while he thrust at the perfect angle. She shattered, and he followed her moments later.

Justus collapsed onto her then rolled to the side. He gathered Derica into his chest, cradling her with care in his powerful arms. He pressed a kiss into her damp temple and whispered barely loud enough for her to catch, "Never again."

CHAPTER TWENTY-NINE

The Savior clenched their teeth, footsteps pounding an angry beat as they descended the stairs again. Things would be much more pleasant if people freely shared the information they were asked for.

There would be no need to resort to other means if cooperation was immediate.

Their shoulders lifted on an inhale and then settled low with a sigh. The dance of firelight from the Savior's torch ebbed and flowed across the stone stairwell. As they approached the bottom, the familiar smell of damp and vellum greeted them. It was a comforting, nostalgic scent that calmed the Savior's frustration slightly.

This time, after the Savior entered the chamber storing precious tomes, they immediately turned left and walked into a narrow hallway, older and more weathered than the surroundings.

It was here that heretics, traitors, and the wicked were kept.

It truly saddened the Savior that the couple was being held here, but they simply needed to give the requested information to improve their lodgings.

Torchlight bounced around the narrow hallway, glancing off the dark metal of the cells that lined the space. The only occupied cell was second to last on the left. In front of the bars stood two figures. Their attire matched that of the Savior—the only difference was the weapons strapped to their waists.

An unfortunate necessity.

The Savior nodded to the two guards, and they filed down the hallway.

"And how are we this evening? Do you have answers for me?" the Savior asked. Their voice was steady and low. Polite.

The couple in the cell shifted and moved toward the bars. They huddled together, squinting at the light of the torch.

The woman answered first. She seemed to have been elected the speaker for the two. "We have nothing else to tell you. Nothing you haven't already heard."

"I disagree." The Savior crouched down so they could peer directly into the eyes of the older couple.

The woman had dirty tear tracks lining her cheeks. Her hair was in disarray. The man was in worse shape. One of his eyes was swollen shut and blood crusted a cut through his silvered brow.

The Savior wasn't a monster. The woman had not been touched.

Yet.

The Savior mused, "I think you have much to tell me yet, but maybe you need some help remembering." They reached into their clothing and extracted a book. "I have brought something to shake loose your memory." They straightened and placed their torch into the timeworn sconce hanging next to the cell. Carefully turning the pages, the Savior found what they sought and turned the pages toward the couple. "I apologize for the quality of the light, but this is the mark I wish to know about. I have every reason to believe it's quite familiar to you both."

The woman gasped, and the man placed a comforting arm around her. She huddled into him for a moment, then turned back, shrugging out of his hold. Her face was hard and her cleft chin didn't tremble when she spoke.

"What have you done with her?"

"Oh, I assure you. Absolutely not one hair on her head has been harmed," The Savior paused, "by me."

The man finally spoke, his voice gruff. "You won't touch her at all if you know what's good for you."

"I don't think you have much to bargain with. I can't guarantee her safety unless you tell me what I need to know."

"We've told you before," the man snarled. "There's—"

"What do you mean *by you*?" the woman interrupted.

The Savior turned, facing away from the cell. They clasped their hands behind their back. "There was quite a miraculous event the other day. The girl was injured, but she is well now." Quietly, they added, "Your son saw to her wound."

A hitching, high-pitched sob escaped from the woman before her husband shushed her.

"Maybe you'd like a visit from him?" the figure asked "We could accommodate him in the cell next to yours. Would that make you more amenable to my questions?"

"Listen here, you will not touch my children! You filthy pile of pig shit, you will not hurt them!" cried the woman, beating and rattling the bars of the cell.

The Savior clucked their tongue. A mother's love was sacred, and it almost pained them to use it in this instance. When faced with unpleasant choices, decisions still had to be made.

The salvation of Veridion depended on the Savior's ability to make those decisions.

Turning back around, they saw the woman sobbing quietly into her husband's chest. Oh, if looks could kill, the hatred in those blue eyes would slaughter the Savior where they stood.

"I will not harm them." Again, the Savior held out the book and the drawing to the couple. "Although, only the boy is yours, correct? The girl is not," they mused.

"She *is* mine. She may not have come from my loins, but she is as much mine—*ours*—as he is," the woman turned her head and articulated with surprising menace.

"I only want to help her," the Savior soothed. "I'm going to help her fulfill her purpose."

"And you think by locking up and abusing her family, you will ensure her cooperation?" the man asked incredulously.

"Assurances are necessary in this world." They waved the book in front of the cell, trying to maintain calm. Anger was not a tool that would help this endeavor. "Now, tell me what I need to know. Please."

They watched as the couple examined the pages, and then looked at each other, silently communicating.

When the man sighed, a thrill of triumph coasted down the Savior's back. *Finally.*

The man pushed the woman behind him again and squared his shoulders. "We will not help you. Do whatever you wish with us, but you will not harm our children with our assistance."

The Savior stepped close to the bars and then sank lower to be level with the man.

"I think it's time for a visit from your son then, hm?"

The couple's faces crumpled in unison. It was almost heartwarming to see such concern and care for their children. They loved them dearly.

That love was jeopardizing them all.

Other arrangements would have to be made.

The Savior straightened, took the torch from the sconce, and walked back down the long hallway. The woman's wailing and the man's tearful attempts to soothe her followed.

They halted at the entrance. The two guards had been waiting.

"Bring him to me," the Savior said.

The guards nodded, hoods bobbing.

Now for the other headache that had been plaguing the Savior.

Opposite the hallway where the couple was being kept, there was another long corridor. It was not filled with cells. A heavy, thick wooden door guarded it; it had been built to keep noise in.

It was failing.

A litany of wails and screams filtered faintly through the oak door.

The Savior placed a palm on the barrier, feeling the reverberation of the suffering inside

"Soon. We will fix this soon," they promised.

CHAPTER THIRTY

Derica burrowed deeper into the blankets, pulling the covers over her head. She pressed her nose into the pillow and breathed in. It smelled heavenly.

Like him.

Her eyes flashed open, and Derica popped up. The covers slid down to her waist and cold air assaulted her breasts. Shivering, she tugged the blankets up to her collarbone.

Her gaze searched the apartment, unseeing for a moment as she remembered where she was. And who she'd been with.

And what they'd done.

"Jus... Justus?" she called, faintly.

Nothing.

Derica flopped back onto the bed and exhaled through her nose.

The tiny apartment didn't have any windows, but Justus had been kind enough not to leave her in the dark.

The lantern he'd lit before their indulgence was still softly illuminating the small room.

A wry chuckle escaped Derica. What had she thought? That they would wake together, profess feelings of love, and live happily ever after?

The smile slid off her face. Staring at the ceiling, she wondered where Justus had gone. She couldn't even tell what time it was. Had she slept through the whole day?

Disappointment suffused her thoughts as she recalled the words he'd spoken while worshipping her body. Derica had let herself hope maybe she could have more with Justus.

THUMP THUMP THUMP!

"Commander!"

Derica squeaked and huddled into the blanket.

THUMP THUMP THUMP!

"Open the fucking door, you Weaver-damned coward!"

She didn't recognize the voice, and she was absolutely not opening the door for whoever that might be.

Derica crept towards the edge of the bed. She stood on quiet feet and tiptoed to the chest where Justus had neatly folded her clothing.

She felt a melting somewhere in the vicinity of her heart. She mentally froze it again.

"The man can fold fabric. That means fuck-all," she whispered to herself as she dressed.

As she laced her stays, a key turned in the lock.

Derica snatched her tunic from the trunk and held it against her chest, backing toward the wall as the door swung open.

"I don't know how you got your rank when you never—" the voice cut off. Derica blinked, and so did the intruder.

"Who—"

"—are you?" they spoke together.

The woman standing in the doorway wore clothing similar to what Justus and his mercenaries wore. Dark, belted breeches, sturdy-looking leather boots, and a plain tunic in a hue that matched her pants. Her skin was a luminous, deep brown. She had a wealth of black hair, made up of small, intricate braids, coiled at the crown of her head.

"I'm Alondra and I'm looking for the commander. Now, who are you?"

"I'm Derica." She doubted that cleared up who she was, but it was all she could offer.

"Derica, hm?" Alondra flicked her stare down to the fabric Derica was shielding herself with. "I'll turn away and let you finish dressing. How about that?"

She nodded, voice stalled in her throat.

Alondra turned toward the closed door and presented Derica with her back.

Trying not to curse, Derica tossed the tunic over her head, and then tucked it into her rumpled skirts. Justus's folding hadn't saved them from wrinkling.

She swiped her damp palms down the front of her skirt and cleared her throat.

"All done?" Alondra asked.

"Y-yes."

"Very good." Alondra turned around and continued her visual inspection of Derica.

Derica gnashed her teeth and started an investigation of her own.

The weapons that hung at the woman's wide hips were different than she'd seen on the other mercenaries. Sleeker. The curved blades on each hip had a subtle, artistic flair, ornate pommels peeking out of their leather scabbards.

"So *you're* Derica." Alondra sauntered toward her and then circled.

Derica turned with her, determined to keep this stranger in her sight.

"Oh, Maz said you were something else, but I was expecting..." she paused in front of the redhead, pondering her with crinkled brows.

"What were you expecting?" Derica said, crossing her arms over her chest and popping out her hip.

Alondra smiled suddenly, and there was an edge to it. An edge softened by the twin dimples that accented the flash of her teeth.

"There it is!" Alondra kept smirking as she turned away, examining the apartment now that her curiosity about Derica was appeased. "So did the commander leave a note? Say where he was going?"

A chilling thought occurred to Derica. Was Alondra meeting the commander here for a tryst of their own?

She observed the other woman moving around the small space. Alondra navigated Justus's dwelling with confidence and familiarity. She strode to the trunk at the end of the bed and opened the latch. Her dark head disappeared behind the lid as she opened it.

"There's really no note?" Alondra asked again.

Derica cleared her throat. "No. Not that I've found." There weren't a plethora of places a message could be hiding.

"Just like the commander. I've never met a man more close-lipped," Alondra said, letting the trunk slam shut. Derica was proud that she didn't jump at the sudden noise.

Alondra sat on the closed trunk and leaned back on her hands. Derica wanted to squirm at how close she was being examined. She settled for crossing her arms and meeting Alondra's frank stare with cool indifference.

Alondra turned her head and glanced at the bed over her shoulder. The covers lay in a messy pile; the rumpled pillows clearly suggested two people had slept there.

The woman's nose wrinkled as she sniffed. With a little huffed laugh, she turned back to Derica. Settling her elbows onto her thighs, Alondra leaned toward Derica.

"So," she whispered, "how was he?"

Derica's mouth hung open.

Alondra laughed at the look on her face. "Oh, you didn't think the commander and I...?" she trailed off, trying but failing to hold in more laughter. "That man is too cold for me. I like my bed partners with a bit more fire. And a lot more to say."

"Like Mazolan?" Derica needed to work on not blurting out every stupid question that popped into her head.

Alondra barked a delighted laugh. "I like you. I knew I would from what Maz and Nyle said."

"Who are you?"

"I'm the head of the Radley mercenary guild. But before that, I was the commander's commander." At Derica's look of surprise, she continued. "Yes, those three idiots used to report to me. But, that was a long time ago now. Hadrian was supposed to deliver some supplies yesterday. He didn't show up. Mazolan and Nyle couldn't tell me where to find Hadrian—which is extremely odd in itself. For the commander not to complete an obligation to the guild? Unheard of." Alondra nodded over her shoulder at the unmade bed. "Now I understand why."

Derica willed herself not to blush, but her cheeks and the tops of her ears heated. She remembered Justus giving that exact reason for inviting her to the market with him. And now it was the next day. With a sinking feeling, she hoped Reid and Father Simond weren't worried and looking for her.

"I don't know where he went," Derica said, proud that her voice didn't betray her embarrassment.

"That's crystal clear, sweetheart. Strange that he was the one who left, though. It's normally his partners that he flings out the door as soon as possible. But then again," Alondra considered Derica from head to toe, "he's been acting differently since his last visit to the city."

"And you know so much about how he treats his partners because...?"

Alondra's lips twitched. "Mazolan was correct, as ever. You are exactly what the commander needs." She shook her head ruefully, "I know because Mazolan is a shameless gossip. They keep me up on the latest about Nyle and Hadrian too. Honestly, I don't know how they collect some of their information." She raised her eyebrows and asked, "Well, since Hadrian didn't tell you where he was going, shall we keep each other company waiting for him? Or I can escort you home, if you'd like?"

Derica warmed to the other woman offering to see her home. She opened her mouth to answer when the door to the apartment opened and faint morning light filtered in from the alley.

Justus stepped over the threshold, holding a cloth sack that appeared full and heavy. He carefully set it down inside the entrance. He looked up and halted when he saw Derica standing in the middle of the apartment and Alondra seated opposite on the trunk.

"Can I assume those are supplies you were supposed to pick up for the guild yesterday, Commander?" asked Alondra.

Justus heaved a sigh and stepped all the way into his quarters, closing the door behind him. "Yes," he answered, avoiding Derica's gaze.

"See?" Alondra said to Derica. "*Much* too contained for me."

Justus frowned. His beard was a little thicker than it had been six months ago, but Derica could still see the characteristic tick of his jaw. She could almost feel it against her skin.

"And what reason do you have for the late delivery?" Alondra asked, crossing her legs and leaning her chin on her uptilted palm. Her eyes glittered with mirth, but her face was smooth and blank.

Justus gazed at Derica for a fraction of a second, then lost the battle and returned her stare fully. His dark eyes heated and flashes of last night flitted through Derica's mind. The feel of his body and the phantom caresses of his lips across her skin. The number of times they'd woken to lose themselves again in the other's body sent another wash of color to her cheeks.

Justus noticed her flush and satisfaction joined the heat in his eyes.

"Interesting," interrupted Alondra, pulling Derica from the spell of his stare. "It's clear what the distraction was. You're lucky this order contained nothing essential."

Voices came through the door, Mazolan's among them. "I'm telling you, this is the last place to look and Alondra would have been back by now if—"

"Maz, don't. We should wait back at the guild," came Nyle's calm tenor. "Don't!"

The door swung open behind Justus, almost knocking him aside.

Maz stood grinning in the doorway, Nyle peering over the demon's shoulder with a pained grimace on his face.

"Ah! The party is here. I told you, Nyle!" Maz crowed and swept around Justus into the apartment.

Nyle looked apologetically at Justus and shut the door behind him.

"Lonnie!" Maz launched themselves at the woman, pecking her with an exuberant kiss on the cheek.

Alondra threw back her head and laughed huskily.

Both Nyle and Justus wore identical looks of exasperation.

Derica's morning had become increasingly entertaining. She tried and failed to conceal a giggle.

Four pairs of eyes focused on her.

Mazolan gasped, rushing to stand in front of Derica. "Morsel!" They gathered Derica's hands in theirs. They leaned in and whispered only for her, "Good. He needs to change if he wants to alter the outcome. Keep pushing him." Mazolan patted Derica's hand before pulling back and withdrawing to sit next to Alondra on the trunk.

Speaking to the demon was always a little like trying to decipher a foreign language. Derica didn't know the dialect and had no clue how to translate.

Alondra and Maz chatted amiably, having dismissed the rest of them.

Derica looked at Justus and Nyle. They were both watching her. Justus appeared to be telegraphing an apology for Maz, and Nyle was cool as always. On closer inspection, though, the tattooed mercenary did look happy to see her. A smile hovered at the corners of his mouth.

"Alondra," Justus cut through the pair's chatter firmly, "why don't you have Maz bring the supplies back to the guild and take Nyle. I'll escort... my companion home."

Nyle couldn't conceal a flinch at the word companion. Mazolan frowned and clucked their tongue while Alondra raised her eyebrows. She stood and jerked a chin at the demon and Nyle, letting them know they should lead her out of the apartment.

On the way by Justus, Alondra reached up and clapped him on the shoulder with a resounding slap. She leaned forward and whispered something Derica couldn't hear. Nyle barked a laugh behind the Commander, and Justus grimaced but nodded.

Nyle smiled kindly at Derica, waving to her before picking up the sack of supplies. Mazolan stepped by Derica and murmured, "Remember. Keep pushing." Alondra was the last out, tossing Derica an invitation to visit the guild over her shoulder. She didn't wait for an answer.

The trio left, and Justus pushed the door closed behind them. He braced his hands against the frame and leaned his forehead against the wood. His shoulders rose and fell as he took several deliberate deep breaths.

Derica moved to occupy the seat Alondra had vacated, waiting for him to turn around.

The abrupt silence after the others' departure worsened with every moment.

Mazolan wanted her to push? She could push.

The surprise and delight of Justus's whispered, tender words from last night withered in the tense moment.

"Companion?" she asked, voice cracking like a whip through the small space.

He sighed against the door and dropped his arms before facing her.

Justus's face was carefully blank and his voice bored as he asked, "You don't think last night entitled you to a marriage proposal, do you?"

Derica reared back, her jaw dropping open.

"Good, I see it didn't. *Companion* seemed accurate and polite," he shrugged. His face was blank, but his eyes...

His eyes still simmered with heat.

Derica didn't know what was between them, but it had defied her attempts to brush off or ignore. At that moment, she became determined to explore whatever this was. She had spent too much of her life holding back, afraid to pursue what she wanted. Afraid to live.

Her face must have given away her stubborn determination because Justus shifted into something like a battle-ready stance—arms loose at his sides, knees slightly bent.

"The words you spoke last night and the way you treat me this morning are at odds." Derica flung the observation like it was a bomb.

Justus scoffed a laugh. "You haven't ever heard of a man being guided by his prick? Weaver, you *are* naïve." His face was granite and his shoulders were tight. Still, his eyes...

"My father was one such man. You didn't strike me as the same type."

"And what kind of man am I? You know *nothing* at all about me—and it should remain that way."

"Why?" she whispered.

"Because you were a warm, enthusiastically willing body yesterday. Through the night as well. I should take the rustic jobs more often if all the women are like you." The second the words left his lips, it was clear he'd crossed a line. "I—"

"Are you done?"

"Done?" His calm facade cracked, and Justus's eyebrows furrowed.

Derica squared her shoulders, "I'm well aware a night of passion does not signify or constitute a relationship beyond the physical. I had simply thought there was the potential for more. I wanted to explore that. But if you're de-termined to be an ass, I'd better be leaving." The words were harder to say than she guessed they would be, and she was surprisingly nervous awaiting his reply.

Justus appeared out of sorts at her declaration. Through the crack in the facade, she saw intense longing, deep sorrow, and frantic anger slide over his features in quick succession. He moved his hands to his hips and stared down at his feet.

It was a peculiar gesture for the man who always seemed so cool—unless he was burning her up with desire. Then, he was flame and unconstrained passion. He had yet to show that heat and fervor unless they were in each other's arms.

Somehow, she knew something was there. It just required coaxing.

A *push*.

"Why?" he asked, voice low, still looking down at his feet.

"Why what?"

"Why would you want anything more with me?"

"You said last night there was a pull. You don't remember?"

Justus looked up, and the longing that blanketed his expression shocked Derica. She wanted to go to him and wrap her arms around him.

"I remember," he rumbled. "But why?"

"You think that pull is one-sided?" she rasped.

The surprise on his face was answer enough.

"But... you don't re—" He cut himself off with an angry groan.

"I don't, what?"

"You don't know what the life of a mercenary is like. The travel is incessant and long. Dangerous, obviously. What kind of relationship, much less a life, would that be for you? For that matter, you don't even know me well enough to consider wanting that."

"You're right," she said.

Justus looked up and something shattered in his eyes. He didn't understand.

"I don't know you well," Derica continued. "I would like to, though. If you would like to give in to the pull—to see what we could be."

The mercenary, the man she'd seen in battle, so competent and fierce, was scared. It was plain in his eyes, in the way his shoulders curled inward, the way he watched her so intently. For her to take back the words, perhaps? For her to condemn his chosen life? To condemn *him*?

Derica would do none of those things.

For she had learned that life was long, and yet so incredibly short. Her mother, who should still be alive, was taken by an unjust sickness. The danger of the Shredded lurked outside of Radley—maybe even within now, too.

Justus looked up to the ceiling, having found no answers on the floor at his feet. His left hand lightly traced the pommel of the dagger he always wore.

The familiar ruby and dark metal chilled her, stalling her thoughts.

Had it been a vision or a hallucination? Maybe a waking dream?

That's all it could have been.

She'd dreamt of death and battle, so her mind had plucked a recognizable weapon from her memory.

That's all it had been.

CHAPTER THIRTY-ONE

J ustus wasn't strong enough for this.

He would rather face a horde of bandits, fight an army battalion alone, or listen to Mazolan pontificate until his ears bled.

He had been offered the thing he wanted most, and his acceptance would only hurt the woman holding out her heart to him.

His heart was already so bruised, so heavy with guilt that it must match the hue of the dark dagger that hung at his hip.

That knowledge didn't keep him from wanting to sink to her feet and worship the gift she offered. Justus already questioned the strength he would need to learn the way she cried out in passion, how she looked when she came apart in his arms, and then walk away. If he gave in, if he explored everything Derica was, he knew—as sure as he knew the cursed dagger always found him—that he would never leave her side.

In the heat of passion, he'd bared his heart. He didn't know what made him think she'd forget the words that had come out of his mouth. He never would. And now she was making it impossible for him to walk away.

First thing this morning, he knew he had to leave. Not just the apartment but the sanctuary of her arms. That was the only action that would clear his head.

Wryly, he wanted to laugh. There was no escaping her—them. Justus was too weak. He was already in her thrall, and he would sink to oblivion in her arms, if she asked.

Justus startled when soft fingers clasped his forearm.

He looked down into Derica's warm brown eyes and felt his determination crack further.

Slowly reaching her other hand up, giving him the opportunity to pull away, she cupped his jaw gently.

He allowed his eyes to drift shut as he breathed in the scent of her. It fired his blood and whet his appetite. He'd forgotten the all-consuming hunger for her. Not just physically, but her laugh, her voice, her scent.

And here she was, offering him the chance to have it all.

"Why are you scared?" she murmured.

In every lifetime, the Weaver-blessed read the Warrior like they were a language only they understood. Although each unique pairing varied when that connection formed, it was always a moment of profound gratitude for him—to have someone who saw all of him—and chose to stay.

This was damned early for her to be reading him so well.

He sighed, succumbing to the comfort of her thumb stroking his chin. "It has been a very, very long time since I have let anyone know me like you are asking to know me."

"And why does that frighten you?" Her voice wrapped around him, coaxing him.

"I am not a good man. These hands," he lifted them, showing her his palms, "are stained with blood—"

"Shh." Derica laid a finger across his lips.

The kiss he pressed to her skin was a reflex from long ago. It kicked his heart into a gallop. Things *were* settling into the familiar much too quickly.

"I don't know everything, but I do know you command the respect of two comrades—people I cannot imagine would follow an unjust man," she said.

"I think that's generous when you consider Mazolan."

She laughed, and the sound eased the tension in his chest. Almost unintentionally, Justus's hand reached up and fingered a strand of her fiery hair. Her laughter stuttered as she watched him rub the skein between his finger and thumb. Carefully, he tucked it behind her ear before stroking her jaw and dropping his hand.

Another brick in the wall around his heart tumbled to the ground.

Last night had damaged that barrier. Once fortified, it was now objectively crumbling.

It was fucking terrifying.

Her eyes were luminous, and her breath puffed from between her lips just a bit faster.

"And if I say yes, how does this work?" he murmured, fitting a hand to the notch in her waist above the bounty of her hips.

"Um," she blinked. "I—I think we simply spend time together. When you aren't away because of a contract."

His thumb drew circles slowly and firmly on the fabric of her skirt. "Doing what?" Her pupils expanded, and his cock started to swell. The memory of Derica wrapped around him last night muddied where he was going with this line of questioning, and he struggled to hold onto his reason.

"Well... you can escort me on my errands for the church. We can—we could attend events together. The Winter Fête is coming up?" she offered, licking her lips as he brought his other hand up, now stroking her hips with both hands.

"Is that all? Hear me when I say this, Derica. There won't be anyone else for me. I know this in my bones. I also know I'm not a safe choice. I am not a *good* choice." He looked deeply into her eyes, making sure she saw the truth in his gaze. "You are safer far, far away from me."

She slowly shook her head, staring at his lips. "I don't believe that."

You never do.

"It's true. But staying away has proved impossible for me," Justus answered. Then he succumbed to temptation and sank lower to take her lips with his.

This kiss was softer than all the ones that came before. It was an unspoken acceptance of more between them.

This kiss was giving and taking in equal measure this time.

But Justus could still feel the frenzy for her that had sprung up the first day he'd laid eyes on her. The one he had denied. It was always waiting under the surface.

He pulled free, a thrill coursing down his spine as she tried to follow him. Justus trailed hot, open-mouthed kisses from the corner of her mouth to her jaw, until his lips were at Derica's ear.

"Turn around," he breathed.

Slowly, she turned in his arms until her back was to his front. The top of her plump ass was the perfect notch for his hard cock, and he barely kept from starting a rhythmic grind.

Not yet.

Justus wanted to reward her for offering him the honor of her heart.

She pushed her hips back into him, seeking his hardness, and he clamped his hands at her waist with a groan.

"No, Derica. You don't need to chase anything this time. I'll give it all to you. I need you to do what I ask though. Can you do that?" he spoke into her ear, her head falling back into the cradle of his shoulder.

Derica nodded.

Tilting her head to the side, he worshipped her neck with his mouth and teeth while he fumbled with the clasp of her skirt. When the fabric sank into a puddle around her feet, he slipped a hand around the front of her, cupping her warmth. He stroked through the delicate barrier of her pantalettes. "Fuck, you're already wet for me, aren't you?" Justus rasped.

With a throaty moan, she turned and pressed her lips into the side of neck.

"Who am I, Derica?" he asked, a breath away from her throat, as he rolled her bundle of nerves between fabric and fingers. Her hips jumped under his touch, searching for more. His cock pulsed in answer.

"*Justus,*" she whimpered.

"Good girl." He strummed her with the side of his thumb while his longest finger teased and stroked her entrance. Reminding her she was empty—promising her she wouldn't be for much longer. "Who are you?" The question slipped from his thoughts and out of his mouth, unbidden. He froze for a terrified moment, holding his breath for her answer.

"Yours," she moaned.

It was the response he wanted, but Justus hadn't been expecting her to say it.

"Yes," he hissed, not able to stop himself from grinding into her plush curves this time. He moved his other hand to her breast, watching the way she overflowed his palm. Working in tandem, he teased her nipple and clit with matching cadences. Taking her earlobe into his mouth, he laved the soft skin with his tongue before breathing into her ear, "I'm so Weaver-damned selfish, I can't even stand the thought of you with another. You are more than I deserve—it's a unique, divine punishment." The words bubbled forth like sea foam from churning waves. They couldn't be contained any longer.

Delivering a stinging bite to the uninjured bend of her neck, he spoke against her skin, "Come for me, now."

Derica tossed her head and ground back into him. He increased the pressure against her clit while pushing her forward with his hips.

When she moaned her release, he could feel the echo of her spasms against the tips of his fingers.

"Good, good girl," he gritted out. Derica was pliant and fluid in his arms now. Scooping her up, he walked the few steps to the bed and laid her on the rumpled sheets. Her chest moved rapidly as she attempted to catch her breath.

She shouldn't be wasting her time.

With surprisingly steady, but rushed movements, Justus divested Derica of the rest of her clothes. He gripped himself through his breeches and stroked twice, hard, before concentrating again on her.

He brushed tendrils of damp hair away from her forehead and took her mouth again. Hands bracketing her head, he levered himself above her to tease and nip with soft strokes of his mouth until she was again squirming and straining.

With a gargantuan effort of will and restraint, Justus pulled back and gripped Derica's nape. He guided her until she was sitting upright.

He couldn't stop himself from bending down and sucking a berry colored nipple. With a whine, she speared a hand into his hair, and his lips pulled into a feral smile against her skin. He teased the nub with his teeth and then pulled back.

"Up," he growled. Derica's eyes had slipped closed, but they fluttered open at his command, a fog of hazed desire dulling her stare.

Justus tugged her hands until she perched on her knees. Her swollen, red lips were a siren song of distraction. He was the hardest he could ever remember being, and the frenzy to be inside her was rolling into a tidal wave, threatening to take him under.

Smoothly as his fervor would allow, he guided Derica until she was facing away from him. He pressed steadily between her shoulder blades until she was resting on her hands and knees. Her lovely, lush ass was in the air and her pink flesh peeked out from between her wide thighs, damp and wanting.

"Weaver above, you'll be the death of me, woman," he ground out.

No, it's the other way round.

Justus shook his head and grounded himself in the warmth of Derica's skin—in the way she moved under his hands, silently pleading.

His fingers frantically pulled at the laces of his breeches. When he undid the placket and freed his cock, the head was weeping and almost crimson.

Derica dropped onto her forearms and implored, *"Please."*

Justus snapped.

Swiping a hand through her center, he reached down and coated himself with her. Justus grabbed her hips and pulled her closer to the edge of the bed. Taking as much care as he was capable, he notched himself at her entrance. And then halted.

"Derica, who am I?" he panted, shaking from the effort to keep still while her heat gloved the head of his cock.

"*Mine*," she answered, trying to push her hips back into him. Her claim was deliverance, reward, and damnation, all rolled into one. Sick, selfish bastard that he was, it sent a bolt of lightning down his spine, shooting his length even harder.

"Yes. *Yes*, Derica." He slid in with one thrust, gasping when he was seated fully. Her answering gasp echoed his.

"Move, *please* move," she begged.

"As you wish," Justus rumbled.

Their gasps of passion resounded off the walls. He varied his depth and rhythm to keep from coming too soon. He needed more of her.

More of her sounds. More of her gasps. More of her pleasure.

He always needed *more*.

Bending, he slipped a hand around her hips until he pinched her clit. Placing an open-mouthed kiss between her shoulders, he licked the salt from her skin.

"Again," Justus growled against her damp skin.

This time, when she shattered, he followed her.

CHAPTER THIRTY-TWO

A fortnight later, Justus knew several things.

He knew he shouldn't have allowed himself to cross the line from physical attraction to emotional attachment when it came to Derica. He knew this would end as it always did—with his hands bloody and his heart broken. He knew he should be more worried about this development than he currently was.

Meanwhile, Mazolan's smug voice in his head was becoming insufferable—in addition to when he saw them at the guild. The sly smirks the demon passed Justus when they crossed paths were beginning to grate.

Not enough, though, to keep him away from Derica.

Justus had invited her to his private apartment yesterday evening, and they'd done very little sleeping. He'd escorted her back to the church early this morning. The journey had been filled with fiery glances and several detours that resulted in one of them pressed up against a wall, whispering soft words and sharing scorching kisses.

The thought had the corner of his mouth hitching in a smile and his cock hardening in his breeches.

That's not how he wanted to walk into the guild, however.

Willing the smile from his lips, he concentrated on shaking thoughts of Derica and her lush mouth and even more lush body from his mind.

Justus thought of burying bodies after battle. He thought of digging latrines. He thought of the time a drunk-off-their-ass Maz had slid into bed with him and clung like a limpet all night long.

By the time he walked into the main hall of the mercenary guild, Justus felt sufficiently calm.

Until he saw Alondra, Maz, and Nyle sitting in the corner, watching him with identical knowing smiles. It was fucking aggravating.

Sighing, he walked over to join his comrades.

"Not you too?" he asked Nyle.

"You know how hard it is to resist getting in on the scheme when Mazolan is this excited," Nyle shrugged with a sheepish smile.

"Why? Why is this..." It took him a moment to come up with a word that wouldn't betray how deeply he was entrenched, "Dalliance! Why is this dalliance so fascinating for you?" Justus frowned at Mazolan. Their fangs flashed brilliantly in a wide smile.

Mazolan leaned across the table and loudly whispered, "Oh, Commander, you *poor* man. You're still denying what this is?" They *tsk*ed and shook their head, pale hair swishing along with the motion.

Justus wasn't sure he could muster a heavy enough sigh to express his weariness. He scrubbed a hand over his face and sunk onto the bench next to Nyle. The tattooed mercenary stifled a laugh, but he clapped Justus on the back sympathetically.

"I like her," declared Alondra.

"I told you!" chirped Maz.

Justus sank onto the surface of the table and groaned into his hands.

Nyle nudged his elbow and leaned in, speaking low and only to Justus. "Don't get too frustrated with them. You know Maz gets their kicks from a good meddling. A happy Maz is a less chaotic Maz—and a happy Maz means a happy Lonnie."

"They give me a headache, Nyle. Such a headache," Justus murmured back.

A thunk on the table had his head jerking up.

A small leather pouch lay before Justus's clasped hands.

Mazolan pointed to the pouch and then grinned wickedly. "Never say I'm not a magnanimous demon, Commander. Willow bark powder for your headache. What's that awful platitude you like to spout before a long job? 'Always come prepared'?" They nodded at the pouch and pushed it closer to Justus. "I know my glee is physically painful for you. Also," their fangs glinted in a smirk, "might help any *aches* from activities." Their eyebrows danced suggestively above their citrine eyes.

Lonnie choked into her ale beside the demon, and Nyle's shoulders shook even though he stayed silent.

"You are unbearable," Justus said, swiping the pouch up.

All mirth drained from Maz's face. "No, I'm trying to right a wrong."

Alondra and Nyle shifted, watching as Mazolan and Justus stared at each other, trying to determine what the other knew. And *how*.

"Lonnie, Nyle," Maz said, not moving their eyes from Justus, "don't you have reports and other horridly boring things to work on? I'd like a moment with the commander."

Everyone was used to Mazolan's mercurial moods, but the pair shifted, hesitant to leave. Justus met their eyes and nodded to both, indicating all was fine.

Or that it would be.

Mazolan waved jauntily as the others left the table and then settled back into a more serious mien. A serious Maz was always a revelation. Justus braced himself for whatever this conversation would illuminate.

The demon leaned across the table, mirroring Justus's posture—hands clasped, forearms braced on the scarred wooden tabletop. "How long have we been working together now, Justus?" Maz only called him *Justus* when they were alone. It was odd, but just another quirk in the long list of the demon's eccentricities.

"Ten years now, at least," Justus answered.

"And after all this time, we've been very careful not to talk about a certain topic. Haven't we?" said Maz.

Justus lifted one brow. "What would that be?"

Mazolan chuckled, and the sound had a dark edge. "Would you like to speak only in questions? That's something demons excel at." They leaned closer to Justus, dropping their voice lower. "While there's much you don't know about my kind, I *do* think you know that, hmm?" Maz asked, tilting their head, studying the commander.

"This topic—go ahead. Let's have it." Justus waved his hand in the air. He was tired of this dance. The last six months were hard enough after finding the Weaver-blessed. If Mazolan wanted to strip him of his secrets... Well, so be it. Being alone with the burden was exhausting.

"Your dagger. You don't think I didn't recognize it the day I met you?"

"I've never tried to conceal that it was of demon make."

"True." Mazolan continued, "Here's something you may find interesting. That dagger? We have legends about it. Tales passed down generations about the demon that helped the famed human Warrior to trap their Weaver-blessed mate."

Justus clenched his hands, knuckles turning white on the table in front of him. Mazolan's sharp yellow gaze flicked down, noting the tension.

"Didn't know your legend was popular with the other races of Veridion?" asked the demon.

Justus shrugged, the action stiff and jerky. "Every human child has heard the tale. It's a favorite of the church and tittering romantics alike. Why wouldn't other races know about it too?"

Ire flashed in Maz's gaze. "In the ten years we've known each other, fought together, I've always thought you righteous and brave—for a human, of course. But I'm happy to take orders from you."

"When it suits you," Justus sighed, already fatigued.

Maz nodded and shrugged. "True. Not every job we do holds my attention. But I didn't think we lied to each other. So let me ask you baldly." The demon swiped their tongue across their lips, the first sign of nerves Justus may have ever seen from them. "Is that the dagger that belonged to the Warrior?"

Justus had never confided in anyone, at least not in this lifetime—about the curse, the Weaver-blessed, or the dagger. He ached to share his guilt and his heartache. Maybe his resolve crumbled because he'd already given in to Derica. Whatever the cause, he found himself nodding, once.

Mazolan's eyes sharpened, and they leaned closer, lowering their voice. "And you?"

"What about me?"

"Who are you?"

Justus held their citrine gaze. "You know who I am."

"Then maybe this is the better question: who *were* you?"

Justus let his eyes close, breathing in through his nose and out through his mouth. When he opened them again, Mazolan was watching intently, patiently waiting for an answer.

"You know. I think you have for a long time." Justus said, wearily.

"I want to know if I'm right. Say it."

Justus ground his teeth, fighting the urge to jump up and abandon this conversation. He could only blame his eroded discipline as he heard himself say, "I was—*am*—the Warrior."

"And that makes her...?" Mazolan asked.

Justus didn't want to voice it. It was hard enough, knowing he'd failed in his effort to stay away and keep her safe. It was even harder to confirm the title that was her death sentence.

"I want to help, my friend. And to help, I need your confirmation. Please," implored Mazolan.

The noise of the guild fell away as Justus's heart rate kicked up. He searched Maz's eyes, finding nothing but keen interest. "You think I haven't sought help before?" Justus scoffed. "You think I haven't searched Veridion for a way to undo this? The lifetime after the curse, I kept a journal as I searched far and wide for answers. I documented anything and everything that could help us escape the fate I'd so stupidly consigned us to. I buried that journal and used it for several more turns upon the Loom—until I finally gave up."

"Commander, let me tell you something that may illuminate my qualifications." Mazolan shifted in their seat and projected a determination that seemed out of place from their normal joviality. "Do you know why I subject myself to living among humans?"

"The demons kicked you out for causing too much chaos?" Justus asked, voice drier than a desert.

"Don't make jokes. You don't do it as well as I do," Mazolan dismissed.

Justus grunted. He thought it was pretty fucking funny.

"I'm not a full-blooded demon." Maz surveyed their surroundings, making sure no one was listening. The grand hall that served as the hub of the guild was never empty, but today it was relatively quiet. Only a handful of the tables were occupied, groups clustered together while clutching cards and swilling ale. There was nothing a mercenary celebrated more than the breath between one job and the next.

When satisfied no other soul was paying them any attention, the demon continued, "I'm half fey."

Justus tried to keep his surprise from showing but failed. Maz took notice, and their eyes gleamed.

"Neither the demons nor the fey want anything to do with a half-breed. For a time, I resided with each race until they discovered my origins and cast me out." Mazolan stared hard before delivering the next piece of information. "*But,* I was able to dredge every piece of useful knowledge from each of my antecedents."

Justus's mind was reeling. Maz didn't seem surprised by Justus's true identity, but they must have suspected for years. The commander never doubted

Mazolan was anything more than an oddly adventurous demon, one who didn't share their kind's disdain for humans.

"After they exiled me, I even tried to sweet talk my way into the dwarven city. It didn't work, but it's still a lovely dream I hold onto." Maz chuckled. "I digress, however. The point, Commander, is that the Weaver is a special point of interest for the other races of Veridion. It would surprise you to learn some of the things they know about your goddess."

"How? How can you help?" asked Justus, voice hoarse with disbelief.

"I hope we can figure that out together," said the demon.

"But, why this interest? I don't understand," Justus frowned, cocking his head and searching Mazolan's enigmatic gaze.

"You're not ready for that answer yet." Mazolan cut him off before he could respond, one light blue finger raised to silence Justus. "Ah-ah! All in due time and all that other cryptic shite. Let me have this. There is a method to my madness. I have a few more questions for you, and then you can go back to staring off and making cow eyes when you think no one's watching." Mazolan brushed their thick braid forward over their shoulder, fingers raking through the tuft at the end. They looked down, releasing Justus from their intense stare for the first time during their conversation. Almost so low Justus didn't hear it, they asked, "Why now?"

"Why now, what?"

"It's surprisingly easy to track the Weaver-blessed and the Warrior through history if you know where to look. The battle at Hederdon. The Plains War." Their fingers moved to the feathered pendant they always wore. "And of course, there's everything the Warrior Queen of Loquamora accomplished in her reign. You're never far from conflict, are you?"

To have such pivotal lives in the Warrior's many journeys among the Loom so succinctly listed made Justus's head spin. Memories swirled, clamoring for his attention. But it was the last that struck him silent.

"That one's painful, is it?" murmured Mazolan. "Is that when it happened then? When you were separated for lifetimes?" Mazolan's fingers twitched around the striped feathers in their grasp. "How?"

Justus gnashed his teeth, loathe to even think about it. It was the single most painful memory—from any of the Warrior's lives.

"If you tell me, I guarantee you the next contract will go smoothly. Not one Mazolan Scheme will be hatched. I will follow orders, to the letter." Their mouth hitched up, two fangs gleaming. "Surely that's worth a little painful retelling?" With surprise, Justus noted the softening of their regard. He truly had the feeling that if he were to refuse this line of conversation, the demon would respect his boundary. For now...

The words danced on the tip of his tongue—poison waiting to be purged.

A rise in the murmuring of the guild hall interrupted the rest of their conversation. The hall occupants were in a tizzy over something that was happening near the front door. No one ever came in or out of the guild by the front, as Justus had told Derica. And parties wishing to hire the guild knew to contact the organization via letter courier.

The banging at the front door was so foreign a sound that no one knew what to do.

Justus looked around but no one moved to see what the noise was about.

"Oh, today keeps getting more entertaining," Maz said with a feral grin, popping up from their bench and bounding toward the door.

"Fuck," Justus sighed. He rushed to follow his comrade.

When he caught up to Maz, they were standing several yards from the front door with their head cocked, listening.

"I think it's for you, Commander."

"Wha—"

That's when he heard the voice on the other side of the door calling his name.

CHAPTER THIRTY-THREE

D erica pounded so hard on the door it brought tears of pain to her eyes. "Justus! Commander Hadrian! Help, please!" She continued banging.

Finally, the entrance swung open, and Justus pulled her into the building. She collapsed against his chest, shaking as she listened to his heartbeat and felt the rumble of his voice under her cheek.

Justus's arms were firm around her back. "Derica, answer me. What's wrong? Are you hurt? Please, tell me what's wrong."

"R-Reid," was all she could force out before sobbing into his tunic.

"Commander, you deal with the leaking human. I'll get Nyle and Lonnie. We'll meet you in Lonnie's office." Mazolan's voice seemed far away, oddly gentler than she was used to hearing.

Justus shielded her from others' eyes, and Derica told herself she could fall apart for a minute. Then she would wipe her tears and show him the letter. When she'd read it, her heart had sunk into her stomach, inciting a panic that had her running through the streets to find help.

To find him.

"Do you need some time, or are you ready to tell me what's wrong?" Justus whispered into her ear, soothing her back with light strokes down her spine.

"I-I'm ready," she said, voice watery.

The mercenary crooked a finger under her chin and wiped her tears with his thumb. He smoothed her hair and placed a hard kiss on her forehead. "Tell me first. Are you well?"

Her vision swam, and she blinked hard. "I'm fine. But, everything is not all right."

"Tell me what happened, and I'll help you however I can."

Derica peeked around his wide shoulders, finding a large hall with mercenaries standing in groups and sitting at large tables. All were openly watching them.

"Am I going to get you into trouble?" she whispered.

"I don't think so. Lonnie's the head of the guild, and she likes you, remember?"

"I didn't know another way to find you. I'm—"

Justus's chest rumbled with a frustrated growl. "Don't you dare apologize for coming to me for help," he warned.

Derica nodded. Licking her lips, she told him, "It's Reid. He's missing. Or taken. I don't know." She fumbled in her pocket with trembling hands, then passed him the piece of paper she had found at the physicians' guild lodgings.

Justus's features hardened, sharp angles thrown into relief as he read the small scrap of paper. "Where exactly did you find this?"

"In Reid's quarters. After you escorted me back to the church, I ran into Father Simond. I was worried he or Reid would be concerned bec—" her cheeks warmed with a blush "—because I didn't come back last night. When I spoke to the father, he said Reid hadn't been to the church today.

"Reid comes to see me every day, even for just a few minutes. When I got to his room though, he was nowhere to be found. His room was a mess, like someone had searched it. I discovered that note on his bed. When I asked the other apprentices if they had heard anything or seen Reid recently, they said no." Derica shook her head, biting her lip. "The way his quarters were tossed, I have a hard time believing no one heard any commotion. But the others were very clear that they hadn't heard or seen anything to indicate Reid was in trouble." She took another shaky breath. "I came straight here after leaving the apprentices' lodgings."

Justus held up the note again. On the torn sheaf of paper, a rough sketch of a location was circled with a time scrawled next to it.

"Come with me," he said, taking her hand and leading her out of the hall and into the corridors of the guild. As they left, several of the mercenaries watched with undisguised interest. Whispers and furtive glances followed in their wake.

"Don't mind them," Justus said over his shoulder. "Mercenaries are a chatty bunch—inside the guild, at least. This will give them enough to titter about for the next month."

He held open a door and gestured for Derica to precede him. "This is Alondra's office, we can speak in here."

The woman Derica had met in Justus's apartment sat behind a desk, papers spread before her. Nyle stood at her shoulder, leaning on the desk. Both looked up when Derica and Justus entered. Mazolan stood propped in the corner, flipping a wicked-looking dagger into the air before catching the hilt.

All the mercenaries nodded or waved at Derica in some measure before dismissing her and focusing on Justus.

Alondra didn't waste any time; she held out her hand, and the commander passed her the slip of paper. She smoothed it and examined it, her forehead pinched with concentration. Nyle leaned in too, a frown decorating his normally smooth brow.

Mazolan swaggered away from the wall to stand over Alondra's other shoulder, cocking their head at the roughly sketched map.

"This is the poorest attempt at a ransom request I think I've ever seen," said Mazolan.

"You've seen many?" asked Derica.

Nyle placed a finger on the scrap of paper, dragging it closer for his inspection. "You'd be surprised how many contracts for rescues the guild receives." He flipped over the map and held it up to the light filtering in from the large window behind Alondra.

"Anything?" Alondra asked.

Nyle shook his head and tossed the scrap back on the desk.

Justus saw Derica's questioning look and supplied the information before she could ask. With a shrug, he said, "Sometimes the paper will have signs or print from something else we can use to pin down who left it."

"There's not much time to sleuth out who left the letter. The time printed on the note is after dusk tonight. I need to know where to go to get Reid back," Derica said.

"Oh, my sweet, naive morsel. I don't think the commander feels like letting you go to this location, and certainly not alone."

Justus rubbed his temples. "Mazolan—"

"Am I wrong? I know how you like to run these types of missions. Backup plans for the backup plans, and a secondary team on standby, am I right?" asked Mazolan.

"You can't!" cried Derica. "If whoever took Reid sees a company of mercenaries, they could hurt him!"

"Derica," Nyle soothed, "the commander is skilled at planning jobs like this. He knows how to conceal our presence. No one here wants to see Reid hurt."

"Who do you want for the secondary team?" Alondra asked Justus.

"Are you listening to me?" Derica grabbed Justus's forearm, forcing his attention to her. "You can't do anything to endanger Reid, and I need to know the plan," she insisted.

Justus's eyes softened, and he cupped her elbows, thumbs stroking her arms. "We don't know the note was meant for you, Derica. Another apprentice, or even one of Reid's mentors could have been the intended recipient."

"The commander does have a point, Derica," Nyle said.

Derica's eyes misted, and her chin wobbled in frustration.

They didn't understand.

They *couldn't* understand.

Reid was all she had. She'd lost her mother, her home, her surrogate family. Derica couldn't take Reid's loss as well.

Her vision started to tunnel, and she tried to catch her breath. The fear twisted in her belly, and her lungs couldn't draw in enough air.

"Whoa—whoa there." Justus grabbed her shoulders and tilted her chin up. Their eyes met, and whatever he saw in hers caused a flicker of alarm in his.

Hastily, Justus grabbed Derica's wrist and brought her hand to his chest. He pressed her palm flat to the wide expanse of muscle. She could feel the thumping of his heart.

"Breathe with me," he instructed. "In." His nostrils flared as his chest expanded under her fingers. Derica couldn't match the movement. She tried to make her body mimic his, but it refused like a recalcitrant child.

"It's going to be all right, just breathe with me, Derica." Justus touched her waist and tugged her closer.

Derica began to turn her head, worried that everyone else in the room would scoff and pity her.

"Ah-ah," Justus murmured, capturing her chin to keep her from looking away. "Focus on me. Breathe for me. Please." He released his grip, smoothing a hand around the nape of her neck, fingers tangling in her hair.

His heart was a rapid drumbeat against her palm. Despite the frantic rhythm, he appeared entirely in control.

"Now. In," he said again.

This time, she pulled in air through her nose, a few unsteady little gulps.

"Good. Good. Out now." Justus's lips formed a small O as he slowly breathed out.

Derica's exhale came out as more of a cough. His fingers stroked the back of her neck, a pleasant distraction to the crushing, twisting, all-consuming panic.

"One more time for me," he said, voice low and smoky.

"I—" she started.

"Shh. Just breathe. Once more."

This time she could pull the air into her nostrils smoothly. Derica matched his exhale, following the rhythm under her palm, and realized her cheeks were damp.

If her body could have managed one more involuntary response, Derica's face would be furiously red. As it was, her breathing hitched back out of sync.

Justus's thumb brushed the moisture from her face. "I will find him. Don't worry. I *will* bring him back to you."

Derica thought he meant to be comforting and to sound heroic. However, it only reminded her why a thick knot of panic writhed in her chest, threatening to choke her.

Another voice said, "Commander, I think this calls for some special intervention."

Justus looked away from Derica for the first time, and her panic ratcheted higher.

He nodded at whoever spoke and stepped back. Derica's hand flopped to her side, and her vision tunneled again.

He was leaving her too.

Something dark and dangerous joined the writhing panic.

Suddenly, her vision filled with citrine.

Mazolan.

Their face was kind as they searched Derica's eyes. She didn't want Maz's kindness though. She wanted *Reid*.

"Morsel, that's enough of that. If you pass out, then Nyle will have to coddle the commander and that's not something I want to see."

Did they think she wanted to have this reaction? That she enjoyed making a fool of herself in front of this capable and steady group?

Did they think she wasn't ashamed of her weakness?

That darkness coiled tighter, and now she couldn't breathe at all. Her chest was expanding, but to no avail.

Tears streamed down Derica's cheeks, and a scream burned in her throat, unable to escape through her clenched teeth.

"*Tsk.* I wanted to give you a way around this. Forgive me." Mazolan stepped closer and stooped so their eyes were level. "I'm not going to hurt you, little morsel. If I damaged a single red hair, I'd feel the prick of the commander's dagger." A deep growl registered behind the demon. "See?" Maz flashed a fanged smile. "I'd be a dead demon, and I very much value my life. It's better to make mischief above ground than six feet under, I say. Filthy human habit, that. Burial. The worms and things—"

"Mazolan!" boomed Justus.

"Right, right, on it," they said over their shoulder. "Come now, morsel, you know that was funny. I expect a good laugh when you're well." They nodded as if it was a deal struck.

Derica's vision was winking in and out. The darkness was closing in. She hoped there was peace there.

"None of that," snapped Maz. "I have plans for you, and there will be no escaping them." Their lips curled, but with her swimming vision, Derica couldn't say whether it was sinister or wry.

Mazolan locked their stare on her, and Derica began to feel... odd.

Their yellow eyes seemed to glow—then burned like coals.

Mazolan spoke, and it was with a voice layered and woven with something else. ***"Calm, human. All will be well."***

The words washed over Derica like the knell of a bell, silencing the fear inside her heart and her head.

Mazolan reached up a slim-fingered hand to her forehead and gently brushed her eyelids closed. The demon stepped closer, and that multi-layered voice now whispered into her ear, ***"Your time will come. You will soon know the power you hold. But not yet. There is more to do—more to prepare—before you are ready."***

A low growl drifted to Derica from over Mazolan's shoulder. They stepped back, and Derica blindly reached out, snatching a handful of their tunic.

"Open your eyes," crooned Maz, taking her hand in theirs.

The crushing weight sitting on her chest vanished. Derica blinked, looking first at Mazolan, then Justus, Nyle with a restraining hand on the commander, and finally Alondra propped on the edge of her desk.

All but Mazolan watched her with cautious expressions.

They squeezed her fingers before releasing her. "Better, morsel?" the demon asked with a flash of fang but a telling hint of concern shining in their citrine eyes.

Derica nodded, swiping her tongue across her dry lips before answering faintly, "Yes." She could fill her lungs with a full, cleansing breath. "Wha-what did you do?"

"Oh, that?" They waved a hand in the air dismissively. "Just a little something I learned before I joined this lovely band. It's why I'm often in charge of interrogations and information gathering. My personality is rather magnetic to begin with—but I know how to make it even more... *influential*, shall we say? Makes me a valued member of the commander's team. Right, Commander?" Maz tossed over their shoulder.

Justus didn't respond. He stared at Derica with an expression that both chilled and warmed her. His dark eyes held such tortured longing. The scar slashing across his lip was white with tension. Underneath it all, however, glimmered a hint of relief.

Mazolan spoke again, "Morsel, no one wants to exclude you from the planning, but would you like to follow me for a brief rest and something to drink?"

Derica blinked in surprise at Maz's offer. Her mouth opened and closed without a sound.

"Derica," Justus's low voice drew her eyes to him, his gaze now dark and stony. "Go with Mazolan? I promise we won't do anything without telling you."

Mazolan extended their hand. She slipped her palm into theirs and, turning her head over her shoulder, held Justus's stare until they were out of the room.

As they walked down the hallway, Maz murmured softly, "Morsel, I know I can come off..."

"Brusque? Trite? Superior? Judgmental?" The selection of words was off her tongue before she finished thinking. Then she bit her lip, ashamed. The demon had helped her selflessly.

Mazolan tossed their head back and laughed, the sound echoing against the stone floor.

"Oh, morsel, you are exactly what he needs."

Derica frowned and opened her mouth to ask, "What—"

"That's a conversation for another time. First, let's get you that drink, and then we can see what the two of us can come up with, hmm? I was going to say I know I can come off in a manner that you humans find off-putting." Mazolan mused, "Curious things, humans. You value your differences—until they become *too* different. I think that's the crux of the rift between the races of Veridion. But," they shrugged, "what does one demon know about healing the world and its long-standing conflicts?"

Derica watched them carefully out of the corner of her eye. Maz wore their patent smirk, but those eyes... There was a barely contained fervor glowing in them.

"I think," she ventured, "you know a great deal more than you want anyone to realize."

Slyly, Mazolan slid those yellow eyes to her. What they were looking for, she didn't know. She was scared to find out.

"And *I* think they could say the same of you, morsel."

With a slow blink, the spell broke and Maz continued on, blithely leading her through the halls of the guild, until they halted in front of wide double doors.

Beyond, Derica heard the clang of metal and the movement of a great many people.

"Stay here. Be gone for the span of a wink." The demon slinked through the doors so quickly, Derica couldn't glimpse whatever lay beyond. She assumed it was a kitchen. There was nothing to do but wait.

It wasn't long until Mazolan slipped back out, carrying two large wooden tankards. They pressed one into Derica's hands. The liquid inside was dark, and steam wafted up from the surface. She sniffed it cautiously, and her eyebrows rose in surprise at the familiar aroma.

"Spiced wine?" she asked.

Mazolan nodded with a smile before carefully sipping from their mug. With a groan, their eyes slipped closed as they savored the drink. They sighed blissfully, "Cook keeps a little batch over the stove, and if I ask very, *very* nicely I can manage to snag a cup every so often. Of course, it did help my cause to say it was for a distressed damsel." They looked impishly over at her.

Derica's vision clouded with shame and fury.

Mazolan's yellow eyes filled with worry. "Morsel, I—"

"No, you're not wrong. I have been useless and passive. If my mother could see—" Derica forced out a breath rather than releasing the sob she was holding back. "I am so tired of *letting* these things happen to me. Reid—" This time she couldn't stop a hiccup and accompanying tear from escaping. "Reid was the last straw. I refuse to sit and wait for someone else to do something when I can help. There has to be something I can do."

"I think that's a perfectly rational response, morsel."

Derica's eyes flew to theirs.

"What? You'd be surprised to learn I felt like that myself once. Action can erase some of that anger and guilt. But it must be *smart*. I don't have any desire to repeat past mistakes."

She frowned at the demon. "Just what are you offering?" she asked.

"I can offer my excellent instincts and years of brilliant experience. It's not an exaggeration if it's true, morsel. I do think it's best if we keep this from the commander, though. I have it on the authority of years long association that he wouldn't allow you to participate in this. And with the commander, it's better to ask for pardon than permission."

Derica's heart beat faster as she absorbed what Mazolan was proposing.

Mazolan placed a hand on the small of her back, guiding her deeper into the guild. "Now, this is what I think we should do. I'll tuck you into a lovely little vacant room here with your spiced wine. You have a good little spot of rest and think on what you can *objectively* contribute to a rescue team of two. In the meantime, I will go back to the commander and find out what the plan is, reporting that the damsel in distress—" Derica yelped a rebuttal to this."—forgive me, a *reformed* damsel in distress—is resting and will wait for them to bring back her precious farm boy. When I learn the plan, I'll volunteer for the solo, redundant backup assistance the commander always insists on. Once I know what our wily leader has up his sleeve, we can run circles around him." Derica knew the demon would rub their hands together if they weren't holding a mug. They positively radiated delight.

CHAPTER THIRTY-FOUR

Derica paced back and forth. The quiet of the room pressed against her ears, the pressure increasing the longer she waited. Her shaky breaths escaped into the yawning stillness, crashing against the silence like waves.

Her back, between her breasts, even the soles of her feet were damp with perspiration.

Imagined scenarios of Reid lying injured—or worse—flashed in the back of her mind.

Justus didn't understand her need to act rather than sit and wait for someone else to remedy the situation. Rather than stay still and silent while the world moved around her. It was a suffocating reminder of the grief that consumed her after her mother's passing.

Derica didn't want to slip back into the muffled pitch-black darkness she'd fallen into. Every time she thought she left the cocoon of melancholy, its siren call tried to lure her back with promises of rest and surcease where nothing mattered. Not even herself.

Her shoulders rolled inward, and she battled that same out-of-control feeling from before. With sheer will, Derica shoved it back.

She was sick of being the canvas rather than the painter. Another soul would not dictate her path, mood, or choices again.

For the longest time she wanted to sink to the ground on the top of her mother's grave and never move again. Forcing her shoulders back and taking several deep breaths—hearing Justus's voice instructing her to breathe—Derica managed an equilibrium.

The fear was still there. The temptation to give up and huddle in the corner had not left. She simply decided to shut them out.

Instead, she made every effort to relish the deafening silence. Because after the wait, she would be *doing* something for once.

A faint knock reached her ears. To Derica's hyper-alert senses, the sound was like a boulder crashing into the placid surface of a lake.

Stepping towards the door, she realized the knock came from somewhere else. Derica turned with trepidation, scanning the room and straining to hear.

The knock came again, this time with a muffled call of "Morsel?"

The knock sounded once more, this time with more force.

There was a wardrobe made of sturdy, dark wood on the opposite wall. Derica moved toward it with hesitation. Standing in front of the carved double doors, she reached out a trembling hand, skating her palm down the seam until she grasped the cool cast iron handle.

A quick yank revealed nothing but clothing. The garments swayed, and the mustiness of stored fabric tickled her nostrils.

A slim-fingered faintly blue hand appeared and waved from behind the clothing. Clapping a hand over her mouth, Derica smothered the screech that climbed up her throat.

"Morsel," the fingers waggled back and forth, beckoning, "let's go."

"Where?" She couldn't imagine where the inside of a wardrobe would lead.

"Now is not the time for questions." With an air of agitation, the fingers snapped twice, before disappearing beyond the hanging garments.

Derica's sigh gusted from her lungs. She should have known the demon wouldn't have collected her by normal means.

A muted, exasperated call to hurry her arse up made Derica grind her teeth. She pushed the doors open wider and gathered the bottom of her skirts. The wardrobe was tall enough that Derica didn't have to bend as she stepped in. Mazolan could have—at the very least—held the clothing aside, so she didn't have to fight through the garments to get to the hidden passage.

Managing not to fall on her face by some miracle, Derica pushed through the secret door. Maz was standing several feet away, leaning indolently against the wall of the tunnel. Lamps illuminated the long hallway, and the tunnel forked about thirty feet away from where they stood. Where the rest of it led, she'd have to wait and see.

"No time to gawk, morsel. We have to get to where we need to be." They levered off the wall and headed toward the fork.

"And where would that be?"

"Why, to the meeting location, of course."

"But I thought—"

"I said *we* were going to find out the commander's plan and then run circles around him. And you know what his weakness is? He likes everything planned, every possibility considered and counted. But you know what kind of shite that thinking is to a demon who can't be bothered with all that nonsense—much less commit to a course of action before the time to act? It stinks worse than the stables after a jousting tournament, morsel." Maz cast her a gleaming look of citrine mischief. "Oh, for the provincial, a jousting tournament is—"

"I know what the fuck a jousting tournament is."

"Beg to differ. If you haven't experienced it, do you *really?* It's all pomp and circumstance. Puffery, if you will. Ah!" Mazolan held up a finger to stave off her interjection. "Puffery may not be a word, morsel, but there's no better one to describe a joust. It's posturing and pandering for entertainment. There's not one event that happens at a jousting tournament that has any true meaning. I like my entertainment as much as the next demon—*more*, even—but all those rules? In *entertainment?* Humans are the most contrary creatures—"

"Mazolan—"

"—I once attended a tournament—not by choice, let me tell you—where the Duke of Lanesby—"

"Mazolan!" Derica's shout echoed through the narrow walls of the tunnel and finally got their attention.

The demon sniffed. "Fine, I can tell you what the Duke did another time. You're probably rather concerned about the plan—knowing the plan and executing the plan. Right?" Mazolan looked at her over their shoulder, one silvery brow arched. When she nodded, Maz inclined their head and started forward again. Before turning right at the fork, they mumbled, *"Two fucking peas in a fucking pod."*

"First of all, puffery is, in fact, a real word." She bit her lip, trying not to laugh.

Mazolan's eyes widened. "It is? I think you're lying." They waved a dismissive hand.

"And secondly, the plan?" Derica prompted, squaring her shoulders.

"Right, the plan is... *the absence of a plan.* The commander is going to set an ambush at the meeting location. When they capture whoever arrives, they will interrogate Reid's location from them. Then, their captive will lead them back to Reid and likely into a trap. And we," Mazolan's voice sounded giddy, "are going to pop up in the middle of that plan and dash it all to pieces."

"And then?" she asked.

"Then we see what happens. No use planning for every eventuality when we can't predict with a certainty what *will* happen. I have a lovely arsenal of tricks and weapons stored in my mind and on my person—my demon?—I digress. I'm confident I can get us into and out of wherever they're holding Reid. There's not a human alive that can outwit me, especially when it comes to entering or exiting a fortified location. This time, with or without a hostage *and* a useless human along for the ride."

Derica had her fill of being called useless. Her temples pounded, her nerves strung tight.

"I am not useless!" The words bubbled up out of Derica's lips. With every casual insult Mazolan flung at her, the volcano of anger and frustration in her chest had come closer to erupting. *Useless* was too close to what her own thoughts whispered.

The cap had blown.

"I'm not a mercenary, and I have no training, but that doesn't make me *useless*. I am not a waste of space or a blight on the world because the skills I *do* possess don't meet your lofty standards." Her words increased in speed and volume the longer she spoke. "I make the best cakes within three villages. I'm a good, loyal friend. I care deeply about and for the people I love."

Mazolan halted and turned around to face her. They watched patiently, taking in everything Derica spat at them. Patience was a look she hadn't seen the demon wear before. The tiniest suggestion of a grin tugged one corner of their mouth, and the smug smile spurred Derica onward.

"Do you know why I have no notable skills—at least by your judgment? Because for the last four years, I devoted myself solely to my mother's well-being. There was no traveling, gallivanting, or *skill development* in my past. I was watching my mother wither before my eyes! I wanted to be with her every moment I could. And when she—" Derica stopped. Her throat threatened to close on the molten rage and sadness spewing from her heart. After a deep breath, she continued, "When she passed, I wanted to go with her. Nothing felt happy. Nothing felt worth doing. Nothing felt worth seeing. I am clawing my way back from wishing I'd died along with my mother! I am doing the only thing I can to make sure that one of the people I care most about in this world stays in it with me!"

The echo of her words traveled through the tunnel. If Derica hadn't been so angry, she would have been embarrassed. She'd never yelled at someone like that in her life. A small voice in the back of her mind urged her to take back the words.

Apologize for her feelings.

Chest heaving, eyes stinging with a combination of resentment and grief, Derica vowed to do neither.

Derica was not going to demure her emotions for anyone else. She refused to accept any opinion of her worth that wasn't her own. She would not apologize or be ashamed of the decisions she made.

Voice low and soft, Derica spoke once more. "I can't fight, and I have no desire to get in the way of the rescue mission. But I have to be there for Reid."

Mazolan stood still and calm in the face of her wrath. The ghost of a grin still played on their lips. If Mazolan replied with some condescending ramble about humans and their pitiful emotions, no one would hold Derica responsible for her actions.

"Are you sure about that? I heard how you helped the commander with those Shredded the night they attacked on the road," Mazolan said.

"I... That was—"

"A reaction to adrenaline? Poor forethought?"

Grinding her teeth, Derica nodded.

"Will you let these things override your common sense again? Jump into a fight you are ill-prepared and untrained for?" Mazolan asked.

Derica shook her head, hands fisting at her sides. With a satisfied nod, Maz turned on their heel and continued down the tunnel.

Derica's jaw gaped open in stunned silence.

"Move your feet, morsel. We have a farm boy to rescue," Mazolan called.

When she still didn't move after the demon was a good distance away, they sighed and returned.

Mazolan nudged her mouth closed with an elegant forefinger. The demon smiled at her, their yellow eyes soft and gentle.

Derica waited for the punchline—to be told she was just a silly human with silly emotions. It didn't come.

"I knew there was fire in you," they finally said. "What you're doing is very brave. I am glad you realize your limitations though. Mercenaries care because they are paid to. Your caring needs no inducement. There is a kind of nobility in that. It is also very human—which is ironic in a way you don't yet know." When Derica frowned at the word *human*, Mazolan shook their head. "Human does not mean weak. There are weak demons. Weak fey. Weak dwarves. One race of Veridion does not own all the weakness in the world. In my attempt to relieve any fretting with humor, I struck a nerve and for that, I am sorry. You are not useless. I see I need to be serious for a moment longer and lay out some directives." For a moment, their eyes twinkled with mirth. "This is what it must feel like to be the commander." Mazolan chuckled, and with a deep breath, straightened to their full height.

Hands clasped behind their back, tone serious and steady, they continued. "You will trust me to see you through this. You will trust me to do what's necessary to get Reid back. If I say hide, you will. If I say run, you will. You must trust me for this mission to succeed. And I must trust you. Can we do that for each other? For Reid?"

Derica considered for a moment before nodding.

"Good. I will protect you, and you will cooperate with my orders."

"And we will find Reid," Derica stated. That was the only outcome she would accept.

"We will." Mazolan inclined their head and inspected Derica.

She tried not to fidget and held the demon's stare.

"Then a little farther." Mazolan moved away from the wall and the pair started moving, this time side by side.

"I need to know more about your no-plan plan if I'm going to do what you need me to," she said, voice low and even.

Mazolan sighed, then started. "Fuck, now I sound like the commander. This being in charge shite is why he must have such healthy lungs. All that sighing." They stroked their chin, considering. "Hmm, yes, I can see that a plan is better when you have a small team, and one team member is supposed to do what the other wants. Some communication is necessary."

"Yes. So. What are we doing?"

"We'll be entering the tunnels that run under the city soon. I'll lead us below where the meeting is supposed to take place. We'll enter the location and bypass the commander with his ambush setup. He won't be able to stop us, because that would reveal their trap. This gives us a failsafe should anything go wrong. I fully expect, if they lead us back to Reid, Hadrian and the others will follow. Nyle will convince the commander to do the sensible thing. You can always count on Nyle for that. A wonderful man. It's damned annoying, rea—"

Derica cleared her throat.

Mazolan barked a surprised laugh. "Oh, you're getting good at that. The commander lets me get a little farther off track before hauling me back though. He could learn a thing or two from you. As I was saying, we'll follow whoever we find waiting for us. I'll do the talking and introduce myself as the soldier you hired to protect you. I'll be doing my best to appear incompetent and non-threatening. I know that seems impossible, but I can be very convincing. Don't be alarmed if I say or do something stupid. That's the point. Just nod and stay silent. I'll get us to where we need to be."

Mazolan stopped speaking when they reached a slope in the tunnels. Clasping her shoulders with care, they turned Derica to face them.

"This takes us to the paths running under the city. Once we leave the vicinity of the guild, there's no turning back. There won't be time. So, I have to ask: are you sure? I won't think less of you if you want to return to that room and wait," Mazolan said.

"I'm sure," she answered.

CHAPTER THIRTY-FIVE

"**R**emember," Mazolan said, "don't react when I say something unbelievably unintelligent."

"I would *never*," Derica murmured dryly.

Maz looked back over their shoulder, their eyes twinkling. "Good for you, morsel." They nodded. "Good for you." They settled their hands on their hips, weapons absent from their belt. Derica almost asked if entering the meeting unarmed was wise, but she told herself to trust the demon.

"Ready?" asked Mazolan.

The pair stood at the foot of an aged metal ladder. How Mazolan knew which ladder they needed when the tunnels in this area were nearly bursting with them, she had no clue. She guessed this would take them to the streets of Radley, close to where the meeting would occur.

"Wait." Derica bit her lip. "One more time."

"Spirits be damned. Again?"

"I need to go over the plan—it *is* a plan, don't shudder like that—one more time."

"We climb the ladder. We pop up onto the street. We blink, all innocent and stupid, when the ne'er-do-wells are startled. We ask if they're the nice people who are going to take us to your poor blond giant. You squeeze out a tear of gratitude and say we must hurry to his side. I will clumsily present myself as your hired protection, but you're not flush in the pocket, morsel. The quality of my fictitious protection will be expectedly lacking. Keep your wits about you and watch me closely. Got all that?"

"But what if—"

"No more what-ifs, morsel. You can't what-if everything to death. Being prepared is all well and good, but there is only so much you can anticipate in life. Now, I'm going up the ladder first. As a precaution. Because I'm mitigating danger, not what-if'ing to the point of paralysis." Without waiting for a response, Mazolan clambered up the rungs. Metal grated against stone. Then light from the oil lamps streaked down.

Derica took a fortifying breath and followed. She accepted the hand Maz offered to help her step off the ladder.

If Mazolan hadn't laid out their plan in the tunnels, the sudden change in her demon companion would have shocked Derica.

Like pulling on a cloak, they assumed a whole new personality and manner. The swagger and mischievous twinkle were gone, concealed under the hood of their thick cape. Gloves completed the task of hiding the demon's unique skin tone. Mazolan's posture was timid, something Derica thought she'd never see. It was jarring enough to make her forget the purpose of their endeavor for a moment.

"Morsel," Mazolan murmured, "don't act so shocked. You'll ruin the plan you insisted I make. Start acting like an empty-headed miss. And, by the Spirits, stop frowning like that. It's too similar to the commander's favorite expression."

Derica concentrated on blanking her face before looking around. She hadn't raised the hood of her cloak. They'd decided their performance would go better that way. Derica and Mazolan stood within a small circle of lamplight in a junction connecting four alleyways. They could have been anywhere in the city. Derica had no clue of their precise location—likely what the ransomers intended.

"Good," Mazolan said, "now try to look less like a general surveying a battle map. *I'm* supposed to be the threat here."

Derica dipped a shallow nod and released the thoughts she'd kept safely locked away. Reid dead or dying—alone and afraid. Reid crying out for help. For *her*. Her shoulders rolled inward, and she pressed her hands into her nervous, roiling stomach.

An owl hooted loud and long from the rooftops and Derica startled, shifting closer to Mazolan.

The demon chuckled, the sound low and dark. "Oh, the commander is quite unhappy with me," they mused.

"How can you tell?" she whispered back, trying not to move her lips.

"That hoot? It's one way we send covert messages during a job. That specific one says 'you fucked up.' That, and I can practically feel flames of retribution licking up my back. Ornery bastard is probably staring at me with death in his eyes at this very second." Casually, Mazolan itched the tip of their nose—with their middle finger.

Derica held her breath, waiting for the commander to jump out of the shadows and haul them off. When nothing happened, her tension increased. The waiting was the worst part.

At least she was waiting here, instead of back at the guild. She wouldn't have to wait for news if...

Three hooded people melted from the shadows, and Derica jumped. Mazolan patted her shoulder, unconcerned. And waved.

"HO THERE!" Mazolan yelled.

Derica's jaw fell open.

"Are we in the right place? We followed that map you left my lady. I hope we're in the right place?" the demon asked, tone cheery.

The trio said nothing and moved closer. Derica clicked her mouth shut and stepped into Mazolan's side until they brushed shoulders.

"Yes, my lady, you are in the right place." The rough, deep voice came from the middle figure. They sounded a bit like someone who had been ill and was speaking for the first time in weeks.

"Oh, good!" said Mazolan. They relaxed their posture into a slump. It was as threatening as a blade of grass. "So, can you take us to her friend?"

"Please," Derica whispered. It was a pathetic appeal. She was ashamed at the authentic desperation behind it.

"Follow," the voice instructed.

She looked to Mazolan, but their vacuous facade was still in place.

"Follow the nice people, my lady," they said, flicking a hand forward nonchalantly.

Doing her best to maintain her own facade—which was merely the outward expression of fear she would normally have suppressed—Derica jerked into action, following a safe distance from the hooded trio.

She could feel Mazolan's stare on the back of her neck. Or, at least, she hoped it was Mazolan's stare. After the demon had shared the coded message about Justus's disapproval of their actions, the burning on her nape could have been from his flinty gaze. Derica would gladly weather his rage as long as she could save Reid.

"I need to know," Mazolan spoke to the back of their guides, "is this part of an apprentice hazing? I told my lady—I said, 'My lady, this has to be a prank. Maybe your Reid will return a little drunk, and a little bruised, but he'll be fine.' You should know that I've known many physicians—been on the end of their needles plenty of times from... brave... battles." They turned to Derica as if to make sure she was aware they were brave. "Yes, very brave. Anyway, I've known a good share of the healing inclined and let me tell you, there is no group in all of Veridion that better hides the way they enjoy a good celebration, some pranks, and a keg of ale." The hoot of an owl sounded—three sharp calls. Mazolan chuckled, the sound barely more than a whisper. "Am I right?" they called forward to the hooded trio.

There was nothing but the strike of their stride on the cobblestones.

"Hmm, it's all right. Probably a trade secret." Mazolan fumbled their hands into their pockets and began whistling a horrible melody—discordant notes that couldn't be called a song by any stretch of the imagination. Derica allowed herself to wince. She'd heard Mazolan whistle before. This was purposefully awful.

The hooded figures halted before a narrow, shadowed alleyway. If they hadn't shown her its location, she would have walked by, oblivious.

The middle figure held out one arm and said, "This way."

Derica's brain screamed a warning. They were stepping into a trap. She didn't know how Justus, Nyle, and the others could follow them. Not without showing the kidnappers their presence. Panic gripped her throat, tying her tongue. She didn't move one step farther. She didn't think her legs would let her.

Maz whispered so low she barely heard it over the frantic pounding of her heart, "Morsel, remember to trust me." Louder, for the benefit of their audience, they added, "Come on, dove. I promise I won't let any spiders get you. I won't even charge extra for that!" Booming a laugh—an inelegant expression for the smooth demon—they turned and looked at the hooded figures. When no appreciation for their jest was forthcoming, Mazolan murmured, "You three need some ale. I'll have a word with your guild later for you, if you like."

Derica shoved her fear down.

Trust Mazolan.

If it meant finding Reid, Derica would walk into any danger. With a deep inhale, Derica stepped into the shadowed alleyway.

On the rooftop, Justus rubbed his temples. His head felt like it would burst. His ears were ringing. He clenched his teeth so tightly, he was positive his molars squeaked.

That Weaver-damned demon. And her.

He could accept Mazolan was the kind to wiggle around orders—but her. Derica sought *him* out for help. She came to *him* crying, scared and needing help. And he'd felt like her champion.

Justus should have known the second she didn't protest staying where it was safe. The Weaver-blessed was different in every incarnation. But one thing they always had in common, a core tenant of their soulthread, was their need to protect the ones they cared about.

Derica was no different. Reid was her closest friend—first in her heart.

A tattooed hand clapped him on the shoulder, and Justus bared his teeth. If Nyle didn't remove his grip, he would remove it for him. Justus would accept no calming, placid, piratical shit from the smooth bastard.

Not right now.

"Commander—"

"Don't. You. Dare," Justus breathed, violence curling under his words like smoke under a door.

"They'll be fine. Mazolan won't let anything happen to her."

Justus's vision edged red at the corners. He was not in the fucking mood. Checking his sword and dagger in their scabbards, he patted his other concealed weapons. Then Justus moved toward the rope ladder hanging off the roof.

Nyle moved in front of him like liquid night, holding his palms out. It wasn't the attempt to halt him that incensed Justus. It was the fucking serene expression on Nyle's *fucking* face.

He snapped.

Knocking Nyle's hands down, Justus stepped forward into the other man's space. He plowed his knuckles into the other mercenary's navel, and Nyle's whoosh of air struck a chord of pleasure, harmonizing with Justus's rage.

But did Nyle go down?

No. Of course not.

The other man hunched over in pain, though.

Sweeping a boot into Nyle's feet, Justus leveraged the other man's position, sending him to the ground. The shingles thumped and rattled, a beautifully discordant sound.

Justus stepped over his prone comrade. He needed to get into that alley. He would rain death and destruction on anyone who might harm Derica.

Nyle coughed as Justus stepped onto the top rung of the rope ladder. He croaked, barely audible, "T-trust Mazolan."

With a snarl, Justus vaulted back to Nyle and crouched in front of his nose. Nyle lay on his side, clutching his stomach. He breathed in shallow pants, mouth tight. Honestly, he was laying it on a little thick.

Justus hadn't hit him *that* hard.

"Trust Mazolan? When is that *ever* a good idea?" Justus spat, looking down at him.

"W-when have they ever failed to do what you wanted?" Nyle gulped air into his lungs, levering himself up. Justus could list every single time Maz got *creative* with orders, but Nyle cut him off. "They," the tattooed mercenary continued, "may use unique methods, but they always get the job done."

"At what cost?" Justus seethed. "Her *life*?" Justus bent forward until he was menacing directly into Nyle's eyes. "Unacceptable."

"You're overreacting. You know you are," Nyle said.

Nyle interacted with the world like it was water and he was a shark's fin. Cutting through it all—affected by little resistance. Justus couldn't imagine that kind of freedom.

Justus had seen and done so much—not only in this lifetime, but all of them. Sometimes, he wondered if the memories would overflow. With every turn on the Loom, he felt his heart and soul harden, coated in another layer of stone. Even before he lost the Weaver-blessed, there was something inside of him that grew colder the more time passed.

Nyle wouldn't cut through him. Justus was too tough, too fortified.

"She's your solution," Nyle said, "and Maz knows that. Don't they?"

Justus narrowed his eyes.

"Mazolan knows exactly who she is to you," said Nyle.

The commander jerked back and watched Nyle, eyes narrowed. He hadn't been there when Justus and Mazolan aired their secrets.

"Anyone with eyes in their skull knows what she is to you. Mazolan may do things differently, but that's how they've always been. They know what's important—*who's* important." Nyle nodded, eyebrows raised.

Justus didn't want to let go of his rage. It was the only thing holding him up. The only thing keeping him from collapsing like Nyle after Justus's fist plowed into his gut.

He'd forgotten how much caring could hurt. How much fear there was in caring.

Nyle saw the change come over the commander—because of course he did.

"We'll get her back. Her *and* Reid. And Mazolan will keep them safe until we get to them."

This time, when Nyle's tattooed hand landed on his shoulder and squeezed, Justus left it there.

CHAPTER THIRTY-SIX

Derica and Mazolan followed the hooded trio for what seemed like an eternity. Every time they made a turn, she expected to find Reid. Her nerves wound tighter and tighter as they moved from one empty alley to the next.

Mazolan was no comfort. They whistled, loud and off tune, while frequently missing turns as they were being led. Derica was doing her best to trust Maz, but they weren't instilling much confidence with their antics.

She supposed that was the point. Who would expect to be outwitted by such an incompetent sword for hire?

Maz's whistling halted. "Ho, my good... hoods," they called forward. "Are we, by chance, almost at our destination? If I had known it would take this long, I would have charged the lady by the hour. Doubt she could have afforded me, had I done the smart thing. I mean, look at her." Mazolan gestured at Derica, but none of the hooded figures turned. "Well, you got a good look before. Not posh, this one. But I'm sure you're familiar with capitalist enterprises. I'm an entrepreneur, really. Trying to make a name for myself—build up a history of satisfaction with those that hire me." They rambled on, "Just curious, you're not planning on requesting an ungodly sum for the return of her friend, are you? That's another thing that might cut into my profit margin. The lady clearly has limited funds." The demon trotted a few steps away from her, closer to the figures. Loudly whispering, they said, "If she had an enterprise like mine, who knows? Maybe she'd have heftier coffers. People don't seem to like women in commerce, however. Quite odd, that. What objection could they have to stimulating the economy and seeing them operating as equals? It's damned odd, if you don't mind my saying..."

Derica tuned out Maz's continued monologue. The hooded figures didn't slow, comment, or otherwise take any notice of their rambling.

Every narrow street they'd led them down could have been anywhere in Radley. There was no indication of their location whatsoever from their surroundings.

She suspected confusion was the purpose of their circuitous route. Derica hoped Mazolan was as talented at tracking and wayfinding as they were at making nonsense speeches.

Derica stiffened at three faint hoots from the roof above them. She cut her eyes to Mazolan, watching for any reaction. Their hood fluttered, a delighted smirk gleaming from its depth—there one second and gone the next, so quickly she could have imagined it.

Mazolan's monologue never stuttered "...Did you know that other races in Veridion have managed this so-called equality humans make efforts towards? Not that you'd know, the way they've shuffled them to the edges of the known world. Honestly, can you blame them for staying far away from that lot? Obsessed with war and violence. Not like you three, I'm sure—"

"CEASE!" thundered one of the hooded figures, finally facing the jabbering demon.

"I understand. You're just not up for a philosophical chat this evening." They nodded, holding their hands out in a placating motion. "So, are we almost there yet? It's as if you've been taking us in circles!" Maz laughed, slapping their thigh. "That can't be true. I'm sure you want us to reach my lady's friend and have this entire business over with. You never did say—was it hazing? I think it's hazing—"

The center figure jerked toward Mazolan, growling. Mazolan yelped and jumped behind Derica, holding her before them as a shield.

Trust Mazolan trust Mazolan trust Mazolan trust Mazolan trust Mazolan trust Mazolan trust Mazolan trust Mazolan trust Mazolan.

The refrain crashed through her thoughts over and over. The words did nothing to keep her knees from knocking together as the figure approached. She cringed back into Maz. Their fingers softened on her shoulders—the only comfort they could give.

Despite stopping only a foot away, Derica couldn't see into the shadows cast by the figure's hood.

"I—" her voice came out thin and warbling. Licking her lips and trying again, she said, "I'm sorry for my companion. I am anxious to see my friend, and my escort is only trying to earn their coin."

In a whisper so quiet, it could have been an aural hallucination, Maz said, *"Most important lesson about plans. They change."* Mazolan's fingers left her shoulders, and Derica had to squash the mental image of the demon abandoning her, returning to the guild minus one red-headed hindrance. A darker thought followed of a knife slipping through her ribs, leaving her bleeding on the cobblestones.

The figure stepped closer, and she peeked around them. The other two were standing placidly, waiting for this interaction to conclude. Mazolan made no noise behind her. Derica stepped back, an icy chill raking down her spine when she didn't feel their hands anymore.

"You hired the loudest, most incompetent sword I've ever seen, *my lady*," the hooded figure before her sneered. "And we will bring you to your friend, rest assured. But, if there isn't quiet for the remainder of the journey, your condition will be less than pristine at our destination. Accidents sometimes happen in dark alleys."

"No more questions," she promised. Her heart was in her throat. Her fingers tangled into frantic knots at her waist.

"We'll be there shortly."

Before the figure could turn around, two shadows slid down from the rooftops. They dropped the other hooded individuals to the ground without a sound. Derica's heart raced faster. Something flashed in the corner of her eye, and then Mazolan was holding a knife to the throat of the one before her.

"Well," Mazolan purred, "I would rather we get to our friend as quickly as possible. Otherwise, the condition in which *you* arrive will be less than pristine."

The figure's shoulders rose as they inhaled sharply. Mazolan's knife exaggerated their point.

"You started taking us in circles. No, don't deny it!" Maz shook the figure, and their hood slipped down.

If Derica had expected this... man—boy, really—to appear evil, he didn't. He was tall and lean. He had unremarkable dark eyes, light hair, and pallid skin. Nothing to outwardly claim they were a kidnapper. She didn't know what evil looked like though. Maybe evil didn't evidence itself in appearance. Maybe it festered inside, like an illness. Or maybe there was a kernel in everyone, and it grew if you fed it.

"Mazolan," Derica reached to stay their arm, "I don't want to hurt this man."

"That's precious, morsel. But I don't think kindness will get Reid back from this one. Whoever he's working with isn't likely to be swayed by your benevolence."

The boy struggled in Maz's hold. The demon pinched his neck, and his eyes rolled back in his head. With a grunt, Mazolan caught him before letting him fall to the ground with a *thump.*

Nyle materialized from the shadows over Maz's shoulder. "Mazolan's right, Derica. We don't take pleasure in it, but sometimes the rough stuff gets better results." He shrugged an apology.

Derica didn't look away from Nyle. Because if Nyle was here, Justus would be too.

"Hello, Derica. Mazolan," growled Justus, walking toward them. "What the *fuck* made either of you think this was a better plan than what I organized? *You*," he addressed Derica, "should be at the guild. Safe."

Out of the corner of her eye, she saw Nyle wince, and Mazolan rubbed a hand over their twitching lips.

This time, Derica's fear for Reid's safety didn't stop her from using her voice. Her temper blasted through, and she let it carry her forward until she stood in front of the commander.

"I only," she punctuated each assertion with a poke of her finger to his hard, wide chest, "wanted to be present when you recovered Reid. I know I am a liability in a fight." Poke. "But you didn't listen to me. I told you what I needed and what I wanted but you," *poke*, "wouldn't," *poke*, "hear," POKE, "me! At least Mazolan *listened*." If the last of her common sense had deserted her, Derica would have spat at Justus's feet. As it was, her finger was still jammed into his sternum. The fact it likely hurt her more than him was another log on the flame of her rage.

Dark gaze cold, Justus bent forward, lowering his head until they were eye to eye. His breath feathered her cheeks and stirred her hair. "I'm sorry you didn't like the plan I came up with but—"

"That's not it! I wasn't asking to operate as part of your team. I merely wanted to be here! If I'm here, I'm not waiting somewhere, alone and imagining all the worst possible things." Her voice wobbled, and she bit her lip, using the pain to ground herself.

"And what you foolishly don't seem to understand is that being present means being in danger. If I'm worried about keeping you safe, Reid wouldn't be my priority." He grabbed her finger with one hand and roughly raked his other through the tail of his hair. His eyes begged her to understand. "You would."

Derica blinked in shock, her mouth agape. Did he truly expect her to melt because of his concern? Did he expect her to titter and simper now that she knew he objected to her presence—merely because *he couldn't concentrate?*

She snatched her hand back. "If you can't focus enough to do something you're hired to do, simply because I'm near, it's a wonder you were made a commander."

Mazolan choked on a delighted laugh, and Nyle sucked in a surprised breath, both of their gazes bouncing between the commander and Derica.

Taking a step back, she squared her shoulders, opening her mouth to continue. Justus stepped forward, closing the space before she could speak.

"No," he said, "you didn't hire us. You came to *me* for help. This isn't a job. This is personal—for us both. This is not just a contract. And you are not only my client." He bent, his lips grazing the shell of her ear. "I thought you wanted more from me—I thought you wanted more from *us*. This is what you get. I don't want to put the woman I—" he cut himself off, dropping his forehead to her shoulder.

Derica's eyebrows climbed her forehead, and her hands fluttered at her side. She wanted to stroke his back, comfort him. Over Justus's shoulder, Nyle shook Mazolan's arm and jerked his head toward the end of the alley. Mazolan frowned and waved the man off. Nyle sighed and hauled Mazolan away by the belt. The demon protested until the shadows of the alley swallowed the two.

"The woman you what?" she whispered.

Justus turned his head into the curve of her neck, breathing her in. He sighed against her skin. "The woman I... care for. This would be personal even if you weren't here. I know how much Reid means to you." His deep voice held the barest hint of jealousy.

Giving into her impulse, she allowed herself to stroke one hand over his shoulders. His clenched muscles softened under her fingers.

He murmured, "I care for Reid's safety because you care about him. Protecting him protects a piece of your heart. I wanted you to stay at the guild because I can't guarantee your safety here." His lips pressed lightly over her collarbone for a second.

"But you're not alone," she said, "and I know to stay out of the way. You don't trust Mazolan and Nyle to protect me and Reid?"

Justus sighed and placed another fleeting kiss to her skin, then stood straight. He began to reach for her waist but curled his hands into fists instead, lowering his arms to his sides. "I guess I have to. There's no sending you back to the guild now. Is there?"

She shook her head. Derica spoke true, and she would see this to the end. She was not going to put herself in danger. If she gave Justus more than a moment, he might argue she jeopardized her safety by accepting Mazolan's help. So, she didn't give him time to think. They needed to find Reid. "No, there isn't," she said, raising her chin and meeting his eyes steadily.

Justus sighed. "Yes. All right," he murmured, more to himself than to her. She saw the wheels turning, the way this complication made him adjust his plan.

Mazolan and Nyle drifted back. They flanked their commander, waiting. Mazolan caught her eye and winked. Nyle rolled his at the demon's antics.

Justus clasped his hands behind his back and laid out the new plan.

Derica watched Mazolan, remembering what they had said. *Most important lesson about plans. They change.*

CHAPTER
THIRTY-SEVEN

D erica was glad Justus didn't have to alter the plan drastically. The
commander delivered the order that Mazolan was in charge of safe-
guarding Derica, his tone brooking no deviations. Derica spoke up to remind
Justus the demon hadn't placed her in danger. Justus merely responded by
glaring at Maz with menace so intense, it was a wonder their braid didn't
crisp.

Nyle and Justus had intervened when it was obvious the hooded trio were
leading them in circles. Mazolan nodded and said they knew, that they were
waiting for the right moment to act. When Mazolan arrogantly thanked Justus for the opening, she was genuinely afraid for the demon's safety.

Holding Nyle between them, Mazolan yelped, "Now, now, it'll all come out
in the wash, Commander! We should get the details from those robed idiots.
I can make quick work of that." It was half statement and half question. They
peeked over Nyle's shoulder, expression contrite. Justus sighed and nodded.
Derica suppressed a smile.

Justus and Nyle brought over the young man the demon had knocked out. Mazolan propped him against the brick wall.

"Mazolan," Justus said, "I want him awake, and I want Reid's location as soon as possible." He waited for Maz's nod, then added, "Whatever it takes."

The demon lowered their hood and rubbed their hands together, crouching before the unconscious man. Nyle, Derica, and Justus stepped back.

Maz woke the man with something between a slap and a pat on the cheek. When the man jerked, groaning, the yellow-eyed mercenary crooned, "Wake up. Mazolan has questions for you."

The man blinked slowly, then cringed into the wall when they realized who woke them.

"Name. Now." Mazolan's demand bounced off the alley walls.

"W-Walden."

"Good, Walden."

Walden paled at the fanged smile Maz offered.

"Answer all my questions, and I won't have to get creative. I enjoy stretching myself as an artist, but the people I interrogate rarely appreciate it." Mazolan leaned forward, and their voice dropped into a slower cadence. "Where are you keeping the lady's friend?"

Walden rolled his lips inward, saying nothing.

Mazolan looked over their shoulder. "Nyle, did you bring my carving knives?" they asked, a frightening gleam in their yellow eyes.

"Wha—no!" Walden threw his hands out, pleading.

Mazolan clucked their tongue and shook their head. ***Then answer the question.***

Nyle leaned into Derica and whispered out the side of his mouth, "A bluff. They do have carving knives, but they're not for this. We don't have time, and Maz knows it." Derica shivered, imagining Mazolan gleefully wielding dual weapons. A small part of her was extremely curious to see how they fought.

"Where are you keeping the lady's friend?" Mazolan repeated.

Walden's eyes went glassy and their response was monotone. "Underneath." Then he pointed behind Derica.

Nyle frowned and muttered, "Back to the east side of the city."

Derica nodded, like she had any sense of direction in Radley.

Mazolan leaned closer to Walden, speaking too low to hear. The quiet was more unnerving than anything. A reserved Mazolan was dangerous. Derica knew this with certainty.

Justus and Nyle were murmuring to each other, and Derica let the conversation drift around her, watching the demon the whole time. Mazolan didn't raise their voice loud enough to be heard again. Contented with whatever they discovered, Maz pinched a spot on the side of the man's neck. Walden slumped forward, suddenly limp and unresponsive.

Derica swallowed past the knot of alarm in her throat. "Is he...?"

"No." Nyle shook his head after a quick scan of the man. "Only out for the next several hours."

Justus shifted, drawing Derica's attention. "We'll leave the trio tied up here. We'll take their robes and head east."

"And that will work?" Derica asked. "You three are larger than they are."

Mazolan joined them, hands in their pockets and swaying back and forth on their feet like they hadn't just interrogated and threatened someone. "Morsel, people see what they expect to see. If we're covered and dressed in these lots' robes, we'll have enough time to get in and find Reid. As we've learned—"

"Plans change," she finished.

Mazolan grinned with satisfaction. "Your education is coming along wonderfully."

Nyle chuckled, and Justus frowned darkly.

With the three mercenaries robed, Mazolan led them to the location where Reid was being held. On the way, Derica let her mind wander hopefully, imagining scenarios of finding Reid safe and sound. When they halted at a dead end, she peered up at the indistinguishable bricks.

"Where are we?" she whispered.

"Shhh," hissed Mazolan, focused on the wall in front of them

Derica rolled her eyes and moved closer to the robed figure with the broadest back. "Where are we?" she asked again.

Before Justus could answer, Mazolan pushed on one of the bricks. With a metallic whine, a grate at their feet slid into a hidden recess.

Nyle bent over, peering into the opening. "This can't be connected to our tunnels. Can it?"

"If they are, I don't want to be the one to tell Alondra," said Mazolan.

Justus waved a hand. "If they are, we have to tell her."

"Sounds like a job for the commander!" Mazolan clapped Justus's shoulder and jumped down into the gap.

Derica gasped, expecting to hear a sickening thud. Instead, Mazolan's hooded head poked back up. "Come on, then. By now, they're probably awaiting their comrades' return. We don't need any more trouble than we're already going to face." The demon's head disappeared, then popped back into view once again. "Stairs. Leading further beneath this building, if I had to guess."

Nyle descended next, followed by Justus. The commander held up a hand to guide Derica down.

"Careful," he said. "It's dark."

Finding herself in a dim tunnel eerily like the one Mazolan led her out of, Derica followed behind Justus, her hand still in his.

Nyle noticed and coughed pointedly. It would look suspicious if they encountered anyone else.

Justus let go with a squeeze, moving farther ahead, closer to Mazolan and Nyle. "We're right here. Nothing will happen to you," he whispered.

"I'm not worried about myself. As I've told you, I'll stay out of the way. I only want to—"

"We know," said Mazolan. "The farm boy. You're here for him." They motioned for the others to follow, and the rest walked in silence. A few yards into the tunnel, a glow grew brighter with every step.

Derica let out a relieved sigh when she realized there were lanterns posted farther in the dark tunnel.

They walked for a substantial length of time—at least it felt substantial to Derica—through long stretches of shadow and brief intervals of light until they reached a dead end. The wall blocking their path was exactly like the rest of the tunnel. A single lantern hung high in the center of a wrought iron hook.

Derica was about to assert they must have taken a wrong turn when Mazolan stepped forward. They started running their fingers over the surface of the wall.

"I think these people might like their hidden entrances even more than the guild, Commander," they chuckled. "We should have Lonnie send them a letter offering our services after this. They could use a security consultation."

"Mazolan," Justus grumbled, "find the Weaver-damned button or lever."

"What do you think I'm looking for?"

Nyle joined Mazolan, both of them sweeping the wall for a loose brick or anything to indicate a hidden mechanism. When they'd made a full pass, neither finding what they were looking for, they stepped away. Mazolan and Nyle both stood, hands propped on their hips, studying the wall.

The tattooed mercenary hummed, considering, and then stepped forward again. This time, Maz stayed back, watching.

Nyle hooked the lantern hanger with one finger, the blue ink decorating his knuckles looking like dancing shadows. Derica held her breath. He pulled, and the hanger tilted down. Faint grinding rumbled on the other side of the wall, and it slid open.

Mazolan humphed. "Lucky guess," they mumbled.

Say what you wanted about the demon, but Derica was glad they were here to lighten the mood. Justus and Nyle wouldn't be using humor to combat any sense of impending doom. Maybe it wasn't even intentional on Mazolan's part. Regardless, she was thankful for it.

Nyle and Justus flanked the door, and Mazolan entered first with a flash of white fangs. Derica was used to the sight by now, but it still struck her as predatory. She wondered if Reid's captors could feel they were being hunted.

Viciously, she hoped they did.

Nyle vanished through the door next.

Justus looked at her, his eyes two black pits in the shadow of his hood. She could tell he wanted to say something—probably to ask her again if she was sure she wouldn't go back. Derica didn't give him the chance, stepping by him to follow Mazolan and Nyle. Justus's grumble of irritation followed her.

She wasn't turning back, and he would have to deal with it.

Derica bounced off a robed back—no telling which of the mercenaries it was—and rebounded into Justus. He caught her with an arm around her waist, and a bolt of heat thrummed through her body. She blushed, happy the darkness concealed her reaction. This was not the time nor the place.

Despite that knowledge, she couldn't keep her fingers from stroking his forearm before she moved out of his hold. Justus grumbled again, the vibration a phantom stroke down her back.

Not the time.

He knew it too because he moved around her, settling in formation behind Mazolan, next to Nyle. Mazolan, with the knowledge from the interrogation, would go first.

"Do they have something against lit spaces?" breathed Maz in the dark.

"Shh," hissed Justus.

Mazolan had a point. Why was there so little light?

"This way," the demon said, leading them away from the hidden door.

They reached a lit juncture. It forked between a staircase and another door. The stairs spiraled upward. The architecture around both was different. The stairs appeared older than the tunnel they'd come from, made of rough, pitted, bleached blocks. Derica couldn't guess how old it was.

"Which way?" asked Justus.

Mazolan inclined their head to the door, and everyone followed. It opened into a sizeable room that smelled like mildew and something Derica couldn't quite place. If age had a smell, that's what perfumed this space. The lighting was just as sparse and their surroundings were still barely visible.

Before entering the larger room, Justus grabbed a torch from the stairwell.

Mazolan looked back, lifting their lip. "Not stealthy," they hissed.

"Not all of us see in the dark as well as you," Justus hissed back. "Fighting blind is—"

"Never wise. I know, I know." Mazolan grimaced.

Tall shelves seemed to go on endlessly around them. Derica stepped closer to the nearest one and reached out, inspecting their contents. Her finger met cool, stiff leather. Trailing her hand to the side, she felt the bump of various leather-wrapped items of varying widths.

Books.

Derica's forehead scrunched into a frown. They were in a library? Reid was being held in a *library*?

A loud noise sounded from the other side of the room, making Derica jerk her hand back. She stumbled into Nyle. Without hesitation, he swept her behind his back, and she found herself surrounded by three alert mercenaries.

It took Derica a moment to think while her heart raced, but the sound might have been a yell, and it hadn't been Reid's voice.

Derica tapped Justus's shoulder and moved closer to speak to him, so her voice wouldn't carry. "I don't think kidnappers would care for my safety quite this much."

"Too fucking bad," he said, voice low and thrumming with tension.

Nyle shifted, looking at his commander. "She has a point."

"Again, too fucking bad."

"Commander," mused Mazolan, "are you sure it wasn't yourself we should have left at the guild? It's not Derica insisting on stupidity right now."

She jolted at the use of her name. She'd become so used to them using her moniker, it was jarring to hear Mazolan address her by name.

The mercenaries lapsed into hand signals—and once or twice, crude gestures—while they argued silently. Finally, the matter seemed to be settled when Justus gestured with exaggerated frustration at Mazolan.

The demon pointed opposite the direction the sound had come from. Derica sighed in relief.

Traversing the wide room of bookshelves, the group stayed to the side of the room, moving toward the corner. A narrow corridor, even older than the area they were in, came into view.

The walls here were visibly ancient—darkened by time, the floors weathered by countless feet. Cells with black metal bars lined the small path, sending a frisson of apprehension down the back of her neck. In the darkness, the cells appeared to stand out among the shadows like macabre sentinels.

There were no faces peeking from between the bars, no hands reaching out for absolution or rescue. No cornflower-blue eyes and gleaming golden hair. It was, at once, a comfort and a source of harrowing panic.

Derica reached forward and tangled shaking fingers in the back of Justus's robe, needing to ground herself in some small way. He slowed slightly, letting her fingers press into his skin through the fabric.

She took a slow, deep breath and then immediately wished she hadn't. At first, two smells tangled in her nose. The air inside the passageway tasted like metal—coppery. Another shallow breath confirmed with certainty it was the scent of aged metal and underneath... salt.

Blood.

Derica's fist trembled against Justus's robe and he stiffened, broadening his stance to shield her.

Nyle noticed and gave him a hard, eagle-eyed look. Justus twitched one shoulder as if to say *deal with it*. If he wouldn't be sensible, Derica would. Justus couldn't afford to appear like a protective captor. At first, her fingers resisted her mental order to release him, but she finally loosened her grip, dropping her hand. Derica drifted back a few steps, maintaining a normal distance.

"Heads on straight, humans," hissed Mazolan in a whisper.

CHAPTER THIRTY-EIGHT

An ember of pride warmed Justus's heart. Derica was doing incredibly well under the circumstances. However, the Weaver-blessed always possessed a will of iron and an inclination to protect the ones they loved.

It was one of the reasons the Warrior lost their heart to the Weaver-blessed in every lifetime. Although Derica didn't remember, their souls had done this dance over and over. The particulars were always different—how they met, what they looked like, their cultural backgrounds. The end result was the same. A communion of soulthreads so deep and intertwined, they termed it a heartthread bond.

He craved it like a man dying of thirst—and he regretted what it would lead to.

Justus called himself a fool for yielding to Derica and the fate he knew was heading for them. He'd lived the inevitability of this struggle time and time again. At least she didn't remember. At least Derica was not weighted by the memory of his betrayal. He did not wish to see her shoulders sag with the burden of guilt he carried alone.

Nyle nudged his arm, and Justus shook his spiraling thoughts away. He needed to be clearheaded. He needed to be Derica's shield because the amazing fool insisted on being here when she should be at the guild.

The four of them stood inside the doorway to the ancient cell block Mazolan led them to. Nyle caught his eyes and jerked his chin. Reaching back, Justus gently pried Derica's fingers from his stolen clothing and signed to Mazolan to stay at Derica's side.

The demon rolled their glinting yellow eyes but nodded. Justus's chest vibrated with a low growl of aggravation, and Derica looked at him askance. He shrugged and followed Nyle deeper into the row of cells.

There was a single lantern casting a tiny circle of light twenty paces away. He and Nyle could barely stand side-by-side as they walked. Each scanned the closest cells as they stepped, ears cocked and steps silent.

Every barred square was an empty cocoon of shadow. The more unoccupied cells they passed, the more unnerving it became. Every time Justus's gaze swept to a yawning pit of darkness, he expected to see a prone Reid, blond hair shining like a beacon.

But there was nothing.

Something hummed in the back of Justus's mind. He hadn't anticipated this pervasive feeling of impending dread. Before a mission, Justus thrived on the intricate planning and mental maneuvering that was part and parcel of his career. A deviation from plan was adrenaline inducing, another way to adapt and overcome. But he currently felt nothing but apprehension and unease.

Justus's and Nyle's breaths were too loud among the eerie quiet of their surroundings. There wasn't even the skitter or squeak of rats.

Reaching the circle of lantern light, Nyle saw them first. He nudged Justus's shoulder, and they moved closer to the bars. It was an older couple, a man and a woman. They were on the ground, bound and gagged in the cell's corner. When the woman spotted the pair of robed mercenaries, she leaned into the man's shoulder, and his head jerked up.

Reid's eyes stared back at him from the man's face, and Justus growled a curse under his breath. What in the Weaver-damned world was going on?

Justus scanned the woman and found some of Reid's features in her face as well, though softened by age and femininity. The woman looked at him with embers of hate gleaming in her gaze. The man tried to put himself in front of the woman, but could not move more than a few inches, limited by his bindings.

Justus signaled to Nyle that the other man should sweep the rest of the cells. The woman frowned when the other mercenary walked off. She likely suspected something was different about them.

At the entrance, scuffling and muffled whispers bounced along the pitted stone floor. He turned his head and found Derica trying to wrestle her arm out of Mazolan's grip. The demon was nearly nose to nose with her and clearly trying to get her to remain where they were. Justus signaled them to quiet, and Mazolan snapped something at Derica before signing an agreement back.

That was when Derica danced away from Mazolan, rushing down the corridor toward Justus. Mazolan jumped beside her, but didn't restrain her progress. The set of her shoulders and the clip of her heels announced her determination.

She thought they'd found Reid.

Derica reached Justus's side as Nyle was returning from the other end of the cell block. The man shook his head quickly, and then chaos reigned.

Derica's red hair glinted in the light of the lantern, and the man and woman in the cell thrashed against their bindings and shouted into their gags. At the disturbance, Nyle and Mazolan jumped to face the hall entrance and drew their weapons from under their robes. Derica grasped the bars of the cell, rattling the door.

The whine of steel and the scrape of the locked cell door had the couple thrashing harder, yelling louder.

"Pip! Tedric!" Derica cried, shocked. Tears glinted in her eyes, and her chin trembled.

As he thought. They must be Reid's parents.

"Open this door," Derica begged. "Oh, please—"

Justus stepped behind her, slipping his palm over her lips, silencing her. The couple in the cell stilled.

"The whole thing has gone bollocks up, Commander," Mazolan said. "This isn't what I was told we'd find. We can't cock it up any more."

Nyle scoffed. "Beg to differ."

Derica thrashed against Justus. He loosened his hold but kept his hand over her mouth. She bit his palm.

"This isn't the behavior you promised me," he hissed into the shell of her ear. Justus was fast losing control of the situation.

"Oh," said Maz, "*now* you care about good behavior."

Derica stopped struggling, but she nipped his hand again.

"Quiet," Justus ordered as he released his grip.

"I don't think that matters, Commander. We should have drawn attention by now," said Nyle. "We need to make this quick. Get them out, have them tell us where Reid is, and then get the fuck out of here."

"I concur." Mazolan nodded.

"Nyle, the door," Justus said, stepping back with Derica. He kept one palm on her back, keeping her in easy reach should she try to wiggle away. Damned woman.

Nyle slipped an instrument into the lock of the cell door. The man and woman—Pip and Tedric—watched with wide eyes. Derica's back shifted in jerking breaths under his hand, and Justus stepped closer.

Footsteps, more than one pair, sounded from the entrance.

"Faster," hissed Mazolan.

"This thing is ancient. I can't risk breaking the lock. Then we'll never get them out," Nyle snapped. However, he stirred the instrument in the lock faster.

Derica whimpered, shrinking back into Justus's chest. He shifted her to his other side, away from the approaching footsteps. "Remember," he whispered to her, "stay out of the way of any fighting." Derica jerked a nod.

The footsteps stopped.

Mazolan tensed, and Nyle paused at the lock. No one spoke. They waited in the silence. Justus focused on catching the tiniest sound in the suffocating quiet. Mazolan looked back at him and nodded, then the demon tapped Nyle on the shoulder. Nyle resumed his work on the door.

"Are they gone?" Derica whispered.

"Doubtful," answered Mazolan, adjusting the grip on their weapon. "They didn't just disappear."

Derica's form shook against Justus's body. He wanted her out of this place. But he wouldn't dare try to haul her away without rescuing the couple first. Otherwise, she wouldn't budge. This he knew in his bones.

When the lock clicked, there was a hushed, collective sigh.

A faint squeal of hinges drew Justus's eye to the back of the cell. He squinted. There was something protruding from an opening in the wall at about shoulder height. *Several* somethings. There was a hiss before something hit the side of his neck; Derica yelped at the same time. Mazolan and Nyle jolted.

Justus slapped his hand to his neck, cursing when his fingers brushed something thin, sending a bolt of pain into the top of his shoulder. The ground started to tilt below his feet.

"No." The words felt thick and too slow on his tongue. Like cold honey. He fisted a hand in Derica's tunic, seeing her weave from side to side. Bracing his feet, he herded her behind him and pressed her into the cell bars at his back.

"Commander," warned Mazolan, shaking their head as if to clear their vision.

Nyle stood as still as a stone. If Justus hadn't seen his chest move, he would have been worried. "Nyle?" he asked, fighting his lips to release the name. They tingled.

The tattooed mercenary sounded like his mouth was full of rocks. "Worst outcome: poison darts. Best? Sleeping draught—we go to sleep and wake up. In what condition that happens would be anyone's guess." Nyle leaned sharply to the left and then righted himself. Only to lean to the other side. With a crack of bone, he fell to his knee and dropped his head.

Mazolan backed up until they stood against the wall beside Derica. "Oh, these shall be some truly horrific dreams. Why can't my mind ever conjure lovely, naked, writhing nymphs? It's always..." they shook their head, sinking onto their ass, "...*always* it's blood and death."

Derica's hand waved into Justus's periphery, reaching to comfort Mazolan, he guessed. He blinked when he saw double. "S-sit," he hissed. Derica didn't have time to follow his direction. He fell to the ground, taking her with him in a tangle of fabric and limbs.

Mazolan barked a delirious laugh. It rang off the walls, transforming into something dark and sinister. At least, that's what Justus thought he heard. It could be the drug coursing through his system.

Derica's hands clutched at his shoulders, and he chased them with his until their fingers tangled. He brought her hand to his numb lips and pressed a kiss to the back of it.

"We didn't find Reid," Derica said, her voice high and thin, drifting away to nothing.

His heart kicked sluggishly, and he settled more of his weight onto Derica. If he couldn't be awake to protect her, then he'd damned well make it hard for anyone to separate them. His unconscious form would be her shelter from whomever or whatever wanted them.

"I know, my heart. I know." He'd let something slip that he shouldn't have. Panic flitted through his brain and then drowned in the encroaching black eating up his thoughts.

Derica's hand spasmed in his and she went boneless against his back. Mazolan was the next to tilt over. As Justus's strength faded—as Nyle dropped to his side on the floor in front of them—he fumbled with his robe and his weapons belt. He snagged the dagger and slipped it into Derica's boot, doing his best not to slice his fingers. He wasn't likely to feel the cut if he did.

With the dark glint of the ruby pommel being the last image he saw, Justus lost his fight and fell into the void.

CHAPTER THIRTY-NINE

Derica's eyes felt weighted. Her body felt like a cage for her soul, not its home. And in the very back of her mind, she screamed at herself to move, to hide—to find safety.

To find Justus.

She jolted with the thought. He had been with her. He had... kissed her hand... and he'd called her... something. Something heart-stoppingly tender.

It fluttered out of reach, dancing through the shadows, veiling her mind in sluggish fog. Struggling to lift her eyelids, Derica fought a creeping panic.

She couldn't see.

She blinked frantically. Light and shapes formed out of the darkness. Her heart beat harder, battering her ribs and sending tingles into her numb extremities.

Reid sat tied to a chair, his ankles and wrists bound by thick twists of hemp. His golden head lolled to one side, his face a mottled canvas of purple and blue. Blood crusted above his lip and the sides of his mouth. The eye not covered by his hair was swollen shut. Derica jerked toward him, realizing her hands and feet were bound in the same fashion when the ropes bit into her skin.

"R—" her voice was a rough garble. Derica swallowed thickly and tried again. "Reid. Reid! Wake up. Oh, Weaver, open your eyes."

He didn't twitch a muscle.

Derica bit her lip hard. She would *not* cry. Not right now. Crying would not save them.

She tried one more time, breathing in deep before yelling his name. Again, nothing. His stillness was all the sudden more terrifying. Frantically, she raked her gaze over him, searching for the thrum of his pulse, the lifting of his chest. It took a moment for her to focus and watch, but his chest finally moved. The breath hardly moved his torso, and it was entirely too shallow, but Reid was alive.

Derica allowed herself to melt into her chair for half a second. Tears flooded her eyes, blurring her view. She blinked, streaking them down her cheeks, dropping onto her collar. The tracks tickled, but she couldn't wipe them away.

Sniffing hard, Derica filled her lungs and yelled Reid's name once more. He didn't move as her voice ricocheted off the surrounding walls, echoes glancing off the ancient walls. A roar answered her yell, tunneling from behind her. Derica whimpered and jerked her chin over her shoulder, eyes searching her periphery. She couldn't even tell if there was a wall behind her. There was simply more darkness.

The roar came again, and this time it raised the hair on arms, sending prickles of alarm up her nape to the crown of her head. Another immediately joined it.

There was something in the dark, made all the more terrifying because Derica could only imagine the horror behind her. Derica faced Reid and tugged at her bonds. She succeeded only in chafing her skin. When her wrists and ankles became slick with blood, she stopped. The sharp point at her right ankle scraped and ground against the joint, making it especially painful to move.

All the while, she kept one eye on Reid. She counted his breaths, hating each moment she waited. Some came on even beats, others arrived later. Her count was a disjointed, broken rhythm of worry and terror. She breathed to match. Several times, it was so long between inhales that dots swam in her vision.

Keeping one ear cocked for any sound, Derica jolted at the scrape of iron and stone from behind her. She stiffened and held her breath. It likely didn't matter if she turned to look at what or who had come, but Derica couldn't gather the courage to peer over her shoulder.

Her eyes squeezed shut as she imagined claws raking down her back, knives slicing her skin, or worse.

With her eyes closed, her hearing took up the burden of her hyper-vigilance. Soft footfalls pattered on the stone. They didn't sound hurried, but neither were they a normal cadence. Someone was sneaking behind her.

Derica breathed slowly through her nose, trembling. She couldn't get free. There was nothing to do but wait.

She flinched away when the steps drew near, anticipating a strike.

The rustle of fabric and scuffling suggested someone crouched next to her. Derica whimpered, unable to contain the sound.

"Shh," they said, voice low.

Derica strained against her bonds, her heart beating so hard she wondered how it wasn't bruising her ribs.

"Be calm," the voice whispered.

It took a long moment for the voice to penetrate the fog that occupied her thoughts, but when it did, Derica's eyes snapped open. She turned to see Balduin kneeling by her side, a lantern at his feet casting them both in golden light. He was the last person she ever thought she'd be thankful to see.

She sobbed, opening her mouth to ask where they were and how the acolyte had found them, when he held a finger up to his mouth and raised his brows. Derica licked her dry, cracked lips and nodded jerkily. His hand awkwardly patted the back of hers. He looked over to Reid, and his mouth tightened at what he saw.

Metal gleamed as Balduin took out a blade. He moved closer to her, bending over her left wrist. "I'll be as quick as I can, but these ropes are thick," he murmured. Derica did nothing but nod. Too many questions crowded her mind.

How did Balduin know where they were and how did he find them? Where was *here*? Did he know why Reid was taken? Where were the others?

The questions filled her mind until they spilled from her lips in a low tumble. The acolyte listened, not answering. He was intent on his task. When one of her wrists finally came free, he clucked and wiped the blood that circled the joint, before moving to her other side.

The roar came again, followed by its companion, and they both froze. Their eyes met and fear passed between them.

Hurry, she mouthed, pleading.

Balduin compressed his lips and nodded, sawing at the rope restraining her right arm. Following the roars, the faint sounds of snapping filaments were explosive blasts in the ringing silence. When her other hand was free, she shook the feeling back into her fingertips and gingerly inspected the rings of rope burns. There was nothing to do for them now.

The acolyte moved down to her feet. She bunched her skirts in her lap, pulling the hem away so he could see what he was doing.

The roar and its companion's echo came again. This time, closer.

Derica and Balduin both flinched. His hand moved the blade across the rope quicker and she hissed when his hand bobbed, the tip of the knife poking through the thin leather of her boots. When her foot was free, Balduin's hands were shaking and Derica practically vibrated with the need to rush to Reid. Balduin crossed in front of her, tripping on an uneven stone. He seemed to fall in slow motion. Derica reached out her hands to steady him—catch him—but her hands snatched empty air.

He hit the floor with a clatter and a gust of breath. The knife bounced out of his hand when his fist struck stone, twirling beyond the circle of lantern light. The blade disappeared, swallowed in shadow to be forgotten in the dark.

Derica's breath rushed in and out of her chest like a blacksmith's bellows. She tried to stand, but with one ankle still bound, she lost her balance and slammed back into the chair. Balduin attempted to push himself up, but cried out in pain when he placed weight on one hand.

His yelp rang off the walls. A second later, the roars came again. The acolyte scrambled up. Their eyes met. The cascade of fear, guilt, and sorrow in his expression chilled Derica's blood.

Gingerly, with careful movements, Balduin padded back to her side. He bent, grasping his lantern in his uninjured hand, and straightened.

Derica's chin wobbled as he looked at her with sadness and a grain of regret. "I'm sorry. May the Weaver be more kind your next turn on the Loom." He turned and silently rushed into the darkness past Reid.

The scrape of metal and stone announced his departure. The roars of rage that followed, closer again, made Derica shake all over. She wasn't sure if she was breathing at all now the way fear weighted her lungs.

When the echo from the roar subsided this time, Derica heard the rush and pound of feet. The sound galvanized her into action.

Her hands were shaking, but she gripped and pulled at the last binding on her ankle. The pain pressing into her ankle kept her from getting her fingers fully under the rope. The thin skin that covered the joint screamed, and her hands shook harder as every tug abused her skin even more.

Derica sobbed in frustration, her vision clouding. She blinked her tears away frantically. She had to get free. She had to get Reid free. And then she never wanted to encounter formless monsters in the dark ever again.

A hysterical laugh bubbled past her lips. It transformed into a cry of frustrated hopelessness as the beat of running feet drummed behind her.

Closer.

Ever closer.

Derica beat at her knees, her bloody wrists leaving wet streaks of crimson on her skirts. Her tantrum served only to waste time, but it hardened her resolve. She bent again over her thighs and tugged the hemp twist. She frowned when she touched the spot that was the most tender, not finding a knot. But she found...

Derica's breath escaped her in a shocked puff of air.

Justus's dagger. She'd never held it herself, but the simple grip and round pommel somehow felt familiar. Derica winced as she lifted the blade free—it left a path of agony as it pressed between her skin and the choke of the rope, slicing as she guided it loose. She began to manically hack at the tether with the blade, trembling fingers slick with blood.

Iron and stone scraped and squealed behind her.

She could cut faster, but Derica was out of time. Whatever or whoever was behind her had come. And there was nothing Derica could do to escape now.

CHAPTER FORTY

"Commander," hissed a voice close to his ear.

Justus moaned. His head ached, and his body seemed heavy. He felt like he'd had the best—or worst—night at the tavern. His tongue was thick, and his eyelids scraped like sand when he tried to blink open his eyes.

A hand patted his cheek firmly, the pressure not quite a slap, but the imminent threat of one was successfully communicated. And then he remembered where he had been last, how they'd all collapsed in the cell block.

"Derica!" he shouted, forcing his eyes open.

This time, the strike to his cheek was a slap. Justus batted the hand away and grabbed a slender throat, snarling. The wide, yellow eyes that met his were more apologetic than worried.

"Told you not to wake him like that, Maz," floated Nyle's voice from behind Justus.

The demon shrugged and went entirely limp in his hold. With an irritated growl, Justus flung Mazolan away and then scrubbed both his hands down his face, scratching the familiar coarse stubble on his cheeks.

Other than feeling like he had imbibed a wagon's worth of ale, his ribs were tender on one side. If he had to guess, he'd say he took a boot to the torso while unconscious. They were in a cell like the one they'd found the couple in, but the stone and metal construction appeared different, newer. Not the same location, then. Based on their surroundings, Justus thought they could be in the same underground area, or somewhere else entirely.

"Nyle?" he asked.

"Present and alive," Nyle answered.

"Mazolan's clearly fine. Where's Derica?" At the passing of her name over his lips, his chest burned with the urgency to find her. He was certain she wasn't safe, wherever she was, and it gutted him.

"If we knew, Commander, we'd tell you. Thank you for inquiring about my health as well," said Mazolan.

Justus pinched the bridge of his nose, breathing out all his fear and panic. It was time to adapt the plan—yet again.

"I know what you're thinking," said Maz. "You're thinking that this is the second time in a row you're having to rework the plan. Am I right? Of course I'm right. This is why I told Derica, the best plan is no plan. What good is a plan if the scenario doesn't fit? I said, 'Morsel—'"

"Mazolan," Nyle snapped, raising Justus's brows, "if you don't shut your mouth—"

"Enough." Justus stretched his neck and gingerly probed the boot-sized bruise on his side. "What have you seen?" Moving slowly, Justus turned around so he could see both Mazolan and Nyle.

Nyle said, "There's been no guards, no movement of any kind since I've been awake. But there are—"

"Quite interesting noises," finished Mazolan.

Nyle rolled his eyes. Justus wondered if the demon didn't hear themselves speak a certain amount of words every hour, whether they experienced physical pain.

"And what noises would those be?" Justus asked. "Any sign of Derica, Reid, or the older couple?"

Mazolan and Nyle shook their heads to his last question, and then the tattooed mercenary held up his hand, signaling silence.

They sat like that for several moments until a dull clamor, very far off, rang through the stone hall.

"Don't like the sound of that," murmured Justus. "How long has it been going on?"

"I heard it first, a few minutes after waking," Nyle said. "It's becoming more frequent. And judging from the sounds, whatever is making the noise is moving—away from us, if I had to guess."

"Surprised that we're not bound." Justus stroked his chin, wondering.

"We were actually." Mazolan shined their nails on their tunic. "As impressive as you two are, your teeth are not efficient tools for escape." They flashed their fangs, the four points glinting in the dim light.

Justus rotated his wrists, nodding his thanks to Maz.

"Nyle, have you tried the lock?" Justus asked.

The man sighed with frustration. "With what? They took anything I could use to pick it."

Mazolan's smile slid off their face. "And I can't gnaw through steel—"

The demon cut off, raising a finger to their lips and cocking their head. Nyle and Justus stilled, waiting.

Justus brought up his knees, resting his forearms and displaying his quite free—if slightly bruised—wrists. Nyle and Mazolan settled into similar poses. Pride thrummed in his chest. There wasn't another pair he'd rather face uncertain danger with.

A hooded, robed figure stepped into the faint light in front of their cell. Draped in drab gray, the same as the other three they'd encountered, there was nothing distinguishing about this person.

"Great Spirits, do any of you have an ounce of individuality?" Mazolan sniffed, wrinkling their nose. "Please tell me your leader wears a big, fancy hat. Or a silk-lined cape. Someone, somewhere, has to have some personality."

Nyle snorted, settling back against the wall. Justus's lips twitched. Never let it be said that Mazolan didn't know how to lighten a mood or break the tension.

The robed person lifted their hands and lowered their hood. Father Simond stared at them—lined, wizened face grim and serious.

Nyle barked a short laugh. "It's always the religious ones."

Mazolan narrowed their eyes, examining the father.

Voice flat and hard, Justus asked, "Where's Derica?"

"With Reid," Father Simond said.

"And that would be...?" Mazolan raised their eyebrows, waiting.

Father Simond ignored the demon. The mercenaries stiffened as Simond reached into his robe, pulling out a thin, leather-bound book.

All the blood left Justus's head, dizziness rushing in. If he wasn't already sitting, he would have fallen onto his ass. He'd never expected to see the journal again. Its pages were weathered and yellowed with age. The tanned hide cover had been a soft, golden brown when it was new. Now, it was a deep walnut, creased and marked by the passage of years. Justus's ears buzzed as he imagined everything contained in the volume.

Simond opened the journal and thumbed through the pages. Justus could barely hear the flutter of the paper over the drumming of his own heart. Mazolan shifted their gaze from the father, watching Justus with interest. He concentrated on keeping his face blank and the panic bubbling in his gut from outwardly showing.

Finding the page he sought, Simond gripped the spine of the journal and showed them the book. Justus did not allow himself to react. He wanted to snatch the journal and feed it to the nearest flame.

"This looks familiar, doesn't it?" mused Simond.

On the page was a sketch of Derica's birthmark. Justus's heart stuttered, and his fingers tingled. His lungs screamed at him for more air.

He'd never expected to see that sketch again. Early after the Warrior damned the Weaver-blessed, they kept a journal, not trusting knowledge would follow them from one life to the next. The Warrior was nothing if not resourceful. When the Warrior and the Weaver-blessed had been separated, they had discarded the book like refuse when the memories within became too much to bear.

Father Simond reverently stroked the leather of the cover. "The Disciples have had this longer than we have been devoted to the Weaver. We have prayed and petitioned the Weaver for a solution to the Shredded plague. Imagine my surprise when I recognized the mark of the Weaver-blessed on a girl from the tiny village of Arlan. The Weaver has heard our pleas and sent us the instrument of our salvation."

"And how will she do that?" asked Mazolan. "There was that odd business with Braiden and you figured—what? You'd trot her around to all the Shredded and have her cure them one by one? And you're going to gain her compliance by kidnapping her friends?" Maz shook their head, mouth hitched in disgust. "As a mercenary, I need you to know this is such a tired plan. No originality whatsoever. Much like your wardrobe. I shouldn't be surprised. I'm not angry, just disappointed."

The gears of Justus's mind whirred. Simond didn't seem interested in the Warrior. His identity was likely safe from the Disciples, but that was no consolation when Derica was in danger.

The father went on, "I want nothing more than to serve Veridion by guiding humans to the benevolence of the Weaver. Some Disciples believe the Weaver-blessed is a boon, sent to heal the damaged threads of the Loom. Others believe that if the blessed one were able to unite with the Weaver, their reunion would heal the afflicted." Father Simond paused.

Justus wanted to rush the bars and bloody the holy man's face against the cage.

The father shrugged, "I am simply willing to do what's necessary for the world's salvation—to see what culminates when the Weaver-blessed encounters a true Shredded."

Nyle laughed without humor. "And how exactly will you unite the Weaver-blessed and the Weaver?"

Mazolan waved their hand, sighing. "The usual way all villains transform anything. Death. It's death, right? Again, terribly disappointed. Humans resorting to two of their favorite pastimes: murder or enslavement." The demon leaned forward and nonchalantly spat at Simond's feet, then clapped, slowly. "Way to overcome established conventions, Father."

Simond's lips curled in disgust, and he backed away from the puddle of spittle. "The populace of Veridion should come before the life of one insignificant woman. The whole Tapestry is of greater importance than any individual thread."

That, Justus thought, is where Simond was wrong. Lifetimes ago, the Warrior decided to cherish the Weaver-blessed for who they were—not as a tool of some formless god. That had been the intent, at least, behind seeking a way to tie the Weaver-blessed to the Warrior. The consequences of that decision stained the Warrior's hands with blood and regret. The Warrior—*Justus*—believed the woman he loved deserved the autonomy of a destiny free from the chain the Weaver placed on her life.

His folly had only gifted her a chain of his own, however.

After so many lifetimes of happiness tainted by tragic ends, he needed to let her go. To free her from the bond the Warrior had placed on the Weaver-blessed.

So he would set her free. He would love and cherish her as long as Derica let him, but he vowed he would not take up the dagger to secure her to his side ever again. Provided, of course, they both lived to see tomorrow.

Resolved, Justus reached one hand behind him, signaling Nyle. Blocking the father's view of his other hand with his legs, Justus signed to Mazolan as well.

"But," Father Simond said, "I don't expect mercenaries to understand putting the many before the few. At least not without monetary compensation, of course." He reached into his robe, depositing the journal and pulling forth a bag. Simond threw it between the bars of the cell, and it landed with a tinkle of coins, spilling a few shining gold pieces. "The church will purchase your silence. Upon your agreement, you are free to go."

Nyle looked at Mazolan. Maz looked back. Then they looked at Justus. All three threw their heads back and howled with laughter.

Mazolan wiped tears out of their eyes. "Do you—" they lapsed back into laughter briefly and then tried again. "Do you know," they said, voice becoming more serious, "what the best part of our career is?"

Simond didn't answer, mouth twisted in distaste.

Justus supplied the answer. "The ability to choose our contracts. Thank you, but we're currently under another contractual obligation. We'll be seeing that job to completion." As he'd told Derica, this wasn't a job. It was personal. But he didn't want Simond aware of that fact.

"Let me phrase my offer another way, then." Simond said. "Derica will serve the Weaver's purpose however she's meant to—"

"You mean," interrupted Maz, "she'll either work some power for you, or she'll die trying. And you are fine with either outcome."

Justus snatched the bag of coins up and lobbed them back through the bars of the cell. "Let me rephrase our refusal: *Fuck you*." The bag smacked the father in the chest and there was a satisfying *oof* as coins bounced to the stone floor

Simond stared at the spilled gold. It was like the mask had lifted, and they were seeing the man behind it. His lips thinned, white lines bracketing his mouth. The tips of his ears tinged a ruddy crimson, and the father's eyes transformed to flat, glittering chips of ice. With obvious effort, he calmed himself—smoothing down the fabric of his robe and picking a loose thread from his sleeve. When he met Justus's eyes and spoke, the words were wrapped in poisonous briars, laid out to both warn and maim. "Derica will not be treated any differently for your failure to comply." Slowly, making a grand show of the gesture, Father Simond raised one hand until his palm was level with his eye. Then he snapped his fingers. "The same cannot be said for you."

They waited for two beats. Then three. Then four.

Nothing.

Mazolan's lips twitched. "Was that supposed to be an order for our deaths? Again, lacking all imagination. Why snap if we aren't going to be beheaded or shot in the eye immediately after? Really, I think you need to talk to Alondra at the guild to hire out someone to teach you how to truly—"

Over Maz's shoulder, a recessed grate in the wall flipped out. A small metal nozzle extended through the opening. Like before, in Pip and Tedric's cell. Icy terror froze Justus's heart in his chest.

Father Simond watched them, stepping away from the bars. He wasn't ordering their deaths. No, much worse. They were going to be unconscious, confined to dreams while Derica fought for her life.

With a roar, Justus rushed the bars, Nyle and Mazolan close behind. He swiped a hand at the retreating father. Justus's fingertips grazed the man's robe, but the steel rods of the cell pulled him up short. Impact like being hit with a cloth-wrapped pebble struck the back of his neck. He fought the descent into darkness. Justus shouted, making sure the sound of his rage rang through the halls of the infernal prison long after he lost the battle to stay conscious.

CHAPTER FORTY-ONE

D erica wanted to move. She needed to see what was coming. Every
nerve in her body shouted a warning urging her to do *something*.

Her limbs locked, refusing to obey, tensing to the point of pain. Her eyes watered, not moving from Reid's abused face.

The faint patter of feet against stone moved like a ripple across water, echoing from all directions. Derica's heart beat too loud in her ears. Was there anything more terrifying than the unknown, lurking in the shadows?

A small, scared voice in the very darkest, quietest part of her mind urged her to close her eyes, to welcome the end. She could see her mother again. Surely before the Weaver took Derica's thread and joined it again to the Great Tapestry, there would be time. Time where she could feel the love that had been missing from her life since the day she'd buried Eleanora.

She loved Reid, Tedric, and Pip for trying to fill the void ripped open by her mother's loss. But she admitted the truth. She'd allowed a piece of herself to go to the grave alongside her mother. Maybe if she let it end here, she could get that piece back. Maybe her mother had been keeping that part safe this whole time until Derica could join her.

Maybe the Weaver would put her back together if she went willingly.

On that thought, Derica took in a deep breath and relaxed. Acceptance was a terribly powerful thing, and, it seemed, her key to overriding terror. As her eyes slid shut, welcoming whatever end might come, Derica saw it.

Reid's fingers twitched. A moan escaped his split lips.

A small sob of frustration escaped her. She mentally gathered the shards of her shattered resolve, trying to repair it. If her hands bled, then she would use the blood as mortar. She would bear those bandages and, later, the scars.

They would serve as a reminder.

Reid moaned again—his eye that wasn't swollen shut fluttered open. Twin snarls whispered into Derica's ears, and she flinched. Whatever had entered the chamber was avoiding the center of the room, sticking to the shadows in the corners. It raised the hair on her arms. Derica felt like prey.

With a wince, Reid raised his head gingerly. He saw her and opened his mouth to speak, but Derica widened her eyes and shook her head, raising a finger to lips. Reid frowned and then immediately hissed at the pain.

Growls—one from the left, one from the right—hit her ears and Derica bit down hard on her trembling lip. Reid stiffened, warily searching the darkness of the room. When nothing emerged from the shadows, he looked to Derica. There were a million questions in his blue-eyed stare, and she couldn't voice any answers right now.

Justus's dagger lay hidden under her thigh. Her fingers twitched thinking about it. With her foot still bound and Reid trapped in his chair, she imagined a fight would mean a quick and bloody death

The desire to give up was a faint call, a tempting offer of relief—a cessation of worry. Heart steeled, Derica let her mind spool out all the options she could think of. Unfortunately, not many presented themselves before danger stepped into the light.

It melted from the shadows. One moment, there was nothing but the shapeless promise of demise, and the next, a Shredded prowled toward them. Its companion still lurked out of sight.

Derica couldn't take her eyes off it. This thing was nothing like Braiden when he was afflicted. Looking into opaque, marble-white eyes, she found nothing human there. The unnerving way it moved was like a cat stalking a bird. A puppet cut from its strings, but enchanted to keep moving—with more grace and intelligence than it should have been capable.

Some thought the Shredded were the living dead. Derica now thought of them as the living damned. They were either a damaged, broken soul torturing and eating away the mind of the person they used to be, or their broken soulthread inside had festered, spreading infection and sapping humanity. Derica was inclined to believe the latter. There was room for hope in that belief.

If she could pluck Braiden back from the cusp of the disease, extraordinary things were already possible.

The Shredded stopped, its feet a shiver away from touching the leg of her chair. A breeze would brush her skirts over the creature's dirty, bare feet. Derica, too scared to breathe, worried a puff of air would provoke it. With unseeing eyes, it seemed to study her. The back of her neck tensed, and her fear swept cold fingers down her body, alternately locking and shaking her limbs.

That foreign voice stirred, the one Derica thought she imagined the night she healed Braiden. Terrified to turn her attention inward, Derica battled the need to look at the threat in front of her.

Reid shifted, and the Shredded's head snapped to him. Reid froze, lips rolled inward and clamped between his teeth. The lines bracketing his bruised mouth went white and his square jaw ticked. His open eye flashed with terror. The Shredded moved, taking a step toward Reid.

Away from her.

The tension from holding its gaze vanished, replaced with regret that its marble-white eyes were now trained on Reid.

Before she could mentally recite all the reasons why this was a horrible, awful idea, Derica spoke. "Stop." Her voice was a dry, thin rasp, but it still filled the space around them.

As the last sound left her lips, the Shredded froze as if it were blanketed in ice. It didn't move a muscle, but she knew she was the sole focus of its attention again. Licking her lips, she waited to see what happened next, fingers curling and nails pressing into her palms.

Come, entreated the voice. The one from the night Braiden attacked her. Derica's neck twinged, a phantom pain from the injury she'd sustained.

Come, it said again.

Come where? How? She was still tied to a chair. If she took the dagger and cut the rope, maybe she'd be able to escape. But would that provoke the Shredded? How would she reach Reid? Derica resolved that they would leave this room together or... not at all.

The Shredded had not moved since Derica spoke. She clenched her fists so hard she wondered if her palms dripped crimson. Then she let go.

Let go of her fear.

Let go of her worry.

She let go of her senses and turned inward.

The physical slipped away. Cocooned in swirling, liquid night, she found a suspended well of glowing starlight. It seemed to breathe, inhaling and absorbing light one second, then expelling it in brilliant sparks that arced like shooting stars the next. The lights danced through the air, never once touching her. The well called to her.

Come.

The writhing mass of velvet night and incandescent celestial fireflies calmed. The well's surface appeared hard and solid as a mirror. If mirrors were made of the night sky.

Come. Take what is yours. What has always been yours.

Derica stood directly before the well, staring down into its glassy depth. Leaning forward, she expected to see her reflection. She gasped at what she saw instead.

It was Derica like she'd never seen herself. Her eyes blazed with an other-worldly fire. Her red hair floated on a breeze she couldn't feel. Soft, golden light limned her, gilding her profile. Derica looked away from the reflection and down at her hands. They appeared completely normal. No ethereal glow. No alarming and beautiful anomalies.

The voice didn't speak again, but she felt its urging growing more insistent. It was a pressure against her skin, a prickling at her nape. What would she set in motion if she obeyed? Would she be giving something to gain something else? Derica knew all things that appear to be too good to be true, are.

She leaned once more over the still, liquid night of the well. Her reflection beckoned, slowly raising one glowing hand, and crooking its—*her*—finger.

Come, before you lose him.

That spurred Derica past her reticence. Reid was in danger. They both were.

Not knowing if this was real or a hallucination, Derica plunged her hands into the glass-still surface.

CHAPTER FORTY-TWO

I f Reid didn't have a monster staring at him and another lurking in the dark, he would have yelled when Derica slumped in her chair, slack and boneless. Instead, he stayed silent, his body a throbbing mass of pain. He suspected he had several broken ribs, and the back of his right calf was suspiciously numb.

He couldn't have imagined that Father Simond would be the villain behind his capture. When Reid realized what the father wanted, he refused—he would have died rather than assist him in taking Derica, too.

Simond, unfortunately, had insurance against that outcome. Simond showed him his father and mother, tied up and imprisoned. His parents' eyes had sparkled with tears when they tossed Reid into their cell. They spent hours together, chained and gagged, unable to speak. There was no soft moment of comfort for any of them in this Weaver-damned maze of horrors.

His good eye watered as he watched Derica for any sign of consciousness and monitored the Shredded. He couldn't afford to blink.

Reid didn't know if it had been mere seconds or minutes, but the Shredded moved first.

It was like the monster stood frozen and then thawed between one breath and the next. Weaver's tits, Reid thought, he didn't want to die mauled by Shredded, tied to a chair. He wanted to die, old and frail, in his bed one day. After living a full life.

The Shredded walked, slow and graceful, its unseeing eyes unfocused and opaque. Reid's skin crawled—he knew beyond a doubt it was watching him. It was taking its time. After all, Reid was stuck like a rat in a trap. There was no way out for him.

That thought broke the cage of his fear. He wasn't coming out of this unscathed. He was going to be lucky if he made it out at all. Better to go down swinging, he decided. Make his Ma and Pa proud. Protect Derica for as long as he could.

Reid braced for the pain, then thrashed against his bonds. Both Shredded in the room roared and pounced, the other nightmare finally emerging from the shadows. Clawed fingers tore into his damaged flesh and his yells mingled with their bellows. Every time the Shredded moved enough to give Reid a proper look, he glanced at Derica. She'd still not wakened. He worried there was more to her descent into sleep.

The Shredded behind him raked its nails across his nape, ripping away his coherent thought. It burned like fire. Reid thrashed against his bonds harder. He had no hope of escape, but he refused to stop. His vision tinged red as blood ran into his good eye. Then the world tilted, and he hit the floor with a crack. Reid landed on his side, still tied to a Weaver-damn chair. The fall rattled his ribs. His shoulder was blessedly numb. In the back of his mind, his physician's training turned over the way he hit the ground, wondering if his shoulder was dislocated. The Shredded fell upon him, hammering and raking blows against every inch of him within reach.

One of the crazed creatures struck for his face and Reid flinched. His eyes widened when he discovered he could bring up his arm and shield his head.

The earlier crack had been the arm of the chair breaking. Dodging blows to the best of his ability, Reid wiggled until the wooden arm slipped loose from his tether. Still lying on his side, Reid snatched up the chair arm and wielded it like a club. The Shredded jumped back and watched with their eerie, opaque eyes. He steadied his grip, waiting for them to rush him again.

This time, they came at him together, like they shared a mind—a united effort to tear him apart. When one demanded his focus, the other danced in and tore at his vulnerabilities. Reid's muscles burned and his fingers trembled around the wooden chair arm.

He couldn't take much more of this. His soul would fight until the end, but his abused body would give out long before then. Reid needed to fight with cunning. He must conserve his energy and make every strike matter.

He bit his lip, tasting blood, when one of the Shredded swooped in and struck his open side. That would be another cracked rib. Reid yelled against the pain, clubbing one in the shin. He knocked its feet together, and it went down.

Reid panted. Taking shallow breaths was all his abused ribs would allow him. The fallen Shredded lay motionless. He got the sense it was shocked, as was its companion. The one still standing didn't approach. Reid lied to himself that they were shaken and held onto the thought like a lifeline.

His breathing was the only sound filling the space. "I'm not scared of you," he said. He didn't recognize his own voice, it was so ragged and thready. Of course, he was scared. He was going to die in this pit, then they would turn to Derica and tear her apart too. But Reid had more to do. He needed to do more than knock one down. He had to end one.

The prone Shredded stayed down. He imagined it was shocked to be hit by a target it once thought was helpless. The one still standing stooped, grasping the prone Shredded under the arms. It dragged its companion into the shadows.

Reid let his eye slip shut for a moment as he breathed deep. A moment was all he got. The Shredded, sans its companion, launched from the dark and attacked again, vigor renewed. When they collided, Reid's chair skidded backward several feet. Farther from the light and Derica, Reid realized, trying not to panic. The shadows felt like a third opponent, ready to trap him between inky fingers of black. Reid strained his vision and attempted to meet every strike with his improvised club. When the Shredded danced back, calculating its next angle of attack, metal glinted for a fleeting second.

Metal would be better than wood, Reid thought. Unless it was only a loose coin. Or a button.

He judged the risk worth it and used the chair arm to drag himself toward the shine. The Shredded did not like this at all, and rushed in. Reid battled it back with renewed determination. His arm burned and shook as he scooted himself along the floor. Finally, the item came into view.

A knife.

He would have to let go of his club. Moving himself a little closer, Reid roared when the Shredded swiped his exposed ankle, slashing skin and exposing tendon. Reid drew back his arm and threw the wooden bar at the creature as hard as he could. The Shredded fell back with a scream that pierced his eardrums.

Reid grasped for the knife. His fingers stung as he grabbed it, blade first, and brought it closer. One slightly dull knife: acquired. Flipping it to clutch the handle, he wasted no time in sawing at the binding on his other wrist. His slick fingers bobbled here and there, and he paid for his clumsy efforts. If he lived, his wrist would bear the scars of this day—at least he thought it was day. He hadn't seen the sky in what felt like ages.

When his wrist was free, Reid pushed his chair upright. His feet were still bound, but he was apprehensive of bending his head and taking his eyes off the Shredded. The Shredded struggled to stand. Reid braced his back against the chair and readied his found weapon.

When it rushed him, Reid caught it in the neck with his forearm while his other hand sunk the blade into its chest. He'd performed minor surgeries with scalpels and sutured wounds with needles. Those procedures were nothing like putting a knife through living flesh, intending to kill. It felt wrong. Even if the living thing was a Shredded.

He gagged, turning his head away. Reid pushed again, shoving the knife deeper. The Shredded fell back and took the blade with it. It lay before Reid, unmoving.

The remaining Shredded screamed from the shadows on the other end of the room. *Stupid*, Reid thought in a daze. He shouldn't have let go of the blade handle.

Reid snarled and dragged his chair closer to the dead body. He bent and yanked the knife free, holding it before him. "I've taken care of one of you. I could do the same again." He didn't even care that his voice sounded weary and entirely unintimidating. He *felt* weary and unintimidating.

Nothing moved from the dark. The other Shredded didn't come for him. Derica was still lost to the world around her, her chin dropped to her chest and her eyes closed. He watched for a moment, relieved to see she was still breathing.

"Derica?" he called. "Can you hear me?" No response. "I'll protect you. I'll get us out. Then we can find Ma and Pa and get the fuck out of this place. I don't know what we'll do after but—" his voice grew rough, and his throat closed. "We'll be together again. Your family will be with you, and you will be with us. Please, Derica."

Nothing. Wait—

Her chest hitched, and her head bobbed slightly, as if she fought to lift it. He couldn't urge her for more or call her louder because the Shredded chose that moment to advance.

CHAPTER FORTY-THREE

The second before Derica opened her eyes, terror clamored across her nerves in anticipation.

In the next moment, she realized one of the Shredded lay unmoving—dead—on the ground several paces away, while Reid grappled with the remaining fiend. Reid, still tied to his chair.

She tried to vault out of her seat, but her ankles remained bound to the chair legs. Fishing Justus's dagger from under her thigh, she bent forward, working on severing the ropes.

"Reid!" she yelled.

"Derica!" he huffed while fending off the Shredded. Metal glinted as he swiped a knife in an arc, and the Shredded jumped back. Reid didn't take his eyes off his opponent as he spoke. "Run away as soon as you're free!"

Derica laughed incredulously. She wouldn't leave him. One foot was free. In a minute, both her feet would be free.

Reid's grunts mingled with the Shredded's animalistic snarls. Its movements lacked all the grace it exhibited before. Something had changed, and whatever that was enraged it.

At the snap of her last tether, Derica stood, swaying on trembling legs. She shook from fear, but also from the lingering effects of the drug.

"Stop!" she yelled. The Shredded didn't pause, forcing Reid to keep defending against its attacks.

Her feet moved without forethought. All she could see was Reid in danger, and she wouldn't stand back as he wrestled with the thing before him.

"Derica, don't!" Reid cautioned.

"I said, STOP!" Derica yelled at the Shredded's back.

She had the dagger in both hands, pointed toward its back as it swiped its clawed hands at Reid. She kept moving forward. When her weapon was a breath away from the thing's back, she shut her eyes, not wanting to see the blade sink into flesh. A strike to her forearm disoriented her, and then her arms shook as the blade sunk into warm flesh.

Derica opened her eyes to a shocked, corn-flower blue gaze.

"No," she breathed. "No no no no-no-no-no-no-no." Derica was terrified to move her hands. She blinked, hoping the tableau before her was an illusion—another dream.

Derica couldn't move. Her fingers were wrapped around the dagger protruding from Reid's chest. His blood ran between her fingers, ruby liquid slicking the hilt of the weapon. A hush descended like a shroud over her mind. Her chest filled with a wail of despair that couldn't rise past the hitching choke of her breath. She directed all of her energy to keep her hands steady, desperate not to cause any more pain.

Reid's hand wrapped around hers. "It's all right. You're going to be all right." His voice was thin and pained, but his face was relaxed. He lifted a shaking hand, holding out the knife Balduin had dropped. "Take this. It's moved to the shadows for now. It will be back."

Derica's vision clouded. "Tell me how to fix it," she sobbed. "Tell me I haven't k-k…" She bit down on her lip until she tasted copper. "Please. P-please tell me I haven't… *Please*, Reid." Her fingers spasmed on the hilt, and

Reid's eyes tightened in pain. Hot tears spilled from her eyes. Words garbled, she pleaded, "*Don't l-leave me.*"

"Never." When she didn't take the other knife, he dropped his weapon into his lap and smoothed her hair behind her ears. His finger trembled slightly, and it shattered something inside Derica. "I will never leave you. But you need to take care of the last Shredded before we can worry about me." Reid suppressed a cough and swallowed with difficulty, but smiled at her easily. Her vision snagged on a speck of red liquid at the corner of his mouth. "Take the other knife. It's going to attack soon. They have a pattern—trust me."

Carefully, slowly, she unwrapped her hands from the pommel of the dagger. She wanted to scream with anger and fear when she saw the dark stains marking her palms.

"Here it comes," whispered Reid.

Derica turned, scraping together her resolve to do what she must. She would kill the Shredded, and then she would find help for Reid. They would find Pip and Tedric. And then they would go far, far away from this place. With trembling hands, she took the other blade from Reid's lap. The feel of another weapon in her hands almost made her gag, and her heartbeat threatened to bruise the inside of her ribs.

The Shredded stepped into the light, and she could feel its hatred coming off of it in waves. Its unseeing gaze shifted to its dead companion, and Derica knew. It was glad Reid was dying.

The gift from the well swelled up within her like a great wave, suspended in place but demanding to be unleashed. Without touching the Shredded, Derica immobilized it with a thought. Her eyes burned with heat and she could peer inside the monster, to its frayed, atrophied soulthread. A small part of her was saddened by the state of it. The larger part gave herself over to the combined maelstrom of fear, rage, and pain in her chest. With a mental sigh, she unleashed the wave. She obliterated the soul with a thought. The empty husk fell to the ground like a limp doll.

Derica felt somewhere outside herself, watching this happen, unable to believe her eyes. She had healed Braiden, but whatever this gift was also had a dark side, it seemed.

Now holding steady hands out in front of her, Derica dropped the knife to the floor with a metallic clang. The golden glow from her dream radiated from her in a thin shimmer.

She turned back to Reid and found him studying her with awe and surprise. The surrounding glow dissipated as her hands fluttered to her sides, unsure what to do or try first. His breathing was coming in shallow pants, and the stain around the dagger had grown. Derica rushed to him. He wouldn't... wouldn't...

"Reid, what do I do?" She sank to her knees in front of him.

"Well, we can't pull the blade out. I'm likely to bleed out that way. And if you move me, that could be worse. I know I have fractured ribs because it's hard to breathe. I think one of my lungs may have collapsed." Reid recited it all flatly, like reading from a list.

The blood rushed from Derica's head, and she swayed. Reid caught her arm and groaned at the movement.

His hand was icy.

Reid smiled, then coughed, wincing. Red streaked down his chin, dripping onto his dirty tunic. "You can go get help, but I don't want to send you away alone. Who knows what else is lurking in this Weaver-damned maze of horrors?"

"You're not helping, Reid." Derica tried to laugh, but it came out less of a chuckle and more a sob.

He stared into her eyes, gaze hard. "Leave me here and take your chances to escape. From what I've seen of the place, stay away from any area that looks old."

"No, I won't!"

Reid's mouth kicked up on one side, and his eyes dimmed with regret. "I won't make the journey. I will slow you down. And if you need to run, I won't be able to follow. Take the dagger and go."

"Take—" she repeated, sputtering. "No! Not without you."

"Derica," Reid took her head in his hands and made her meet his one-eyed gaze, "I can't follow you out like this. It's not your fault. It was an accident." He coughed, more blood dripping from the corner of his mouth. "If you find Ma and Pa, you tell them it was an accident, and I fought as hard as I could. And tell them I love them. Just as much as I love you."

Derica was openly sobbing now. She let her head fall to his knee, and she wrapped her arms around his leg, pressing her tears into the rough, dirty fabric of his breeches. "I can't, Reid. I can't. I was going to g-give up, but then you moved and I couldn't. I couldn't give up because of you, so why are you allowed to do it?"

He pressed her head into his leg, roughly smoothing her hair. Reid groaned and jerked. When Derica tried to lift her head, he held her still. "B-because, you daft woman, I'm not giving up. My body has, though. If I try to leave with you, I will just place you in more danger than you would be alone. And that is unacceptable to me." Reid's voice was watery as a cough racked his frame. Derica tried to pick up her head, but he still wouldn't let her. "I don't want you to remember me looking like this. Remember me dancing in the square. Tell my parents to remember me laughing at the dinner table."

"I don't want to *remember* you. I want you to be next to me in the square. I want to sit with you at your parents' table."

"We can't all have the things we want, Derica. You want to live, you have to be willing to get hurt. I don't want you to walk through your days as a ghost, missing me. Not like when Eleanora passed. Promise you won't do that again. Or I'll find a way to escape the Loom and haunt you until the end of your days."

Derica choked out a croaking laugh. "If that's what you want. I promise." She hugged his leg tighter. His skin was alarmingly cold. If she could keep him warm a little longer...

Reid's fingers tangled in her hair and stopped moving.

Derica's heart kicked, and she jerked her head up. He didn't hold her down or keep her from looking this time. His head lolled back, both eyes closed.

Derica exclaimed a wordless cry. He'd taken the dagger from his chest and laid it in his lap. He didn't move, and the dark stain of blood had soaked through his tunic. She brought her hand to his chest and gingerly pressed, seeking the beat of his heart. Not a single thump greeted her fingertips.

"I promised!" she hissed, helpless rage bubbling and mixing with her grief. "I p-promised." She didn't know why those were the words she repeated, but they were the ones that tipped off her tongue over and over again. "I promised, and I thought we'd have more time. How could you leave me, Reid?" She sank into his lap, afraid to let him go. "I won't leave you. I can't bring Pip and Tedric this pain. How could you ask this of me?"

He didn't answer. She knew he wouldn't, and it gutted her. She lay with her arms around his waist and her head cushioned on his cooling thigh. Her eyes slipped closed, salty tracks wetting the fabric beneath her cheek. "It's not fair. I don't want this end for you. I don't want this grief. I don't want this pain for your family. We don't deserve it. *You* don't deserve it. You don't deserve it, Reid."

Against her closed eyes, dim golden light flickered. This was nothing like the soulthread of the Shredded she'd seen. This was a soul at the end of its time here. This is what death looked like.

"Reid?" she whispered, feeling her lips move, but seeing with another sense.

The thread pulsed brighter briefly, then darkened. Reid's soulthread was picked and actively fraying as she watched—withering bit by bit. Derica imagined her hands reaching out to the thread and repairing the damage, shoring it up. Making the thread whole again.

It is not the same to destroy as to turn back from the hold of death. There will be a cost for this, said the voice from the dreams.

"Anything. I will pay anything," Derica said.

And so the terms are accepted.

Behind her closed eyelids, Derica saw hands that were hers, and yet not, pass over the soulthread. Everywhere they touched, the thread was smooth and glowing once more. Healthy.

Whole.

Reid's fingers twitched, and Derica gasped. She lifted her head and cried out to see Reid's chest moving regularly and deeply with breath. His shirt was still stained and wet, but when she tugged the fabric, she could see the skin of his torso was unmarred. His other injuries were still present.

Was that the cost? He would live, but the other injuries he had sustained would remain?

"How?" Reid croaked, blinking dazedly.

Derica shrugged. She didn't know. But she would find out.

They both startled as footsteps rang through the room.

"What a pleasant surprise," a familiar voice said. "I would apologize for the ordeal you've both been through, but I now see it was necessary. I hope you'll forgive me."

Reid gathered Derica to him, as if to protect her. Derica stared in shock as Father Simond stepped into the light.

"You did this?" she asked. "Why?"

"It was a test more than anything. And you passed. Splendidly, if the," Simond eyed the two dead bodies of the Shredded, "decor should tell the tale. Truly marvelous. You are going to be the savior of Veridion."

"What are you talking about?" Derica asked.

"Derica, he's the one who kidnapped me. He took my parents too."

Derica was too stunned to speak. Reid squeezed her, giving her some small comfort. Simond simply stared, waiting for her to speak.

"Why?" she said.

"Because you, dear girl, are the Weaver-blessed."

Reid jerked, but didn't let her go. Her nails made half-moons on his abused skin where she clutched him back.

A hysterical laugh bubbled from her lips. "You must be daft."

"So you didn't rip the soulthread from that one," the father flicked a hand at the fallen Shredded, "and bring Reid back to life?"

Derica opened her mouth, but not a word came out. She had done those things. But did it mean she was the Weaver-blessed?

She licked her lips. "That's a myth. A pretty story circulated by the Disciples."

"Mmm, it may be true that we perpetuate the tale, but it's not one we created. There is nothing but truth to it," Father Simond said.

"If I'm the Weaver-blessed, then what do you want with me?"

"My child, that's the wrong question—it's not what I want with you. You should ask why the Weaver would grant you this power and how they intended you to use it. You can heal the world of the blight of the Shredded. I know this because the Weaver guided me to you so that I might help you in your holy mission."

A chance to heal the sick, Derica thought. To help others, like Braiden.

"Don't, Derica," Reid whispered, as if he knew what she was thinking

"Derica," Simond said, "can you forgive me for the measures I went to show you the depth of power you have inside?"

Derica thought of Reid, cold and still. "Never," she spat.

Father Simond sighed. "Then I can hope you learn to see past it, because you are the only one who can save us all."

Slipping from Reid's grip, Derica stood and approached the father. He blinked in surprise, and Reid hissed for her to stay away.

When she was close, but far enough for comfort, Derica spat at the father's feet. His eyes darkened with anger, and his lip twitched briefly in disgust before smoothing back out.

"I want Reid's family freed. I want the mercenaries freed. Give me back my family and my friends... and I will consider what you want."

"And what makes you think you can bargain here?"

"Because I am the one with the power you want to use. If you could take it and use it yourself, you would have. You require my cooperation. This was not the way to gain it. So, I am asking. Give me back the people I care for, let us leave, and I will return to you willingly... These are my terms," Derica said, recalling the voice from earlier.

Reid protested, but she shushed him with a glare. She could see it; Father Simond was considering her deal. He was turning over options, considering alternatives.

"And what if I threatened to kill one of those people every hour until you accepted?" he asked.

Derica flicked a look to the Shredded. "I have mastered death. You might very well be in danger right now."

"Mastered death, hmm? I think you have much to learn. But if this will gain your total and complete cooperation, then you have my word. I will release your companions to you on the provision that you return to me in a fortnight. Do we have a bargain?"

Derica measured him with a look. This was the best she could hope for without more bloodshed.

"And if you don't return, there will be consequences. That should go without saying, of course. But I don't want to be accused of hiding the particulars. You say you've mastered death? Have you paid its price?"

Ice danced down Derica's spine. How could he know?

"Oh, I can see you have questions for me. I will answer them all when you return in a fortnight. Do we have a bargain?" he asked again.

"Derica!" Reid said.

She ignored him. "We do. I will return to you in a fortnight."

Simond smiled. "Then follow me. We will collect your companions and see you safely out."

CHAPTER FORTY-FOUR

Justus awoke slumped against a wall, shoulder to shoulder with Mazolan and Nyle. They were outside, and the sun struck his eyes, stinging. He hissed, vision watering. When his sight cleared, however, he thought he was hallucinating.

Derica crouched before him, rumpled and stained, but her flame-colored hair was brilliant as always. Her eyes searched his worriedly.

"Am I dreaming?" he rasped.

Derica's specter shook her head.

"I don't believe you," he whispered.

The mirage reached for his hand. He inhaled sharply then held his breath in anticipation. Soft fingers stroked the back of his hand. He snatched her palm and drew her into his lap.

Derica—it was actually her—squirmed. "Not a dream," she murmured. Her voice was a meal he didn't know he was starving for. It hummed along his nerves, loosening tight muscles and easing more than his worry.

It felt like the earth was shaking. Until Justus realized the tremors were his. Derica's hand stroked down his back. He couldn't tell if she was trembling too, or if he was responsible for the way her touch juddered over his back.

He pulled back, taking her face in his hands. Her eyes were glassy, but she appeared uninjured. He scanned his companions—rousing—and grimaced when he saw Reid between his parents. The man looked like he'd gone ten rounds with a giant. Cuts, bruises, and claw marks covered him. One eye was swollen shut. Reid cradled his ribs like they were broken. If Lucinda, the guild's healer, had her way, he'd be in a full body bandage soaked in some foul-smelling herb tincture. *The smell is a necessary evil,* Luci always said. For a fleeting moment, a grin tugged Justus's mouth upward.

Revenge. Served cold.

Justus frowned at the large bloodstain covering Reid's tunic. There was a slice through the fabric, but no wound underneath.

Derica swayed in his hold, and Justus steadied her. Compared to Reid, she was practically pristine. However, there were dark stains on her clothing and pink slashes on one of her forearms.

"I'm sorry," he croaked, pulling her head into the crook of his shoulder. "I'm so sorry I couldn't get to you." He said it to Derica. But he remembered when he'd said it to the Weaver-blessed before. With another name and face. As they turned cold and still in the Warrior's arms.

The memory racked his body with another tremor, and he gathered Derica closer. "I'm sorry, my heart." He whispered the words into the crown of her head.

Her shoulders shook, and she gripped him tighter, his dirty tunic becoming damp with her tears. Derica didn't make a sound though.

"I have you," he said. "You're with me. You're safe." He stroked her quivering back and spoke low. To him, the aftermath of battle was familiar, a weariness that only the sight of death could bring. He wished she'd never had to experience it.

Nyle shifted next to him and inspected their surroundings. When he frowned with concern at Derica, Justus signaled silently behind her back that she appeared fine and that they needed to get back to the guild.

Derica shifted in his lap, and Mazolan grunted. "Morsel," Maz rasped, "watch those sharp little heels around my soft parts."

Derica didn't respond and when Mazolan saw why, their eyes flickered with sympathy and understanding. Nyle and Mazolan both stood. They moved gingerly for a moment, searching for injuries from their second drugging. Both seemed fine. Better than Derica, Reid, and Reid's parents by far.

Justus pressed a kiss at the corner of her eye, her tears a salty stain on his lips. "Can you move back for a moment? Then I'll carry you to the guild. We need to get somewhere safe. You can't go back to the church."

At the mention of the church, Derica shook so badly her teeth rattled. She didn't look ready to talk about what had happened or what she knew about Father Simond. He squeezed her, then slowly let her go. Trying not to wince at his damaged ribs, Justus stood and then helped Derica up. He didn't care if his chest burned like a lance was stabbing through him. No one else would carry Derica to the mercenary's guild.

When Justus swept her into his arms, he groaned, but only once. When Nyle and Mazolan looked at him questioningly, coming forward, he frowned, warning them off. Mazolan shrugged and helped Nyle with Reid. The man's parents seemed enthralled by the demon. They both watched Maz, listening as they gave instructions. Justus suspected there was some power at play to calm the pair. Whatever got them to the guild as fast as possible was fine by Justus.

By unspoken agreement, all were quiet the whole journey to safety. The saltwater stain on his tunic dried, and Derica was asleep in his arms when they entered the guild.

CHAPTER FORTY-FIVE

Maz watched as guild members shepherded the bloodied human to the healer, along with his parents. They tried to take Derica too, but Justus snarled and snapped like a dog with a bone. Lucinda wasn't scared of him, quite willing to smack him on the nose, but she must have decided it wasn't worth the battle. With a disgusted huff, she ushered Reid and his family away.

Nyle and Mazolan hovered, waiting. Justus looked at them and each knew exactly what he was silently asking.

Nyle clapped his hands, and Mazolan jumped up onto a table in the guild hall. "Get out, you looky-loos! That's been enough excitement for the month for all of you!" Mazolan punted a pint of ale off the table. One of the apprentices caught it full in the chest. Unlucky for them, it had been half full. "I'll tell Alondra you're all lying around on your arses while there are jobs to be completed!"

That was the one that finally cleared the hall.

Just the trio and the sleeping woman remained. Justus looked down at Derica—who would have quite a story to tell them when she woke up. As one, they moved toward their room.

In the guild, they shared a room where they bunked on brief stays in Radley. The commander had his separate rented lodgings for longer, personal leave, as did Nyle. As for Mazolan, they preferred to be near the obnoxious humans they knew, rather than strangers they didn't. Maz liked the guild lodgings just fine when the other two were away. And it gave them time to visit with Alondra.

Nyle held open the door for Justus. Mazolan followed, shutting it after everyone filed inside. With a groan, Justus laid Derica on his cot.

Her fair skin was a blotched, pink mess of tear tracks. Her closed eyes were puffy, and her red hair was a chaotic halo of snarls.

Justus weaved. Nyle snatched out a hand and steadied the commander. Justus tried to shrug him off but only tipped the other direction.

Nyle clucked his tongue. "You need to see Lucinda. Or you'll be no use when Derica wakes."

"I concur," Mazolan nodded.

Justus frowned and opened his mouth to protest—so Mazolan helped him make the right decision. They stepped forward and lightly struck the commander in the ribs. To the man's credit, he didn't collapse. He did whiten like a freshly washed sheet, however.

The look the commander flicked Mazolan could have singed their eyebrows. "Go," Mazolan waved. "Go with Nyle to see Lucinda. Get bandaged up. I'll watch over her."

"I don't know that I like that idea," said Justus.

"So, your ribs aren't broken? Or at the very least, cracked? Seems like you should remember what that feels like. Happened to you two years ago now?" Mazolan asked.

Nyle pinched the bridge of his nose and sighed. "Maz is right—" the man pointed a finger at Mazolan to halt their crow of victory "—the quicker you let Lucinda bind your ribs, the quicker you can be back here. Derica's in the guild. She's safe. And Mazolan will stay with her."

Justus finally capitulated, and Nyle guided him from the room. After watching Justus put Derica into his cot, it was clear the commander should not have carried her, much less a thimbleful of water, to the guild. If Mazolan didn't know Justus was the Warrior, they'd think it was disgustingly stubborn nonsense.

But, they thought, moving to crouch beside Derica, it all made sense when you realized who this sleeping woman was.

More than Derica. More than the Weaver-blessed.

They were sure their fangs were out in an unseemly display of glee, but they couldn't be bothered to conceal their mirth. Mazolan loved nothing better than knowing what others didn't. And there was definitely something they knew about Derica no one else did. Not even the woman herself.

They gently tucked a stray hair away from her face and studied her. You'd never know by looking; they'd done such a good job binding themselves to human form.

"Yes," Mazolan said softly, "you have much to tell us when you wake. And I have something to tell you. I know who you are." Derica turned away in her sleep, exposing the mark that had put her in danger from Father Simond. "Oh, Derica, little breaker of fate, you poor girl. You're the Weaver."

ACKNOWLEDGEMENTS

It might surprise you to know, but I could argue that a second edition book is just as much work as a first edition. Despite the story essence remaining unchanged, this book feels like it carries an entirely different aura now. At least, that's my view. And there are some very important people I need to thank for supporting me and this book's journey.

Always, to my mom and sister, thank you for supporting me in this dream. I'm so grateful I have the both of you. Nikki, if it weren't for you, this book would never have been published at all.

Andrea, you embraced my characters so well and so lovingly, it was the most logical thing in the world for me to approach you about a cover. I won't ever be able to put into words how much I appreciate the art you've given to me, my readers, and my characters. I look forward to many more projects together in the future.

Cam, Agus, Kyla, and Ash: you continue to be the most wonderful friends and I love every day we get to chat about books and whatever else strikes our fancy.

Cady, this book brought us together, and I can't imagine going a day or week without talking to you now. Whether that's chaotically sending writing snippets or Astarion content, I'm so happy I get to call you my friend.

Lex, I don't know if this counts as taking the train for another spin before pulling back into the same station, but CHOO CHOO. Thank you for being the ideal ADHD writer friend who gives the kindest, most needed advice. I can't wait to prop AIM next to Breaker on my shelf someday soon.

Hannah, thank you for being the kindest author friend. You helped ground me when everything felt like doom and chaos before publishing my first edition, and I can't thank you enough for listening and offering your industry knowledge.

Cianne, handing you my manuscript for evaluation was one of the most nerve-wracking things I did early in my author journey. You helped me so much with figuring out my story. I absolutely believe there wouldn't have been a first edition of Breaker without your insight.

Tiana, Maria, Franki, Sarah, LB, and Lauren, I'm grateful to have "met" you all early in my writing journey. Thank you for the encouragement, book chats, and author commiseration.

A blanket thank-you to everyone I've met and formed a friendship with through bookstagram. This book would not have happened if I hadn't found community there.

You. Yes, you. Thank you for reading my debut novel (repackaged and improved). As an independent author, you've made a very tangible impact on my writing journey by reading this book. I hope you loved it, and I hope you'll stick around to see what happens with Derica, Justus, and the rest of the gang.

Lastly, if I could make one small request: please review this book after you read it. I don't have a marketing department (the team is just me, my ADHD, and a Canva subscription). A review or recommendation goes so so far.

From the very bottom of my heart, thank you.

ABOUT THE AUTHOR

R.M. Derrick has always had a love for fictional worlds and a dream to create them. She has a particular passion for stories that give the page/screen/voice to characters in larger bodies. Plus size people deserve representation in media.

When not occupying her imagined worlds, R.M. is a 30-something desert-dweller who believes in the magic of words on paper, the stimulating power of caffeine, and the supreme satisfaction of a Happily Ever After. She lives with her family and adorable pitbull terrier in the southwestern United States.

You can catch up with her at www.rmderrickauthor.com for the latest news about Derica and the gang.

Milton Keynes UK
Ingram Content Group UK Ltd.
UKHW010641270324
440147UK00018B/295/J

9 798986 066646